madeleine reiss

ZAFFRE

First published in Great Britain in 2019 by
ZAFFRE
80–81 Wimpole St, London W1G 9RE

Copyright © Madeleine Reiss, 2019

A CIP catalogue record for this book is available from the British Library.

ISBN: 978–1–78577–092–0

Also available as an ebook
1 3 5 7 9 10 8 6 4 2

Typeset by IDSUK (Data Connection) Ltd
Printed and bound in Great Britain by Clays Ltd, Elcograf S.p.A.

Zaffre is an imprint of Bonnier Books UK
www.bonnierbooks.co.uk

To my dear sisters Tania and Thomasina,
with love and gratitude for all the ways they enhance my life.

Prologue

Summer 1990

YOU WOULDN'T HAVE SEEN THEIR hideaway unless you knew where to look. The entrance was down three stone steps and obscured by a tangle of ivy and clumps of flame-coloured montbretia. The garden outside – balding lawn, decaying wooden furniture and stumps of things in pots – hung breathless under a fiery blue sky.

'It's hotter than a witch's arse out here,' Tina said. She shifted a little and some of the water in the washing-up bowl slopped over the edge.

'Stop wriggling. I'm not going back into the house to get more water.' Lottie dug her elbow sharply into her sister's side. 'For your information, the correct expression is *it's colder than a witch's tit*. The whole point of witches is that they're not human and therefore not warm-blooded.'

'Did you know you say "For your information" about a hundred times a day?' Tina said. 'Anyway, you're not in charge of words. If the witch didn't have a top on but was wearing furry pants, she might have cold boobies and a hot bottom.' Tina put her toes over Lottie's and her sister jerked away as if she had been burned.

'Keep your feet away from mine!' Lottie said, shuddering. 'It's bad enough having to share the bowl with you. You probably have verrucas.'

Beside them, Mia sighed. She was fourteen and well beyond the age when she should be sitting with her two younger sisters in a bunker with her feet in a washing-up basin. People with proper lives were seeing out the heatwave under umbrellas by stretches of water and drinking from tall glasses brought out to them on trays. Mia imagined the drinks sweating and misty from the fridge and the way the cubes of ice would ring as they hit the sides of the glasses, the sound prompting the women to tilt their sleek heads and suck from white straws.

'Stop arguing about stupid things, and please don't say arse and tits and boobies,' she said. 'It's very immature, not to say derogatory to women.'

'Yes, Tina, stop being so childish,' Lottie said triumphantly.

Tina frowned. 'I actually *am* a child.'

'I was a lot more mature than you are now when *I* was ten,' Lottie answered, pulling up the neck of her T-shirt to wipe her forehead. She was a whole twelve years old.

Although it was far cooler in the bunker than it was outside, where the sun was merciless, the air was thick and heavy with the scent of the earth. It wasn't sweet the way soil could be when you dug into a new patch, but smelt as if there was stuff mixed up in it that was rotting.

'It's a bomb shelter,' their father had said, when they had moved into the house the year before and walked the length of the garden together. It had been built a long time ago in the dusty, crumbled world they had seen on TV. They imagined London with hollowed-out houses and men in drab uniforms, their chests strapped across with webbing, and women with a battling look piling up the bricks and pulling the corrugated metal roof across, then covering the whole in rubble and turf so that it couldn't be seen from above.

'It's probably best we get the shelter checked out before you go in,' their father had said, although to their knowledge he hadn't and they had used it as a refuge almost from the beginning.

'Do you think that place is safe, Joe?' their mother Lynne had asked once. She had been jolted out of her disinterest by the fact that her own children had invited the twins from next door into their den and she knew she was supposed to be *in loco parentis*.

'It would have fallen down by now, if it wasn't,' their father had replied, shrugging. She had smiled the special smile that she only used when she was talking to him, the one that made her look softer and younger.

'Do you think we can go back in yet?' Lottie asked Mia. 'The water in the bowl's getting warm and I'm sure it's riddled with germs from Tina's feet. I want to fill the bath up as cold as it will go and sit in it up to my neck.'

'I'll go and check.' Mia padded along the pathway to the back door of the house. Her wet footprints were sucked into the thirsty stones as soon as they were planted.

She opened the door a little way and listened. It seemed quiet at first, but she had long ago become accustomed to the deceptive silences that seemed to mark an end but turned out to be only interludes for regrouping and rearming. Sure enough, it seemed the hostilities were not yet over. There was the sound of something smashing against a hard surface and then a screeching sentence – the words loud but difficult to make out – then the sound of agitated panting as if something was being gathered and marshalled before the next volley. Mia shut the door quietly and went back the way she had come.

This time the stones burned the soles of her feet, but she barely noticed.

'I think we should give it a bit longer,' she said. She rolled up her jeans and placed her feet once more into the basin next to Tina's wide toes, tipped with chipped pink varnish, and Lottie's narrow, slightly bent ones, webbed on one foot between the first toe and the second. It was better here than it was inside the house, and at least they had each other.

'We're sister soup!' Tina said, smiling.

Chapter 1

Present day

TINA WAS IN THE WINDOW seat and Lottie had to bend across to get her first view of America. The bay was the colour of pewter and there was a dull, intermittent sheen on its surface. She could see the dense column of a rainbow, its arch hidden by low cloud, rising out of the water.

'It's a sign our trip is going to be incredible,' Tina said.

Lottie was less sure. 'It's the wrong sort of rainbow,' she said, 'you can't see its curve.'

Tina laughed derisively. She always got a little mocking when she'd been drinking, and she had started early at Gatwick Airport.

'We're on holiday,' she had almost shouted when Lottie had tried to dissuade her from having a fourth glass.

'You can multiply the effect of alcohol by at least five when you are on a plane,' Lottie had said, and looked aghast as her sister grabbed the flight attendant's hand to get his attention.

'Definitely not gay,' Tina had whispered when he had moved on, just a shade too loudly – and then, just like that, as if he had caught a virus from her red-wine breath, the blond, soft-bellied attendant was in her thrall. He brought her iced water and nuts she hadn't asked for and then, with an agonised glance at his tight-haired colleague at the other end of the aisle, he slipped Tina his number on a napkin.

'I shouldn't really be doing this,' he had said. His voice had an eager sibilance that was off-putting, but Tina had laughed as if she was delighted.

Later Lottie noticed that Tina let the number fall from the table and didn't bother to retrieve it.

Lottie thought that maybe the secret to attracting men was not to want them – that and having long legs and wide, deceptively limpid eyes and a delicately freckled face. Everyone always said that the sisters were very alike to look at, but Lottie knew herself to be a smaller, less glossy version – the freckles not quite as captivatingly spaced, her eyes set a little deeper in a narrower, less open face. They shared the same mouth – a narrow top lip that curved upwards so that even in repose they looked as if they were smiling.

'Valentina's the beauty of the family,' their mother had announced once. Tina had just bounded into the living room, her cheeks flushed by the wind and an hour of vigorous kissing. One of the twins from next door had turned from blotchy and silent into pale and enigmatic, seemingly overnight, and had become the object of Tina's almost clinical attention. Even though she had only been about fourteen at the time, the youngest sister had launched herself firmly into the mysterious world of love – much to the disgruntlement of both Lottie and Mia, who felt that by rights she should have waited her turn.

'Valentina has the unpredictable nature that all truly beautiful women possess. Carlotta, you're the clever, grounded one. You will never take risks and no one will ever make a fool of you, and Mia . . . well, Mia combines the best of all of us. She gives herself to others. She's my good, incorruptible girl.'

Lynne Ward had spent an important year of her life in Perugia – *I found my true sensuality there* – and ever since had espoused all things Italian, even in the selection of her daughters' names. The younger girls had shortened them so they sounded less conspicuous, but Mia's name didn't lend itself to diminutives. Lottie often thought that ordinary Sunday afternoon, the fug of sweatshirt uniforms drying on radiators and the clock ticking down to Monday, was when who they were and who they were going to be had been laid down for all time. Tina made a virtue of her unpredictability, which often manifested itself as a kind of selfish disregard for other people. Lottie was aware of her own, often craven, cautiousness that she sold as being sensible. Right to the end, Mia too had remained in character.

Tina wobbled slightly as she pulled her bag from the overhead locker. 'I think I'll need a nap this afternoon.'

'I expect *I'm* going to have to drive,' Lottie said.

'Well, that's just the price you have to pay for not knowing how to have fun,' Tina answered, not bothering to pull down the top that had ridden up during her exertions to reveal a taut stomach adorned at the belly button with a ruby stud.

'What would have happened if we'd both got pissed?' Lottie asked.

But Tina either didn't hear or had decided not to answer. She was already shouldering her way down the plane, people automatically moving aside to accommodate her. The smitten attendant's smile faltered as she passed him without a glance.

At the airport car hire, instead of the white Ford Mustang convertible that Tina had booked, they were offered a lurid yellow one.

'I booked a white one. It absolutely *has* to be white,' Tina said, drawing herself up to her full five-foot-ten-inch height and sounding more British than Dame Maggie Smith.

'The yellow's not so bad,' Lottie muttered. She felt sorry for the young man with bitten nails and a face shaped like a spoon who was clearly struggling to maintain the appropriate American cheer in the face of such obstinacy. Her sister shot her a furious look. Lottie knew that Tina had set her heart on this particular car.

'It's the only vehicle suitable for a road trip of this kind,' she announced.

Tina could be a pain in the arse.

'I'm staying here until the car I booked is found for us,' she said with such decisiveness that it was futile to protest.

Sure enough, after another ten minutes, the right car miraculously appeared. Tina was gracious in her triumph.

'I knew there must have been some mistake,' she said, smiling warmly at the young man. By then he had the softened, relieved look of someone who had been unexpectedly released from a pair of constricting shoes.

'Enjoy your trip, ma'am,' he said, as if he meant it.

Lottie had little experience of driving on the right, nor of automatic cars. She was terrified as she navigated her way out of the airport with Tina issuing instructions from the satnav on her phone – often a little too late, causing Lottie to have to make sudden, sweating turns. She drove tentatively down Highway 101, ignoring the cars that overtook them with horns blaring. Tina stuck her finger up and grinned ferociously as they went by, which made Lottie feel even more anxious. After a while Tina got bored of glaring at the other drivers and put on the Spotify list she had created for the road trip. She started singing along to the San Francisco section – Chris Isaak's 'San Francisco Days' and 'Don't Marry Her (Fuck Me)' by The Beautiful South. She delivered the title line of this song with such enthusiasm that Lottie told her to shut up or she wouldn't drive a moment longer.

Lottie was so intent on the road that she barely dared look to the right or the left – but she could feel the sea alongside them. Then, in the far distance, there was the Golden Gate

Bridge, with its epic, rusty stretch. She saw the word 'DREAM' made out in blocked, glittering letters against a hillside and thought perhaps she had imagined it. The sky was patched with cloud, brighter now than it had been on their arrival, but still shifting and unpredictable.

With the roof of the car down, Lottie's first impression of San Francisco was of its many odours – coffee, incense, cedar, spicy meat, garlic, weed, shoe leather – and the constant shifts of perspective, hill and then slope and sudden views of sea.

'I remember it more than I thought I would,' Tina said, looking around her as they drove.

Lottie sighed inwardly. She knew Tina was enjoying the fact that she had been to America before and knew more about it than Lottie did. There had always been this rivalry between them – a kind of jostling for attention, a determination to make the other aware that they were in possession of greater knowledge or deeper feeling. She wondered whether it was what all sisters did. She couldn't remember having ever felt it with Mia, but then Mia had been different.

Lottie had a sudden memory of another trip: the three of them in the back of the unreliable family car. She couldn't remember where they had been going – all the journeys that took them from one barely known place to another had merged in her mind. Their parents had been shouting at each other; being in a car had been one of their many triggers into acrimony. She had been scared that they were going to crash and Mia had taken her hand under the ragged travelling blanket. She, in turn, had held Tina's sweaty little palm. They had been comforted by the touch that linked them, knowing they were strong enough to withstand anything as long as they had each other.

Lottie stole glances out of the window as she navigated the roads. There was a sign announcing a yard sale – a great number of dusty velvet lampshades were lined up on some porch steps, watched over by a man smoking a joint on a battered leather sofa. There were girls with tight bottoms and loose, sun-kissed hair, and houses painted the pastel colours of nursery bedrooms. Gaudy bougainvillea arched here and there, and small trees filled the fronts of houses in smoky clouds of gauzy pink. Shops advertised cures for all ills – indigestion, acne, menopause and heartbreak.

'Were you happy here?' Lottie asked.

'Yes,' Tina said. 'I had a great year.' She had put on an enormous pair of sunglasses so it was hard to read her expression, but she seemed suddenly subdued. 'It's the perfect city to set off from. This time tomorrow we'll be on the road.'

'When are Tim and Rachel expecting us?' Lottie asked.

'Around about now.'

Lottie stopped rather too suddenly at an intersection, to let a group of men in red dresses and pigtails cross the street in a great whooping rush. Tina clutched the handle on her door with an exaggerated intake of breath.

'Feel free to take over if you think you can drive so much better,' Lottie snapped. She was tired from the journey and was experiencing the unpleasant, muffled feeling in her ears that flying always gave her. She thought longingly of tea and her bedroom at home, with its peaceful shades of grey, and wondered again at the impulse that had made her agree to this crazy expedition. It wasn't as if she had the time to spare. She was getting married in three weeks and there were a thousand things that needed her attention. She began to itch at the thought of the wedding favours as yet unselected and the honeymoon outfits she hadn't packed.

'Keep your hair on,' Tina said, flicking up the mirror in the visor to check her face. 'We're almost there. I think it's a left turn after that warehouse-type building.'

They drew up at a house painted cream and brown with steps up to a railed veranda. They pulled their cases from the boot – Lottie's neat and black with efficient wheels, Tina's grubby and straining at the zip, making a great rattling sound as she pulled it along the pavement.

'Do you think it's all right that we've left her in the boot?' Lottie asked.

'We can't schlep around with her every time we stop anywhere.'

'But what if someone steals the car?'

'I've decided it's OK and so you have to, too,' Tina said loftily.

I must have been stark raving mad to agree to this trip, Lottie thought. It's going to be a slow, agonising torture. They barely had time to knock on the door before it was opened and a tiny woman dressed in blue hurled herself at Tina.

'Oh my God! You look exactly the same! Still absolutely stunning.' Rachel smiled. 'Come in, come in. This must be your sister. Isn't she just like you? Did you have a good journey? I'm so, so happy to see you.' All this was said without drawing breath and while hustling them inside. 'Is it too early for a proper drink? Yes, it probably is. But who cares? We have to celebrate. Tim will be back from work soon. He's just dying to see you. If I remember right, you were more than a little fond of a gin and tonic. Can I make you one now? Or do you want to eat? I have lasagne. I've actually cooked in your honour. You know I don't do that for just anyone.' She gave a great, rumbling laugh – a sound that was startlingly odd coming as it did out of such a diminutive person.

Rachel was made up of a series of circles – round face, wide eyes, rosebud mouth, bobbing curls, plump arms heavy with bracelets which made expansive, curving, excitable gestures. Lottie quailed slightly in the face of such uninhibited vigour. She hoped that not all Americans were prone to such excesses of energy or she would not survive the trip.

Later, when they had showered and changed, and just as the rather glutinous lasagne was about to be served, Tim arrived back. He was as quiet as his wife was voluble, but in his studious, blinking, round-shouldered way, he seemed just as pleased as Rachel to welcome the sisters to his home.

'Tina stayed with us for a few months, while she was studying here,' he said. 'We had a ball.'

'I thought you lived in San Francisco for a whole year while you did your internship?' Lottie asked.

'Oh, after a while she moved in with Spike,' Rachel answered.

Lottie looked at her sister, who had got up and was inspecting the photographs on the wall. 'I've never heard about a Spike.'

'Well, it was a long time ago now,' Tim said. 'It's been at least seven years since Tina was here.'

'Was he a boyfriend, Tina?' Lottie asked, smelling a mystery. Sometimes she thought they knew almost nothing about each other. She wondered exactly when the closeness between them had gone. Things changed when you were not watching, like a once-hefty dune diminished by the wind or a vibrant flower kept between the pages of a book, which falls out, years later, as a shadow of itself: you only noticed differences when you looked in the same place.

Tina didn't turn. 'Mm, kind of.'

Sensing a slight awkwardness, Tim tactfully changed the subject. 'You're unlucky to miss the boys,' he said, 'although I realise that other people might not see it that way. I sometimes forget that not everyone is as besotted as we are. They are staying with my mother for a week.' He pointed to a picture of his progeny: two solemn-faced boys with carefully combed hair, standing shoulder to shoulder in matching purple T-shirts.

'Which means we are child-free and carefree,' Rachel said, 'and we thought you might like to come along to a party we've been invited to this evening.'

'If you're too tired, don't worry,' Tim added hastily. 'We'd be happy to stay in with you guys. Maybe you want an early night.'

'Jet lag is best managed by just pushing through. We'd love to come – wouldn't we, Lottie?' Tina said this in a meaningful way, so even though she had a headache, Lottie nodded with what she hoped was the right amount of enthusiasm. She had, after all, signed on the dotted line. She only had herself to blame.

I, Carlotta Ward, soon to be married to Dean Fowler Watt, agree to cancel my boring old hen weekend (Denim and Diamonds . . . Seriously??) and go with my dear sister Valentina Ward on a two-week road trip in America instead. We will set off from San Francisco and fly back from Park City and hire a car for the bits in between. I confirm that I will say YES to every single challenge.

Chapter 2

LOTTIE WENT UP TO THE roof terrace to get away from a middle-aged man in a pork-pie hat and flip-flops who had demonstrated a dim grasp of the need for personal space.

'I could listen to you all night,' he had said, leaning towards her. His breath was musty like worn money and his face was soft and creased on one cheek, as if he had been lying on a rough surface and had just woken up. 'British people always sound so polite. It's real sexy.'

To be fair to him (and Lottie always did her best to be fair), there wasn't a lot of space available anywhere in the house. The living room was heaving with bodies, and in the smaller, adjacent rooms the guests had claimed every single surface, even the floor. Pretty much everyone seemed to be drunk or high on something. They moved too quickly and said things in earnest, frantic voices that she couldn't quite catch. Her ears were still not functioning at full capacity. The women at the party were conspicuously younger than the men, who all seemed to her to be a little predatory and yet also strangely capering, like people who were in the grip of a desperate, unstoppable joviality.

Her life with Dean mostly involved seeing the same people in the same places, and the fact that she was not tied to anything or anyone except for Tina made her feel uneasy. She was used to knowing exactly where she was, but here, everything was new. She wondered what Dean was doing right at this moment. Sleeping, probably, since it was gone midnight back at home. He was careful to get his allotted eight hours.

'I don't function well on less,' he always said, his neat beard well oiled, the whites of his eyes bright. She thought of him tenderly – the way he curled his body in their bed, the duvet between his legs, his fists clenched despite her continually reminding him to relax. She felt suddenly lonely. She had lost sight of her sister more than an hour ago. Tina was probably somewhere in the crush on the dance floor; she always made it her mission to be at the centre of the action, as though she needed to be held up in the movement of things, in case slowing down would cause her to falter and fall.

The city around her glittered in bits and pieces; it was dusk and the lights were not yet all illuminated. The view from the roof was cut across by a great sweep of raised road, which curved off into the distance. Beneath the pillars of the highway, a man and a woman were sitting on the bonnet of a truck, sharing a bottle of wine. The traffic moved above them in a continuous flow. In the corner of the terrace a firepit burned, fed with kindling and coal by a man in black jeans and a dark jumper. Lottie thought he had the look, with his close-fitting clothes and compact body, of a burglar, someone athletic yet debonair like Cary Grant – who could move across roofs and slide from balcony to balcony, as comfortable in this shining landscape as a cat. Or maybe it was simply that she was in America and on a roof.

'Are you Tina's sister?' the cat burglar asked, and Lottie jumped at the sound of his voice. She felt a rush of embarrassment that she had been caught staring at him.

'Yes, I am,' she said. As he walked towards her, she saw that he was much less polished than his movie counterpart. He looked as if he could have done with the attentions of a barber. His hair was a little too long and curled on his neck and his stubbled jaw bore no resemblance to Cary's smooth cleft.

'You're so alike,' he said. He looked at her intently and she had the familiar feeling of being compared, perhaps unfavourably, to her younger sibling.

'I'm not nearly as beautiful,' she said and immediately wondered why she had said something so cringingly self-deprecating.

'I'm not sure that's altogether true,' he said. He smiled at her, and all of a sudden the movie-star looks were there again. He had dark, clever eyes and a way of holding himself that she recognised as confidence. She always noticed this quality in others because she lacked it herself.

'How do you know Tina?' she asked.

'I'm Spike. We hung out for a while when she was younger,' he said.

Tina thought that perhaps the jet lag was catching up with her after all, despite the two lines of coke she had been given by one of Rachel's friends, a statuesque woman called Fay. Fay was dressed in a boiler suit unbuttoned to the waist and when she had bent down to the table, Tina had seen that one of her nipples was threaded through with a twist of glinting copper wire.

She pushed her way off the dance floor looking for Lottie. She sighed; she was probably hiding away somewhere. The trouble with her sister was that she was just so terminally cautious. She always had been, even as a child.

Tina remembered a wood and a river. All three of them had been there. She couldn't recall now which of their temporary homes this particular wood and river was associated with. They had never stayed long enough in any one place to form attachments, and after a while she had discovered it was easier not to start things because then you wouldn't miss them when you moved on. She had once rejected a neighbour's cat that had taken a liking to her, even though she had wanted so much to pick it up and feel its body beating. I can't like it, she had thought. I can't save bits of meat from supper and feed it from my cupped hand. I can't set out a cushion for it on the deep windowsill, which catches the afternoon sun. If it starts to expect meat and sun it will mourn their absence when I can no longer provide them. It was better that she didn't set in motion a process that could only end in loss.

In the unnamed wood a tree trunk had toppled over the river, the weight of its fall embedding it safely on either side of the muddy bank. The sturdy path over the rush of water had been an invitation she couldn't resist.

'Don't do it,' Lottie had said, her eyes anxious. 'You'll fall.'

Tina had ignored her and stepped on, enjoying the sickening way the wood gave slightly under her and the speed of the water moving below. She had turned when she reached the middle, executing a triumphant pirouette, and laughed at her sister's face, made pale by worry and the green shade cast by the trees. However many times Tina had run back and forth over the log, demonstrating its strength, Lottie had refused to attempt the crossing and had eventually walked away by herself. Mia, torn between staying and enjoying the bridge or ensuring that Lottie didn't get lost, had gone after her. It hadn't seemed so much fun after they had gone. There was something silly about teetering along a bit of wood if you didn't have someone to watch you doing it.

When she had discovered her unexpected windfall, her first thought was that the money could pay for a trip for her and Lottie. She had been surprised that the notion had come to her as suddenly as it had. Tina and her sister had not seen much of each other in recent months, and they had never

20

been on holiday as adults together before, but the more she thought about it, the more sense it made. Being away would give Lottie the opportunity she so clearly needed to work out if her upcoming marriage was really what she wanted. Tina didn't think Lottie had thought it through; she seemed to have just acquiesced to her redoubtable, but extremely dull, boyfriend's wishes. She couldn't understand why Lottie was even bothering to get married. It wasn't as if anyone in the family had made a success of the institution. Their parents' union had been a disaster, and Mia's had sealed her fate. Getting married was something to be avoided at all costs.

'Dean proposed to me at the top of the Shard,' Lottie had said, as if this was proof positive of the depth of his feelings, rather than the act of someone desperately short of imagination. Apparently some people had been doing yoga in the viewing gallery at the time of the romantic encounter. Undaunted, Dean had still got down on one knee and presented her with a ring, while thirty women doing the downward dog had cheered at them from between their legs.

'Please come,' Tina had said, when she had rung her sister to explain the plan. 'We'll have fun, just the two of us. I guarantee adventures. Just think: California, Arizona, Nevada, Colorado . . .' She rolled the names around her tongue as if they were delicious.

'I've got so much to do,' Lottie had replied. 'I can't afford the time – nor, for that matter, the money. We're spending so much on this wedding.'

'I'll pay for the flights, the accommodation and the car. You can buy the drinks. Live a little,' Tina had said. 'We'll wear hats and take chances. You know it makes sense.'

'It makes absolutely no sense. Besides, how can *you* afford it? Have you just got a big photography commission or something?'

'Unfortunately not, although it can only be a matter of time. I'm expecting a call from Beyoncé any day now.'

'Maybe you'll be doing the triplets photo.' The smile was evident in Lottie's voice.

'I'm stocking up on yards of net as we speak.' Tina laughed. 'No, the truth is – and this will probably make you choke, since you know how unlikely it is that I have ever paid insurance on anything – but I just got an eight-thousand-pound PPI payment. Couldn't even remember I'd had the credit card in question.'

'And how is it that I, who have never bought anything unless I had the money in the bank, get not a penny?'

'It's only money I've already spent, even though I didn't realise I was spending it – because unlike you, I don't have a ledger in which I write up every single pair of knickers and toothbrush I buy.'

'I thought the point of this phone call was that you were trying to sweet-talk me into your hare-brained scheme to drive around America moments before my wedding. If so, you're not being particularly successful.'

'Don't be so boring. I'm offering you the trip of a lifetime, gratis, free, no strings attached.'

'There are always strings attached when it comes to your suggestions, Tina.'

It had surprised Tina that the sharpness of her sister's tone hurt her as much as it had. She didn't have to do this. There were a hundred better ways to spend the money.

'What will the trip be *for*?' Lottie had asked, as practical as ever, as if you needed a reason to have fun and see something new. She was so fatally immersed in thoughts of ribbon colours and bubble machines and garters that she had lost all sense of perspective.

'Does there have to be a reason for everything?' Tina had answered. 'Can't we just take some time out to enjoy each other's company?' She didn't think Lottie would have responded well if she had said, *I think the man you want to marry is a bit of a tosser, so I'm taking you away in the hope I'll be able to change your mind and get you to cancel your wedding.*

But Tina knew that she was not being completely honest, even with herself. There was something else she wanted from the trip beyond trying to convince Lottie that getting married was a terrible idea. There was a practical issue that needed to be resolved, of course – but she was also looking for some kind of resolution, a landing place. She couldn't articulate exactly what she meant by that; she had never told anyone – it didn't fit with her 'I can leave anything behind' persona on which she so relied – but when she was tired, or simply when a day had not turned out the way she had hoped, Mia came to her. She was often there, in the corner of Tina's eye, conjured up on a breeze or in the half-light of the evening. The shape she took was not her final one, but rather that of the child she had once been, with her sweet, round face with its inward, distracted gaze, as if she was standing with one foot in a dream. It wasn't that Tina wanted the haunting gone – there was comfort in it – but she wished the ghost of her sister would come to her peacefully and without blame. What she was about to say to Lottie felt like a risk. She took a deep breath.

'We'll be in America on what would have been Mia's forty-second birthday,' she said. 'We'll drive through the locations of all her favourite movies. You remember the code ... *A cowboy must never shoot first, hit a smaller man or take unfair advantage. He must be gentle with children, the elderly and animals.*'

There was a silence at the other end of the phone. Tina thought perhaps this was not what Lottie wanted. She knew herself how much easier it was to shut down all thought of Mia.

'I remember.' Lottie's voice lost its tone of resistance and became gentle. '*A cowboy must never go back on his word or a trust confided in him.*'

They were both quiet, acknowledging the gap where Mia's contribution would have been. Tina could hear her voice with its clear, earnest cadence ... *A cowboy is clean about his person in word, thought and deed. He respects women, his parents and his nation's law.*

It had been like this ever since she had gone – the childhood rituals that had been carried on into adulthood were now always incomplete. She was not there to lead them as they walked in single file in strict age order (although Tina had always tried to get in front). Jokes were missing their punchlines. The poems they had learnt were without their central verses. Home-made cakes lacked their secret, vital ingredient.

'The Cowboy Commandments are a litany of misogyny and racism,' Lottie said over the phone.

Tina ignored her. 'We could even perhaps do what we promised her,' she said.

Lottie didn't answer. Tina could imagine her sister somewhere in her ordered house, that small frown between her eyes, her fingers picking something up and setting it down again in its place.

'I suppose I'll do it,' Lottie said at last. 'I'll do it because of Mia.'

Chapter 3

'HAVE YOU SEEN LOTTIE?' SHE asked Tim. Unshackled from children, he had drunk deeply from the vodka luge and was looking blearily around the party through misted spectacles.

'I think I saw her go upstairs,' he said.

Tina looked into various rooms, most of which were piled with coats and lovers, before discovering a further set of steps up to the terrace. She was sure this was where her sister would be; the girl had always had an unhealthy interest in fresh air. Night had fallen while she had been inside, and she was surprised by the depth of the dark and the way the city showed itself in shining waves, bright at the front, falling away along its slopes into a smeared, velvety gleam.

She was right; Lottie was hiding away up here. Her tidy black dress with its white collar was unmistakably out of place in this costumed city. She was talking to a man who was leaning with her against the railings of the terrace.

'I've found you!' Tina went up behind her and put her arms around her neck in the stranglehold they had perfected as children. That was the thing about sisters – you always knew just how to hold them and exactly where to push to get the expected reaction. Lottie hated being taken by surprise. It wasn't until Tina had let her protesting sister go that she turned to look at her companion.

'Hello Tina,' Spike said.

A sudden flare of shock took her words away. She told herself that it was simply that she hadn't been expecting to see him. He looked just the same. Slightly older around the eyes maybe, a little less hair and more forehead – but everything else was unchanged. It wasn't until this moment that she realised just how well she remembered him. He still had that slightly protuberant left ear. She had once pinned it back with a bulldog clip as a joke.

'It's been a very long time. Seven years, I think,' Spike said, sensing his advantage.

'I thought you'd moved away from San Francisco,' she said at last. She was aware of Lottie looking at the two of them with curiosity.

'I did,' he said, 'but then I came back. I missed the smugness of the locals and being freezing cold at four o'clock in the afternoon, even in summer, and the terrifying cost of renting an apartment.'

'Are you still looking for little stones?' Tina asked.

'Yep. In fact, I'm going to Mexico in a couple of weeks' time on a field trip.'

'He collects pebbles,' Tina said, turning to Lottie in explanation.

'I'm actually a geologist with a particular interest in meteorites.' Spike's voice was good-humoured. 'But why split hairs? Tina's right – basically I look for bits of old iron.'

'It sounds very interesting,' Lottie said.

Tina yawned ostentatiously. 'It is if you're the sort of person who finds crawling around on scrubby ground riveting.'

Spike smiled at Tina, and she scowled at him. 'It's good to see you haven't changed. I've been hearing about your road trip plans from your sister. It sounds as if it's going to be quite an adventure.'

'Yes, it will, actually,' Tina answered sharply. She wondered if he was making fun of her.

'I wish I could come along,' he said, ignoring the edge in her voice.

'Three's a crowd. And besides, I'm sure our little trip will seem tame since you've seen it all before.'

'Travelling without children?' he asked.

'Neither of us has children,' Tina said.

'I see,' he said.

'I don't think you actually see much at all,' Tina retorted. 'You never bloody did.'

'Shall we go back inside and get a drink?' Lottie said. 'Why are you being so rude to him?' she whispered, as Spike led the way back inside.

'I've always brought out the best in her,' Spike said, without turning round.

*

Back at the party Tina disappeared with a tall woman dressed in what looked like a workman's overall. Lottie did her best to mingle. She attempted to dance a little, but she felt foolish and inhibited. She wondered why other people seemed to lose themselves so effectively, swaying with their eyes closed and their arms above their heads in a way that should have looked stupid, but somehow didn't. She could never seem to get her body to do what she wanted. The group next to her were doing moves to 'Blame It On the Boogie' in a great, grinning line, all with synchronised hand gestures. I just can't, I just can't dance, Lottie thought, and was relieved to see her sister making her way towards her.

'Shall we call it a night?' Tina shouted above the noise, and Lottie let herself be taken by the hand and pulled out of the room.

It was early October, and the city dripped slow rain from its curving metal staircases and elaborate plasterwork. Cars sparked water, the sound of their tyres like sticky tape being pulled away slowly. Lottie could smell the sea –a briny, slightly oily odour, as distinct as the spices and smoke of the daytime.

'Let's walk back,' Tina said. 'I don't think it's very far.' She was shivering a little in her tiny dress that barely covered her bottom. She fumbled in her bag and brought out a thin scarf that she wrapped around her shoulders. Lottie refrained from reminding her that she had suggested Tina should bring a jacket; even she knew she had to rein in her tendency to be pompous.

'So what's the story with Spike?' she asked.

'I met him when I was here last time.'

'Well, I know that! I was just wondering what happened between you. Didn't you live with him for months?'

'Just because I lived with him doesn't mean I was sleeping with him. Rachel was pregnant and being sick and I felt I'd outstayed my welcome at their house.'

'Something happened between you. I could tell by the way you were talking to each other.' Lottie might be a stiff on the dance floor but she could recognise intimacy when she saw it, and her sister had definitely had sex with the cat burglar on at least one occasion. Tina had gone into haughty hair-touching at the mere sight of him.

'It was just a fling. It was years ago and meant very little. I had several relationships – if you can call them that – while I was living here.'

Lottie had no trouble imagining the swathe a thirty-one-year-old Tina must have cut through the local male population. A man had once driven into a lamp post at the sight of her sister marching down the street in shorts – a story their mother was fond of recounting with a kind of envious glee. Lottie herself had only slept with three men, including Dean. They were getting married on the tenth anniversary of their first kiss.

It had been autumn. The wet leaves had slid under their feet and a bonfire with a chemical tang was burning somewhere near. In the park, the pear tree they were standing under still retained its fat, golden fruit and a girl, too old to be there, was moving backwards and forwards on a swing, bouncing her feet along the spongy stuff they put down so that children didn't hurt themselves. It had been a clumsy kiss – she had turned her head slightly at the last minute so that his mouth had landed on the corner of hers. But the second one had been better, and the heat of it had sent them home smiling and touching shoulders on the tube. In his room in the draughty shared house he had unbuttoned her coat and placed his hands on her waist and looked at her as he pulled her skirt up slowly. She had been amazed, both by his confidence and the depth of her longing. Despite the grey, unforgiving light, which came solidly through the curtainless window, and the housemate in the next room, she had forgotten and then found herself in him.

'How do you know that you'll want to sleep with him forever?' Tina had asked once, after a not particularly successful drink out which Lottie had arranged in an attempt to get her sister and her boyfriend to know each other better. 'It's not as if you have much to compare him to.'

'I just know,' she had said, and she did know, although there had been times over the years when she had allowed herself to wonder how it might be with someone else. Despite the way she loved him, there was a little tug sometimes from the things she would never now know. It was a bit like finding the perfect house and rejoicing that you can live in it forever, but feeling wistful on certain summer days that you were never going to live by the sea.

'I would hazard a guess that it was a little more, for him at least, than a fling,' Lottie said now, scrutinising her sister's profile. 'And you looked as if you had seen a ghost.'

'Stop staring at me!' Tina said, with exasperation. 'I can feel your eyes boring into the side of my head. You're wasted at that homelessness charity. You should work for the police. You'd force people to admit to all sorts, even things they hadn't done.'

Lottie smiled. 'I'll get it out of you in the end.'

Chapter 4

'YOU DO THE FIRST STRETCH, and I'll take over in a couple of hours,' Tina said, as she settled herself into the car. 'I'm feeling a bit rough at the moment.'

After saying goodbye to their hosts, they had had their first American breakfast in a café round the corner, Lottie tucking into a pile of pancakes topped with berries and maple syrup while Tina picked at a piece of toast.

'Where's our next destination?' Lottie asked.

'This trip is not about having an itinerary,' Tina said. 'It's about stopping when we feel like stopping. We can drive all day, or stay in one spot, just as the spirit moves us.'

'I'd rather the spirit didn't move us to spend the night in some lay-by, or up a track with a dead end,' Lottie said.

'Remember you agreed to say yes to everything. You even signed the document. Challenge One is for you to give up control. I know it's difficult for you, but let go of your addiction to timetables and maps. Allow yourself to just be, and see what turns up.' She fiddled with her phone and the melodic strains of the Red Hot Chili Peppers singing 'Road Trippin'' filled the car.

Lottie had always had an irresistible impulse to master her territory. Looking back, Tina thought it was as if Lottie could only come to terms with their regular moves if she was able to exactly record her environment. She would tear out pieces of paper from her exercise book and Sellotape them carefully together along their edges to make a large enough expanse to fashion a map. She would give grand names to even the most insignificant of things; a curved hedge was called The Green Crescent, a bus shelter became The Silver Cave and the downward slant of a road was The Great Fall. Each of these places was recorded and colour-coded in elaborate keys at the bottom of the page. The dotted lines along the streets, looking like Hansel and Gretel's dropped crumbs of bread, traced the routes they had taken. The map would be marked with things only Lottie had noticed: a house that looked like a bearded face, the slavering hound of hell who guarded the post office, the totem pole lamp post strung about with colour photographs of missing cats.

Tina could still see Lottie crouched on the floor, drawing her way back home. If all the maps her sister had made were laid out next to each other, they would represent a strange sort of a world where motorways became paths through woods and rivers rushed through back gardens – that was what it had felt like when they were children. They had never really known how far things stretched, and where what they had to know began and ended.

'I hate it when you say things like "just be",' Lottie said now. 'It makes you sound so vapid.'

'Only you would think to use the word vapid in casual conversation.'

'Well, it does. All that let's-go-where-the-wind-blows-us stuff makes me cringe,' Lottie said. 'And anyway, I thought going to the party last night was Challenge One.'

She was distinctly anxious about what Tina might ask her to do. She had found the party last night quite challenging enough.

When she had told Dean about the plan that she should acquiesce to whatever Tina told her to do, he had been incredulous. 'Under her hippy-dippy disguise,' he'd said, 'your sister is bloody power-mad. Why the hell are you agreeing to let her manipulate you?' She had been lying on her stomach at the time and he had been kissing the Finnish flag along her back. She had been struggling to identify its particular, subtle configuration. When it came right down to it, flags were pretty much all the same. At his instigation they sometimes played this game after sex. She found it endearing, but also ridiculous – a teacher and a charity worker's idea of post-coital tenderness. She smiled now to think of how Tina would mock it: *Christ, even sex with him involves having to LEARN something.*

She wasn't sure herself why she had capitulated to the challenges – only that she had heard the eagerness in her sister's voice and it had reminded her of what they had always done. The three of them had bound themselves together with avowals and promises, with demands of overt demonstrations of faith.

If you climb that tree to the very top, if you run across the level crossing, if you kick Mark Savage's ankle, we will live forever.

She remembered them sitting in the bunker on some quiet weekday evening, cutting the tips of their fingers with a Stanley knife and rubbing their bleeding hands together.

'We promise we will always stick together, come what may,' Tina had declared. She'd been dressed in a sheet, with a plastic flowerpot fastened to her head with an elastic band, the mistress of ceremonies, even then. She wants to test me as we used to test each other, Lottie thought. She thinks my life is dull and she wants to show me something else. It touched her to think that Tina wanted to share what she knew, and so Lottie had given in.

'God, no!' Tina said now. 'That was nothing. Your tasks are going to be things that really take you out of your comfort zone. But don't worry, I'll ease you in.'

Lottie's heart sank. She was aware that her comfort zone was a very narrow sliver of land, barely enough for a patch of lawn. She didn't trust her sister's concept of easing in. Easing in was a foreign notion to the woman who had once stabbed a man with a fork between his fingers, fastening him to the table, because he had put his hand on her leg. He had been married, but still – Lottie would have struggled to do more than blush and move away.

'We have to know where and when we are going to sprinkle the ashes,' Lottie said. 'We have to have that as a destination, at least.'

She had been trying not to think about it too much, but the idea that they were carrying what was left of Mia in the boot of their car made her anxious. She worried that a bump in the road or a sudden stop might dislodge the lid, that the gaffer tape she'd wrapped around it would not be strong enough. It was typical that it had been her, not Tina, who'd had to smuggle the thing into America in her suitcase.

'Why does it have to be me?' she had complained. 'I'm sure it's against the rules to bring ashes across borders. They might think it's drugs.'

'Because you look like the sort of person who would never do anything wrong,' Tina had answered, grinning wickedly.

Mia had made the transit safely. She was now tucked up under the carpet of the boot with the spare tyre, a precaution that Lottie had insisted on, despite Tina's derision. It was strangely painful to think of the fragments of her being carried along a road she had never seen.

'We don't know exactly where we are going to put her,' Tina said. 'Only that it has to be in Monument Valley at "Landing Rock", wherever that is.'

'That's the place Dove and Tache found the baby, right?'

'Yes. Just before they are ambushed and Dove gets injured and Tache goes back for him.'

'*Dove, so named because he is anything but peaceable, and Tache, who had the smallest moustache in the world,*' Lottie quoted.

Films had been a protection and an escape throughout their childhood, and they knew Mia's favourite movie by heart. They had latched on to westerns after Mia had come back from a jumble sale one day at the age of twelve with a box filled with videos of them – *Red River* and *High Noon* and *Butch Cassidy and the Sundance Kid* – Mia had loved them all, even *Hopalong Cassidy*, which everyone knew was a bit boring. The one she watched the most often was *Landing Rock*, the story of two brothers avenging the death of their murdered father.

'Why do you like it so much?' Lottie had asked her once.

Mia had smiled. 'I like the fact that where they get to is not where they set out for.'

'*If you think you are going to go and die on me, you'd better think again. The baby has just dropped a load in his diaper,*' Tina and Lottie said now in unison, and laughed.

'It's strange that she liked all that shooting and murder,' Lottie said. 'Not to mention the subjugation of women and Native Americans.'

'I think she liked the fact that in pretty much every movie the hero rights a wrong. In the process he has to fight the enemy, who is often someone a bit like him.'

'Yeah. The moral code is always clear, even if you might not like some of the ways the protagonists go about doing what they think's the right thing.'

Tina didn't answer, so Lottie continued.

'I think she saw herself in the role of the avenger. She was always trying to be good.'

'Stop talking now, I've got a headache,' Tina said.

Her sunglasses were on again even though it was foggy, and she was moving her head very carefully as though she thought it might topple off her neck.

I won't mention the red wine and the vodka and the cocaine, Lottie told herself. She didn't want to be a nag. Last night, her sister hadn't been able to fall asleep once they had finally got back to the house, which had turned out to be much further away than they had thought. By then Tina had been wired and frozen to the bone. They were sharing the double bed in the guest room, and Tina had shivered and wriggled beside her for at least an hour. Every time Lottie thought she was falling asleep, Tina would say something else.

'I can't get warm.'

'All I can see when I try and count sheep are their shitty bottoms.'

'What do you think is better – being blind or being deaf?'

'Do you think Trump's pubes are the same colour as his hair?'

'Tell me something interesting.'

'Describe what dull Dean is like in bed, that should send me off.'

'I'm too tired to talk,' Lottie had replied, her scratchy eyes firmly shut.

'Does he go down on you?'

'Fuck off, Tina.'

'I can't get comfortable. I'll never be able to sleep,' Tina had moaned. 'Do you remember that imaginary place I invented to escape into when dearest Ma and Pa were going at it hammer and tongs?'

'*Please* stop talking.' Lottie had tried to muffle her ears with her pillow. Her sister's words recalled the feeling of being in a siege that was so much part of her experience of childhood. They used to close their door on the rage that made downstairs a dangerous, shifting place, and the three of them would gather at the bottom of one of their beds, the sheets over their heads, pillows piled like hills and valleys. Without any props, they had been able to see and describe the place that lay there in front of them. *Bedtown* was a scattering of red-roofed houses that lay in the valley between two mountains. The graveyard had wafer-thin headstones. Shadowy cats, pale as ghosts, sat on the rims of bins. In the sweet shop the spun sugar shone in crimson and cobalt blue, the same colours as the church windows. The clothes emporium had dancing mannequins decked out in sequins and lace. The heart-shaped swimming pool was decorated with bunting and a flume twisted down into foaming water. White horses with green ribbons in their manes carried people up and down the mountain slope to the school on the other side of the mountain. A full moon, brighter than any sun, lit the town.

It had been Tina's masterpiece.

Looking sideways at her sister sitting slumped and sleeping in the passenger seat, Lottie felt a wave of affection for her. She was glad of it. It had been many years since they had spent any quality time together or talked properly. Maybe the trip would do them good after all.

Lottie hardly noticed leaving San Francisco. One minute they were on the bridge – the cables rising as they approached the first tower – lifting them towards the sky and then curving slowly downwards before ascending again, like the verses of a song, and then the city was behind them. She could see little more than the car in front. The landscape on either side of the road was blanketed in a dense, drizzling fog, but she knew they were driving by the sea because she could smell the salt of it and hear its swell. Not having any visible markers meant it was hard somehow to get a handle on the time. The further she drove, the further she felt from home. Dean would have done almost a full day's work by now. He always stayed far longer than he should at the school, preparing lessons for the next day or seeing pupils who needed a bit of extra help.

'You're so committed to your job,' she once said to him when he had eschewed a night out in favour of marking essays. She had often suppressed a disloyal impulse to wonder what, exactly, teachers had to work so hard at. It was pretty much the same lessons over and over again, wasn't it? That was what she remembered from her own schooldays, anyway.

'I should be committed, you mean,' he had said jokingly to her. 'Only a fool would persist in trying to get Year Nine to see the poetry in *Macbeth*. They would much rather be left alone to sit in the gloom of their bedrooms looking at women's bodies or blowing someone's head off with a machine gun. I'm surplus to requirements. They think I'm too old to understand the lure of flesh and violence.'

He had a precise way of talking, a kind of puckering of his lips and a tendency to stroke his facial hair that made him look as if he was taking the piss. But it was only himself that he mocked. He loved the children in all their grimy insolence and wouldn't have swapped his job for any other.

'Perhaps we should have a baby,' he had said the night before she left. She knew by the diligent way he had set about making love that he wasn't really happy about her going, although he'd tried to hide it. They had often talked vaguely about children, but the time had never seemed quite right. As a couple they had always been slow off the mark. Getting together in the first place had been an elaborate, indecisive dance. It had taken them three months to kiss each other, five years to decide to move in together and another three to renovate a kitchen, which only had half a floor and a rotting wooden draining board. Unable to decide on a honeymoon destination, they had postponed it indefinitely. Lottie couldn't fathom how other people made up their minds about things so quickly. Making choices felt fearful to her and she had fallen in love with someone who understood – and facilitated – her indecision. His gentleness, which she knew others (including Tina) took as weakness, had been what had attracted her to him in the first place. She loved it still, although she knew that in holding each other so carefully they were sometimes in danger of holding each other back.

She thought of the coil embedded in her womb, its plastic and copper T-shape, like a cul-de-sac, repelling the advance of life. They had probably missed their chance for children now. She was forty. Not old, but not young anymore. The imprint of the bed sheet on her face lasted longer than it used to and something was definitely happening to her knees. In any case, she couldn't really imagine herself as a mother. She had read somewhere that when you bore a child, they left vestiges of their DNA in you after they were born, so that you were not the same as you were before they set up residence in you. They took your cells with them, too, and passed them on to their children in their turn. It seemed that everyone was a mixture of all that had gone before.

A few miles before Monterey, the sun came out and Tina woke with a little startled gasp.

'Have I been asleep?' she asked, her face soft and puffed from sitting with her head hanging down. She looked around her. 'Let's stop for lunch when we get into town. I'm starving.'

Chapter 5

THEY FOUND A DINER BY a stretch of beach, on which a pile of elephant seals dozed in the sun. In the sea the creatures looked sleek and purposeful, but on land they were beached and blubbery, their whiskered faces and dark eyes displaying a comical contentment. They made sounds like someone gargling mouthwash and butted heads and scooped up sand and dragged their sluggish bodies across the beach, leaving a smooth pathway in their wake. People passed by, crammed into strange, canopied vehicles, and the sea beyond sucked at the legs of the pier.

Lottie and Tina ate burgers twice the size of the ones at home, served to them by a young woman with a hairsprayed fringe so rigid it formed a jutting ledge over her forehead. A thin man was sitting in the corner, working his way steadily through a giant mound of waffles as if he was playing out a bet that he couldn't gain a stone by the afternoon.

'Right!' Tina said with her mouth full of chips. 'It's time for Challenge Two. Your first challenge was to stop being such a control freak. Now we need to build on that.'

'Oh, God. You'll give me indigestion.'

'I want you to make conversation with that bloke over there.'

'What, him, in the corner?'

'I don't see anyone else around here,' Tina said, with a smirk. 'Do you?'

'What shall I say?'

'It's up to you. You invent the lines. Don't look so horrified. Although you often act as if we do, we don't actually live in an age when women can't talk to men unless they have been introduced at a ball.'

'I can see why you get yourself into the situations you do.' Lottie looked covertly at the man. He was of an indeterminate age with a face like a fox. He had a pointed nose and wispy facial hair and eyes just a shade too close together.

'And I can see why you don't get yourself into any situations at all,' her sister answered, scooping a glob of tomato ketchup onto her finger and licking it off. 'I want to see your seduction technique in action. I'm guessing it's going to be a little rusty.'

'God, you really do have the most disgusting manners,' Lottie said. 'I'm surprised your dates don't run off in horror after sitting opposite you at a dinner table for a few minutes.'

'Don't think that if you start insulting me I'll forget the matter in hand.' Tina reached over to grab a handful of Lottie's chips. It was lucky she was attractive, Lottie thought;

otherwise she would never get away with behaving like a pig. She swallowed. She couldn't fail so early in the expedition. She would never be able to survive her sister's contempt. She would have to do this bloody silly thing. She cleared her throat.

'Excuse me,' she said, and then realised that her voice had come out as a squeak, so she coughed. 'I'm sorry to disturb you, but I don't suppose you know if there is anything particularly interesting that we could visit while we are here? We're tourists.'

'Jesus,' Tina muttered under her breath, 'you sound as if you are about a hundred and three.'

The man raised his head and surveyed them. He slowly wiped his mouth with his napkin. 'Depends what y'all find interesting,' he said. He pushed his plate away from him and stood up, carefully placing his chair back under the table.

'Genius. One question from you and he loses his appetite and abandons his waffles,' Tina whispered.

Lottie was mortified. There was nothing she found harder to bear than her sister being proved right.

'I believe John Steinbeck lived and wrote here,' she said, smiling hopefully.

'Yeah, that is so,' he answered. He sloped past them to the door.

'It's a very beautiful place,' said Lottie, desperately, even though she had seen almost nothing of the town barring some corpulent seals, a few chubby tourists and an awful lot of ugly signage. What was it with Americans and signs, anyway? They seemed to want to announce everything, and if they couldn't use big voices they used big letters instead. Today, however, they had just hit upon the only American who didn't want to say anything at all.

'Yeah, it is that.'

'And so much marine life.' She was clutching at straws now.

'Yup, there is,' he said. Then he went out and shut the door firmly behind him.

Tina rocked back and forth with mirth. 'You should give lessons in how to attract men!' she said. 'People would pay good money to see how not to do it.' She scooped up the last of the chips into her grinning mouth.

'I'm not trying to attract men,' Lottie said. 'I have a perfectly good one at home.'

'I didn't mean I wanted you to have sex with him. I just wanted you to unbend and flirt a little.'

'He was probably repelled by your table manners. And anyway, are men really fooled by all that touch-your-hair-and-look-at-their-mouths garbage? If I was a man it would turn me right off.'

'I'm only teasing,' Tina said, relenting. 'He was a miserable sod. Probably suffering from cramps on account of the waffles. I wouldn't say you passed the challenge with flying colours, but at least you didn't duck it.'

*

They set off down Route 1 towards Big Sur. Lottie was glad that her sister had taken over the driving because the road was winding and precipitous. She was able to sit back and enjoy the fog-trimmed mountains, covered in feathery grass and pinkish succulents, and the sudden views of the sea, wild against craggy black stone. In the tiny space afforded between cliff and deep water, it felt somehow that they were between elements. There were palms and roses; the exotic and the familiar side by side in this light-veiled landscape. And then there were so many trees – redwoods and laurels and oaks and others she didn't know the names of.

They stopped by the roadside for a pee. Tina was exasperated that Lottie wouldn't squat by the car door with her, but insisted on wandering down a path out of sight of the road.

'I get stage fright!'

'What've you got to hide?' Tina shouted after her, leaning against the bonnet of the car and puffing on her vape. Lottie had forbidden its use in the car; she had said she couldn't stand the sucking noise it made. Tina had simply replaced one addiction with another and now the taste of inhaled liquorice vapour seemed to be more delicious to her than tobacco.

'I think you're very oral,' Lottie had said, in that reprimanding way that so annoyed her sister.

'Damn right I am. All the best things involve the mouth, if you know what I mean.'

'You're also obsessed with sex.'

'By the dreary look of Dean, it might be better if *you* were a little more interested in it.'

'I have a very satisfactory sex life, thank you very much.'

Tina watched her sister's progress down the track. After a ridiculous amount of deliberation, Lottie finally found a place behind a shrub and Tina smiled to see the way she spread out her cotton skirt like a woman in a painting by Constable, so that she could piss decorously beneath its folds. She had developed this technique as a child. 'Anyone who catches sight of me will think I'm just enjoying the landscape,' she had announced when she complacently demonstrated the trick, sitting like an eighteenth-century lady while a trickle appeared from beneath her skirt and snaked its way through the grass.

There was something unwavering about Lottie that Tina found perplexing. She couldn't understand how anyone could be as certain as her sister seemed to be about life. There was a part of Tina that envied it. It must be restful to know exactly what was coming next. Lottie had found the work she wanted to do – a laudably useful role as a fundraiser for a homelessness charity. Her house was a symphony of greys and blues. She was a mistress of the low-calorie casserole. She ran six miles every other day, come rain or shine or the very occasional hangover. Perhaps most perplexing of all was the way she seemed so sure that she had found the person she wanted to be with forever. Tina thought Dean was rigid and domineering, not nearly good enough for Lottie – but she was set on him, and on the ghastly white wedding dress with pearl buttons and lacing up the back that would surely make her resemble a trussed leg of lamb. Lottie had shown her a picture of it, touching the image on her phone as if it was something precious.

'Now you make sure you look after her,' Dean had said to Tina at the airport in his teacher's voice.

Tina thought it was unlikely she would ever find anyone that she actually wanted to commit herself to. She thought about her current lover, a fellow photographer who was away more than he was at home. The part-time nature of their relationship suited her. Absence sharpened a passion she suspected she would not feel as acutely if he were more readily available. Sex with him kept its urgency – its weekend, freewheeling, champagne-and-celebration feeling – and never quite had the opportunity to descend into predictability. Even so, the last time she had seen him she had been aware of a new timorousness, something perilously close to need that had made her falter. She liked men, enjoyed the thrill of the chase, loved sex with the ones who bothered to put the effort in, even valued the companionship – it was nice, after all, to have someone to wake up with and accompany to parties and gigs – but she found relationships extraordinarily difficult to sustain. It just required too much . . . energy, and in any case, when a certain amount of time had elapsed (usually around the four- or five-month mark), she often found the man in question was lacking in some way or other. The hero in bed turned out to be limp in his dearth of ambition. The clever, funny chap who could transform the making of a salad into an entertainment had two young children that sucked up his time. The guy that pulled out chairs and remembered what she had said on previous dates was fatally attached to his mother. It seemed there was always some flaw to turn her heart or her mind. Besides, she was far from perfect herself. She couldn't imagine there would be any man who would be able to absorb all that she was, the few good bits and the far greater number of things she was ashamed of, things which kept her awake at night.

When she looked again, Lottie had disappeared from her pastoral perch, so Tina got her camera and followed her down the track. The air smelt of juniper and sage and verbena and gorse, and the light was golden like honey. She found her sister in a little cove. The sea, heavy with maroon kelp, was quiet here, sheltered as it was by a stony outcrop. Lottie's face was glowing. Tina took a close-up picture of her so that only half of her head was in the frame, the freckled skin around the side of her nose, a section of the mouth they shared, one eye, wide and greenish in the sun, and the sea lying behind like a promise. She didn't know how lovely she was.

'It's so abundant!' Lottie exclaimed, gesturing to the tangled, complex water, the mass of raptors sweeping overhead and the bountiful, herby track. Even the tumbled rocks were heaped in generous mounds.

'The land of plenty,' Tina said.

'If you were a sandwich, what sandwich would you be?' Tina asked as they got back into the car. As a child, Mia had been obsessed with this particular game, as if, even then, she had been trying to work out what it was that exactly defined her.

'I can't believe you are still thinking about food!'

'Go on, play the game, sis.'

'I'd be an avocado on wholegrain bread.'

'How drearily healthy you are! I'd be a pastrami and crisp bacon on rye with lashings of mayonnaise and some fat pickles,' Tina said. 'Being as we are in America, and all.'

They travelled the impossibly beautiful curves of the road, view after stunning view, each better than the one before. They drove to the sound of Ray Charles's gospel version of 'America The Beautiful', The Mamas and the Papas singing 'California Dreamin'' and Lana Del Rey's moody 'West Coast'. Tina insisted on having the roof down despite the chilly edge in the air and so they cranked the heating up, which made Lottie feel profligate and a little wild.

At around seven they found a suitable overnight stop at a glamping site in Big Sur and took possession of a yurt. Lottie, who had been getting anxious about where they were going to stay, was relieved when Tina suddenly turned off the road. She still couldn't quite come to terms with her sister's spontaneity. Their accommodation had a polished wooden floor and two beds with faux-fur throws, and a lit stove in the centre.

'It's the epitome of *hygge*,' said Lottie, looking around her in delight.

'What is hooga?' Tina said, throwing her suitcase onto one of the beds.

'It's a Danish word that means recognising special moments and celebrating them. It's also about being cosy. A *hyggekrog*, for instance, is a little nook you can snuggle up in.' Lottie unzipped her suitcase to reveal neatly arranged, rolled-up clothes.

'More like a Danish marketing ploy to make us buy all those bug-ugly beeswax candles and scratchy socks. Less hooga and more hooey.' Tina surveyed Lottie's suitcase. 'My God, have you brought anything on this trip that isn't navy or black?'

'It's easier when everything matches,' Lottie said peaceably.

'OK Miss Matchy-Matchy, let's hit the hot tub before we eat in the yurt-shaped restaurant.' Tina pulled off her red shorts and orange sweatshirt. Her body was beautiful, pale-skinned and narrow-waisted, and Lottie was painfully conscious of the persistent roll around her own middle that wouldn't budge however many hours she spent running.

'Are you not wearing a costume?' Lottie asked.

'Challenge Number Three: sit naked in a hot tub. No towels or beach cover-ups allowed.'

'But what if someone comes by?'

'Just say hello and ask them to join us,' Tina said, grabbing a bottle of red wine from the provisions rucksack (a travelling essential, according to Lottie, who had planned to fill it with healthy snacks – but Tina had had other ideas) and two wine glasses from the cupboard, which had been *hygge*-ified with scorched doors.

The hot tub was positioned at the side of the tent and had a view of the sea and the beginnings of a sunset, rose pink now but soon to bloom into a startling orange. Tina walked out like a queen and plunged in. Lottie followed a few moments later, hastily submerging herself so that she was in bubbles up to her neck. She gave a sigh of contentment.

'It's like heaven, isn't it?' Tina said, pouring the wine.

'What if we have to get out of the tub and go somewhere?' Lottie asked, looking around her. The place was quiet, but every now and again someone emerged from a nearby yurt to go to the toilet block or the restaurant, or to walk along the road by the sea.

'Why would we have to do that?'

'Or say the stove caught fire and we couldn't get back into the yurt?'

Tina palmed her forehead. 'I've lost count of the number of things you worry about . . . fire, floods, running out of drinking water, cutting your tongue when you lick envelope flaps, exploding cookers, garlic breath, the fluid levels in your ears and not having enough clean knickers – and that's just a few of them, not to mention showing even a small section of your body.'

'It's all right for you. Your body is perfect.'

'I have no breasts to speak of, my bum is square and, unless I really concentrate, I walk with my feet turned in. I think you have a far sexier body than mine.'

Lottie made a disbelieving face. 'I promise I'll try and relax,' she said, allowing her neck and arms to emerge. She took a gulp of wine. 'This is like a glamorous version of sister soup.'

'I remember you used to accuse me of having verrucas.'

Lottie smiled. 'We were all so close then.'

'Mia kept us together,' Tina said, her voice sombre.

They could no longer see the sea, only hear it. From where they were sitting, the waves sounded like the night traffic in San Francisco.

It was true, Lottie thought. Mia had always been the glue. As three sisters, they had had their own language and their own strength. Three was the perfect number. Three was the Holy Trinity, three wishes, Three Musketeers, Three Graces, three harpies, three witches. Mountains and rivers and bridges came in threes. Even crops were grown in three-sister formations, the corn providing the height for the beans to climb up, the marrow giving ground cover so that the other two plants could thrive. When they were children they had once made up a triangle, the sturdiest shape of them all. If you took away one corner of it, it was simply a line going nowhere.

'We became like a stool with only two legs,' Lottie said.

Tina nodded sadly. 'Yes, we did.'

Chapter 6

THE NEXT MORNING WAS MIA'S birthday and her shadow hung over them. Lottie disappeared for a run and Tina walked along the beach taking photos. Her heart wasn't really in it. The sea, which had seemed so beautiful the day before, was drab under a cloudy sky. The sand was covered in weed – horrible stuff with green blisters, still unpleasantly moist. Pelicans swarmed in the air, occasionally diving head first into the water as if suddenly losing power. The awkwardness and distance between her and Lottie had risen up again now that the first excitement of being on the road had worn off. It had been stupid of her to imagine that the trip was going to move something on between them. She wasn't even sure what it was that she had hoped for.

They were too different now. It was more even than a difference of personalities. You could love people whose idea of fun was rubbing their Lycra-clad thighs together like locusts on interminable weekend bike rides, or people who had a special Hoover for cleaning out their car, or who wrote letters to the paper about the dearth of taxis. Hell, you could even love a Brexiteer as long as they didn't talk about it. What was harder to deal with was not being able to find a way through to the common ground, the stuff that bound you together, even if one of you enjoyed spending high days and holidays dressed up as a Tudor wench.

Lottie had stopped running and was sitting on the edge of a wall, looking out to sea. She felt too tight and miserable to really get going, and she had only managed a mile or so before despondency had shut her legs down. Running usually liberated her and silenced the querulous voice in her head.

You should be doing this. You have forgotten to do that. Why do you always say the wrong thing? Does the mole on your back look bumpier than it did last week? Is there really a point to any of this?

She supposed she should try meditation or mindfulness, both advertised at her local community centre, but sometimes her thoughts seemed unstoppable. Surely any intervention would only offer a brief respite, the way a beaver-built dam in a river only holds fast until the first spring tide. Besides, sitting cross-legged making uninhibited sounds with strangers was not something she felt she could comfortably do. She wondered if the day would ever come when she would listen to her thoughts and there would be no commands or criticisms, only the unchaotic sparking of joy or of noticing what needed to be seen. Somehow she always got in the way of herself.

She had taken the job at the homelessness charity because she thought it might make a difference to people who had nothing. She had also hoped it might put her worries in perspective, having to contemplate on a daily basis what it was really like to have no sure and safe place to be. The stories the homeless people told her about the inevitable steps downwards, the small increments that led to a scrap of cardboard by a hot air vent, moved and dismayed her but did nothing to switch off her redundant static.

As she stared at the sea, grey today and moving gently as if brewing something, she wondered if she had always been like this.

'We have to get rid of some of this stuff. We haven't space in the car,' her mother had once said, getting ready for a move to another town by tipping the entire contents of her desk drawers into bin bags. Lottie could still remember the feeling of panic their loss had engendered. The maps, the journals of holidays, the scraps of things cut out and glued – these were what helped her to make sense of what was otherwise confusing. What she did, what she had always done, was to establish routines, set things down so that they were clear and unambiguous.

Mia had helped. She'd had the gift of seeing to the heart of things, of making dramas and anxieties seem not so bad, just annoying or inconvenient but easily surmounted.

Nothing was ever the end of the world to her – until, of course, it had been.

With a little twist of pain, Lottie thought of how beautiful Mia had been as a young woman: tall and strong, with the kind of curves that denim was made for. She had a long neck and sloping shoulders and a round, dimpled face and the Ward girl curving top lip. She caught the eye, not because her beauty was dazzling, but because it surprised you. She had stealth beauty. The kind that makes people feel clever for noticing.

'Here you are!' Tina exclaimed, appearing suddenly from round the corner and sitting down on the wall. 'I've been looking for you. I thought you had gone running in the other direction.'

'I've barely run at all,' Lottie replied. 'I've just been sitting here, thinking.'

'What have you been thinking about?'

Lottie paused. 'What makes us the way we are.'

The wind picked up slightly, knocking the wading birds off balance and catching up the sand so it misted the surface of the beach like steam.

'I don't think I actually know who I am,' Tina said, with surprising openness. 'I'm quite hard-working, loyal to my friends, impulsive, unromantic, grumpy – but I'm getting on for forty and I still feel half formed. Look at me, I'm still dressing like a teenager.'

Lottie looked at her sister. She was wearing a bra top under a checked shirt that doubled as a dress.

'You look beautiful,' Lottie said. 'I need to get something that isn't black, white or navy. I feel so ordinary next to you.'

Lottie didn't much care what she wore. She chose plain clothes simply because it was one less thing to dwell on in the morning. She had no flair for putting things together, but she knew it would make her sister happy to imagine she was having an impact. It made her feel suddenly tender towards Tina, to be able to offer her this.

Her sister lit up gleefully at her words and grabbed her hand. 'Right, that's Challenge Four sorted. We're going to hit the shops!'

Lottie laughed. 'That's not much of a challenge.'

'It is when I'm in charge of it,' said Tina in a slightly menacing tone.

They packed up the car and set off with Lottie at the wheel. Simon and Garfunkel were spinning out their gentle ballad 'America', which echoed Lottie's mood this morning with its mournful theme of searching for something when you didn't quite know what you were looking for. They stopped at a small strip of shops – the kind you find at regular intervals along pretty much any American highway. In the car park, a hummingbird hung over some hibiscus, its wings beating so fast that it seemed, for all its sophisticated motion, as if it wasn't moving at all.

'This one looks promising,' Tina announced, leading Lottie into the type of shop she never normally even noticed, set as she usually was on purchasing a replacement pair of jeans or a black jumper. There were tiny T-shirts and bejewelled shorts and wispy dresses made up of little more than a couple of straps and a pocket. Tina plucked garments off hangers as if she was catching butterflies and hustled Lottie into a changing room.

'It's OK if I vape, right?' Tina asked the startled attendant, leaning back in a chair luxuriantly, a cloud of mist swirling around her.

'Well . . . it's not strictly . . . um . . . permitted,' the woman ventured. She was wearing high-heeled shoes with spikes, which looked as if she had just trodden on a hedgehog, and a bright red pinafore dress, which added to the general roadkill look.

'I feel like Richard Gere in *Pretty Woman*,' Tina announced, ignoring the shop attendant's objections.

'A ruthless, misogynistic, middle-aged man obsessed with material things who pays a woman for sex and then pays her some more to become his wife,' Lottie hissed from behind the dressing-room curtain.

'OK, Hugh Grant then, in the scene when that American person is trying on wedding dresses.'

'So you're a floppy-haired idiot who can't keep it in his pants, who chooses a numpty in a big hat who is so daft she doesn't even know that it's raining, over Kristin Scott Thomas?'

'You really need to lighten up a little, Lottie.'

There was the sound of urgent scrambling from behind the curtain.

'I'm bloody well not coming out in this one!' Lottie shouted.

'Come on. Reveal yourself. Remember you're on challenge time.'

There was a muffled groan and then the curtain parted to reveal Lottie, bright red in the face, her normally groomed hair in a state of disarray. She had squeezed herself into a tube of animal-print Lycra.

'Your breasts look magnificent!' Tina announced, provoking another moan from her sister.

'I look like a leopard that has just ingested an impala,' she said, tugging at the dress.

'OK, OK. It's not for you. Move on!'

The next showing was a minuscule dungaree dress with a startled rabbit embroidered on its bib.

'Why have you been hiding those legs?' Tina said.

'Tina, I'm a forty-year-old woman.'

A slip dress made out of something that looked like foil was rejected for its fire-hazard properties. A gauzy blouse and shorts met the same fate for their nipple and camel-toe exposure. Lottie pulled a terrible face in an all-in-one littered with bumblebees ('I look as if I have some kind of a rash'), and posed sarcastically in a floral frock that had more than a hint of alpine upholstery.

'That's the one!' Tina said, fifteen outfits later. Lottie was wearing a deep orange, slightly off-the-shoulder dress cinched at the waist with a broad leather belt.

'Are you sure I don't look like a satsuma?' Lottie asked, but she was smiling. Tina also persuaded her to buy some loose blue silk shorts with big pockets, and a yellow top to go with them.

'We are sartorially sated,' Tina said, tucking into a greasy grilled cheese sandwich in the café next door.

'Thank you,' Lottie said, 'although I'm not altogether sure that Dean will like them. He prefers muted colours.'

'You surprise me,' Tina said, 'and here I was thinking he favoured purple leather.'

'He's not as boring as you think he is,' Lottie protested – and then laughed at the qualification in her own words. 'He's just not flashy. He doesn't need to be because he knows who he is.'

'Is that why you like him so much?' Tina asked.

'Partly. He never falters.'

'Are you sure you're not mixing up a strong sense of self with inflexibility?'

'I don't think so. He's just sane, when so many other people don't seem to be.'

She remembered a train journey back to London. They had been at a wedding somewhere – there was a period of their life when they always seemed to be at weddings – and they had been sitting next to a group of young men drunk after a night out. The ringleader was louder than the rest, with a highly coloured face that was only a few years short of ruined, and a meatiness about him that made you want to look away. In the row of seats in front of them was a man who had the uncoordinated, bewildered look of someone struggling with a disability; his white neck and ugly anorak marked him out as a person who was used to being the focus of derision. The florid man started ripping up pieces of newspaper, chewing them noisily and then spitting them at the back of the man's head, cheered on by his companions. The man in the anorak winced each time the pellets hit, but did nothing to stop the onslaught. Everyone else in the compartment was looking studiously out of the window. Dean had stood up and tapped the assailant on the shoulder. 'Don't be a dickhead,' he had said, looking him in the eye when he turned.

He had been shoved back into his seat for his trouble, but his action had shifted the mood on the train. Other people had started to murmur about ringing the police. One woman tutted loudly. Another held up her phone threateningly. In the end, after gazing around with a piggy-eyed belligerence, the tormentor shrugged and sat down. Lottie had been so proud of Dean she'd held onto him all the way home. He was a good person. She felt a little rush of happiness at the thought that they would soon be married.

Tina and Lottie drove back into Big Sur and took a walk in a patch of redwood trees. These were smaller than the ones found further north, and yet still magnificent with their great fluted trunks, frequently hollowed out at the base and providing shady caves for bats. Breaking through the tops of the trees, the sun struck the path in front of them in great slices of light, so that it seemed to their dazzled eyes that the world was a series of lines and segments. Lottie was not sure if she was imagining the smell of incense that insinuated itself sweetly through the odour of mushroomed wood and dank earth.

'If you were a landscape, what would you be?' she asked Tina.

'I'd be a great, straight beach with a boardwalk in the middle, and people would stroll and cycle and skate down it, and in the sky would be hundreds of kites with coloured tails.'

'I'd be a forest,' Lottie said. 'Something like this one, but with more water around, so you could hear it wherever you were, and the ground would be soft under my feet.'

'You are an utter weirdo,' Tina said, laughing. 'Who wants squelchy ground when you can have golden sand?'

'What landscape was Mia?'

'Oh, I don't know . . . a field of sunflowers, or perhaps the South Downs with their rolling acres of poppies.'

'I think her landscape was something much darker.'

It was typical of Tina to put a convenient gloss on things. Poppies and sunflowers! Even now she couldn't bear to look squarely at anything. She had been right to describe herself as half-formed, Lottie thought; she was still a child. The fondness Lottie had felt for her sister earlier in the day was replaced by irritation. Lottie should be at home, making the most of her days of leave, working out seating arrangements and buying shoes, not walking through this wood with a person who had spent most of her life pretending that everything was all right when it wasn't, and that all you had to do was to keep on collecting things – men, travel destinations, hilarious anecdotes – as a barricade against, actually looking at anything.

It was ironic, when you thought about it, that Tina had become a photographer, which above all other jobs surely demanded keen and extraordinary observation. And yet she was good at her trade, particularly her portraits of women. Tina's photographs revealed her sitters' personalities clearly, as if she had somehow made them show more than they wanted to. She had always taken photographs of the three of them when they were children – balancing her camera on walls and chairs so that she could be in the picture too. Every year she took a special one on New Year's Day, wherever they happened to be. She slotted the photographs into a series of plastic folders so that they could be unfolded in date order, the clothes and hairstyles changing, the backgrounds almost always new, the early closeness morphing into the stubborn solitariness of adolescence, the alliances, the arms around shoulders seeming permanent since they were recorded there, but always shifting in real time. Despite the changing backgrounds and the way one or other of them stood slightly apart, whether one frowned and the others smiled, it was always clear that they were utterly linked.

Lottie couldn't remember when Tina had stopped taking the photographs. Looking back, it seemed to Lottie that the end of that yearly ritual had been the first stage of letting Mia slip away.

Chapter 7

LOTTIE COULDN'T BELIEVE TINA WAS hungry again. Maybe it was her energy that gave her such a large appetite. It was only when Tina collapsed into one of her sudden sleeps, head down like a switched-off toy, that she stopped moving. The rest of the time she was either talking or gesticulating or asking to stop and walk somewhere. Lottie was still angry at what she perceived as her sister's flippancy about Mia, although her irritation had been somewhat assuaged by the purchase of a large wooden horse sculpture from a shack they had stumbled upon in the woods. The man who had made it had been so ingrained with dust he looked a little like one of his own creations. It was beautiful, with its flared nostrils and wild mane, and she hadn't been able to resist. Especially because she knew that it would irritate Tina.

'Bloody fantastic! Now we've got a flipping great lump of wood *and* an urn of ashes,' Tina had said, in a disgusted tone of voice.

The horse was now sitting on the back seat strapped in by a seat belt.

They rejoined Route 1. After the mottled shade of the trees, the light was almost Mediterranean, as if they had passed through an invisible boundary. Already the earlier soft mists had moved into memory and the sea had changed to a jaunty turquoise.

They stopped by a working pier with sinks and taps for rinsing fish and pelicans on posts. In a salty, brisk seafood outlet they ate bowls of clam chowder and white fish fried in olive oil, fragrant and new from the ocean. They toasted their trip with bottles of Amstel Light. There was happiness, somehow, in the air, even though they had been mired in a kind of discontent such a short time ago. It was like that with sisters, Lottie reflected: you moved from love to annoyance and back again in seconds. Beneath their feet the glass floor revealed the lazy perambulations of seals and fish in silver clouds, moving as one.

The road smoothed out and lost its showy curves, the cliffs giving way to barren, rounded hills and plains of cattle. The Beach Boys sang 'California Saga', and in the sky a plane had left the smudged words 'Open For Business' across the blue. In Morro Bay Tina bought them matching cowboy hats.

'We've got to get into costume,' she said. 'Do this thing properly. Mia would have wanted us to be cowboys.'

Lottie could tell she was making an effort. She offered a feeble protest, saying that it would make them look like tourists, but capitulated when Tina placed the hat on her head and fastened it firmly under her chin. They wandered down a street of shops selling shells and trinket boxes and slabs of fudge. There was a huge extinct volcano peak, over five hundred feet high, planted out in the bay. According to the leaflet, it was twenty million years old and one of nine. The other eight were now submerged under the water. Lottie thought of the landscape below their eyeline, mountains and valleys and plants moved by the water as if blown by the wind. Dean would like this town. There was something orderly about it that she knew would appeal to him. He was a man who stored the screwdrivers in strict size order in his immaculate toolbox. Sometimes she would deliberately put things in the wrong place just to rile him.

'Do you think I'm boring?' he'd asked her once, after she had teasingly paired his socks into mismatched days of the week, Monday toes tangled up with the Friday ones.

'No, I don't,' she had answered. 'You're just a little predictable.'

He had smiled and nudged her out into the garden and they had made love in the hidden spot on the lawn between the shed and the row of bamboo. His face had been full of her even though he was already late for work. Afterwards, he put on a pair of the mismatched socks and left the house whistling. The memory of his triumphant gaiety made her smile now.

She was distracted from her thoughts by the sight of a giant conch shell, glinting at her through a shop window.

'No. Just no,' Tina said threateningly, seeing the direction of her gaze. 'We'll have to hire a trailer if you carry on like this.'

Lottie regretfully tore herself away. They walked on in silence, enjoying the sun on their arms and the sense of not having to be anywhere in particular. It struck Lottie that she was getting accustomed to Tina's relaxed approach to travel. There were certain compensations for not knowing where you were going.

'What do we have in common?' Tina suddenly asked.

'Umm, well . . . we both like cheese. We like making stuff.'

This latter thing was certainly true. All three of them had always had restless fingers. They kept themselves occupied with glue and wool and beads, a hundred projects started and never quite completed.

'And freckles. We all have freckles. Do you remember we once joined all of Mia's freckles up with a magic marker when she was asleep? We made constellations on her face – I can't believe she didn't get mad.' Lottie smiled. 'We have freckles, and we know the names of the stars,' she said firmly, as if she was trying to convince herself of something.

Up ahead of them, a man was bending over the open bonnet of his car. As they approached, he shut it with an angry bang and turned round.

'Fucking hell, it's Spike!' Tina said. 'What's he doing here?'

Almost at the same time, he saw them too, and his face broke into a broad grin. There was a slight tensing of his body before he relaxed into his greeting.

'Well, howdy!' he said, indicating their hats.

'Are you following us?' Tina asked.

'No, I'm not, although I admit it kinda looks that way,' Spike said, rubbing his hands, which were dark with engine oil, against his jeans.

'So why are you here?'

'I'm due in Mexico in a couple of weeks but I have some vacation to take. So I decided on the scenic route.'

'And you just happen to be in the exact same place as we are on the exact same day?'

'It looks like I'm some kind of stalker, doesn't it?'

Lottie thought the man did rueful extremely well. He smeared a trail of grease across his forehead.

'I'd lay money on it,' Tina said grimly.

Lottie smiled. 'We are, of course, delighted to see you.'

'Well, I'm not bloody delighted,' Tina said.

'I know how it seems, but seriously, I wouldn't even be here now if my car hadn't broken down. I was aiming for an overnight stop just beyond Guadalupe. I've got a friend with a house near the beach. Thought the two of us could hang out and do a little fishing.'

'Well, good luck with that,' Tina said. 'We've got to be on our way.'

'Will you at least stop and have a coffee with me? I've rung the local garage and they're coming to look at my pile-of-shit car.'

'*I'd* like a coffee,' Lottie said. It was not very often that she had the upper hand, and she wanted to play it to the full. She was curious to know exactly what had happened between Tina and Spike that meant that, every time her normally laid-back sister saw him, she acted like a cat on a hot tin roof.

Tina looked furiously at her.

'What was it you were saying about taking things as they come?' Lottie said. 'This is a perfect example. We bumped into Spike, which is something we were not expecting.' Tina made a kind of humphing sound, not so dissimilar to the noise the seals had made in Monterey. 'And so now, according to your own philosophy, we should go with it, right?'

'OK,' Tina said ungraciously, 'but we'll only stay for a short while.'

They went into the nearest place, an eco-bakery of the kind that Americans called 'cozy', its walls advertising poetry slams and jam sessions, the slamming and the jamming all presumably taking place among the woodblock tables and hanging bunches of chilli. Lottie was amused to see the way that her sister insisted on ordering a cup of coffee to take away, as if she couldn't bear the thought of actually sitting down at a table with Spike. In the end it was clear that she felt a little foolish standing at the counter with her cup in her hand, and so she joined them with the same look on her face that she had worn as a child when she was thwarted in any way. She had always been a terrible loser. She would cheat and lie her way to victory, doing whatever she needed to do to get around the board, or to the winning post first. She would trip you up if it meant she would win the race.

'You're so competitive it's scary. You actually have the characteristics of a psychopath,' Lottie had said once, when it was discovered that Tina had Blu-Tacked winning cards to the underneath of the table during a game of rummy. Lottie had developed a fondness for books about serial killers.

'It's better to read something than nothing at all,' their mother had said when she discovered a book about a man who specialised in melting faces by Lottie's bed.

'You're just as competitive as me,' Tina had answered. 'It's just that you are passive-competitive. You pretend you are not competitive, but you actually are.'

'For your information there is no such thing as passive-competitive. There's only passive-aggressive.'

'Well, you're that too,' Tina had said.

'So where were you two heading next?' Spike asked. He really was incredibly handsome, Lottie thought. The kind of handsome that she often found intimidating, but somehow, on him, wasn't. He wore his beauty with a kind of nonchalance, and his clothes looked as if he had pulled them from the back of the car and put them on. She supposed there was no call for looking smart when you spent your time on dusty, wide-open spaces looking for black rocks.

'We're going where the spirit moves us,' Lottie said, giving Tina the side-eye and making Spike laugh.

'I've heard that somewhere before,' he said.

'All the best road trips are spontaneous,' Tina said stiffly, her hauteur somewhat diminished by a moustache of coffee foam.

'Well, I hope you guys aren't going to spontaneously drive off a cliff or anything.'

'We're going to sprinkle our sister's ashes,' Lottie said. 'She was really into westerns, so we are taking her to Monument Valley.'

Tina looked at her as if to tell her to shut up.

'Oh,' Spike said, 'I'm sorry. I knew there was a third sister, but I didn't know she had died.'

'She died three years ago,' Lottie said, ignoring her sister's repressive look.

'How old was she?'

'Thirty-nine.'

'What happened? If you don't mind me asking.'

'She died suddenly,' Tina said, in her I'm-shutting-down-this-conversation voice.

'That's so sad. Well, I hope you find her a good resting place.'

Just then his phone went.

'Ah, the mechanic is with my car, I'll be back in a moment.' He hurried out of the café.

'He's nice,' Lottie said.

'If you say so,' Tina said.

'What happened with him? Did you have a relationship that went wrong?'

'Something like that,' Tina answered.

Tina could still clearly remember the first time she had seen him. She had been out with a group of friends, fellow Brits that she had hooked up with in San Francisco. One of them, a scientist, had previously met Spike through his work and stopped to say hello. It wasn't his looks that had first caught her attention; it was the life that sparked off him. He didn't stay talking long, only enough time to exchange some pleasantries, but after he had walked on, she remembered feeling brightly and uncomfortably alive, as if something coarse had grazed her skin. She didn't think he had even noticed her.

It seemed, however, that he had. A week or so later she had been at The Fillmore, seeing a band she had never even heard of. She'd only gone because there had been a spare free ticket. Someone had tapped her on the shoulder as she was waiting to be served at the bar and she had turned round to see him standing there. She had felt the same impact as before, but this time she noted the shape of his face – an almost cartoonishly perfect jawline, a sensual mouth and dark eyes that were not quite symmetrical, the slight dissonance making him even more striking.

'He's actually very arrogant,' Tina said now, although she knew her description wasn't quite fair. He certainly wasn't without vanity. Like many handsome men, his looks sometimes made him lazy. His emphatic beauty often acted as a substitute for the effort less well-proportioned men put in. He was used to being looked at, being favoured, but she knew his handsomeness was a lucky sideline in him rather than a defining characteristic. It wasn't quite that he was arrogant – more that he was unbending. You were either in or out. There was little room for manoeuvring. He reminded her of Lottie, actually, in the way he made up his mind and stuck to it.

'He doesn't seem that way to me,' Lottie said.

'You're quite smitten.'

'Don't be silly. Not smitten, of course not. He's just quite impressive. That self-contained way he has about him. The fact he doesn't seem to notice how breathtakingly gorgeous he is.'

'Oh, he notices all right,' Tina said.

In the far corner of the room, a poetic battle had commenced. A man and a woman – she dressed in kimono and hair ribbons, he already sweating and pinkish in a cloak – were spinning Shakespearean riffs.

'I think it's probably time to go,' Tina said.

Just as they were getting up, Spike came back in.

'The car is a no-hoper. It's going to cost more to fix it than it's worth. I've told the man to take it away to be scrapped.'

'Oh, that's such a shame,' Lottie said.

'I guess I'll have to hire a car. I might have to scratch my idea of taking the leisurely route to Mexico and go back to San Francisco.'

'Perhaps it wasn't meant to be,' Tina said.

She swept out of the café. Lottie trailed behind her, casting apologetic glances over her shoulder.

Back at the car, Tina put on her dark glasses and revved the engine impatiently as Lottie got in.

'I feel sorry for him,' Lottie said.

'I wouldn't waste your energy,' Tina said. 'He'll be fine.'

'Couldn't we just take him part of the way with us?' Lottie said.

Tina scowled. 'No, we absolutely could not.'

'It might add another dimension to our trip,' Lottie said, as Tina pulled off with a showy screech of tyres, one hand holding her hat on.

'I wonder what darling Dean would say to see you so taken by another man,' Tina said, and Lottie subsided into silence.

A mile or so down the road, Tina drew into a lay-by.

'Actually,' she said, 'it might be a good idea if we take him along.'

Lottie was astonished.

'What's brought about the change of heart?' she asked.

'I think that Spike Linden could be just the thing we need on this trip,' Tina said.

She made a risky three-point turn and headed back the way they had come. Now that her sister had capitulated, Lottie wasn't feeling quite so sure about the decision. Ten minutes ago she had been all for it, partly because Tina was so resistant to the idea. Her sudden reversal was a little puzzling. Tina might be a free spirit, but she could also be extremely calculating, and Lottie wasn't at all sure that her present calculations were benevolent.

'Maybe this isn't such a good plan after all,' she said.

'You can't change your mind now,' Tina said. 'Challenge Number Five is you have to agree to take Spike with us.'

Back in Morro Bay, they found him unloading his rucksack from the back of his car. The mechanic from the garage was reversing his truck into position so that he could tow it away. Tina drew up alongside him.

'I've been prevailed upon by my better half to take pity on you,' Tina said, tilting her hat to the back of her head. 'Do you fancy hitching a ride with us?'

Chapter 8

SPIKE HAD BEEN SURPRISED TO see them again in Morro Bay. The screech of their departing tyres had sounded pretty final to him.

'No, I couldn't impose. This trip is a sister thing, isn't it?' he had said, trying to read Tina's inscrutable face behind her sunglasses. 'I've decided to take the train back to San Francisco and get a ride to Mexico in a week or so with one of my colleagues.'

'What about your fishing excursion?' Lottie asked.

'The fish aren't going anywhere,' he had said, pulling his rucksack onto his back. It weighed a ton.

'Get in,' Tina had said, revving the engine. 'You've got exactly five seconds to make up your mind.'

His immediate impulse had been to walk away. He disliked being faced with ultimatums of this sort. Tina's brand of spontaneity had always contained an element of coercion. She had fixed ideas on what constituted living life to the full, and often derided as dull the people who didn't fit in with her vision.

'All that saving and scrimping,' she had once said with disdain after visiting some friends who had been proudly showing off their new apartment. 'All those years of monstrous doing without, just to live in three rooms with a view of a supermarket.'

He hated the fact he remembered so much of what she had said all those years ago. It felt like a weakness in him. She hadn't changed at all. She still had that maddeningly superior way about her, the same disregard for other people's feelings. Her sister seemed to be a less fixed and softer character. He detected a humour in Lottie's face, a kind of wry self-deprecation that was singularly absent in Tina, who had always taken herself far too seriously. This was ironic, considering she claimed to make things up as she went along.

'We'll feel bad abandoning you here,' Lottie said.

It was the kindness in her voice that finally made him decide to heave his bag onto the back seat and get in.

'Mind my horse,' Lottie had said, and he wriggled in alongside the thing, his feet resting between its wooden fetlocks.

On the freeway just past Pismo Beach the coast was suddenly expansive. The palm trees and luxurious villas looked more like the South of France than America. Here the waves rolled in orderly ranks beyond smooth pavements on which people in expensive jackets were pulled along by silky dogs. Further along, towards Guadalupe, a vast, agricultural valley stretched around them, striped with rows of crops. Endless

83

fruit stalls – strawberries and yet more strawberries – lined the road, their hot, candy sweetness combining with the woody odour of cut celery. Long lines of sprinklers misted the horizon. The road ran through a small town – a library, a grill, a garage with towers of tyres, Kmart, a bridal shop – and then continued on, stopping eventually at a car park. Beyond that lay the ocean and a moonscape of dunes.

'Shall we get out and have a walk?' Tina said. 'Apparently we've got supper in the famous provisions rucksack.'

'Bread, cheese, wine and doughnuts,' Lottie said. 'All the most important food groups.'

Tina sighed. 'You can take a girl out of her comfort zone, but you can't stop her endless tendency to shop.'

'If I hadn't shopped for a few basics, we'd have gone hungry.'

'We'd have found *something* to eat.'

Lottie was looking up at the sky, which was thick with birds. 'Yeah, we could always have roasted a pelican.'

The three of them set off walking through the empty dunes. Where the massive, wind-blasted stretches touched the ocean, the spray from the waves met the blown sand so that land was sea and sea was land. This salty, gritty mingling had a kind of whistling music – the implacable, endless movement making up a single chord.

'It's so utterly beautiful,' Lottie said. 'It's barren and yet full at the same time.'

'A little further along the coast there's a buried Egyptian city. The set from Cecil B. DeMille's *The Ten Commandments*,' Spike said. 'Once they'd finished filming, they tried to blow it up, but that wasn't very effective, so they kicked a bit of sand about and abandoned it. Every now and again archaeologists or beachcombers come upon a sphinx's head or a foot belonging to Ramses the Great, but most of it is still down there – plaster of Paris walls and statues and pyramids.'

'How peculiarly American,' Tina said.

'There are also hundreds of different species of wildlife, some only found on this coast,' Spike said, slightly defensively.

Tina smiled to herself; this was an old battle between them.

'If England is so much better, so much more *sophisticated*, I don't know why you don't just go back to the land of carpets and clouds and cruddy bacon,' he had said once, when she had been derisive about something or other – the Halloween mania for orange plastic, or the way people were always so needlessly enthusiastic. 'No one is actually *making* you stay here.'

'You're making me stay here,' she'd said, and he'd laughingly pinned her down in the bed. She could still remember the way he had held both her wrists in one hand, as if her fingers were a bunch of flowers.

They found a sheltered spot and sat down to eat a sandy picnic. The sky changed from cornflower blue to a misty purple. In the shallows, under the ledges of the dunes, plovers picked their leggy way, dipping their heads to the Pacific Ocean as if paying homage to its shining breadth.

'Do you want to stay the night at my friend's house?' Spike asked. 'I could give him a call and say I'm bringing you along. He has the space, and he has a soft spot for blondes. You don't have to do any actual fishing.'

'I'm not sure,' Lottie said, looking round at her sister. 'I'm under Tina's command. She's calling the shots on this trip.'

'You surprise me,' Spike said, smiling to take the sting out of his words. 'She's usually so accommodating.'

He threw some crumbs from his doughnut up in the air. A swarm of birds gathered instantly, called from their arduous work of pecking and pulling through wet sand by the lure of fast food. The sun was lowering itself down into the water, its shine making a glittering pathway from the horizon to the shore.

'Remember, we can leave you by the side of the road whenever we want to,' Tina said. 'I could wait for some particularly inhospitable terrain and boot you out.'

'I rather like the fact I'm at your mercy.'

Tina gave him a hard stare and his confident grin faltered. She had always been rather fierce, something she usually kept hidden under a veneer of happy-go-lucky insouciance. That first time he had spoken to her properly at The Fillmore he had sensed her steel, despite the legs (still beautiful, he couldn't help noticing) on show beneath the small dress, and that way she had of scanning your face as if she was thinking which bit of you to lick first. He had noticed her immediately, even though she had been part of quite a large group. He didn't think she had looked at him once. There wasn't a shortage of attractive women in San Francisco – the town produced them as readily as it produced fog – and yet even this first glimpse of her had set up a kind of longing in him. It had been as if he had suddenly rediscovered his appetite after a spell of being indifferent to food. He remembered walking on, leaving her behind, feeling as if he had been deprived of something. When he saw her again at the concert it was as if his hunger had called her up.

'You're Bob's friend,' she had said, after he had tapped her on the shoulder. His heart had skipped. It made him a little ashamed to think how eager he had been, how happy to discover that she had noticed him after all. He bought her a drink. They never made it back to their seats, but stayed talking at the bar. He had been oblivious to the crush around him and the elbows impatiently digging into his side. That thing happened that he had previously thought was only the fantasy of delusional people – he felt the world sliding away. It had been love at first sight – something else he had always been sceptical about – although it had taken him a little time to recognise it as such. That evening, all he had been aware of was the need to be near her, to listen to what she was saying. Afterwards, on the way home – he had walked in the rain to try and quench some of the heat in his body – it hadn't been her beauty that he had thought about most, but the way she had explained herself to him with a kind of shy seriousness. It had seemed at odds with the wild hair and the bare shoulders and that mouth, turned up at the top lip as though she was always smiling.

'Well, shall I call or not?' he said now. 'It's getting late and I'm sure you don't want to start looking for a place to stay.'

'We can always sleep in the car,' Tina said.

'Oh, let's not,' Lottie said. 'I always think someone is going to knock on the window and freak me out. I have a bit of a thing about people pressing their face against glass.'

'Oh my good God! That's another addition to your ever-growing list of neuroses.' Tina turned to Spike. 'OK. Ring your friend. He'd better have lots to drink.'

'Don't worry about that,' Spike said. 'He's the host with the most.'

He got up and paced up and down a little distance from them talking on his phone while Tina buried Lottie under a mound of sand and commanded her to lie still so that it didn't crack.

'Right. We're sorted,' he said, moments later. 'Greg can't wait to meet you.'

They walked back to the car in the purpling light, Lottie trying to get the sand out of her clothes all the way.

It was dark by the time they reached the house. It proved tricky to find, even though Spike claimed to have been there before. It was set back from the coast road, along a bumpy track that wound its way past small clumps of trees and a few tumbledown shacks. They caught a glimpse of the white swoop of an owl and two coyotes, standing stock-still, their eyes shining in the car headlights. An enormous, wrought-iron gate opened at the press of a button, and they drove up to a house that would not have looked out of place on an English country estate. It was massive and red-bricked, with pillars and trees in pots at either side of the wide front door. In the lights that suddenly flooded the drive, they could see that there were medieval-style imps extending long tongues, flanking the edge of the crenellated roof.

'Greg's father was in love with all things British,' Spike said, by way of explanation.

The door opened and a small, dark-haired man stood in the light.

'What took you so long?' he demanded, and gave Spike a great bear hug in greeting.

'So these are the beautiful sisters,' he said, looking closely at them, and then placed an arm around each of their shoulders. 'You were not wrong, my friend, you were not wrong. They are exquisite examples of womanhood.'

Lottie bristled at his words and fixed him with a stare.

Greg spoke like an American who was trying to impersonate an English person, and at first Lottie thought he was mocking them. When confronted by people from Britain, some Americans seemed to fall into a kind of Billy Bunteresque Tourette's of 'crikey' and 'cheerio' and 'what ho, mate' – but it soon became clear that this was Greg's usual way of talking.

He led them through a hallway the size of Lottie's entire house, lit with Hogwarts wall sconces and lined with oak panelling.

'What an amazing place!' Tina said, although Lottie could tell by the tilt of her mouth that she had already decided to hate it. She was always going on about authenticity, and Lottie was pretty sure that she would take a dim view of this Disney version of a stately home.

'Any moment now we will be greeted by a man in a bow tie holding a tray,' she hissed into Lottie's ear, as Spike and Greg went on ahead into a sumptuous room in shades of gold and cream. There was a vast window at one end, through which the night swimming pool glowed like kryptonite.

'I thought cocktails!' Greg said, approaching a bar at the end of the room. 'What do you ladies fancy?'

'I'd like a margarita,' Tina said. Lottie said she would too, but only because she couldn't think of the names of any other cocktails.

'So how did you two meet?' Tina asked, settling herself down on a sofa.

'We met in a bar,' Spike said. 'We bonded over whiskey sours and rocks. Greg collects people, along with everything else. You name it; he has a collection . . . geological specimens, first editions, paintings, boats, art deco boxes, coins.'

90

'You are forgetting my prized collection of PEZ dispensers,' Greg said. 'I'm still looking for the extremely rare blue-helmeted astronaut from the 1982 World's Fair.'

'I've got a couple of Mutant Teenage Ninja Turtle ones I could send you,' Lottie said.

'That's very kind of you,' Greg said, smiling. He had an extremely sweet smile and she revised her earlier opinion that he was a bit of an idiot.

'What work do you do?' Tina asked, which was the exact question she had told Lottie that you should never ask anyone because it was boring and elitist.

'I'm a dilettante,' Greg replied. 'The tragedy of my life is that I cannot seem to settle on one thing. How do people choose?' He seemed genuinely perplexed.

'Most people are only good at one thing,' Spike said. 'The problem is you can turn your hand to anything. This guy here has built boats. He paints. He's written a screenplay. He's even invented a bike light that switches on and off with a click of the fingers.'

'It's not an advantage, you know,' Greg said. 'I'm still waiting for that moment of revelation. The day I wake up and decide *this* is what I really want to do. Since I'm now forty-five, it's unlikely ever to happen.'

'What are you doing *at the moment* is a better question to ask Greg,' Spike said.

'I'm seeing how long I can hold my breath under the sea. I've managed nine minutes, but the world record is twenty-two minutes and twenty-seven seconds, so I have a way to go.' Greg laughed, as if he was aware of how absurd he sounded.

'How do you maintain all of this?' Tina asked, waving her hand to indicate the house. Lottie winced. Her sister often mistook being outspoken with being tactless. Lottie had the British aversion of talking about money.

Greg seemed unperturbed by Tina's question. 'My father was very, very rich. I now live off the fact that he invented a cardboard box that could be stacked into lorries more efficiently.'

They drank a lot more as the evening ran on, and everyone but Lottie smoked some dope. They ate biscuits and grapes, golden and cold from the fridge, and cheese that Greg said he'd had sent to him from France.

Still later, when Lottie was just thinking it was time perhaps to go to bed, four or five other people arrived. The music was ramped up and everyone got into the pool. Tina was first in, diving straight-legged off the board in a striped swimming costume that looked as if it had come from a fifties movie. Greg had produced it from what he called his 'guest cupboard', which Lottie thought was perhaps the grandest thing about the whole grand set-up. He found her a costume too – a pretty red one with a scalloped neck and back – but she didn't want to go in. She thought she might drown given her state of inebriation.

She must have dozed off on the sofa, because when she woke Tina was dancing with Greg, dressed in some sort of a diaphanous robe. Their bodies were very close together and his head was resting on her shoulder.

'Where's Spike?' Lottie asked.

'Gone off somewhere,' Tina said. Greg raised his head and looked at Tina as if she was the missing PEZ dispenser. He cupped his hands around her face and kissed her on the mouth. She stopped dancing and kissed him back. Lottie thought it was probably best if she left them alone.

On her way to the room where Greg had deposited her suitcase earlier, Lottie met Spike half way up the stairs. He was sitting, staring into space.

'Hello,' he said. 'I'm drunk.'

'Me too.' She sat down next to him. Through an open window somewhere, Lottie could hear the barking of sea lions and the sound of the waves. She vaguely wondered what the view would be like when they woke up and saw it in daylight for the first time. She didn't like the feeling of not knowing exactly where she was. She felt a sharp longing for Dean. She wanted to be held by him in their familiar bed with the picture of the girl with a pearl earring on the wall and the cushions they had chosen together lined up on the pine chest.

'Why is your sister such a pain in the butt?' Spike asked.

'She isn't really,' said Lottie. She wanted to be loyal, although she had so often asked herself the same question. 'She just pretends to be.'

'I wish she'd stop pretending then,' he said. 'I'm not altogether sure I'm going to be able to do much more of this road trip.'

'Oh, you have to stay with us,' Lottie said. 'You can't leave me alone with her!'

He laughed and put his arm companionably round her shoulder. 'I'll stay for you then,' he said, and Lottie felt an unexpected, traitorous triumph.

She was in a deep sleep, ensconced behind the damask drapes of her four-poster bed, when Tina shook her awake. The lights in the room had been switched on. She had forgotten to close her shutters, and when she parted the curtain she could see the sky only just beginning to lighten.

'What time is it?' she asked.

'Never mind that,' Tina said. Lottie could see she had taken something. Her eyes were all glittery and she had a hectic flush on her face. 'Greg knows exactly where that Egyptian city is buried. We are going to get ourselves a sphinx!'

Lottie felt her heart sink. 'Can't it wait till proper morning?'

'Get dressed. It's Challenge Six.'

It seemed that Greg had woken Spike, too, and they stumbled out of the house together. Greg seemed utterly sober, dressed immaculately in a tweed suit. He looked incongruous, as if he had appeared from a time capsule. They got into his truck and set off back down the track. Lottie wasn't happy about being in a moving vehicle with a driver who had been drinking only a couple of hours before, but she supposed they couldn't come to much harm with no other cars around, on a road that was clearly only used by Greg himself. Spike groaned every time they hit a bump.

On the beach, Greg passed them all torches and trowels. The man was a marvel of organisation. He did some sort of complicated pacing, turning left then right and counting his steps aloud. Beyond them the sea was dark and massy, like oil.

Greg held a torch in each hand and pointed the beams into the sand. 'Right!' he said. 'Start digging here.'

Ten minutes of fairly half-hearted scraping later, they hit upon something hard. The discovery put new vigour into their efforts and they dug eagerly, shovelling the sand that poured back into the hole almost as fast as they emptied it. Under the torchlight a terracotta ear emerged, and then the side of a face. Spike put the tip of his trowel underneath and forced it upwards.

'King Ramses' head,' said Greg with satisfaction. 'It's been there for getting on for a hundred years. In America that passes for an antiquity.'

'You knew exactly where it was!' Spike exclaimed. 'You've found it before, haven't you?'

'I had a rough idea.'

They shook the sculpture free of sand. It was a little damaged on one side, but other than that it was intact – almond eyes and aquiline nose almost as real as a proper marble effigy.

'Can we keep it?' Tina asked.

'Surely it belongs to the town,' said Lottie. 'It would be almost like looting.'

'You're quite right,' Spike said, looking at Lottie approvingly. 'We should bury it again.'

Tina gave them both a disgusted glare. 'You two are so tedious,' she said, and stalked off back to the truck.

Chapter 9

'**D**ID YOU SLEEP WITH HIM?' Lottie asked her sister.

Neither of them had woken until midday. The view from the balcony of Lottie's room at last revealed its stretch of beach and sea, white-foamed and pastel-coloured, with steady, gentle waves that slid over the sand.

'We slept in the same bed,' Tina replied.

'So you didn't actually have sex.'

'Not as such,' Tina said. 'We did some other things.'

'Do you find him attractive? You didn't seem to earlier in the evening. Or was it just a drunk fuck?'

Tina did one of her scary – to Lottie at least – head swivels. It reminded her of a dog suddenly smelling blood.

'That's the trouble with you, right there. You are small-minded. Mean.' She mimicked her sister's tone of voice. '*Was it a drunk fuck?*'

Being mimicked was one of the things that always riled Lottie. She remembered Tina doing it as a child and even now she couldn't resist rising to the bait.

'I don't talk like that! I was just wondering why it's OK for you to go to bed with a man you met five minutes before – why behaving like a slut is somehow transformed into being a free spirit when you're the one doing it?'

Lottie wasn't even sure why she was arguing. She didn't really care that much who Tina decided to sleep with. What really annoyed her was the way Tina cloaked what was pretty pathetic behaviour in an aura of virtue. Lottie knew the implication was that she, by contrast, was shut-down and unadventurous.

'I don't think Spike was that impressed,' she said.

'Who gives a fuck what Spike thinks?' Tina said. 'You'd better Skype that droopy fiancé of yours, before you forget he even exists.'

'What the hell are you implying?' Lottie almost shouted.

Both of them were standing up now and panting at each other across the table.

'*Spike wasn't that impressed,*' Tina said, imitating Lottie again. She smiled nastily; Tina was the mistress of the horrible, fuckwit, annoying smile. Lottie couldn't remember when she had last felt this angry. It was as if she was a child again and had that same quivering sense of being terribly wronged and not being able to articulate the injustice. Usually she was the one who sucked things in and smoothed things out, but Tina had always been able to probe her soft spots, to winkle out the very things she wanted to keep hidden and under control.

'*Lottie fancies Boris Jarvis! Lottie thinks that poo comes out of her fanny hole! Lottie's wearing a bra even though all she's got are a couple of raisins!*'

'I seem to have hit a nerve,' Tina said. 'At least there appears to be some feeling in that buttoned-up chest of yours.'

'For your information, letting it all – and I mean *all* – hang out is not a sign that you have feelings. It's a sign you're a shallow, self-centred arse.'

'Ahh, so she's fallen back on that oft-used phrase "For your information". I was wondering how long it would take for you to start *informing* me of things.'

It came out of nowhere. It was as if Lottie was watching someone else as she drew back her hand and slapped her sister in the face. It was as hard a blow as she could manage from the other side of the table. The impact left finger-shaped marks on Tina's skin. Her sister didn't move.

'I'm sorry,' whispered Lottie. 'I shouldn't have done that.'

'But you did,' Tina said.

Just then they were greeted by voices from below.

'Look what we caught!'

Beneath the balcony, Greg and Spike were beaming and holding up a giant fish. It shone silver in the sun, its mouth drooping open, the life almost still in it.

'Well done!' Lottie got up and leant over the balcony, although she found it difficult to summon up any enthusiasm. She thought of the feel of the fish, the slippery drag of the scales, the slight give of the flesh, and felt sick.

'That's lunch sorted,' Greg announced. He was wearing some sort of complicated fisherman's smock with bulging pockets and a waxed, feathered hat. Spike was in shorts and a baseball cap and carried the fishing rods over his back. Neither of them looked as if they had missed out on any sleep.

'See you downstairs,' Greg said, and the pair of them disappeared from view.

'I'm going to have a shower,' Tina said, and she swept out of the room on the wings of righteous indignation.

Lottie felt ashamed of what she had done. She didn't think she had ever hit anyone before. Even as children the sisters had never progressed much beyond the occasional shove or sly pinch. Her interactions as an adult might have sometimes caused her to clench her teeth or to send evil looks in the direction of the drivers – almost exclusively male – who swung out in front of her in their cars, but nothing had ever stirred her to real violence. She knew where hate got you. She had seen it at first hand, the disgusting, dribbling dance of it. The way it made you feel as if nothing in the world was safe. Maybe, she consoled herself, it was different when you hit your sister. Sisters were not the same as the other adults in your life. They came from the same weaving, the same story. It was almost as if you were hurting yourself.

She felt a sudden need to talk to Dean. Her uncharacteristic act of violence had shaken her. He would surely be back from work now.

When he answered the Skype call, his face on the screen of her iPad made her feel like crying. Without her there he had forgotten to check his hair; it was sticking out the way it did when she didn't remind him to wet it and press it down in the morning.

'Hello, my darling,' he said. 'How are you getting on? How's that sister of yours?'

'I've just hit her,' she said.

He looked surprised. She loved the way his eyebrows rose as he widened his eyes. 'That's not like you,' he said. 'What did she do?'

'She was mimicking me,' Lottie said, feeling foolish.

'Well, we all know we should never do that,' he said gravely. Then he smiled, the ends of his mouth hidden a little by his moustache.

'You need to give your hair a trim,' she said. 'I can't see your whole mouth.'

'Never mind my hair. What's it like? America, I mean.'

'It's beautiful, much more beautiful than I ever imagined. It's like being inside a wide screen all the time. The edges seem further apart than they do in England.'

'I miss you,' he said, carefully upbeat. She knew he didn't want to make his missing her a source of blame.

'I wish you were here. We went to Cannery Row,' she said, knowing that he would appreciate the reference. Dean quoted something about the light and the noise and the dream-like quality of the famous street. He knew the first lines of hundreds of novels. It was his party piece.

'The whole of America feels a bit like a dream,' she said.

'Where are you now?'

'Near Guadalupe,' she said. 'The dunes are massive and everything smells of strawberries and I'm just about to go down and eat some fish.'

'You look so beautiful. Is that a new dress?'

'Yes. Tina chose it.'

'It suits you,' he said, putting his hand up as if he thought he could touch her. She blew him a kiss.

'I love you. I've got to go. I'll call you again soon.'

Switching off his face invoked another wave of melancholy. She really needed to get a grip. She was in America, and supposed to be having the time of her life on a trip Tina was paying for. She loved her sister. Whatever had happened in the past could surely be mended somehow. She wondered briefly why she hadn't mentioned to Dean that they had acquired a hitchhiker. It wasn't that she felt she had anything to hide; it was more that she wanted to protect him from feeling the insecurity he sometimes seemed prey to. She thought again with a stab of guilt about the way Tina's skin had bloomed with the mark of her fingers. She would go and apologise properly to her now.

Chapter 10

Tina wasn't in her room, so Lottie followed the sound of voices downstairs to the huge kitchen. It was decked out in steel and solid-block wood surfaces, as if it was lying in wait for an army of chefs.

'Ah, finally you emerge!' Greg said. He was in a striped butcher's apron and wielding a knife. 'Look at this beauty! A truly fresh fish glistens like this. The flesh should be pearly-white rather than grey.'

Of course, he was as expert at the filleting of fish as he was at everything else he attempted. He had sliced it along its belly and its innards, darker than she imagined, lay in a shining, tangled mass on the table. Lottie felt another wave of nausea. She vowed to avoid margaritas and cheese and ill temper in the future. She tried to catch her sister's eye, but Tina was looking studiously away from her. All signs of the ravages of the night before had been smoothed away by her shower. The mark on her cheek had faded, too. She was looking beautiful in gingham shorts and a tight, halterneck top that showed off the skin of her arms, already turning a little golden.

After lunch, they hit the road again. Tina gave the wooden horse a sly kick. Lottie, to whom she had spoken only the bare necessities since their row, was driving. Spike was sitting in the passenger seat wearing Lottie's cowboy hat. The two of them were as thick as thieves, she noticed sourly. Laughing at each other's jokes, passing a cup of coffee back and forth. Even with the roof of the car down, it was hot. Raptors wheeled around in the relentless blue sky, looking for the absent breeze.

Greg had been oddly formal when she'd left. 'Thank you for visiting,' he had said, as if she was a relative he had been duty-bound to put up. She had been a little offended by his apparent coldness, but when she had stretched out to kiss him goodbye, she had felt him tremble.

'Where's the wife?' she had asked the night before, as they lay together amongst the tangled sheets. He had given her body the skilled attention he seemed to give everything, although she knew even as he touched her, smoothing her skin with his competent hands, that this would only last until he noticed something else. As he plunged between her legs, he demonstrated his ability to stay down without breathing, if not for twenty-two minutes, at least long enough for her to resist and then let go.

'I had one for a while,' he said, his subsided penis lying snugly against his thigh. On the wall opposite the bed a stuffed owl stared, and through the open window she could smell the iodine of the ocean.

'What happened?'

'We were very young. Barely out of college. On the second anniversary of our wedding, she leant over the restaurant table as if she was about to wipe soup from my face, and asked me when I had last thought about her. I didn't understand what she meant. I said something about how I had spent the previous morning choosing the diamond bracelet I had presented to her as an anniversary gift. "I don't mean that," she said. "I don't mean actions. When did I last stray into your mind? Tell me one time recently when you were driving somewhere or reading a book and the thought of me made you soften or even harden. I'd take that," she said. I couldn't find the right answer. It seemed to me that it was enough to think about her when she was there in front of me. It was a misunderstanding. I thought she was happy but it turned out she was lonely. I've never risked it again.'

'I get that,' she had said, touching him on his already absent face. They were not dissimilar. She recognised in him her own need not to dwell, to move on and keep moving.

She looked out of the car window. She had been more shocked than hurt by Lottie's blow. It wasn't the sort of thing she would have imagined her sister doing. Lottie was verging on priggish in her earnest desire to do the right thing. The evils of plastic drinking bottles, the opening divide between the rich and the poor, the criminal use of logs in wood burners, the greed of bankers, the disinterest of politicians, men who touched waitresses, the imminent extinction of the bee all filled her with outrage. She was right about almost all of it (Tina was indifferent on the matter of burning wood), but it would be just so much more *restful* if she could switch it off from time to time.

'What's going on with you two?' Spike asked, turning round to look at Tina as if he thought she was to blame.

'Nothing,' she said.

'Oh, come on. You haven't said a word to each other for hours.'

'I behaved rather badly,' Lottie said, in that prissy way she had that made Tina want to gnaw on her own tongue.

'I can't believe that,' said Spike, grinning at Lottie. 'I thought your younger sister was the badass. What did you do?'

'I hit her,' Lottie said. She managed to make it sound rather cute, as if she was a kitten who had not quite learnt how to control her claws.

'The hitting thing is not good. You can't fall out on this trip,' Spike said. 'Why don't we stop and sample some wine? You two can drink a loving cup.'

'I'm not sure I want to drink any more after last night. Perhaps we should all go easy today,' Lottie said, which immediately made Tina feel like getting drunk just to spite her.

In Los Alamos, a small town with Victorian hotels and shopfronts that still bore evidence of their western past, they stopped outside the tasting room of a local vinery. Between walls decorated with architectural salvage and pictures of grapes, Spike and Tina set about seeing if they could work their way through every wine on offer. Lottie swilled a little Grenache around the inside of her mouth and spat it out into the bucket.

'I'm going to explore some of the antique shops,' she said, after about ten minutes.

'Don't, whatever you do, bring back anything larger than a silver fork,' her sister shouted after her.

The wine kept coming, the deceptively small glasses adding up. Before long Tina realised that she was getting drunk. She needed something solid to eat. The fish at lunch had been delicious – soft-fleshed and crisp-skinned – but one small fillet and a peppery salad wasn't enough to sustain her.

'Mmm, this is a nice one,' Spike said. 'Blackcurrant, damson, wet rope and just a hint of soil.'

'You don't know what the hell you're talking about, do you?'

'I know what I like,' he said, and looked at her. For a moment she thought that he was flirting with her, then she remembered the way he always used to look intently at her just before he spoke, as if he was working out which version of events she would find most palatable.

'How did you get on with Greg?' he asked, looking into his glass of wine as if he had found something floating in it.

'Well enough,' she said.

'He said to me he thought you were sad.'

'What, sad as in pathetic loser?'

'No. He was quite taken with you, actually. Sad as in dejected and distressed.'

'I don't know what he's on about. If anyone's sad, it's him, living in that great, empty pile of a house with its cabinets of coins and clutter, dressing like he thinks he's Bertie Wooster.'

'Greg's come to terms with what he is,' Spike said.

'Meaning he thinks I haven't? I don't think one evening of chat and some sex is enough to qualify him to make an assessment of my psyche.' Tina knew she had crossed the point from mild inebriation into full drunkenness. Her words were beginning to get away from her and the architectural salvage on the walls was looking ever more lopsided.

'How was the sex?' Spike asked.

'Mind your own fucking business.'

'You're right. That was inappropriate. It was the damson talking, not me.'

'You've still got that sticking-out ear,' she said.

'It's the reason for my extremely acute powers of hearing.'

'I want you to do something for me,' she said. She was slurring her words now.

'Oh yes? Carry you to the restroom? To the car?'

'I'm perfectly capable of looking after myself, thank you very much.' She disproved the truth of her words by reaching for her glass and missing it completely. 'I want you to seduce Lottie. You're good at that sort of thing, right?'

Even through the mist of wine, Tina could see that she had astonished him. His eyes went wide and his perfectly formed jaw slackened.

'What did you just say?' he asked.

'I want you to pretend you're falling in love with her.'

'Why the heck would I do that?'

'Don't make such a fuss. She'll be back in a minute and I want to get it sorted before then.'

He looked angry. 'You *are* sad in a pathetic loser way.'

'It's not a big deal. She's about to marry a complete no-hoper by the name of Dean Fowler Twat and I just want to test her devotion. If she can resist you with your sticking-out ear and that irritating way you have of making people feel important, then I'll wash my hands of her. She can marry him if she really wants to. The most interesting fact about him is that he knows the first line of one hundred and twenty novels.' She cackled so much she nearly fell off her chair.

'You really are a piece of work,' Spike said.

'Will you do it, though?'

'No, I fucking well won't.'

The door of the shop swung open and Lottie came staggering in with an alabaster vase on a plinth.

'Oh, bloody hell!' Tina exclaimed. 'You can leave that behind for a start.'

Lottie surveyed the damage. 'Looks like I'm driving, then.'

Chapter 11

'IF YOU WERE AN ANIMAL, what kind of an animal would you be?' Tina asked.

Lottie rolled her eyes at Spike. In the rear-view mirror, she could see Tina slumped in the back seat with the alabaster vase on her lap. They had already had to stop once so that she could throw up, and Lottie was worried that she might actually vomit again into her new antique.

'I'd be an albatross,' Tina announced. 'Flying over the surf. Forever shunned as an unlucky talisman.'

'More like a buzzard,' Spike muttered.

'I heard that! What would you be, Lottie?'

'I don't know . . . a beaver?'

Tina spluttered with laughter. She was dragging maniacally on her vape, but Lottie had given up remonstrating about the noise. Tina was unreachable in her current state.

'Beavers are very industrious,' Lottie said.

'Your beaver isn't,' Tina said.

'You're so childish,' Lottie replied. 'Where shall we make our overnight stop?'

'We'll follow the road,' Tina said, putting the vase down and getting to her feet. She spread out her arms as if she thought she was on the *Titanic*.

'Sit the fuck down,' Lottie said.

'Let her fall out,' Spike said. 'If I was an animal, I'd be a lion and eat Tina.'

'Shut your face, Meteorite Boy. You're a weasel.'

Solvang was decked out like a Danish town with half-timbered buildings and gabled roofs. There was a replica of Hans Christian Andersen's house, a copy of the statue of the Little Mermaid, trinket shops with faux-Scandinavian façades and several non-functioning windmills.

'This place gives me the creeps,' Tina said. 'It's like being on a film set.' She still wasn't altogether steady on her feet.

They walked around, searching for somewhere to stay. They looked through windows at bars that appeared to have fires blazing in the hearth and candles flickering on tables, but on further investigation turned out not to have front doors. In a shop window there was a line of children's costumes on headless dummies – all braces and daisy ribbons and weird aprons. Frosted Danish pastries shone on trays as if they were radioactive. An empty horse-drawn carriage driven by a tiny man with a face the colour of pickled herring clipped slowly down the street.

'Where are all the people who actually live here?' Lottie asked. Almost everyone was wandering around as they were, looking bemused, as if they had been expecting a fairy tale and been delivered a parking lot with a few plastic beams and a surfeit of clogs.

'Challenge Seven!' Tina announced, pressing her face to the glass of a gift shop window.

'I'm not doing a challenge today,' Lottie said.

'For your information, Miss Information.' Tina burst out laughing and half slithered down the window.

'We need to get her into bed,' Lottie murmured to Spike.

Spike took hold of Tina's arms. 'You're scaring the locals.'

Tina pushed him away. 'Going clip, clippety-clop, on the stair, so there!'

'Let's just find a hotel,' Lottie said, aware of the curious glances of passers-by.

'Right! Today's challenge is . . . you have to go into that shop.' Tina indicated an establishment across the road with a suspiciously bright thatched roof. 'You have to steal – *steal*, mind, I'll be watching – a pair of china clogs and a windmill.'

'Oh, don't be so ridiculous,' Lottie protested. 'What good could it possibly do to get arrested?'

'That's the challenge . . . *not* get arrested. Use your clever little fingers' (here she waved her digits in the air in demonstration) 'to slip them into your handbag. Like the Artful Dodger. Distract them. Use misdirection. Wave hankies around. If you want, I'll create a diversion.'

'This isn't one of your best ideas,' Spike said, although Lottie saw that he was trying not to laugh.

'It's not funny,' Lottie said to him, feeling cross that he clearly wasn't going to support her objections. With them both gleefully egging her on, she knew the battle was lost. She crossed the road with the other two following behind, and went into the shop. The tinkle of an alpine bell heralded her arrival. Fortunately the place was fairly busy with aimless tourists trying to get a slice of the Danish dream by purchasing a tankard or an apron adorned with a Viking. She fingered a miniature pair of clogs joined at the heel by a ribbon and looked around her furtively. What the hell was she doing? The sensible thing would be to walk out of the shop right now. Sod it if Tina thought she was lily-livered. She didn't want to spend the night in a gable-roofed police station. She was eyeing up the windmills when she heard a shocked exclamation coming from the shop counter. She turned to look at what the open-mouthed cashier was staring at. Outside, Tina had pulled up her T-shirt and was pressing her bare breasts to the window. Everyone was staring at the spectacle in fascination.

'Jeez Louise,' said a startled man in socks and sandals. 'That's not something you get to see every day. This town is sure beginning to grow on me.'

'Look away *now*, Stanley,' said his companion, a woman with sharp eyes and a stomach bristling with zip-up bags.

'Maybe it's just a Danish thing,' he answered, still transfixed. 'Don't Danish folks like to barbeque in the nude?'

Out of the corner of her eye, Lottie saw Spike pull Tina away from the window. Her breasts left little mist marks on the glass.

'We may celebrate all things Scandinavian, but we certainly do draw the line at *that*,' the shop woman said, flicking her long plait back over her shoulder, as if she was throwing a string of sausages to a dog. Despite her reluctance, Lottie felt Tina had worked extremely hard to create a diversion, so she grabbed the required items and exited the shop hastily, while it was still in the grip of Breastgate.

She wasn't sure why she was running. Her arms and legs tingled with delight. She might just have found herself a new hobby. Not that she would ever rip off small businesses – except for today – but the weekly supermarket shop could be made so much more interesting by the acquisition of an unpaid-for jar of mustard – not the harsh, canary-yellow stuff, but the one with mustard seeds in it – or perhaps a sliver of smoked salmon or those pots of ground-up olives. My God, what the hell was happening to her? Any minute now she would be holding up a bank. Tina was turning her into a delinquent.

Breathless, her skin singing, she ground to a halt beside Spike and Tina.

'Let's see the goods,' Tina said.

Lottie opened up her bag to reveal her contraband.

'One windmill and one pair of clogs as ordered,' she said triumphantly.

Spike was shaking his head. 'I'm on a road trip with a couple of madwomen,' he said.

*

Once they had checked into their hotel, Lottie waited until Tina had fallen asleep, then crept out under cover of darkness to post ten dollars through the letterbox of the shop that had suffered the crime.

Chapter 12

LOTTIE BALANCED THE COFFEE POT on the tray and kicked the door open with one foot.

'I brought you breakfast,' she said, as Tina took the pillow from her head and sat up. 'Have you forgiven me yet?' She put the tray down on the side table.

'I'm still thinking about it,' Tina answered, biting into a Danish pastry.

'I shouldn't have hit you. It was a very cruel thing to do.'

'Yes, it was,' Tina replied, pastry flakes on her chin.

'If I say sorry, will you say sorry too?'

'What have I got to say sorry about? I could have walloped you back, but I've got more restraint.'

'You were winding me up. You know you were.'

'I was only giving voice to my suspicions,' Tina said.

'Listen,' Lottie said, sitting on the end of Tina's bed. 'I'm in love with Dean. I know you don't think much of him, but he's marrying *me*, not *you*.'

'Thank the lord,' Tina said. 'Be honest, he doesn't like me either, does he?'

'You haven't had a proper chance to get to know each other. You've been abroad for so much of the last few years. He's a bit suspicious of you. Thinks you're perhaps not the most reliable of characters. I think he imagines that you might lead me astray.'

'As if I would do such a thing,' said Tina, opening her eyes wide in a parody of innocence.

'You're not fooling anyone, least of all me. I *know* you, remember.'

Tina's hand had been behind almost every childhood disaster. Lottie scrolled back through the breakages, the spillages, the close shaves, the tantrums, the tricks, the truants, the break-ins and the break-ups and the times when things just plain spun out of control. Tina had never quite thrown off her habit of inventing new worlds. She would create stories about the people around them – wild romances for the plainest of teachers, mysteries spun from an overheard scrap of conversation.

The summer she turned thirteen, Sandbag Stomach Man, who lived in the house across the road and had a tendency to linger by the window in hefty silhouette, became the focus of one such tale; Tina swore blind that she had seen him kill someone with a knife.

'I didn't see any such thing,' Mia had said, 'and I was standing right beside you at the time.'

'He did it when you turned away. He was as quick as a flash. I think it's his wife he killed.'

Sandbag Stomach Man's wife had been a source of fascination to them all, since she was seldom seen coming in and out of the house, nor at the local Co-op, where pretty much everyone could be found. They would get occasional glimpses of her peering through the gap in the net curtains. At Tina's instigation they took it in turns to watch the house for signs of the wife. Lottie recorded all activity, or lack thereof, in the back of her diary. Three weeks went by without a single sighting.

'Perhaps we should call the police,' Mia said, even her steadiness troubled by the vividness of her sister's descriptions.

'I could see the knife above his head. He brought it down like *that*.' Tina demonstrated the fatal blow. 'I could see the blood on his vest. It splattered all over his stomach.'

'What we need to do is draw him out,' Tina decided. 'That's what they do in films.'

She wrote a series of letters and posted them through the letterbox, insisting that the other two come with her as back-up.

Dear Neighbour, we know what you have done.

Confess all and you will feel better.

Where is your wife?

One afternoon, Sandbag Stomach Man was waiting for them behind his front door when they rattled the latest missive through the letterbox. He pulled Tina inside, and so Mia and Lottie followed. They knew they couldn't allow her to face whatever horrors the house concealed on her own. Close up, he wasn't nearly as scary as they had thought he was. He smelt a bit and the edges of his vest were a little crusty, but he seemed much smaller than he did through his lighted window.

'I thought you might like to meet my wife,' he said, leading them into a bedroom.

Mia took hold of her sisters' hands. 'I really think we should go home.'

'You're not going anywhere,' he said. One of his top teeth stuck out like a mini elephant's tusk. The dim bedroom smelt sweet, like puffy Haribo hearts. There was a rack of clothes and a clock on the wall with a picture of a bird in the centre. As its hands reached four o'clock there was a scratchy sound of a blackbird's song. His wife was lying in bed propped up by a triangular pillow. She held the blanket against her chest with shining, knuckled hands, as if she was aware, even now, that she had visitors and had to make sure she was covered up.

'She's ill,' he said and touched her head. Her eyes were barely there. They had become lost in the pull of her flesh. Her neck, thin in a nightgown, was tendrilled, like the roots of a tree.

'I'm sorry,' Tina said. They backed out of the room, but Sandbag Stomach Man didn't seem to notice their departure.

A month or so later, on a rainy Sunday afternoon when their parents had sent them upstairs and there was nothing to do but stare out of the window, they saw her come out at last. There were only two men to carry her flimsy body, which was zipped up into a bag that looked like the one they kept the tent in.

'She's the first person I've known who has died,' Tina said, unwilling still to relinquish the glamour of it.

'You didn't know her,' Mia said, drawing the curtain as a mark of respect.

'You might think you know me, but you don't,' Tina said now. 'Not anymore.'

'I'd like to know you better,' Lottie said quietly. The truth of her sister's words saddened her. 'I think Mia would have wanted us to stick together.'

'If Mia had wanted us to stick together, she should have tried harder to live.' Tina got up impatiently, slopping her coffee on the bed sheets. She pulled off the T-shirt she'd slept in, then walked around her bed and began rootling in her exploded suitcase. Lottie wished she could be as comfortable in her own skin. Perhaps being unselfconscious went hand in hand with being unheeding.

'It wasn't anything to do with not wanting to live. You know that, Tina.'

'From where I'm standing, it was everything to do with not wanting to live.'

'It wasn't a choice.'

'It felt like one,' Tina replied, pulling random clothes over her head. She tied her hair back with a silk scarf without looking in the mirror, passed some cream over half her face and still managed to look stylish. It didn't really matter what she chose to wear, Lottie reflected; she just had that impervious grace that made people want to be near her – hoping, perhaps, that some of what she had would rub off on them. People were attracted to beauty.

She knew they were travelling to dangerous ground, so she changed the subject. She wanted to avoid another row now that they were being civil to each other.

'What do you think?' asked Lottie, giving a twirl. She had matched her new blue shorts with a white shirt, tied at the waist.

'You look great,' Tina said. 'Now, shall we hoick that oik out of his bed and hit the road?'

As they turned from the coast into the wine county of Santa Barbara, the sun seemed to solidify. It glazed the cracked tarmac of the road in a hard glare. To their left, the distant mountains were dimly shaped and, in the foreground, rolling, dun-coloured hills were bisected with white tracks leading to flat-roofed buildings. There was so much space to spare that it seemed the occupants of the land couldn't polish all that was there. At the backs of the houses there were well-tended pools shaped like amoeba, and green-leaved plants and plastic-cushioned loungers that were wiped clean of their truck dust every day. At the front, among the limp flags, were piles of rusted barrels, tractors, oil drums, boats resting on gravel and lopsided caravans.

The yellow road began to soften into vineyards. The plants, turning red and gold now, exactly hugged the curves of the hills, as if stitching the landscape together. From the forecourts of farm buildings and the insides of barns came the smell of fermenting grapes, a yeasty, rancid odour that was almost unbearable when you were close to it. A mile or two further down the road, the scent remained with you, but mingled with the dust and the diesel smell of the tankers sloshing past, fat-bellied with wine, it became so perfumed and exquisite that you longed to go back.

They drove past fields of pumpkins, waiting for their inevitable fate at the hands of children, who, in less than a month from now, would be disembowelling them with spoons. Then there was what felt like an abrupt transition from lushness into a desert landscape. They closed the roof of the car as the wind picked up and turned on the music – a joyful James Brown singing 'Living in America', followed by Kim Wilde's scratchy voice grinding through her half-hearted teenage rebel song. There were several ugly, low-lying towns, dwarfed by billboards and full of travelling dust. The clouds were sketchy and looked as if they had been scraped on the sky with a fingernail. Outside a Burger King a man was filling his tanker up with a long, neon-orange hose. On a cracked piece of tarmac a boy bounced a ball against the palm of his hand.

'Challenge Eight – at least I *think* it's Eight,' Tina said, 'is to drive down this road blind.'

'Don't be stupid,' Lottie replied. 'When I agreed to say yes to everything on this trip, I wasn't agreeing to commit suicide.'

'Don't be a chicken. There are hardly any cars and it's about as straight as a road can be.'

True, the low road stretched out ahead, broken only by slight rises and falls and the occasional raven, stirred into clumsy, reluctant flight by their approach. To the left were mountains, too far away to break the monotony of the land-scape. To the right there was scrubby vegetation in colours of dim mustard and bruised pink. The passing telegraph poles were the only indication that they were moving at all and these glancing blows, identical and exactly paced as they were, served only to reinforce the illusion of time standing still, as if they were caught between two-minute markers on a clock. Lottie got the sense that somewhere, beyond the unchanging horizon, proper life was happening.

'I'll hit a pole,' Lottie protested.

'Not if you keep going straight,' Tina said. 'I'll guide you.' She leant over from the back of the car and fastened her scarf around her sister's face. Lottie immediately slowed to a crawl and stopped. Spike groaned.

'I'm getting out,' he said. 'I'd rather walk than travel with you two.'

'If you get out of the car, we are not coming back for you,' Tina said. 'Right, now, foot down!'

Lottie's instinct was to refuse. She was a cautious driver even at home, never going above the speed limit and punctilious about ensuring two clear chevrons between her and the car ahead.

'Do I really have to?'

'Of course you don't,' Spike said.

'If you don't, you will have failed,' Tina said implacably.

Lottie did not like failing. She thought that perhaps if she moved her head slightly, she might be able to see enough to get by.

Almost as if Tina had read her mind, she tightened the knot on her blindfold.

'I hate you,' Lottie said, and she felt as if she meant it. Every argument and feeling of distrust, every disappointment seemed to come sharply into focus. Why was she allowing herself to be treated like this? She had the despairing feeling that she and her sister would be stuck like this in an eternal standoff, unable to move forward or go back, frozen forever by the distance between them. In the end, it was a feeling almost of panic that set her into motion. She moved forward, slowly at first and then a little faster. She was briefly scared, and then she put her foot down recklessly on the accelerator. She held the steering wheel tight.

The car hummed around her. She could feel the vibration of each telegraph pole through the open window as if they were markers guiding her. She floored the accelerator and was gratified to hear a nervous edge to Tina's laugh.

'How fast am I going?' she shouted. She felt as if she could drive like this forever, and that when at last she stopped they would have arrived at the place that was waiting for them over the horizon.

'It might be a good idea if you slowed down a little,' Spike said.

She ignored him. She felt invincible.

'Steer to your left,' Spike said, and she complied, imagining in her mind's eye the curve of the road.

There was a sudden loud sound of a horn, and she felt the steering wheel being taken over and turned violently. Something big passed them by. Lottie felt the car shake. She slowed down and pulled the scarf from her head.

'What the hell was that?' she asked, looking behind her at the rear end of an enormous truck. 'I thought you said the road was empty.'

'It came from nowhere,' Spike said. 'One minute the road was clear. The next it was almost on top of us.'

'There must be a dip in the road or something,' Tina said.

Lottie pulled over into the verge and they all got out. They were laughing and talking loudly the way you do after a near miss. Lottie yelled with her head back and spun round and round. Tina cartwheeled along the side of the road. Spike pushed at her so that she fell protesting to the ground. Then, just as suddenly as it had come, Lottie's feeling of exhilaration passed and she felt wobbly and tearful. She walked a little way through the scrub. The light was lemony. She could taste grit in her mouth.

Tina stretched to relieve the stiffness in her joints and tied her hair back again with the scarf. Spike leant against the bonnet of the car, drinking a Coke.

'What's going on with you?' he asked her.

'What do you mean?' she said. He looked as if he belonged on a billboard – the glint of the sun on the glass bottle, the slope of his legs, the way he was looking off into the middle distance as if contemplating the greatness of America.

'The way you keep goading your sister. This stupid idea of getting me to pretend to fall for her to see if it will break up her relationship. You are many things, Tina, but I've never thought of you as someone cruel.'

'You don't understand me,' she said. 'You never have.'

A week or so after their meeting at The Fillmore, he had rung her up. 'I can't stop thinking about you,' he'd said and she had been instantly wary of his openness, the way he was so quick to say how he felt. She would have assumed it to be an American characteristic if she hadn't already slept with three people in San Francisco who had been far more measured.

'Do you believe in love at first sight?' he had asked her as they sat together on a balcony in the harbour on their first date. He had chosen an expensive restaurant and dressed carefully for the occasion – a pale linen suit with creases around the knees.

'No, I don't,' she replied, wondering if, after all, it had been such a good idea to agree to meet him. He was undeniably handsome. His shoulders were broad in his jacket and he had a mobile, intelligent face and a sturdy grace that she found sexy, but there was an earnestness about him that made her uneasy. She was accustomed to men who were more polished and more indifferent.

They hadn't eaten very much of the slivers of glistening food, piled in artful heaps on black plates, but she had drunk a lot. She was in the habit of getting drunk before she made love. It made the transition from small talk to skin so much easier. In his messy apartment littered with papers and socks and the odd lump of rock, he had kissed her slowly, touching her face, twisting his fingers through her hair, as if he had already found all that he wanted. She remembered feeling impatient at his carefulness. There was something grateful in the way he touched her that threatened her precarious desire. She wanted a reflection of her own, alcohol-fuelled lust – something quick and hard and over and done with. She had pushed him back on the sofa bed and unzipped his trousers, pulling them down only as far as necessary. She had climbed on him, her silky dress gathered at her waist, her hand holding aside her pants so that he could enter her quickly. She wanted to avoid the slow business of undressing – the stripping of layers and the awkward wriggles and pluckings which felt too much like intimacy. Even then he had held back, slowed her down, moved in a deliberate, searching way that had made her cry out and grind against him. Afterwards she had wanted him gone so that she could relax properly, but he had fallen asleep with his arms around her and she hadn't felt she could wake him up.

'So explain it to me,' Spike said now.

'You will be doing Lottie a favour if you stop her marrying Dean. She can do so much better.'

'I don't think it's any of your business who your sister chooses to marry,' Spike said. 'It's certainly not any of mine! Besides, I would hardly think that you are an expert in successful relationships.'

'By that I take it that you see success as having settled down with someone who bores me with a couple of children who will suck me dry and then spit me out.'

Spike looked at her and then shook his head.

'You really don't have a clue,' he said.

'I don't know why you're taking the high moral ground. I don't see any evidence that you've found your own happy ever after. You're still drifting around the way you always did.'

'At least I'm open to the possibility,' he said.

She was infuriated by his tone of disappointment, and the way his eyes slid over her as if he had hoped for more.

'I'm open to everything,' she said loftily. 'It's the way I live my life.'

'Well good for you,' Spike said angrily, draining the last of his drink.

'What's the matter?' Tina asked.

'Nothing at all.' He got back into the car and stared stonily ahead. He always had a fine line in sulking. He made injured silence into an art form.

She turned away, looking out into the grassland. Her sister was wandering around, looking like she had lost something. She thought she was probably searching for a shrub to pee behind.

'Lottie!' Tina shouted. 'It's time to go.'

Chapter 13

AFTER THE TOWN OF MOJAVE, Route 14 turned into Route 395 and revealed a spectacular display of red mountains, ice-white salt marsh and flashes of yellow flowers. In the distance, the craggy, monumental peaks of the Sierra Nevada Mountains were the colour of a pigeon's wing. This new sense of perspective in the landscape seemed to bring with it a lift in spirits. Spike had emerged from his moodiness and Lottie was singing along with Johnny Cash and eating red strawberry laces as she drove.

'I think we should stop at Lone Pine,' Tina said, consulting her phone. 'It's in the Alabama Hills where some of Mia's favourite films were shot – the dire sarsaparilla-drinking *Hopalong Cassidy* but also *High Sierra* and *Ride Lonesome*.'

'I don't mean to be crass, but where exactly is she?' Spike asked. He had been vaguely worried about the whereabouts of Mia's ashes since he had joined them. He considered the two sisters easily mad enough to have mislaid the urn somewhere or to have it rattling around in the picnic bag with the remains of their lunch.

'Her ashes, you mean?' Tina said. 'She's safely stowed away with the spare tyre.'

'I'm sorry, but ... what was it she actually died of?' Tina hadn't sounded as if she wanted to talk about it anymore, but if he was going along on this trip he felt he should at least know the history of the person they were carrying with them.

'Heart failure,' Tina said. She turned to look out of the window. The evasive tone in her voice made him think there was more to the story than she was letting on. She looked sad. The light hit her face in a series of beautiful angles. He hated the fact that part of him wanted to reach out and touch her. He thought of the way she had looked at him just before she had left his apartment for the last time. She had stood in the middle of the room, the sun burnishing her, the way it was now, and she had stared at him blankly, as if he were a stranger.

They passed a hill with the letters 'LP' scored into its side, and a cemetery with a white monument and neat gravestones lined up like beehives. Lottie thought that perhaps it would be better if they had somewhere definite to put Mia. A place with her name clearly marked so that they could return and place flowers. There was something a bit random about driving into the middle of nowhere and leaving her there.

'When I die, I want a great big white angel on my grave,' Tina had announced, long before death had any real meaning for them. The conversation had taken place after they had wept through a movie in which a burial site had been marked only with some tied sticks. 'I'd like to be cremated,' Mia had said, 'and put under Landing Rock.' Lottie could remember them mocking her. Mia had been so easy to tease; she'd had a kind of innocent gullibility that was made for taking the piss.

They drove past a rustic sign announcing the town. Next came a diner called Seasons with a wooden merry-go-round, a number of timber-clad buildings with saloon doors embellished with cartwheels, and some life-sized models of cowboys peeping furtively out from under hats. They found a motel that sat crouched below the mountains, looking vulnerable to the mass above it. After a brief squabble about who was going to get which room, the three of them went to the Museum of Film History next door and watched a documentary about the westerns made in the Alabama Hills. Tina issued her ninth challenge, which was for Lottie to try on Gregory Peck's cowboy hat. She managed about three giggling, terrified seconds before she whipped it off again and replaced it on its pedestal, just a second before the curator came back into the room. In a shop that sold cowboy paraphernalia, they fingered fringed boots and deerskin gloves. Lottie ignored Tina's suggestion that she should get Dean some chaps and her comment that 'he'll look sexy riding you', settling on a sturdy leather belt instead. Both Tina and Lottie bought western shirts embroidered with birds and roses. Afterwards, they sat in a bar by the highway. The light was pinkish and soft, and a stream of curvaceous, shining trucks passed by like movie stars.

'What you guys doing tonight?' A red-faced man with a wide, childlike smile stood over them with a fistful of leaflets.

'I'm not sure,' Lottie said. 'We thought maybe we might go and get something to eat.'

'Well, you might just be in luck,' the man said. 'There's a buffet and a dance three blocks from here starting right about now.'

He handed them a flyer on which there was a series of footprints that meandered in pairs across the page, interspersed with lurid-looking pieces of meat, as if there had been a crime in an abattoir. Tina was grinning, and Lottie knew that she was condemning the man because he'd pronounced buffet with a hard 't'. Here was another example, if she needed it, of Tina claiming to be a go-with-it free spirit, when in actual fact she was a complete snob.

'I think we should go,' Spike said. 'You two can put on your new shirts and get the authentic American experience of steak and square dancing.'

Lottie smiled at him. She liked his enthusiasm and the clever way he managed to keep Tina on her toes. Anyone who could do that had to have a certain resilience and grit. Tina had resisted her every interrogation about what had happened between them – 'It was nothing,' she had said, in her most superior voice. 'Just one of those episodes that happen when you travel.' As if she thought Lottie had no experience of such things, tucked up as she was in her safe, long-term relationship. Tina had no idea of the depth of Dean's tenderness, the way he championed even the smallest of her endeavours and listened with close attention to all she had to say. When he introduced her to people he acted as if they were fortunate to meet her, and after a frost he went out in his dressing gown and scraped the windscreen of her car clear. Tina had never been with anyone long enough to understand the things that tied you to each other.

Showered and dressed in their cowboy best, they presented themselves at a restaurant just off the high street. The tables and chairs had been set up around a dance floor, where three circles of people were being led through sashays and swings by a man with a microphone and a Stetson. By his side, a nimble little woman was playing the fiddle with her mouth set as firmly as the line of her bow. Most of the people were wearing what looked like their work clothes and danced with the abstracted air of people who were as familiar with the turns and bends as they were with brushing their teeth or taking the bins out. The participants caught up each other's arms with inward, self-absorbed faces, as though the linking and looping were not so much a dance as a social obligation. Lottie felt overdressed in her western shirt and hat, as if she and her companions were intruding on a well-worn ritual.

'I hope they don't think we're taking the piss,' she whispered to Tina.

'You're too self-conscious, that's your trouble. Relax a little.'

There was nothing that made Lottie tense up more than being told to relax by her sister.

'Shall we dance?' Spike asked, doing a formal little bow that made Lottie laugh.

'I don't know the steps,' she said.

'Come and join us,' the man with the Stetson said.

'Three isn't a good number,' said Tina. 'You need a partner. I'll sit this one out.'

'Can't I sit and you dance with Spike?' Lottie said.

'Nope. It's Challenge Ten time.' Tina moved over to the table and began helping herself to fifteen different types of meat.

'Come on,' Spike said. 'The guy will talk us through the steps.'

So Lottie got up and followed Spike. One of the circles broke to let them in, and after a few agonising minutes when she didn't know which direction she was supposed to be going in, she found herself carried along by the others. Before long she had grasped the basics. When it was their turn to hold the arch at the head of the line, she and Spike grinned at each other.

'It's fun, right?' he said, and as the dancers passed under their arms, she felt a new lightness. She loved the pattern of the steps. There was no need here for any of the sort of self-expression she found so difficult on other dance floors. These moves had been done a thousand times in this exact and solemn way. Spike's arm encircled her waist and then spun her round; she wove in and out of the standing men to find him again.

'You're good at this,' he said, before he let her go to step between the ill-fitting jeans and dowdy skirts. Spike looked over to where Tina was sitting. A man was bending over her. She arched her neck up at him and fiddled with her hair (why did she always feel she had to flirt?) and then got to her feet and allowed herself to be led into the circling dance. He watched her leaning into the man, all slanting smiles, touching him on his arm, his shoulder. Her partner was wearing a white shirt open over a ruddy neck and had the victorious air of someone who has just successfully lassoed a wild horse. Spike met up with Lottie again. She looked flushed and pretty in her rose-strewn shirt.

'I think I need a drink,' she said, and so he took her arm and led her up to the bar. They got cold beers and sat back down at the table.

'Tina seems to be having fun,' Lottie said. She had a strange way of drinking from the bottle with her mouth sealed over the top of it, so that her cheeks filled and she couldn't breathe and made a gulping noise as she swallowed. Spike looked for Tina again, and saw that the dance had broken up into pairs. She was swaying in White Shirt's arms, her hands clasped around his neck. The man in the Stetson was singing 'Moon River' in a strange nasal tone. As she turned, Tina caught Spike's eye and smiled. He didn't smile back.

'Tell me about Dean,' he said to Lottie. 'What is it about him that makes you want to marry him?'

Lottie pulled her hair away from her hot face. She was just as lovely as her sister; it was only that she was in the habit of thinking she wasn't. Tina was arrogant to think herself so much more attractive. She did her sister a disservice. He had no intention of capitulating to Tina's deluded plan, even though he had begun to think that it might be entertaining to make her see the error of her ways. Tina thought everyone was as shallow as she was. He wished there was some other way to tell Lottie that she was easily her sister's equal in looks and far superior in character.

With Tina, he'd thought he'd found the person he wanted to spend the rest of his life with. The way she always held herself slightly back from him had only added to her charm. He had liked the thought that he might have to work hard to properly discover her. I'll never be bored, he had thought, as he had watched her sleep one early morning – her face had been animated by some feeling from a dream. He was devoted to the way her hair curled over her ear and her lips, swollen by sleep to a new softness.

When she awoke, opening her eyes to find him looking at her, she'd seemed startled. 'Have you been sitting there watching me?' she had said. 'That's slightly weird.'

'Why don't you move in with me?' he had said. He leant over and kissed her and she had pulled him to her. The light from the window had set her pale skin gleaming and he had touched her as if he never wanted to feel anything else, or be anywhere else but there with her, her body rising to meet his, the smell of her sharp and sweet.

'Well, will you then?' he had asked later as they walked around town, trying to find the dress he wanted to buy her for her birthday. He could see it in his mind's eye – tight-fitting at the waist and made of some luminescent green material, the colour of adamite or agate.

'Will I what?'

'Move in with me, live with me,' he had said. This step felt like an important one. He had never lived with a woman before. He looked at her. Her green eyes were flecked with gold. She was a marvellous, perfect thing.

'Well, Rachel and Tim are very absorbed with their growing bump. I feel as if I might be getting in the way,' she had said, and if he had wanted something more than this practical reaction to his suggestion, he hadn't shown it. He had picked her up in the shop and swung her round.

'We're moving in together!' he had said to the shop assistant, wanting to share his happiness.

They had toasted the decision with champagne at the Wave Organ in the bay. Tina hadn't been before and loved the fact that the sculpture was hard to find, hidden from sight until you walked to the very end of the jetty. They had listened to the strange sucking and drumming of the tide through the periscope-like pipes, the music of the sea overlaid with the boom of distant boats and the voices of the people who passed by. They had watched the sunset sitting on the ruined lumps of granite and marble. He remembered the moment as one of intense happiness, almost too great to bear.

She arrived at his apartment the next day in a taxi with one box and a couple of bags. Her few possessions barely took up half a cupboard, but the sense of her filled and transformed the place.

'Dean's so kind,' Lottie said shyly, flushing a little under Spike's sudden scrutiny. 'And he knows such a lot but is never, ever boastful. You know those people you meet who make you feel as if you don't know anything or that you are lacking in some way? He never makes people feel like that. He always makes them feel better about themselves.'

'It sounds as if you two are perfectly matched,' he said. Out of the corner of his eye, he could see Tina approaching. She must have given her companion the brush-off since he was nowhere to be seen. She was an expert at making people think they mattered and then turning cold. She could really do with a dose of her own medicine. He leant across the table so that his face was close to Lottie's.

'He's an extremely lucky man,' he said, smiling at her, his eyes on her mouth. Lottie would surely see through him in a moment. She had way too much sense to fall for moves like this, and it was clear she was madly in love with her fiancé. He was surprised to see her look startled. He had thought she would just laugh at him and he would be able to show Tina just how little she knew about her sister.

'What are you two whispering about?' Tina asked, sitting down. Her skin had a sheen of sweat on it and the hair around her forehead had gathered into tight curls.

'This and that,' Spike said airily, assiduously avoiding Tina's curious look.

'I expect he's boring you rigid about rocks,' Tina said.

'I would actually like to hear about meteorites,' Lottie said.

Spike was grateful for the supportive way she spoke and the way she rested her chin attentively on her hand as if she was really settling down to listen.

'What would you like to know?' he said, mainly because he wanted to piss Tina off. When he had seen some of his colleagues in action, talking about their latest research to anyone who would stand still, as if they had spent the last year under a rock themselves and had lost any sense of proper perspective, he'd learnt not to do the same.

'I don't even know exactly what a meteorite is,' Lottie said.

'They are lumps of matter that land on earth after millions of years of travelling. Some of them are as much as four and a half billion years old. They start out life as space debris – usually shards of comets or asteroids, but sometimes bits of the moon or Mars – and become shooting stars when they fall through the friction of a planet's atmosphere. Those that survive and make it all the way to earth are called meteorites.'

'How come people don't get killed by them falling out of the sky?' Lottie asked.

'Well, potentially they could. But most of them are small by the time they've been bashed and burned, and in any case they often end up in the ocean. There are reports of a cow or two getting killed, and a man was injured when a sizeable one came through his roof.'

'Do you know where they are going to land in advance?' Lottie asked.

'It's very hard to predict. Although there are several times a year when the earth moves through a meteor shower, it's still hard to tell if or where they'll land.'

'I find it difficult to get my head around something going on a journey that lasts such a long time,' said Lottie. 'All those thousands of years of hurtling through space and then they land up on some scrubby bit of ground.'

'Sounds a bit like our road trip at times,' said Tina sourly.

Chapter 14

ELVIS WAS SINGING 'HOW GREAT Thou Art' as the road circled and descended, unfolding deeper canyon layers. The mountains were dark in the distance but moved into the light in shades of yellow, ochre and crimson. In between the wind-ridged mounds, the salt lakes gleamed with an unearthly white.

They had set off early that morning, hoping to arrive at Death Valley National Park before the full heat of the day set in, but already the sun was blistering – melting the edges of the landscape so that everything looked soft and clay-like. The tarmac ahead seemed to bulge and buckle beneath its retaining neon stripe, its surface shining as if it was wet.

Lottie felt her eyes fill with tears. There was no other reaction possible to the strange beauty of it all. It was so ample, so gloriously, impossibly expansive, that she could barely look at its richness. She had the sense that she used to get sometimes as a child, late at night, of being overwhelmed and losing control – a feeling of swelling and turning over and over down a slope, with nothing to catch hold of to stop her fall.

How Mia would have loved to have seen it, she thought. She had a sudden memory of the way her sister used to open her eyes wide when something pleased or surprised her, as if to see as much of what was on offer as possible. Lottie felt a sudden anguish, an impact that slammed so heavily into her it almost took her breath away. If she had been able to act differently, if she had *been* different, Mia might still be with them. She would perhaps be looking out of this window now and sharing the wonder of veined mountains and wide skies.

As she had many times before, Lottie told herself she had done her best. It was the only way to make her pain more bearable. She had certainly done more than their warring parents. They'd always been so fatally entangled that nothing outside the endless recriminations of what he'd done and what she'd done could penetrate that mesh of blame and betrayal. It had made them insensible to anything else.

As a child, and then a teenager, Mia had borne the brunt of all of that. Ever vigilant, she had been the one who had hustled her sisters from the room when she had felt the air change. Lottie remembered how suddenly it used to happen. All it took was a look, a certain sharpness of tone or a weary complaint and there would be a tangible shift. This rearrangement of the atmosphere had a prickling feeling and a smell, as if something sour had crept through the gaps under the doors or down the chimney. Suddenly the house felt bitter and precarious.

'Don't listen,' Mia used to say once they were in their room with the door shut. 'Don't listen. Think of something else. Think of the ponies with green ribbons in their manes and the dancing mannequins.' Sometimes she used to sing the songs they heard on the radio – 'Ice Ice Baby' and 'U Can't Touch This' and 'The One and Only'. She had a terrible voice (the music teacher at school had told her she could be in the front row of the choir because she had pretty eyes, but she must on no account let a single sound come out), but she would stand on the bed, fists balled up by her sides, and bellow until she had drowned out the shouting and the sudden crashes and the terrible silences which were worse than what had gone before.

They made a brief stop at Badwater Basin. There they walked across the surreal stretch of salt that crunched under their feet as if they were walking on crisp snow. This terrain had no softness to it. The crystals had swollen and cracked into weird geometric shapes and the desiccated expanse felt merciless. Lottie could feel an echoing dryness in her mouth and a kind of bone-deep weariness.

'Are you OK?' Spike asked Lottie.

'I'm fine. Why?'

'It's just that you seem a little quiet.'

She squinted at him with her hand covering her eyes. After a period of rain, followed by a few days of this heat, the new layer of salt was blindingly white and she wished she had brought her sunglasses. Tina had walked on ahead and was lying on her stomach, taking pictures. They both stood and watched her for a while.

'You're so much easier to be with than your sister,' he said. 'You're much kinder.'

'She's much kinder than she lets on,' Lottie said, instinctively protective. It was one thing to moan about your own sister – it was pretty much written into the job description – but she didn't really feel comfortable when other people criticised Tina.

'She hides it well.'

'So, what happened between you two?'

'What has she told you?'

'Nothing much. She clams up every time I ask her about it.'

'She betrayed me,' Spike said, looking away. He paused. 'Do you see that mark on the mountain? That's sea level. It shows just how low-lying this location is. Another volcanic shift and it will sink even further.'

'What do you mean, betrayed you?' Lottie asked.

'You'll have to ask her,' he replied. 'Put it this way: I think I fell for the wrong sister.'

Lottie laughed. She figured that his words were simply a knee-jerk gallantry, the sort of thing that men said to women when they couldn't think of anything else. But he was looking at her with those shrewd eyes of his, and she felt a jolt – a small, almost inconsequential shift in her stability. I need a cold drink, she thought. All this hot whiteness is making me feel strange. What was that passage in the Bible about

Lot's wife turning round and being transformed into a pillar of salt? If she lingered here much longer she could imagine becoming calcified, too.

Tina turned round and walked back to them. 'It's amazing,' she said. 'I've taken some close-up pictures of the crystals and they look as if they are blooming, like strange, bleached broccoli.'

Tina seemed to expand in the sun. Her skin glittered and she had draped a green scarf over her head and shoulders. It made her look both robust and glamorous, like an old-style movie star hanging out on location, still beautiful despite the inhospitable terrain.

'Can we go somewhere and get a drink?' Lottie said, wishing that she cared less about how drab she felt in her sister's shining shadow.

At Stove Pipe Wells, a small settlement of tourist services – a hotel, a general store and a couple of places to eat – they parked the Mustang near a sign warning them not to feed the ravens. Spike went into the store to buy the drinks, while Lottie and Tina waited outside.

'You two British?' a woman asked. She was small and whip-thin, dressed in a black shirt firmly tucked into black jeans, which made her coiffured head look all the more incongruous. Her hair was a bright, Ikea yellow, the colour of road signs warning of dead ends, steep slopes and alligators, and was teased into stiff waves.

'Yes, we are,' Tina said.

'From London?' She had an odd, brisk way of talking and small, shining blue eyes. 'Ever been to Clarence House?'

'No. I don't think it's open to the public,' Lottie said.

'It is every August,' she informed them. 'Been there three times myself. Seen the china and the clocks and those itty-bitty spoons.'

'That's nice,' Lottie said politely.

'Althorp?'

Lottie shook her head. Tina went off into the shop to find out what was taking Spike so long.

'Frigging hell, you've been nowhere at all!' the woman exclaimed, hooking her thumb into her belt. She noticed that the woman had an ostentatiously large belt buckle made up of the letters 'DS' entwined in a rope motif.

Lottie tried a placating smile. 'You know how it is when you live in a country – you tend not to do the tourist things. I don't suppose you've ever walked across the salt flats.'

'If I'm gonna be fried I want to be covered with oil and lain down by the sea,' the woman said.

'Yes, quite.'

'You have something of her, actually,' the woman said, peering at Lottie more closely, 'in the shape of your face, the way your eyes are set.'

'Something of who?' Lottie asked, wishing that the other two would come out. Her tongue was sticking to the roof of her mouth and the heat was making her feel dizzy.

147

'Diana,' the woman said. She spoke as if she thought Lottie was a little obtuse. 'Princess Diana.'

'No one has ever said that to me before!' Lottie laughed, but stopped when she saw the woman was deadly serious.

'A haircut and some eyeliner and you could be her twin. You've got that same peaches-and-cream complexion, although you would have to do something about them freckles.'

To Lottie's relief (why was it she always got stuck with the loons?), Tina and Spike finally emerged from the shop holding dewy bottles.

'Well, it's been nice meeting you,' Lottie said.

'You sound just like her too, all soft and classy. Would you like to see my truck?'

'You drive a truck?' Tina asked. Lottie opened her bottle of water and poured it down her throat.

'It's the one just over there,' the woman said, pointing to an enormous white lorry with the obligatory multiple sets of shining headlights and a silver trim.

'We're in a bit of a hurry, actually . . .' Lottie began.

'I'm Stacey, by the way,' the woman said, extending her hand to each of them. Her palm was hard and a little dusty. She led the way across the road to the car park and they followed.

'You sisters?' Stacey asked.

'Yes,' Lottie said. 'I'm older by two years.'

'You got the looks. She got the attitude,' Stacey remarked, which made Lottie smile. 'Which of you does Keanu Reeves here belong to?' she asked, jerking her thumb in Spike's direction.

'Neither of us,' Lottie said, and then wondered why she had been so quick to reply.

'He favours my sister,' Tina said, smiling cruelly at Lottie, who stared back furiously.

'He's got good taste then,' Stacey remarked, opening the door of the truck and climbing up.

'What are you carrying in your truck?' Spike asked.

'Pig,' Stacey said shortly. 'I can fit in two of you at a time. You girls come up first.'

Every inch of the walls of the cab was covered in photographs of Diana. A blonde-haired doll in an off-the-shoulder gown swung from the mirror, faded pink silk roses trimmed the edges of the seats and a single candle in a gold holder was positioned on the dashboard.

'Wow!' Tina said. 'It's quite the shrine.'

'She was the best person who ever lived,' Stacey said, clasping her steering-wheel-worn hands together. 'She was just like I am. She was always looking for somewhere to be. Trying to get a little peace.'

After Spike had had his turn admiring the cab and they had declined her offer of a ride, they said they had to get back on the road. She let them go reluctantly.

'I'd try lemon juice on your freckles,' she said to Lottie, waving them off.

'She's crazy,' Spike said as they got into the car. 'I sincerely hope the "pig" she referred to is in rasher form. She didn't seem in any kind of rush to make her delivery.'

'You've got a fan there, Lottie,' Tina said.

Because Lottie was still feeling a little unwell, they decided to cut the day short and find a motel. Old Masters was a *Psycho*-style establishment with rooms set in a U-shape around an artist's palette-shaped pool. With the sell line *'Each room a work of art'*, they didn't have high hopes of the décor. Tina thought it unlikely she would be able to sleep in the Picasso-themed studio that she was sharing with Lottie, with its luridly geometric bed linen and a giant reproduction *Weeping Woman*. Spike claimed to be delighted with his Titian nude and bosomy pillows. While Lottie took a nap, Tina and Spike sat by the pool with beers and books. Tina's thriller wasn't thrilling her much and she looked covertly at her companion through her sunglasses. It appeared rock gathering had kept him fit because he looked pretty good in his shorts.

Tina recalled a day they had spent together after she had been living with him for a couple of months. She hadn't thought of it until now. Remembering was what she had been afraid of when Lottie had first suggested they take him with them on their trip. It must have been a weekend, because neither of them had had anywhere particular to go. They had slept in and made love and eaten cinnamon bagels in bed. If she shut her eyes, she could still taste the spicy sweetness of the dough. The rain was running in oily splashes down the window and the darkness was gathering. They had decided that there was absolutely no point getting up and putting clothes on since there was so little left of the day. Before him and after him, she had always disliked lingering in bed, but he had brought out a slothful side in her. With time on their hands, they had touched each other slowly, the lust they had so recently sated renewed by the rain and the dim room.

'I love you,' he had said as he moved over her. 'I've loved you from the first moment I saw you.'

It had been on her lips to reply in kind, but she didn't. She thought perhaps she loved him too, although the feeling was mixed up with the sensation of his hands on her. What if the time came when his touch no longer made her arch towards him? It had happened before with other people. She was familiar with the doubts and the impatience that crept into the spaces left by a cooling desire. How did people put their time and their hearts into something that wasn't properly tested? It was like buying an old car without looking at the engine, simply because you liked the colour, and setting off on a long journey with nothing more substantial than the hope that what was carrying you to your destination would continue to be roadworthy. Things changed all the time, and you couldn't rely on love lasting. Mia had given her heart so easily. She could have had anyone, and yet Rick had been her choice – the person she had decided to cleave to and invest in.

'There's just something about him,' she had said to Tina when she had returned after an early date with him to the flat in London they had briefly shared. 'He seems so tough, but really he's vulnerable.'

Mia had been wearing a dark blue dress with a pattern of flowers on it and her hair, loosened by the wind or his fingers, had escaped from the pins holding it back. She had looked, with her bright eyes and flushed cheeks, as if she had been in the grip of some great moment of revelation. Even then, Tina had wondered what the advantage of vulnerability was when it was allied to toughness. There surely couldn't be anything creepier than looking into an adult face and seeing the innocent blankness of childhood, and yet it appeared to draw some women in. It had worked on Mia, anyway. It had been the potential of the boy she had clung to when she was confronted by the reality of the man. Tina felt the old, helpless anger burning through her again.

'What are you thinking about?' Spike asked now, and she was startled back to the present. In the pool a semi-deflated swan was drifting round and round by the filter, while the ice machine in the reception area spat cubes into a tray.

'Nothing much,' she said.

'You looked real pissed about something,' Spike said.

'I'm just thinking that you need to ramp up your seduction of Lottie,' she said. 'I'm so glad you have taken the task on, but you're being too subtle. Start giving her soulful looks. Tell her she looks beautiful, that kind of thing. You're a master at it.'

'Am I?' he asked, looking at her with a serious gaze.

'Second nature,' Tina said breezily.

'Be careful what you wish for, Valentina,' he said.

'What do you mean? And don't call me *that*.'

'I don't mean anything,' Spike said. 'I'm just saying.'

'I hate it when you just say things.'

'What would happen if I really fell for her? She's lovely.' He didn't think it would happen but he wanted to dent Tina's complacency. She was just too annoyingly sure of herself.

'Be my guest,' Tina said, although for the first time since she had devised the plan, she felt a moment of doubt. Spike was certainly more interesting than dolorous Dean, but she didn't plan on him becoming a permanent feature.

'That's big of you. You do realise there's something a bit weird about pimping out your sister like this.'

'I'm just ensuring she keeps her options open.'

'OK. I'll fall in love with your sister, if that's what you really want.' Spike felt an unexpected sense of desolation – it was clear that Tina was completely oblivious to anyone's feelings but her own.

'Great . . . although I doubt you will. She's not really your type,' Tina said.

'She's beautiful, kind, clever, what's not to like?'

'She's too earnest for you. You prefer your women to be a little more challenging.'

'I just want someone nice who sticks around and shares things with me. Someone unafraid of life, who's ready to make the most of everything.'

'Did you know that Lottie is scared of getting her hair caught in zips?' Tina said. 'And bee stings and rabies and sepsis and inhaling sequins and a million other things?'

'That's kind of cute,' he said, goading her. 'She doesn't seem scared of the things that really matter.'

'Are you saying I am?'

'I'm saying nothing,' Spike said. He stretched out on his sun lounger, revealing his flat stomach and the V-shaped tendons disappearing into his shorts that Tina had always had a weakness for. He looked so maddeningly comfortable that she got up and scooped the wasted ice cubes up in a towel and tipped them into his lap. He jumped up and grabbed hold of her and made to throw her into the pool. At the very same time as trying savagely to extricate herself, she wanted to stop moving and allow herself to be held. Then the water took her, and the mobile phone she had tucked into the pocket of her shorts, and she cursed him once again.

Chapter 15

THEY WERE MAKING FOR A car park near the beginning of a trail that took them through the Golden Canyon and Zabriskie Point to a possible place to camp a couple of miles beyond. They had registered their intention to stay overnight in Death Valley at Furnace Creek, and hired rucksacks, a tent that was large enough for three – although Tina had told Spike he had to sleep outside – a stove and sleeping bags. Lottie had scrupulously read the information about what was allowed and what was prohibited and made a list of the necessary equipment. Tina had been patient enough until Lottie had started to go on about camping pans and spare socks and poring with unnecessary attention over the map of trails. Then she had lost interest and wandered out of the shop to take pictures of some children who were doing handstands in a line against the supermarket wall. She loved how joyful their faces looked, with their hair hanging to the ground and their eyes half closed, their toes pointed in their sandals.

She put her camera on the ground, took a deep breath and swung onto her arms. For a moment she thought she wasn't going to be able to get her legs up, but then something in her loosened, her hips hinged and, just like that, her legs were resting against the wall. She remembered the rush of blood to her head and the bulging, crazy inversion of her gaze. The small girl next to her looked sideways and gave a cheer.

Emerging laden down from the shop, Spike saw Tina's handstand and something in him turned, as if he too was looking at the world upside down.

She had never told him she loved him, but he had hoped that one day she would. He was a patient man. Part of him had admired the fact that she didn't give in easily to sentiment. He had had other relationships in which the word had been used loosely, without any real or lasting feeling. *I love ham sandwiches. I love Barcelona. I love pearl earrings. I love you.* There had been days when they were together when he was sure she had been on the brink of saying what she felt, days when he would sense an uncharacteristic, worried tenderness, but she always pulled away at the last minute, diverting them both with a joke, or picking up her camera to take a picture of something that had caught her eye. She had taken a lot of pictures of him. He had always been surprised by the moments she chose to record. He never looked as he imagined himself to be in her photographs. There was an imprecise, off-kilter quality to the images, as if she was trying to work something out.

He had thrown all the photographs away along with the other bits and pieces she had left behind her – a half-bottle of lemony perfume, a brush still wrapped with her hair, a T-shirt she used to wear in bed – anything that had the potential to trip him up and set the pain jangling like a stubbed toe.

He had replayed the scene over and over again. Each time he tried to remember if Tina had showed even a trace of guilt, but in his memory her face was always lacking any kind of real remorse. The man she had slept with hadn't been anyone special. Spike couldn't even remember now exactly what he had looked like. He had been a friend of a friend who had taken to hanging around. Dark-haired, a sweater always round his shoulders, a little too talkative. A chancer. The kind of man who made a point of laughing loudly at jokes and who always drew attention to the fact that he was buying the drinks. Someone who insinuated himself into groups where no one really knew him but accepted him because they assumed he must be there at someone else's invitation. Spike would never have known about it if a working weekend away had not been cancelled, and he hadn't arrived back at the flat when she wasn't expecting him. Like a sap he'd bought wine and flowers, and turned the key in the lock with a sense of pleasant anticipation. A weekend he would be able to spend with her after all stretched ahead. He hadn't called. He had wanted to surprise her. She had been a little under the weather and he had wanted to do something to cheer her up. Take her to the beach, perhaps, or to that Moroccan restaurant she liked which was rigged out like a tent, which gave him cramp in his legs because they had to sit on the floor.

She turned when she heard the door open, and for a moment she stared at him. He had seen her shock and something that might have been regret, a ripple of feeling in her face, the words starting and then dying on her lips. Then she had gathered herself and adopted a kind of blank defiance. She got off the bed, her hair tangled, her beautiful skin flushed the same way it did when he touched her. She had moved slowly, with no attempt to hide her body. There had been no apparent shame in the almost languorous way she had picked up her shirt from the floor and put it on. The man had covered himself with a sheet and made a strange sort of snorting noise, half way between laughter and fear. After several moments in which Spike had stood frozen looking at the scene – the window open, the curtain moving gently in the breeze – he'd shut the door and walked out of the apartment to the nearest bar and drunk himself stupid.

When he got back five hours later, she had gone.

'Acting your age again,' he said now as she swung herself upright, grinning and flushed. He would not show her how she still affected him. All that was done.

They parked the car and packed rucksacks and distributed provisions and set off on the trail. It started as a narrow, intermittently paved track between layered rocks, their strata pushed upright in slender slivers and blooming with occasional clusters of white, spiked quartz. The surfaces of the rocks were rippled with petrified sand, as if they still retained a memory of water over them. After a quarter of a mile or so the view opened up slightly to reveal glints of green and gold and slender, twisting side paths down which waterfalls had once spilled out into lakes. Ahead of them, beyond the ochre sandstone mounds, the Red Cathedral loomed, its surface scored with cracks and folds like the scrolled stonework in the walls of a gothic church. When they stopped to look back, taking the opportunity to have a quick drink, the weathered slices and mounds of the Badlands appeared soft, like floral foam; as if it might be possible to stick your fingers through them.

'It makes me feel sort of holy,' Lottie said, and for once she thought she had silenced the querulous voice in her head. What she could see around took up all the space inside her.

'Thank you for bringing me here,' she said to her sister.

Tina smiled and put her arm around her shoulder and they stood together, silent and perfectly aligned. Lottie wished it could always be like this.

For all her tricky ways, Tina had a great capacity for creating joy. When they were younger, it never felt as if anything could properly start until she was there. She had the knack of setting life in motion somehow. She would arrive at any gathering, inevitably late, always full of some story of disaster or triumph, always funny and opinionated and unmistakably present. She could just as easily cast a cloud over everything if she was in a bad mood.

'What do you think of him?' she had asked Lottie in one of her loud whispers when Mia and Rick had gone into the kitchen. They were at their mother's house, the dark, misshapen little cottage in Ilfracombe into which she'd moved after finally splitting up with their father. Lynne and Joe had lived on together in a perpetual state of deadly skirmish, long after the sisters had grown up and left home. For years they had behaved like creatures in captivity, who, unable to escape their cage, had developed the teeth-grinding, sore-licking habits of animals driven mad by their imprisonment. Even after they split up they couldn't embrace their new freedom, but instead worried away at the scabs left by their confinement.

'He's good-looking,' Lottie had answered.

'I'm never a big fan of winsome charm,' Tina had replied. 'I always think it's hiding something under its floppy fringe.'

'He seems dead keen on her, and I've never seen her looking so happy. She's positively glowing!'

Mia did look great. She'd shed a stone that she didn't really need to lose, but it had made her face look high-cheekboned.

She'd swapped her boho blouses and ragged jeans in favour of neat, belted dresses and heels.

'Yes. She is clearly getting laid regularly. I don't know. It's just that we hardly ever get to see her these days.'

'You're so contrary,' Lottie had said. 'You've been telling her she should concentrate less on work and more on her love life for years, and now that she seems to have found someone, you're being all critical!'

'I'm just reserving judgement, that's all,' Tina had replied, knocking back a huge lemon drizzle gin.

The path continued upwards and curved round the base of Manly Beacon. There were parts that had sheared away and the fall to their right was fairly precipitous, so that they had to be careful where they put their feet. At one point Lottie, dazzled by looking up at the monumental surface of the cliff, almost tripped and Spike caught hold of her.

'Mind yourself,' he said. 'We don't want you getting hurt.' He smiled at her and adjusted her hat, which had been knocked sideways by her stumble.

'You've got some golden dust on your face,' he said, rubbing the side of her cheek gently with his fingers. She was surprised to find herself leaning into him, and had to make herself turn abruptly and walk on. She felt uncoordinated, as if her almost-fall had triggered a weakness. At Zabriskie Point, they sat down on their unnecessary anoraks and ate bread and cheese and drank beer and looked at the view – the bright mounds of the Golden Valley, the duller, softer folds of the Badlands and in the distance, beyond the alabaster gleam of the salt flats, a purplish mountain range. The sky was a celestial blue and full of hawks.

'It makes me want to sing,' Spike said, spreading out his arms to encompass the hills and the sky and the feeling of being there.

'Don't spoil it,' Tina answered.

They weren't allowed to camp near Zabriskie Point, but they had identified a track leading down from the hill and walked for a further mile and a half to a flat, sandy spot. Here they had an expansive view and the benefit of two huge rocks on either side to shelter them. They set about making a camp. Lottie took methodical charge of the tent, Spike stored the water and unrolled the sleeping bags and got the stove lit for coffee, while Tina sat on a blanket issuing vague instructions.

'I've never been much of a Girl Guide,' she said. 'I've always left all that to Lottie. She enjoys doing things like washing pans with a bunch of twigs.'

After a while she deigned to blow up the air mattress she had insisted they bring and then lay flat on it, looking up at the sky.

'I'm just going to see if I can find some stones to weigh the sides of the tent down,' Spike said. 'It can get pretty windy at night.'

Tina sat up and they watched him walking off into the distance.

'What happens if we have to, you know . . . poo?' Lottie asked. 'It says in the list of rules that you have to dig a hole with a trowel, and we haven't brought one.'

'You could fashion one out of a flat stone and a piece of wood,' Tina said. 'Didn't you once get a badge for that?'

'You always mock my time in the Guides, but it taught me a lot of useful stuff.'

'When did you last have to use a reef knot, or make a bridge out of straws?'

'You never know when skills like that will be needed,' Lottie said. 'I think I'll just wait until we get back to go to the toilet. I haven't got a digging implement and besides, I think the landscape is too open to properly relax.'

'Your challenge today is to poo in the wild,' Tina said, grinning.

'How will you even know whether I have or not?'

'I'll know,' Tina said. 'Meanwhile, how about putting your catering badge to good use and rustling me up something to eat?'

'Cheese or pastrami?' Lottie answered, dragging the provisions rucksack out of the tent and delving inside.

'Cheese, and one of those little bottles of wine we bought please,' Tina answered, giving a great stretching yawn. 'I'm done in. It was quite a walk.' She made room for Lottie on the mattress.

Lottie was aware of her sister's scrutiny as she fished around in the bag.

'I can feel your eyes burning into the side of my head,' she said.

'That's usually your trick,' Tina answered.

'It doesn't get me anywhere. You're so secretive.'

'What do you want to know? Try me,' Tina said, biting into her sandwich.

'I want to know what happened between you and Spike.'

'Why are you so interested?'

'Because you're so strange around him,' Lottie said, stretching out her legs. She was gratified to see that they had lost their white gleam and looked almost tanned.

'I'm not the only one.'

'What do you mean?'

'I saw that little exchange between you earlier. You stumbling into his arms, accidentally on purpose.'

'You're talking rubbish.' Lottie moved further away down the mattress. But as she spoke she remembered that small, almost instinctive tremor, the way she had felt dazed after he had touched her face, as if for a moment she had forgotten who she was.

'Am I?' Tina said unrepentantly, taking a swig from her bottle. She had plaited her hair and it lay in a golden coil around her neck.

'OK. I find him attractive,' Lottie admitted, feeling a little flutter of panic as she said the words. Just saying it out loud made her feel as if she was betraying Dean. 'But it doesn't mean anything. I think that Ryan Gosling is attractive, but that doesn't mean I don't love Dean.'

'We are not on a road trip with Ryan Gosling,' Tina said. 'More's the pity.'

Lottie laughed. 'I'm having fun, you know,' she said, and leant over and tugged on Tina's braid playfully.

'You always used to pull on my hair as if you were ringing a bell,' Tina said, but without rancour. 'I'm glad you're enjoying yourself. This is what I wanted, us being close again. Sharing stuff.'

'I know,' Lottie said. She moved along the mattress so that she was sitting next to her sister again. They drank wine and stared at the view. The sky was softening, and it was so quiet they could hear the creak of the rocks contracting and the stealthy rustlings of creatures emerging from their daytime shelters.

'Do coyotes bite?' Lottie asked.

'Yeah, they're like rabid dogs.'

Lottie pushed her playfully on the shoulder. 'You can almost see Dove and Tache riding over the horizon,' she said, gazing around her.

'We're not in Landing Rock territory yet.'

'But there's a sense of it here – the sweep of the horizon and the dust and the colours. You can imagine seeing the shapes of men on horses suddenly appearing on hills and hearing drumming music. You know, that scene where they're tracking the man who murdered their father and the world around them feels so wide and lonely, and although they are tired they can't stop.'

'Spike let me down badly,' Tina said suddenly. 'Just when I needed him the most.'

'How did he do that?'

'He didn't want our baby,' Tina said.

Lottie turned and stared. Just then Spike appeared from behind one of the rocks. He looked wild-eyed.

'What's the matter?' Tina asked.

'I've been bitten. By a rattlesnake.'

'Are you sure?' Tina asked.

'I saw it a second too late,' Spike said. His face was white. Blood was pouring down his leg.

'Where's your phone?' Lottie asked.

'There's no signal here,' Spike said. 'I've tried.'

'Should we bandage your leg up?' Tina said, helplessly. She was never good with injuries and the sight of blood made her feel sick.

Lottie was already bending over to examine Spike's leg. 'I can see the three puncture marks. We should let the wounds bleed. Some of the poison might come out. Sit down, Spike. You need to stay as still as possible.' She led him over to the mattress and he collapsed on it.

'You are *sure* it was a rattlesnake? Could it have been a prickly cactus or something?' Tina asked hopefully.

'I heard the bastard rattle,' Spike said. 'It had an unmistakable looping motion. Like a slinky toy.'

'You could die, right?' Tina said in a panicked voice.

'Only if it's left untreated,' Lottie said. 'Then the poison can start to affect vital organs. We have to get him to hospital as quickly as possible.'

'How much time have we got? Do you know, Spike?'

'I think it's about an hour before it starts to do serious damage,' Spike said. He had started to sweat profusely.

'We could try walking him between us,' Tina suggested. 'We're bound to reach somewhere with mobile phone coverage.'

'I don't think we're supposed to move him – the poison will get round his body quicker,' Lottie said. 'There's a road near Zabriskie Point. The other side from where we came in. I remember a car park there on the map. It would be better if one of us walks that way until they get mobile coverage. The other could stay here and look after him.'

'I'll stay,' Tina said. 'You have a better sense of direction than me. I'll probably wander around in circles.'

'OK.' Lottie grabbed her rucksack and a torch. It was already getting dark and, although she had a pretty good idea of where she had to go, she didn't want to wander off the trail and get lost or fall off a cliff. 'Make sure you keep his leg lower than his heart. In a few minutes, bandage him lightly – there's a first aid kit in the tent.' She looked down at Spike. 'I'll get help, I promise,' and she set off at a run.

'Watch where you're going!' Tina shouted after her, sounding so terrified that if the matter had not been so serious, it would have made Lottie smile. A few moments later she was completely alone and the light was draining away. She tried not to think about coyotes.

Chapter 16

'TALK TO ME,' SPIKE SAID. His eyelids had started to droop and the area round the bite on his leg had already become red and swollen. Tina got the first aid kit and took out a bandage.

'Does it hurt?' Tina asked.

'Like fuck,' he answered.

'Lottie will get help,' Tina reassured him as she wincingly placed the dressing against his skin. 'She's just about the most reliable person I know.'

'How come you find it so difficult being together?' Spike asked. 'It seems to me that you are always on the edge of pulling away from each other. Come on, keep talking. Distract me.'

Tina hesitated. 'I think we blame each other for Mia's death.'

'What happened exactly?' Spike asked.

'Shh, don't speak. You've got to stay as still and calm as possible.'

Tina was talking to herself as much as she was talking to him. She wished she had her sister's fortitude. She was pathetic in a crisis. Tina poured some water onto a T-shirt and placed it against Spike's forehead. He was burning up.

'I'm thirsty,' Spike said, and so she fed him a few sips from the bottle.

'Lottie didn't say whether you should drink or not, so don't have too much.'

'You've kept these nursing skills hidden up till now,' Spike said. 'When I had dysentery after a trip away you told me to stop being a wuss.'

'Men always make a song and dance about being ill,' she said.

'So beautiful, but so hard-hearted,' Spike said.

'Stop talking,' Tina said.

Spike was trying to get to his feet. 'I think I'm going to be sick.'

'Don't move. If you have to chuck up, do it from a sitting position. I knew I shouldn't have given you that water.'

It was dark now, and the sky was studded with stars. In the distance, Tina could see the green glow of Vegas. She thought about Lottie, blundering her way through the dark. Spike lurched sideways on the mattress and lay down with his eyes shut. He looked as if he had fainted.

'You're not going to die on me, are you?' Tina asked, her terror rising. What would she do if he slipped into unconsciousness? What would happen if Lottie wasn't able to get help in time?

Spike opened his eyes. 'Would you even care?' he said.

'Of course I would,' she said. 'Keep your eyes open. I need to see your eyes.'

'Always been my finest feature,' Spike said. His speech was a little slurred.

'What can I do for you?' Tina asked desperately. 'Should I suck the wound?'

'I'm cold,' he said, although he looked feverish, and so she laid down with him on the mattress and put her arms around him to keep him warm.

'Almost like old times,' he said.

'Shut up, fuckwit,' she said, although her heart was beating so fast she thought it must be audible. While she hadn't been watching the moon had slid above them, and shone with an implacable blue light.

'In other circumstances, this would be quite romantic.' Spike tried to laugh, but instead leant over the edge of the mattress to be sick.

'There, there,' she said to him, as if he was a child. How long had Lottie been gone? Ten minutes? Twenty? How far into his body had the poison reached? She had a sudden vision of the way Spike used to come up behind her and rest his head on her shoulder as if there was no more comfortable place in the world.

'Tell me the story of *Landing Rock*,' he said.

So she told him the tale of two brothers who set out to avenge their father's death and retrieve his stolen gold, but who ended up going on another journey altogether.

'They didn't get the gold back, and killing their father's murderer brought them no satisfaction – he was a pathetic little man – but they found an abandoned baby and they saved each other. It's like Mia used to say, the quest is always different from the one you imagine you are on.'

At some point in her narrative, Spike had slipped into unconsciousness. She carried on lying beside him, praying to the moon that it might sway the tide of Spike's blood and keep him safe.

Lottie kept running, the torch held out in front of her. Every so often, she would stop to catch her breath and check her mobile. She looked at her watch. She had already been gone for at least three quarters of an hour. A tiny, pale antelope looked at her from behind a rock, and she could hear the sound of creatures flying above her – ravens probably, or maybe bats. She was sweating. Although it was cooler than it had been during the day, it was still warm enough to hamper her progress.

She could feel something sharp in her rucksack bumping into her back. Why had she brought it? Tina was right, she was too cautious. It was not as if she was going to need to stop and make a fire or use her penknife to fillet one of the big horned sheep that clustered on these hillsides. She had always been prepared for every single potential emergency, except the one that really mattered. When it had come to the crunch, she had fallen so far short. She felt the desert around her – the sinking valley and the warped, slowly shifting mountains, the borax and the gold still in the hollow spaces beneath her feet. When it came right down to it there was nothing to hang onto: everything was unsafe and unpredictable. Everything changed. Maybe even her feelings for Dean. As she ran she thought of the way his face had looked after the first time they made love. He had been shining as if he had lost his old skin and found a whole fresh layer underneath. He was the one for her. It was decided.

The phone was still obdurately giving out its no coverage message. It was now over an hour since she had left the camp and she had run a lot of the way. She didn't understand why she hadn't reached the road yet. On the map it had looked fairly straightforward. Just as she was deciding that maybe she had taken a wrong turn, she heard a car horn in the distance. It was the most comforting sound in the world.

'Are you still with me?' Tina asked Spike. He didn't reply.

He's going to die, she thought. He is going to die on this mattress with the stars and Las Vegas shining on, oblivious. She felt for the pulse in his neck. It was faint under her fingers. It reminded her of another pulse she had sensed deep inside her, many years ago. At the time she had told herself she was imagining it. It had only been a scrap of something at that stage, after all. A little bundle of DNA, intricate and folded, like noodle strands before they separate in boiling water.

'Is it even mine?' Spike had asked, his face strange and hateful.

'Of course it is.'

'How can I possibly believe you?'

'Because it's the truth.'

She would have preferred his anger. This muted, disdainful version of him hurt her more than any other incarnation could have.

'I feel sorry for you,' he said, turning away from her with his arms crossed. He looked out of the window as if he was praying for a diversion – a sunset they could wonder at, a passing carnival float or the march of an invading army – but they were stuck with themselves and this room and a terrible pressure in her throat and chest. The ragged, rising pain gave her something to push against. It kept her upright. It made her find the words.

'I want it,' she had said. 'I want to keep it.'

'Do what you want. You usually do.' His face was flushed, the anger more visible now. She made some sort of move towards him, but he put out his arm to fend her off.

'I don't ever want to see you again,' he said.

She had slept with Rory the day after she had discovered she was pregnant. She hadn't even liked him particularly. She found his loud confidence and the way he kept touching her arm almost offensive. In the restaurant, his bluish jaw and straining shirt had turned her off, and yet she had maintained a façade of beguiled interest – laughing at his terrible jokes, acquiescing with a little flirty purse of her lips to a dessert she had no stomach for. She had worked wilfully through the dreary tropes of seduction, despite her lack of desire – the brush of his foot under the table, the touch of his hand on her thigh, the tucking of a strand of hair behind her ear, the terrible, grim, twinkling emptiness of it all. He had pushed her against the washbasin in the restaurant bathroom, his blunt fingers eager and his cock straining against his shiny trousers. She had let him fuck her in a public toilet and then again the next day in the bed she shared with Spike. And all the while, through the grunting skirmish of it, she had wondered why. After Spike had burst in on them and she'd sent Rory, noisy and peevish, away, she had wept as she washed herself between her legs, feeling a new tenderness that went beyond the soreness of unwanted sex all the way inside to the little nub of him and her.

After she'd told Spike about the baby, she had gone back to England. For a month or so she'd waited, thinking he might contact her. When he didn't, she phoned him every day for a fortnight, but he never answered her calls. She changed her mind almost daily about whether or not to have an abortion. It was clear that Spike did not want to be part of her, or their baby's, future. She was scared of the thought of becoming a mother with no one to support her and yet she couldn't, somehow, relinquish the possibility. She put her palm to her stomach as she lay in the bath one night and felt her child floating with her, and she understood that what she really wanted was to love and care for this scrap of her, however difficult it would be.

When she was about ten weeks pregnant and she had started in a tentative way to look at other babies in prams and imagine her own as flesh and bones rather than a phantom, she woke to terrible period pains, which were so hard and fast they felt like contractions. In the toilet the blood of what she and Spike had made trickled down her legs. She reached automatically, well trained as women are, for tissue to stem the flood and to clean the floor – just a mishap, a girl thing – and the staggering weight of her loss caught her by surprise. Her sorrow made her mad for a while, in that quiet, almost unnoticeable way, easily hidden behind laughter and activity. It made her feel all the time as if she was falling. Even now, when she allowed herself to think of it, her heart flinched at the memory of lying in bed, her hands on her stomach, feeling emptied and ashamed.

The silence was suddenly filled with sound and light. The dust rose so that it filled her nose and mouth. The sparse vegetation trembled and then flattened. A little distance away a helicopter wheeled, searching with efficient lights and movie razzmatazz. She got to her feet, waving her torch in the air.

'We're here!' she said, as if they could hear her. 'We're here. He's still alive.'

Chapter 17

HOSPITALS ARE STRANGE PLACES AT two in the morning. The pain and panic is still there, tangible in the drawn curtains and the occasional, ominous swing of a door, but it takes on a quiet, night-time aspect, as if illness too has to obey the sun. Tina and Lottie were on their third cup of luke-warm coffee.

'You were like Lara Croft,' Tina said. 'Running through the desert and then hitching to Furnace Creek to ring for help.'

'I'm not so sure,' Lottie said, smiling. 'I thought for a while no one was going to stop for me on the road. In the end I had to stand in the oncoming traffic, waving my arms around.'

'I might even ease up on the challenges,' Tina said. 'But only for today.'

Lottie dug her in the ribs, making her coffee spill on the floor. 'It can't have been easy staying with him either,' Lottie said, wanting to make Tina feel as if she had played her part. 'Were you scared?'

'Shitless,' Tina said. 'I thought he was going to die.'

'What did you talk about?'

'I told him the story of Tache and Dove.'

'Thank God the rattlesnake bite was as shallow as it was, otherwise he might not have made it.'

'Would you have run so fast if it had been Dean's life at stake?' Tina asked slyly.

'Of course I would!' Lottie said, indignant. 'I would even have run fast to save you.'

'Just admit you fancy Spike.'

'I'm not a teenager, Tina,' Lottie said. Yet she had to admit to herself (but never to Tina) that she had felt a bit like one over the last couple of days. She was alarmed by how terrified she had felt at the sight of Spike, deathly pale, hooked up to all sorts of machines. His naked chest had made her want to put her hands on him. She didn't know what had got into her. She hardly knew him. It was probably something to do with being away. People always behaved strangely on holidays. One of the three men she had had sex with was someone she had met on a holiday in Paxos. He had taken her snorkelling and fed her raw sea urchin with a little spoon he kept in the pocket of his trunks. She had known as soon as she had seen the spoon that this was a well-worn ritual and that the man lived tidal fashion, taking his pick from the over-sunned women who came on the boat from Corfu to spend a day or two on the tiny island, buying linen tops and staring longingly at the brown-legged men washing down the decks of Russian yachts. And yet she had gone with it. She was just a bit dazzled by Spike. That was all. It was a road trip crush and when the road trip was over, it would pass. Dean was reality. Spike was just a holiday hologram.

'I'm not sure there's any point hanging around any longer,' Tina said. 'The doctor said he was comfortable and the best thing was to let him sleep.'

After alerting the medical team, Lottie had been taken back to the car park by an obliging ranger and had then driven to the hospital. 'Shall we go back to *every room a work of art*?'

'Yeah. I'm absolutely knackered. I might even be able to sleep beneath the *Weeping Woman*.'

Back at the motel, Tina and Lottie ate the burgers they had picked up on the way, sitting cross-legged on their beds.

'This is the most delicious burger I have ever eaten,' Lottie announced, her cheeks distended with bread and pickle.

'It's because you've had a brush with death,' Tina said. 'It sharpens your senses. What we should really do after eating this is get some dope off the creepy bloke in reception – he's already offered me some, along with the somewhat unappetising prospect of sex – and have a swim in the pool.'

'We should really wait until we've digested our food. We could get cramp,' Lottie said. 'Anyway, I thought you said you were tired.'

'Right there you've lost your Lara Croft crown,' Tina said. 'Do you think she ever says, "*I can't swim across this alligator-infested swamp because I've just nibbled on some pulled pork*"?'

'Lara Croft doesn't actually eat, you numpty.'

'Cramp after eating is a myth, along with spiders that climb up plugholes and vampires.'

'How come blokes just come up to you and offer you dope and sex? He barely even looked at me.'

'He knows you are taken. You have that pursed-mouth, I'm-in-a-relationship look. Not to mention that less-than-vulgar, itsy-bitsy diamond on your finger.'

'It's actually from Tiffany's,' Lottie said. 'And he doesn't look to me like someone who notices a great deal.'

'He looks like someone who spends his days peering at porn. He probably has a gecko in a reeking tank at home.'

'Won't we wake the other residents if we swim at this time of night?' Lottie asked, in a worried fashion.

'Have you even seen any other residents? This is like the place time forgot. Maybe Creepy Boy has murdered them all and stuck them in the walls.'

Lottie started laughing, and then stopped suddenly.

'I've just remembered something,' she said. 'In all the chaos it slipped my mind. What were you saying, before, about a baby?'

'Go and get the dope. You might have to give him a hand job to get it, mind.'

'Do I have to? It wasn't me that he offered it to.'

'You're back on challenge time,' Tina said.

'If I go, will you tell me about the baby?' Lottie asked.

'You are in no position to bargain, sis. Go get the weed.'

Creepy Boy was asleep when Lottie went into the office. He was sitting in his chair with his head lolling backwards, his narrow black T-shirted chest rising and falling to the sound of his snores. The remains of a pepperoni pizza and several empty beer bottles littered the desk. Lottie coughed meaningfully. He came to with a start and looked around him in surprised indignation as if he had expected to wake somewhere quite different.

'Sorry to wake you,' Lottie said.

'I wasn't actually sleeping,' he said. 'I was meditating.'

'Well, sorry to disturb your meditation then.'

'How can I help you?' he asked, becoming suddenly officious, as if he had belatedly remembered what it was he was actually supposed to be doing. This job that was only supposed to have lasted a couple of months, enough time to get some money together to travel, had somehow transformed itself at some point into what he actually did. It was impossible on his wages to save enough for the airfare to Thailand and keep himself in weed and beer, and in any case the girl he was supposed to have been travelling with had dumped him for a football player. He still felt actual pain when he thought of her dark, uneven hairline and her breasts that had exactly fitted into his cupped hands. He scooped the remains of his supper into a tissue-filled bin and then raked his fingers through his hair as if he was pulling himself upright.

'You told my sister that you might be able to give her some . . .' Lottie trailed off.

'Yes,' he said, looking suddenly wide awake. He smoothed his hands over his chest with a smirk. He had the air of a man who had moments ago been contemplating an arid desert and was now gazing on the Promised Land.

'I take it you ladies are looking for some company?' He pronounced 'ladies' with an extended 'e' as if he thought he was playing the part of a rake.

'Oh no, no,' Lottie said in alarm. 'No. Sorry. I was just wondering if you might be able to sell us a couple of joints.'

'Oh, OK,' he said, looking crestfallen. 'Am I right in thinking the other one is of the same mind?' he said, the hope not quite extinguished in his chest. The ice machine made a grinding sound and deposited its load into the tray.

'Yes, my sister is of the same mind,' Lottie said firmly.

'Sisters!' he said wistfully, reaching into the pocket of his jacket and pulling out a couple of bent spliffs. 'I'm Chip, by the way.' He said it as if he knew she wasn't interested in his name or in anything else about him.

Lottie felt a little sorry for him. 'You could always join us,' she said. 'Just for the company, not, you know . . .'

'Well, strictly speaking I'm on duty,' he said, as if there was a horde of people clamouring at the door to spend the night with pirouetting ballet dancers and milk-pouring Dutch maids and almond-eyed pre-Raphaelite women.

'I'm sure you would be able to hear the phone and the door if we stay outside,' Lottie said, wondering why she was working so hard to persuade him. It was just that he was a teenager

182

with spots around his hairline and the kind of dog-eared look that spoke of lack of love. It also seemed harsh to just take the weed and run. She liked to think she had better manners than her sister.

'The phone hasn't rung since Monday,' he said, 'and that was only the ice machine mechanic saying he couldn't make it.'

'There you are then,' said Lottie, encouragingly. 'No one is going to come at this time of night – or morning actually,' she added, looking at her watch. It was three o'clock and it seemed they had missed their chance to go to bed.

Tina rolled her eyes when Lottie came back to the room and explained that she had invited Chip to join them.

'If you want a job done,' Tina said.

'He's very lonely.'

'So was Norman Bates,' Tina replied.

They changed into their swimming costumes and joined Chip, who had laid out the joints and a couple of beers with as much ceremony as if he was catering for a grand banquet. The sky lightened and they got stoned, even Lottie, who had declined to join in until Tina had fixed her with a look. Chip, who turned out to be a great raconteur, regaled them with stories about the guests who had stayed in the motel – a man who had had sex with fifteen different women during a three-day stay (Chip had enviously counted them in and out); a troupe of synchronised swimmers who had rowed with each other the entire time; a couple whose room had been discovered to be a treasure trove of stolen goods; and a man who had blocked his toilet with bagels. Sometime around daybreak they swam in the pool, trying out synchronised swimming moves while the sun gained strength and set the water glittering.

'This has been the second-best night of my life,' Chip said, as he left them to resume duty in the reception.

'What was the first best?' Lottie asked.

'I haven't had it yet,' he replied.

When they finally went to bed, Lottie put her head up from the pillow and said, 'You were going to tell me about the baby.'

'I lost it,' Tina said. 'I wanted it so much, but I lost it.'

'I didn't know you wanted a baby.'

'Neither did I.'

'Did you break up with Spike because of it?'

'No. We broke up because I slept with someone else. I think maybe if I hadn't, he would have wanted the baby as much as I did. I'll never know now.'

Just before she went to sleep, Tina imagined the room that they might have made, with stars on the ceiling and lambskin underfoot and a baby with one sticking-out ear, lying with her eyes wide open, waiting to be held.

Chapter 18

'DOES IT STILL HURT?' Lottie asked.

'It's a bit sore and swollen, but I'm feeling a lot better.'

Spike was sitting up in bed eating the chocolates that Tina and Lottie had bought him from the gift shop.

'It was really scary,' Lottie said.

'You did phenomenally well, going and getting help like that. Thank you so much.' Spike caught hold of Lottie's hand. 'It might have ended very differently if you hadn't had the guts to find your way in the dark. It was very brave.'

Lottie blushed and tried to extricate her hand, but he kept it in his grip.

'I was quite brave too,' Tina said. 'You were sick on my trainers.'

'You were amazing,' Spike said hastily. 'Both of you were. I'm an idiot for blundering around and getting myself bitten. I should have known better.'

'Yeah,' said Tina. 'For someone who's used to desert conditions, it was careless.'

'I think I was a little distracted,' Spike said. He looked at Lottie, and she pulled her hand away.

Tina smiled. It looked as if Spike was doing what she had asked of him. The man was definitely a pro. He wasn't going to let a tiny thing like a snake bite get in the way of romancing Lottie. Her sister looked more than a little flustered. It surely wouldn't be long now before she would have to admit that she liked Spike, and if she confessed to that, then surely she couldn't go ahead with the wedding? Tina had been right all along; Lottie wasn't as convinced by drippy Dean as she claimed to be. Spike wouldn't even have to force his pretend feelings to a conclusion – he wouldn't have to sleep with Lottie or anything. The job would be done if it just made Lottie see that she couldn't possibly be properly in love with Dean if she was even attracted to someone else. Tina would have to take Spike aside and warn him not to go too far; she didn't want her sister starting to believe that Spike was actually in love with her, or she would be hurt when his affection mysteriously cooled. Besides, if she was really honest with herself she didn't like the idea of them getting together. It would just be too weird. She had a sudden memory of the way they had lain together on the mattress two nights ago, her arm over him, her body spooned against his back, trying to keep him warm. She shook it away. She had just been frightened that he was going to die, that was all. The fleeting feeling of closeness, of rightness, had been prompted by the drama of the moment, nothing else.

*

'Have they said when you will be well enough to leave?' Lottie asked.

'I should be OK by tomorrow,' he answered. 'I'll have to have a crutch and some painkillers, but it's going to hurt for a while wherever I am, so I may as well be with you guys.'

'You won't be able to drive,' Lottie said. 'Perhaps you should go back to San Francisco.'

Even as she said the words, Lottie felt a sense of loss. If he went home now she was unlikely ever to see him again. He would go back to his life and she to hers. Perhaps, after all, it was for the best. If he went away, she would recover her senses. It was a little like having heatstroke; a day in a darkened room and the sting would pass. She had been meaning to Skype Dean again, but hadn't been able to bring herself to. She had settled instead for a series of jaunty little texts.

Tilting at fake windmills in Solvang. Bought you a cowboy belt! Just seen the fattest man on the planet. Eaten grits . . . never again.

'Are you trying to get rid of me?' Spike asked, doing that lingering glance thing that she found so disconcerting. It didn't seem possible that he was interested in her, not when he'd known Tina. Although she had to admit, when he looked at her, he made her think that she wasn't so plain after all. Dean was always telling her she was beautiful, but

187

sometimes she thought it was just habit talking. She would try and catch him out occasionally, just to check he was still actually looking at her rather than making do with the idea of her he had become accustomed to. 'What am I wearing?' she would sometimes ask before a night out when he had already told her she looked nice, tucking her body out of sight behind a door. 'You can't expect me to describe a dress,' he would say, or, 'I think it's almost certainly blue.' When she laughingly complained about his lack of proper attention he would say, 'You always look beautiful. Every day. It's a fact.' And she knew he thought her so, but just sometimes she wanted him to be carried away. To catch sight of her in a certain light, in a certain dress, and be overwhelmed. It was unreasonable of her to value his steady regard, the sturdy way he loved her, and then expect him to behave impulsively, even theatrically; he wasn't made that way. She felt ashamed of her vanity. She liked to think of herself as a serious person, but she was clearly anything but. Spike made a groaning sound as he moved his leg and she was jolted out of her reverie.

'No, not at all,' she said, deliberately not looking at her sister's grinning face. 'I just don't want you to overdo it.'

'That is such a British phrase!' Spike laughed. 'The British absolutely hate the idea of anyone exerting themselves or being seen to try too hard. *So vulgar! Just so much and no more,*' he said, putting on a terrible English accent.

'I see that your close shave with death hasn't improved your infantile sense of humour,' Tina said.

'We'd better go,' Lottie said hastily, keen to prevent Tina and Spike starting to snipe at each other. 'We've got to retrieve the tent and all the stuff we left behind, otherwise we'll be facing a hefty bill from the hire shop.'

They walked back to their campsite. The trail was easy to navigate in the daylight, and Lottie was alarmed (but also secretly gratified) to see that there were a couple of places where she could easily have fallen and hurt herself if she had taken a wrong turn. Once they reached the campsite, they ate the remains of what hadn't been nibbled at by what Tina said was almost certainly coyotes, and drank lukewarm beer.

'So, how are you feeling about your wedding?' Tina asked.

'I'm worried about the things I haven't done yet. Dean said he would deal with it all, but I don't feel completely confident. I've left him in charge of ordering the flowers so I'm not sure what we'll end up with. Something orange and purple, probably.'

'I don't mean how you feel about the preparations. How do you feel about the prospect of marrying Dean?'

'I'm looking forward to it,' Lottie said, but her tone didn't match her words.

'You don't sound as if you are,' Tina remarked. 'Perhaps the fact that you've been together for ten years and *not* got married is a sign that you've never been really sure.'

'It's the exact opposite, Tina. It's *because* I've been with him a long time that I know I want to marry him. It feels like a real commitment. A proper promise to each other and not something we've just rushed into. It'll be great when it actually happens.'

'Is that what you really think, or what you hope you'll think?' Tina asked.

Lottie fell silent and Tina didn't prompt her. They stared at the view – the landscape that had already become familiar to them. Tina wondered if they would be able to find this spot again if they returned at some time in the future. She resolved to take pictures of it before they left. It felt to her that something significant had happened here, although she couldn't quite say what.

'Do you think that the fact you are attracted to another man means that you can't really be in love with the person you are with?' Lottie finally said, her eyes troubled. With her hair released from its usual tight ponytail and her arms tucked around her knees in a childlike pose, she looked young and vulnerable.

'I think it might make someone think very carefully about committing themselves,' she said.

'I feel so confused,' Lottie said in a small voice.

'What are you confused about?' Tina asked, putting her arm around her sister's shoulders.

'I really like Spike,' Lottie said. Her eyes were full of tears. 'I like him more than I should do if I'm getting married to Dean.'

Now that the words were out, Lottie looked terrified. I've fucked up badly, Tina thought. This hadn't been in the plan. What she had envisioned was a harmless bit of flirtation that wouldn't lead to any great feeling, but only serve to cast doubt on the upcoming marriage. She had never imagined that Lottie might actually fall for Spike. She needed to tell Spike to stop the pretence before the situation got completely out of control.

'But how can I cancel the wedding?' Lottie asked. Her face was wet with tears.

'How can you go through with it unless you are completely sure?' Tina said.

'A wedding is a huge thing. It's like, once it has been put in place there is no stopping it.'

'I think you should think about whether Dean is really the person you want to spend the rest of your life with.'

'I've always thought he was,' Lottie said pitifully. 'I've loved him from pretty much the first time I spoke to him. He came up to me at a party and asked me if I wouldn't dance with him. It made me laugh, and so we went and sat on a wall outside the house and talked for hours.'

'Sometimes you can just get carried along and before you know it you are tangled up in something you are not even sure about anymore.'

'Why have you never been in a long-term relationship?' Lottie asked abruptly. 'Don't you want someone?'

'You have to be certain it's going to last, and I've not had that with anyone.'

As she said the words, Tina remembered how it had felt when Spike had wanted nothing to do with her and the baby, the black days and weeks afterwards when he hadn't returned her calls. It had been the one time she had laid herself open and it hadn't ended well.

'But how *can* you be sure?' Lottie rubbed her face with the sleeve of her dress. 'There's no guarantee. There can't be.'

'So why get married at all?'

Lottie stared at her and then shivered as if a chill wind had risen up from the scrubby brushland.

Tina undid the nozzle of the mattress and pressed her elbows down so that it started to deflate with a hiss. Lottie jumped to her feet and began pulling at the guy ropes on the tent. Tina knew that she always felt better when there was something concrete to do, and so she came to help her. They wrestled for a while to get the tent that had come out so easily the day before back into its narrow bag.

'Challenge One-Hundred-and-Fifty-Three,' Tina said. 'Sing with me.'

She was pulling insistently at Lottie, who was holding fast to the sides of her chair. Tina was boisterously drunk – her hair was wild and she kept going over on the heels of her nasty pink cowboy boots. She had spotted them in the window of a charity shop in Lone Pine and claimed she couldn't live without them, even though they were a couple of sizes too big. Her loud voice, the ludicrous boots and her red mini-skirt and white crop top had already attracted a lot of attention in the bar. Lottie figured she might have to drag her sister home, and was relieved they were only a couple of blocks from the motel. Lottie would never have said anything to Tina, but for the first time ever she thought that she looked a little old to be dressed as she was. Until now, Lottie had considered her to be living, breathing proof that women could wear whatever they wanted, and it was with a shock that she realised that for once her sister didn't look great. She chastised herself for her thoughts; she never wanted to be the sort of person who judged other women for what they looked like or what they wore. There would be much less store set by the firmness of flesh and many fewer hours wasted filtering yourself into what passed for beautiful if women all stuck together and wore red mini-skirts and told more people to fuck off. It was men who benefited from women's insecurities, but it was often other women who created them. She loved the fact that her sister was an unstoppable force – although at this precise moment she wished she would quit trying to make her sing karaoke. In Lottie's opinion, karaoke was the invention of the devil designed for the delusional and the drunk.

Still, a challenge was a challenge. She allowed herself to be hustled to the microphone, and, prompted by Tina's meaningful stare and some half-hearted cheers from the floor, began singing along to 'Just Like A Pill'. She hated Pink's self-conscious defiance, but despite herself the lyrics did their work, and she soon found she was yelling them as loudly as

Tina was. She put her arm around her sister's waist and they moved together. In that moment, the past slipped away and all the blame for what they had and hadn't done went too. They were just sisters, jumping up and down in a bar, gleeful and dishevelled, making the most of life.

Chapter 19

'IF YOU WERE AN ITEM of furniture, what would you be?' Spike asked. He was sitting in the back of the car, his injured leg protected by a rolled-up blanket beneath and a towel on top.

'That's such a boring question!' Tina said. She was hanging out of the car window to vape, because Lottie refused to drive any further if she could hear her inhaling. She said she didn't want to share the car with Darth Vader.

'I'd be one of those old desks with lots of little hidden drawers,' Lottie said.

'I'd be a glass-fronted display cabinet,' Spike said.

'I'd be a bidet,' Tina said.

'That's not strictly speaking an item of furniture,' Lottie said.

Tina pulled her head back into the car. Her hair had been blown into a mass of tangles.

'OK, if I can't be a bidet, I'll be one of those cocoon chairs that swings from the ceiling.'

'Suitably unstable,' Spike muttered, and then grimaced as they went round a corner and his leg came into contact with Lottie's wooden horse.

'I thought we were never going to get away from Furnace Creek,' Tina said. 'It's as if the god of road trips had decided we were going no further.'

'Where have you put the world's worst piece of memorabilia?' Spike asked.

'In the glove compartment,' Lottie said, shuddering slightly.

When they had dropped the tent off at the hire store they had been accosted again by Stacey the trucker. Goodness knew when she actually did any deliveries, because she seemed to spend most of her time hanging around in car parks. As soon as she had seen them, she had scuttled across, her hair incandescent in the morning light, her chest emblazoned with a lurid photograph of Diana looking demented in a tiara.

'I was hoping I'd see you again,' she said, her gaze fastening itself fervently on Lottie. 'I've got something I think you should have.'

Despite their protestations that Spike was waiting in the car and that they really had to get back on the road, she insisted on ushering them to her truck. She had scrambled inside and, after a couple of moments, slithered to the ground again holding something wrapped in tissue paper.

'It's the only thing I have that she actually touched,' she said and carefully unveiled a small piece of grey rubber.

'What is it?' Lottie had asked, politely bending over to examine it.

'It's Diana Spencer's school eraser,' Stacey said in a reverent tone of voice. 'I got it on eBay.'

'How do you know it was actually hers?' Tina asked. Lottie scowled at her.

'It came with a certificate,' Stacey said.

'Absolutely authentic then,' Tina said, and Stacey nodded firmly.

'I want you to have it,' she said to Lottie. 'You could be her double.'

'Oh no. I couldn't possibly!' Lottie exclaimed, looking dismayed. 'It's so precious to you.'

'That's the reason I want you to have it,' Stacey said, waving Lottie's protestations away. 'It will make me happy to think of it with you. Mind you don't let it fall, or anything. You've got to keep it carefully so her fingerprints don't come off.'

'Well, thank you,' Lottie said. 'But can't I pay for it, or give you something in exchange?'

Here Tina had given her a scandalised look.

'There *is* something, actually.' Stacey reached into her pocket and extracted a Swiss army knife, and Lottie instinctively took a step backwards. Stacey pulled out a tiny pair of scissors from the side of the knife.

'Could I have a little piece of your hair?'

'That's a bit strange,' Tina had said, but she was grinning as if she found the idea hilarious.

'I'll just take the smallest curl,' Stacey said, and without waiting for Lottie to reply she darted forward and cut off a lock of her hair, which was hanging loosely on her shoulders. Lottie's hand went instinctively to her head.

'I'm thinking you're her reincarnation, see?' Stacey said, and carefully wrapped the curl up in another piece of tissue.

'I'm really not,' Lottie protested. 'I was actually born before she died.'

'It could be delayed reincarnation,' Stacey said, with a cunning look.

'Yes,' Tina said, smirking. 'It's very possible that any day now you will wake up, Lottie, and discover a taste for see-through skirts and guinea pigs.'

'We really must go,' Lottie said.

'Where are y'all going next?' Stacey asked.

'Las Vegas,' Lottie said.

'Well, enjoy! Don't lose all your money! Me, I'm going home – a place called Chloride, just a few miles away. You should visit sometime.'

'That would be lovely,' Lottie said.

'You do know you're not actually Diana, don't you?' Tina had asked as they walked away. 'You don't have to be so bloody polite to everyone. The woman is a bona fide certifiable loon.'

'I think we should call you Diana from now on,' Spike said now. 'You are as beautiful as she was.'

198

He watched the back of her neck flush at his words. She had tied her hair up to hide the missing lock, and her skin looked pale and delicate. Tina turned and looked crossly at him from the front seat of the car and he grinned unrepentantly at her. She had accosted him earlier that day while Lottie was packing up the car and saying goodbye to Chip.

'You need to ease off now,' she had said. 'Lottie's really beginning to think you like her. You've done what needs to be done – which is make her think twice about marrying disastrous Dean – so now you can cool it.'

'Who says I don't like her for real?' Spike had said. 'She's lovely – and, what's more, she saved my life. There's not many people you can say that about.'

'Stop being a prat,' she had said and stalked off, her nose in the air.

Spike looked out of the window. There was nothing growing in this landscape and the pale hills were monotonously uniform. Lottie was ballsy and had integrity and, although she tried to hide her body all the time, he found her soft curves sexy. He was sure that she would never treat him the way Tina had – she was far too kind. She was a proper grown-up with none of her sister's capriciousness. He had enjoyed his years of being single, but increasingly he was feeling as if he wanted something permanent – someone to have children and settle down with.

His leg ached suddenly, as if it was reminding him of something.

'I can see Vegas!' Lottie exclaimed, and he looked ahead at the dim sprawl of the city. Without its lights and at this distance, it looked nothing special – a few greyish blocks in the dusty sun, surrounded by desert. They drove slowly, past shopping malls and construction sites and unprepossessing houses. On the strip, the traffic was even denser. They had the chance to see at close quarters the swarms of people who passed along, looking both vague and purposeful, clutching jugs of cocktails, and the reality-defying casino hotels – the MGM Grand, the Bellagio, Caesar's Palace, Treasure Island and the Mandalay Bay Hotel, from which a man on the thirty-second floor had once fired more than 1,100 rounds into the concertgoers below. The monumental buildings were sliced and trimmed and sharp-edged, and yet curiously blank for all their architectural embellishments. In between the wedges and curves of steel and glass, huge screens flickered and fountains vomited sheets of thick water into lakes. From the hectic green shrubbery a thousand amplified songs poured out. Some things looked like relics from a less sophisticated time when people were impressed by replicas of the Eiffel Tower and the Statue of Liberty and the Pyramids. Others were so new that they hadn't even been unpackaged yet, and shone beneath protective layers of plastic. The whole place hummed with a strange reverberation. It was a little like the sound of the sea, but without the ocean's rise and fall, only a constant swelling clatter, like the sound of a million hammers hitting a hard surface.

Tina had rung ahead and booked a penthouse suite at the Wynn, fortunate to secure the room after a last-minute cancellation.

'It's only one night, so we can have a touch of luxury. Besides, I need a decent massage, my back is killing me.'

At the entrance to the hotel, they took their cases from the car. Lottie handed the keys to the valet, feeling grand but just a little guilty. The man was sweating in his grey waistcoat and he had something wrong with one of his legs, which gave him a strange swaying walk. Inside, the hotel had left no surface unembellished: the floors were mosaic and the carpets were woven with flowers, and there were vast vases of red roses and pink orchids and acid-green foliage. Glass chandeliers and huge mirrors hung everywhere. Their penthouse was creamy and cocooned in thick material; the double bed and the single had generously upholstered headboards, the carpets were springy underfoot like new turf and in the bathroom there were piles of bouncy towels. After the motel near Furnace Creek, this seemed like giddy excess. Lottie felt a bit uneasy about having to share a room with Spike, but the space was big enough to spread out. It wasn't as if they would be actually sleeping next to each other or anything. Spike put the TV on. Tina ordered champagne. They drank and watched the evening light turn the sides of the Trump International an evil, glinting gold – and then the whole city was suddenly illuminated, as if a massive master switch had been turned on.

'I think we should dress up,' Tina said.

After putting his whole head under the tap and shaking himself like a dog, Spike waited in the sitting room for Tina and Lottie to get changed. Tina chose a red, thin-strapped dress and heels, and Lottie – after a great deal of indecision – settled on a pale blue dress that belonged to Tina, and added a purple belt and gold scarf.

'It's good to see you are embracing colour at last,' Tina said. 'I hardly recognise Miss Matchy-Matchy that I set off on this trip with.'

'I guess I've changed a little,' Lottie said.

Tina gave her an appraising look. 'Yeah, in more ways than one.'

Lottie didn't answer, just stared at her reflection in the mirror. She looked as if she barely recognised herself.

'What are you going to say to Dean?' Tina asked.

'I don't know,' Lottie answered. 'There's nothing to say.'

'So, you're just going to go ahead with the wedding?' Tina asked incredulously. 'As if you feel exactly the same about him as you did before?'

'I do feel exactly the same about him,' Lottie said. 'He hasn't changed.'

'But *you* have. You've woken up.'

Lottie turned round and looked at her sister. Tina thought she looked sad.

'Maybe I've fallen asleep. I feel as if I'm in some sort of a dream.'

'You can deny it all you want, but you're not the same as you were nine days ago.'

'Has it really only been nine days?' Lottie tightened the back of her earrings – a pair of green tasselled beads that she had purchased in Furnace Creek, which brought out the golden sage colour of her eyes. 'Mia was sure, wasn't she? She never seemed to feel any doubt.'

'She said she couldn't live without Rick, if that's what you mean by sure.'

'That's what love is, isn't it? That feeling that you couldn't survive if you lost that person.'

'I wouldn't know.' Tina got up and stood by her sister at the mirror. She put a dark red lipstick on – an almost purplish hue that made her look suddenly harder and more polished. She pressed her lips together to spread the colour and looked at herself dispassionately. 'I've always thought it a weakness to be so co-dependent,' she said. 'I think it would diminish me to rely so much on someone else.'

'Mia didn't rely on Rick,' Lottie said.

'No – how could anyone have relied on someone as fucked up as him? It was more that she gave herself to him so completely that she lost sight of herself.'

Lottie flinched at her sister's words. They conjured up a sudden memory of Mia a year or so before her death. She and Lottie had spent a rare day together. At that stage Mia had been married for about six months. She had only informed her sisters about the wedding after it had taken place. Rick had sprung it on her without any preparation. Mia had thought they were just going for a short excursion, but it turned out they were headed to Gretna Green. He had said he wanted them to be alone, somewhere far away. She hadn't understood why their family and friends couldn't share their happiness, or why he hadn't given her the chance to wear something special, but she had, as always, fallen in with his plans. She had sent Lottie and Tina a picture of the pair of them standing framed by a concrete stone arch. She in jeans with a wilted flower behind one ear and Rick holding her around her waist with both his arms. *I'm so happy*, the caption had read. She had used six heart emojis.

It was very seldom that Mia could slip away, but Rick had been working somewhere out of town and so the sisters had been able to meet in central London. They had done some shopping and had lunch and then taken the tube to Waterloo.

'I want to see the river,' Mia had said, as if she was thirsty for the sight of water. She had been talkative, almost feverish all day, moving from subject to subject as if she couldn't settle on anything. Lottie hadn't seen her for a few months and she had become excruciatingly thin – her collarbones sharp in a round-necked T-shirt, her beautiful hair cut in a new, short style. She had been moving away already then. Why didn't I see her properly? Lottie asked herself now. Why didn't I say something? Do something? Instead she had accepted at face value Mia's story of a new exercise regime and healthy shakes.

'Rick thinks I look like Audrey Hepburn with my hair like this,' Mia had said, touching her head tentatively, as if it was sore.

'I've always seen you as more of a Marilyn Monroe type.'

'Rick doesn't much like curves,' Mia replied, and then she had done that thing she always did, diverting attention from herself by asking questions – 'How's work?' 'How are you getting on with Dean?' 'Has he asked you to marry him yet?' – and Lottie had started to talk about her own life. Mia had listened, seemingly calm, taking her hand at one point and holding it between hers. She had been kind and reassuring as she always was – the vital third leg of the sister stool, the one that kept the edifice upright. Lottie had been able to see in the newly narrow face the same light sweetness it had always had. When they parted – 'I need to get back home before Rick does' – Mia had hugged her tightly. She had always been demonstrative, but this embrace felt fierce and different.

'You do love Rick, don't you?' Lottie had asked, just before Mia turned away.

'I love him more than my life,' Mia had answered, smiling, and Lottie had allowed herself to be reassured. She had watched her walk away like a good child, her shorn head neat and her back straight.

Outside the hotel, the air was warm and foetid. It smelt of petrol fumes and perfume and something unidentifiable but carnally sweet. Things swam in and out of focus like a piece of film shot from the back of a moving vehicle. The neon glare of the signs, so many words – *Lady Luck, Cigars, Flamingo, Frontier, Circus, Cocktails, Nuggets, Cleaners, Weddings, Stardust, Las Vegas, Las Vegas, Las Vegas* – and the fluorescent cocktail glasses, the high-kicking women's legs, the giant decks of cards and the gleaming dollars – all created a strange effect. Lottie felt as if she was not in darkness or daylight but another sort of illumination altogether. It was similar to the eerie, electric shine that comes sometimes before a storm and feels a little like the end of the world.

Although they were walking at a normal pace, with Spike hopping gamely along on his crutches, the distance between them and the next glittering hotel never seemed to shorten. There were so many people going nowhere with them, all looking upwards and outwards as if trying to discover the exit. She saw an emaciated Elvis in a white suit that hung off him as if he was shedding his skin. A little further along the pavement, a girl in a bridal dress was being sick into the gutter. A fountain sprang suddenly into life with a Beethoven symphony and splashing foam that touched her arm as something hot. She had expected a glittering energy, and she felt it in the cars that cruised down the road, men on stag weekends howling like dogs, and in the frenetic, remorseless display of money and muscle and merriment – but there was also a curiously deadened, eviscerated quality to the air that reminded her of Death Valley's salt flats.

'My feet are killing me,' Tina moaned. She took off her shoes and walked barefoot, her feet vulnerable and pale amid the heedless rush.

They stopped at a bar to eat tacos and drink tequila.

'I don't think I can move any further,' Tina said once they were outside again, inspecting the pavement-burned soles of her feet. Spike was all hopped out too, so they hailed a cab and made their way back to the hotel among the hooting, yelling revellers and the occasional silent slide of cream limousines.

Back at the hotel, revived by the air conditioning and the gleaming hush of the lobby, Tina suggested they go to the casino. They made their way to a red-carpeted, swag-curtained hall, in which people were sitting alone at slot machines or gathered round blackjack tables in intent silence, while dealers flipped cards with clean, cuffed hands.

'What kind of a gambler are you?' Spike asked Lottie.

'I don't know,' she said. 'I've never done it.'

As if on cue, Tina rummaged around in her leopard-skin handbag and pulled out a handful of money.

'I've got a hundred dollars in five-dollar notes for you to gamble with,' she announced.

'No. Keep your money,' Lottie protested. 'I hate the idea of wasting it.'

'Your challenge this evening or this morning – I'm a little foggy on the actual time of day,' Tina said, 'is to spend all of it.'

'What if I lose it all? I don't even know what to do!'

Tina ignored her.

Lottie enjoyed spending money, although her own acquisitiveness sometimes made her guilty when she knew there were so many people living without even the basics. She thought of her last big purchase – the wedding dress, cellophaned and pearly and hanging in the back of the wardrobe, hidden away where Dean couldn't see it. She had spent more than she should have done on that. She hadn't even been aware of being particularly interested in such things – she had certainly never been a girl who had dreamed about her wedding and having the whole white-dress-and-speeches rigmarole – but when she had seen herself in the corseted satin sheath, with a diamanté hair clip curved over one ear and buckled shoes that tied with ribbons around the ankles, she had fallen in love with her reflection. She had never thought of herself as beautiful, but there was something so seductive about looking like you never usually did and never would again.

She quailed a little now at the thought of the dress and the as yet unseen flowers and the hundred and fifty wedding guests who must by now have chosen their own outfits and bought gifts. A wedding was not something you could just cancel. It was impossible. Besides, it was what she wanted. What they both wanted. She knew how Dean would look as she walked towards him in the chapel of his old Cambridge college. Tina had reluctantly agreed to give her away since they knew their father wouldn't make the journey from Spain and their mother had suddenly and bitterly decided she hated weddings. Lottie could imagine Tina on the day – drunk on champagne, wearing the despised grey silk dress Lottie had chosen. Dean would have that half-embarrassed, half-proud look. He would probably stroke his beard and shuffle his feet and make a joke under his breath to his brother, who was to be his best man. He often became flippant when he was nervous. She knew him so well. Her feelings for Spike, so chaotic she barely knew how to describe them, were only a foolish fantasy. She couldn't believe that she had told Tina that she was attracted to him.

Now she shrank from the sight of her sister's gleeful face. Being extravagant for your wedding was one thing, but actually gambling money away felt wrong.

'I'll teach you all you need to know,' Spike said. He took her arm, and at his touch she felt that traitorous agitation again. It wasn't desire. It was more like a kind of fear. 'It's easy as long as you can count to twenty-one.'

They took up the three empty spaces at one of the semi-circular tables and the dealer nodded at them. He was a florid-faced young man with a receding hairline and a collar and bow tie that seemed a little loose for his neck.

'You kind of scratch the table if you want a hit – which means another card – and you put your palm flat and wave it slightly from side to side if you want to stay,' Spike explained. 'The idea is that you have to beat the dealer by getting a hand nearer to twenty-one than he has.'

Tina bought a handful of five-dollar chips.

'We're just assisting,' Spike told the dealer, who nodded again. Lottie wondered if dealers were forbidden to talk.

'Place your bet,' Spike said. 'Put one of the chips in that little circle.'

Lottie's first two cards were a queen and a six of hearts. The dealer's upturned card was a king. She looked enquiringly at Spike and he shrugged.

'The decision is yours,' he said.

Tina caught the eye of a waiter and ordered whiskey sours for them all.

Lottie tentatively scratched at the surface of the table and was dealt another card, an eight of spades.

'Bust,' Spike announced, and the dealer's hand moved smoothly over the table and took Lottie's chip away.

Lottie lost the next five hands.

'See,' she said despairingly. 'I told you I would be no good at this.'

She tried to stand up, but Tina pulled her firmly back down into her seat.

'You haven't spent all the money yet.'

Lottie gave a heavy sigh and received her next two cards. This time she won. It seemed her luck had finally changed because she beat the dealer in the next ten consecutive hands. Spike advised her on the finer points of splitting and doubling up, while Tina exhorted her to bet higher. Lottie began to feel a weird calm. The chips piled up slowly. Raised to her feet by whiskey and excitement, Tina cheered her on. Lottie lost two hands.

'Perhaps I should stop while I'm ahead,' she said.

'Just one more go,' Tina said. 'It's better to leave the table a winner. Put all your chips on the next hand.'

'What, *all* of them?' Lottie asked. The silent dealer looked at her questioningly.

'Every single one,' Tina said, and so Lottie piled them up. She wasn't even sure how much she was betting. This was tantamount to throwing money away.

The cards came flicking out of the 'shoe'. Lottie could barely look. She blinked at her hand. She thought at first that she was seeing things. She appeared to have an ace and a king. Her flattened hand wobbled involuntarily. The dealer turned his card up, and Tina gave an excited scream.

'Now's the time to quit,' Spike said, grinning.

In a daze, Lottie said she was leaving the table and the dealer scooped up the chips and handed her some money, which Tina snatched from her hand.

'You've won over two thousand dollars!' she said, flicking through the notes and extracting a couple for the dealer.

'You keep it to cover some of the cost of this trip,' Lottie said, feeling dizzy but elated.

'That's very kind of you – but first we are EATING and SHOPPING.'

Spike picked Lottie up and spun her around.

They ate lobster and truffled risotto by a pool, and drank a bottle of the third most expensive champagne on the menu. Afterwards they staggered, giggling, round the shops and realised how little their money could buy in this shining, vertiginous world, where a handbag the size of a matchbox cost more than six months' wages. Lottie wanted to keep the money but Tina ignored her and bought them each a Dior silk scarf and leather bracelets studded with crystals and a flamingo-splattered tie for a protesting Spike.

'I love *and* hate Las Vegas,' Tina said.

'What exactly *is* the time?' Lottie asked. The hotel was as it had been when they first arrived, people milling in the lobby, the bars and restaurants still full. The same listless people were sitting in front of the same slot machines. It could have been midday or midnight, or any other hour in between.

'I don't think time actually passes at all in Vegas,' Lottie said. 'When we leave we'll discover that it's still the same date as it was when we arrived.'

Back in their suite, Tina crashed out in the bedroom, but Lottie was still on a high after her success and didn't think she would be able to fall asleep. She and Spike drank peppermint tea and watched the lights of the town through their floor-to-ceiling window. From this distance it looked as if the neon was somehow organic – a kind of luminescent moss growing over the buildings and roads.

'I can't decide whether it's really beautiful or really ugly,' Spike said. 'It's just the sort of landscape that I tend to try and avoid, but it's strangely attractive.'

'Imagine a huge meteorite flaming through the sky and landing slap bang on the strip,' Lottie said. She was curled up on one of the chocolate-brown velvet sofas with her shoes kicked off, the air conditioning cooling her swollen feet.

'They would probably just scoop it out and fill it with blackjack tables,' Spike said.

'It can't be long now until you have to peel off and join your team in Mexico,' Lottie said, deliberately keeping her gaze averted from his.

Spike thought she looked beautiful in her gauzy blue dress. Her lipstick was smudged on her smiling mouth. He felt a little drunk from the whiskey cocktails and champagne and the sound of Vegas – that swelling, disorientating clatter that he could still hear all the way from the top of the hotel. He thought she was waiting for him to say something. He could see it in the watchful curl of her body and the way she looked away from him when she spoke. He had a brief picture of Tina's face looking furiously at him from the front of the car when he had complimented Lottie that morning. He knew it was pathetic but he couldn't help thinking how angry she would be if he and Lottie got together. It riled him that Tina assumed he would do exactly what she told him to. She thought she could control everything.

'I'll have to go in a couple of days,' he said. 'It's going to be hard leaving you.'

'I know Tina can be an old bag, but I think she's secretly glad you came along.'

He smiled at her deliberate misinterpretation of his words.

'I meant you in particular,' he said. 'Not you as in the both of you.'

She put a hand up as if to ward him off and stood up. Her eyes were wide. She looked like a creature that had been caught in the headlights of a car.

'Don't,' she said. 'Please don't do this.'

'I gather from your sister that you are having second thoughts about the wedding,' Spike said. He stood up too and came closer to her. He could feel the agitation in her body. 'If I've got the wrong idea, just tell me.'

'I don't know what I want,' Lottie said. 'I don't know what's happening to me. It's like I have lost myself somehow.'

She looked so upset and confused, so unlike her usual calm, certain self, that he felt suddenly contrite. He should have learnt by now not to take any notice of what Tina said. She had always twisted the truth.

'It's just pre-wedding jitters,' he said, stepping back. 'Forget I ever said anything. You're going to go home and marry Dean. I should have known you're nothing like your sister. Forgive me.'

'What did she say to you?' Lottie asked. Her arms were stiff by her sides and she looked as if she might be about to cry. He inwardly cursed the booze and Vegas and Tina's machinations.

'She just intimated that you were having doubts, that's all. And I got carried away. You're so lovely and Vegas is so freaky and I'm such an idiot.'

He thought she was going to say something else. She stood for a moment as if she was poised to flee, but didn't know which direction would bring safety.

'Go to sleep,' he said. 'Don't give it another thought,' and she turned away and went into the bedroom.

Chapter 20

'LOOK AT THE VIEW OUT of the window! And the ridiculous carpet and how deep the bath is.'

Lottie was wafting her iPad around the hotel bedroom, showing Dean the magnificence of their suite. Tina was still asleep and Spike had gone out somewhere.

'You're making me feel dizzy!' Dean said. 'Stop walking around and sit down and talk to me.'

Actually speaking to Dean was something that Lottie had been trying to avoid. It was far easier to enthuse about her surroundings than to engage in conversation, but she settled on the sofa and switched the view round so that she could see him. He was standing in the playground of the school where he worked. She could see the climbing wall in the background, and every now and again a hunched young person in a black blazer would lurch past. She noted that he had had his hair cut and her heart was smitten at the sight of the way the barber had tufted his hair into a mini-quiff. He was wearing his blue checked shirt – the one that would never stay tucked in, but always hung an inch or so below his V-necked jumper.

'How was your walking weekend?' she asked.

'It was exactly the same as it always is. No dog this year and Simon got a stomach upset, but business as usual,' Dean said, smiling.

Every year Dean went to a cottage in Scotland with the same group of four male friends. They had been going away for the last fifteen years and had developed a raft of traditions. During the day they walked up hills and in the evening they sat in the local pub drinking an exact five rounds. Lottie often teased him about the ritualistic aspect of their trips – the way they always linked hands around standing stones and intoned the same strange song, which was designed to invoke wandering Celtic spirits. After a long walk they would roll up their trousers and sit on the edge of the bath with their feet dipped in a lavender-infused water. As each year came and went there would be new additions and new stories which were embroidered upon – the day the dog ate a whole packet of butter; the Belgian man they had met at the top of a hill who had caught them mid-packed lunch and remarked that he could not understand the British obsession with 'ze cheese and ze onion'; the year they all got wrecked and hung naked from the beams in the living room. She had always thought of this with a kind of indulgent tenderness – amused by the way these men tied themselves to each other with habit and history, but now she felt a little impatient.

'Don't you ever want to go somewhere else?' she asked.

'There would be a riot if I even suggested it,' he replied. His smile faltered. 'Are you OK? You look a little pale.'

'I'm fine. Just had a late night, that's all. I won a load of money playing blackjack.'

'It sounds as if you are having an exciting time,' Dean said, a little wistfully. 'You'll be bored when you come home.'

'I won't have time to be bored. We will have exactly five days before the wedding.' As she said the words, Lottie felt a kind of roiling motion in her stomach, as if she had eaten something that didn't agree with her.

'I've arranged all the flowers, you don't have to worry about that at least,' he said. 'I went for bright in the end. Irises and some orange ones with a name I can't remember, something like gerbil, but that can't be right. Long stalks. Like flowers designed by children.'

'Gerbera,' Lottie said faintly, thinking in a distracted kind of way about how they would clash with the pale pink touches she had chosen so carefully. What did it really matter anyway? It was just a day, and the flowers, whatever their hue, would shrivel and lose their lustre in the end.

Just then the screen was obscured by a shock of red hair and a grinning face. 'Who you talking to, sir? You'll be late for class, sir. Sir, I thought you said mobile phones made people "witless".'

'I'd better go,' Dean said. 'I love you.' His words elicited a mocking, elongated exclamation from the now invisible student and then the screen went blank.

A moment later, the door banged shut and Spike appeared with orange juice and bagels crammed with smoked salmon and cream cheese and a new walking stick encrusted with plastic crystals. With another lurch of her stomach Lottie thought of how terrible it would have been if Spike had come back in the middle of her conversation. How would she have explained it to Dean? How could she explain any of it to herself?

'I thought I'd save on room service by going out and getting breakfast myself,' he said. 'Besides, I wanted to get some air, although Vegas doesn't really do air.'

He was determinedly breezy and avoided looking at Lottie. Nothing had happened, after all. Spike was right – it had just been pre-wedding nerves. It was common enough. One of her friends had gone to the airport on the morning of her wedding and taken the next available flight regardless of the destination. She'd ended up in Iceland. The friend was now happily married to the man she had abandoned at the altar.

Tina emerged from the bedroom, yawning and rubbing her eyes. 'I thought we'd do downtown Vegas for a bit before we leave the city,' she announced, pouring herself a large glass of juice. 'See the street art and visit the world's most famous sex shop.'

'I'd like to see a bit more of Vegas, but I'm not sure about the sex shop,' Lottie said predictably.

'It is a continuing source of wonder to me, Lottie, that you ever actually relaxed enough to have sex.'

Tina tried to catch Spike's eye and share a conspiratorial look, but he was fiddling around with bagels and juice.

'I always think that "adult shops",' here Lottie used her hands to demonstrate the apostrophes in an irritatingly pedantic way, 'are for people who like other people to think they have no inhibitions, when in fact they are so clueless they imagine that strawberry-flavoured panties are actually something a woman would want to wear.'

'Don't say panties,' Tina said, shuddering. 'It is almost as terrible as *gusset* and *moist* – words that make the inside of your mouth shrivel up.'

'Whatever,' Lottie said, shrugging. She seemed out of sorts this morning and there was definitely some sort of atmosphere in the room. Spike had hardly looked at either of them.

'If you decide you *are* going to marry Dreary Dean,' here Tina gave a meaningful cough, 'you'll need something more alluring for the honeymoon than the M&S nighties you are probably thinking of taking. I'd lay money that Dean has a fondness for a nurse. He looks the type that's secretly yearning for a bed bath.'

'We're not even going on a honeymoon,' Lottie said, and Tina rolled her eyes.

'Seriously? You have the perfect excuse for an extended break and decide not to take it! Well, a nurse's outfit will come in handy even if the pair of you are so lacking in imagination you are stay-mooning.'

Despite Spike's charm offensive and the fact that Lottie had admitted being attracted to him, it seemed to Tina that Lottie was still planning on going ahead with the wedding. She couldn't detect any particular closeness between her and Spike – if anything, Lottie was acting a little frostily towards him. Perhaps she had decided she didn't fancy him after all. It was as if Lottie felt that since she had set the whole wedding thing in motion there was nothing she could now do to stop it. How could she be crying one minute at the thought that her wobble over Spike meant she was not sure about Dean, and the next talking calmly about her honeymoon? Cancelling a wedding was a huge, embarrassing thing to do, but it wasn't nearly as catastrophic as tying yourself to someone you weren't sure about. There must be a way of making her see what a terrible mistake she was making. Tina couldn't give up yet. She still had a week to make her sister see the error of her ways.

In Amore, Tina tried on a variety of costumes. Spike had taken himself off to the sports bar next door. 'I don't really think this is an activity I should share,' he had said, hopping to the exit on his blinged-up stick with the look of a man who had found himself in the right place at the wrong time.

Tina tried on a ridiculous cheerleader outfit complete with pom-poms and crotchless knickers, followed by a PVC Catwoman suit. Lottie mostly just stood and laughed, but was finally forced into a zip-up nurse's outfit with matching stockings as part of the challenge.

'Dean will be in raptures,' Tina announced.

'Don't you think it's a bit retrograde to dress up like this for the titillation of men?' Lottie asked, protesting as Tina handed her a leather thong.

'Not if you want to do it,' Tina said. 'Some men really like dressing up, too. I once had a boyfriend who enjoyed wearing a rubber playsuit.'

'I'd really rather not hear about it,' Lottie said. 'Dean says he likes me to be natural. I think he'd be embarrassed if I showed up looking like a cartoon.'

'Don't you believe it,' Tina said. 'Men are simple creatures. They are easily impressed by even the suggestion of lace. You could parade around in a couple of doilies and it would do the job. It makes them think that you're making an effort, and that's always a turn-on.'

'Don't you sometimes think you let playing games with men get in the way of actually allowing yourself to love them?' Lottie asked, her serious tone somewhat diminished by her red-crossed headband worn by no real nurse anywhere.

'There are no games between consenting adults that are anything but healthy,' a voice suddenly announced. Tina and Lottie parted their cubicle curtains to find themselves confronted by an ancient-looking woman in a feather boa and fake green eyelashes.

'I'm wondering if you ladies need any help,' she continued. 'I always find our British customers take a little longer to embrace the merchandise.'

'No thank you, I think we've pretty much settled on what we want,' Tina said, a little offended by the slur.

'A British clergyman invented the sock. An American company developed the nylon stocking,' the woman continued. 'It tells us all we need to know.'

'I'm sure people were wearing some version of stockings in medieval England,' Lottie said.

'They were just kind of bandages,' the woman said dismissively, 'worn for warmth, not visual appeal.'

'I've never met a stocking expert before,' Tina said waspishly.

'Is my wife boring you with her encyclopedic knowledge of fetish fashion through the ages?' A man appeared, looking just as extravagantly crumpled as his partner in a white suit and platform boots.

'We seem to have wandered into *The Rocky Horror Show*,' said Tina in an undertone.

'Are you guys here on vacation?' he enquired, apparently unperturbed by Tina's rudeness.

'Yes, it's my hen road trip,' Lottie explained, rather taken by the shop's eccentric proprietors. 'I'm getting married at the end of the month.'

'Well, good luck to you. We've been married for fifty-two years,' he replied, putting his arm around his prickly wife.

'Wow,' Lottie said. 'What's the secret of your success?'

'Having an endless supply of vibrators?' Tina asked, still disgruntled.

'Hell no, we grew out of all that a few hundred years ago,' the woman replied. 'Sex is all very well, but there's nothing to touch being able to laugh with each other.'

'That and knowing when to tune out,' the man said, and she gave him a friendly shove that almost made him topple off his boots.

'My recipe for a long and happy marriage is actually very simple,' she said, the queenly tilt of her head suddenly revealing the beautiful shape of her face. 'If you want it to last, you have to choose it over and over again.'

'If you were a fast food, what would you be?' Lottie asked.

Tina had decided to delay their arrival at the Grand Canyon by taking a detour via Route 66. 'It's iconic,' she had announced, brushing aside Lottie's objections about how much time it would add to the trip.

'I'd be a bacon roll from a truck stop,' Tina said now.

'I'd be a carton of clam chowder,' said Spike.

'I'd be a banana,' Lottie said, ignoring the derision from her travel mates. 'It comes sealed up in its own packaging. Completely hygienic.'

A few miles further down the road, both Spike and Lottie fell asleep. Tina turned down Sheryl Crow's 'Leaving Las Vegas' and looked sideways at her sister. She had her head jammed against the window, a mouthful of hair obscuring her face. Tina took her eyes off the road for a second and gently extracted the clump of curls. Lottie barely stirred. It wasn't like her to sleep in the car. She must be really tired. Lottie believed Tina to be a reckless driver and had until now remained beadily vigilant. She had the annoying habit of making sudden startled exclamations. 'What? What?' Tina would ask, looking to see the source of the alarm – and Lottie would point at a junction in the distance or a car parked by the side of the road. She had once yelled out at the sight of a dog lolloping along the edge of a field. 'It might suddenly decide to dart out into the road,' she had explained to an incredulous Tina. 'It could well be a deaf dog.'

Tina looked in the mirror at Spike. He had wrapped a blanket around the alabaster vase and was using it as a head-rest. He was supposed to be parting company with them in two days, although his leg was still hurting and he was doubtful about how much use he was going to be to the team in Mexico.

'You won't be able to walk far, but you can wait at the base and sift through the rubble,' she had said to him earlier, keen to let him know she wanted him gone, although there was a part of her, a part she fought hard against, that made her feel desolate at the thought.

'And there I was thinking you were actually enjoying my company,' he had replied, yawning and stretching to reveal a brown, toned stomach. She was sure the display of skin had been deliberate, like a peacock fanning out its tail, or one of those Amazonian frogs puffing up its neck into a bulging goitre in an effort to attract a mate. He was suffering under the misapprehension that he was utterly irresistible.

'What happened to the baby?' he suddenly asked from the back seat, startling her. She hadn't realised that he had woken up. 'Did you decide to get rid of it?'

'How like you to use that disgusting expression,' she said furiously.

'Well, it's always been easy come, easy go with you, hasn't it?'

Spike had no idea why he was talking to her as he was. He had never before thought about abortion in those terms. He understood that as a man the relief or the pain or something infinitely more complicated would only ever be felt by proxy. He would never have to say, 'This is what I want,' and set in motion something that could never be changed. He wouldn't feel a presence and then an absence in his body and know that he had wrought it.

He just wanted a real reaction from her, something more than the mocking flippancy that she had shown towards him so far on their trip. He had thought that this desire to unsettle her, to have some sort of impact on her, had worn off long ago. After she had gone back to England, he had struggled with the loss of her for more than a year. He had been so close to phoning her on numerous occasions, but the memory of her in bed with that man had always stopped him at the last minute. He had also ignored the calls she had made to him. He couldn't risk being hurt like that again.

He had eventually tried to move on. It was what people did. It was only in poems that lovers pined and died from broken hearts. There had been other women since Tina, some more important than others, although none had really stuck to him the way she had. Time had just stacked up until she had become part of his past and there was no way back, like an old bridge tumbling into a widening river.

'I know you don't really care what happened, but I didn't have an abortion. I lost my baby,' Tina said.

Spike was shocked both by this new piece of information and by the sadness beneath her combative tone.

'It broke me, although no one even knew it had happened,' Tina said. 'There was a life in me for a while and then it went away. I was left feeling as if I'd been abandoned.'

There were tears in her voice. It wasn't like her to show so much of herself, especially not to him. If she had revealed the true extent of her feelings at the time, would he have behaved differently? He tried to remember how she had looked the day she had come and told him she was pregnant.

What he recalled most clearly was her defiance. What had she said exactly? She had said she wanted to keep the baby, but it had seemed to him at the time that what she had really wanted was to hurt him. He thought she had been saying she wanted the baby, but not him. Perhaps he had misunderstood. In his work he knew that it was only by patiently accumulating knowledge based on observation and experience and remaining open to infinite possibilities that any real progress could be made, and yet it seemed as if he had in this particular instance jumped straight to judgement. His sadness caught him by surprise. The sense that he had lost something that had been partly his seemed more real to him now than it had at the time. He had just been hurt and angry then. He wondered if things might have turned out differently if he had picked up the phone and talked to her.

'It just wasn't meant to be,' Tina said quietly.

In the front of the car, she stared fixedly at the road. The sense of what might have been was always there. She saw the peanut shape of her child's head, the whorl of pale hair and her wide-eyed, unblemished gaze as vividly as if she had actually been able to hold her.

Despite what she'd said to Spike, she couldn't help feeling that what she had lost was exactly what she was supposed to have had, and the life she was living now was one that was never intended for her. She wondered if part of getting older was coming to terms with the knowledge that where you found yourself was not at all where you had planned to be. Perhaps everyone was completely lost, and it was just that some people were able to hide it better.

'Never let them know you are a tourist,' had been her mother's travel advice when Tina had started to go abroad for work. 'It lays you open to being ripped off.'

Lynne had been wrong about that as she had been about so many things. Travelling without a map, pretending you knew where you were going, only sent you down a dead end.

'Isn't this the town where Lottie's number one fan lives?' Tina asked. Hearing her name, Lottie sat up, suddenly awake. They had arrived at Chloride – if the ghostly place could be considered a destination. It was an old mining town that had, in its glory days, boasted seventy-five silver pits. Now parts of it lay abandoned. There was an empty jailhouse and a crumbling train depot and a vintage garage, but despite first appearances it was clear people still lived there. Lopsided signs made up of a patchwork of wood advertised beer and barbeques. Many of the houses were worn and unlovely, although it was evident that the inhabitants shared an artistic impulse – glittering bottles and twists of metal swung from the boughs of trees and fences were festooned with garlands of rusting colanders and old farm implements. In one front yard a giraffe made of old drums and lumps of spiked concrete stared at them with bottle-top eyes. In another, parts of a Hoover had been fashioned into an emu and a dustbin lid was painted with a grinning face. Buildings, roads, trucks and junk artworks were all covered in a kind of dusty veil, as if the whole place needed picking up and giving a good shake. Beyond the first clump of houses, in the centre of the town, the sense that things were not quite as they seemed was reinforced by a mocked-up western scene with saloon doors and wonky porches.

'Mia would have loved this place,' Tina said.

They parked the car and wandered through on foot and, as luck would have it, were just in time to witness the midday shoot-out. Two paunchy men in battered hats faced each other along the road and then solemnly shot several, presumably blank, rounds at each other. One of them staggered dramatically, clutching his chest, and then fell to the ground amid a smattering of applause. They ate grilled turkey on sourdough sandwiches in Yesterdays – a beamed barn with a dingy mural on the wall and a few white-haired men propping up the bar – and then drove to the visitor centre on the edge of the town where they got instructions on how to get to the boulder art painted in 1966 by Roy Purcell. They drove across a cattle grid and along a dirt track road, and stopped when the car started bouncing around too alarmingly. Spike stayed in the car because his leg was playing up, but Tina and Lottie got out to explore.

They walked a mile or so further along until they came upon some surprisingly bright stones, painted in the style of Native American art with goddesses and snakes wrapped around trees and a blue dog with a heart in his stomach. On one of the boulders, the words 'The Journey, images from the inward search for self' had been painted in a curly script.

'They're so bold-looking in this hazy light,' Tina said. She scrambled a little closer to take some photographs, while Lottie sat on a flat rock by the side of the track waiting for her.

'Are you sad our parents aren't coming to the wedding?' Tina asked, when she had slithered back down. 'That's assuming, of course, that the great event is actually going to be taking place,' she added, unable to resist another opportunity to unsettle Lottie. She didn't know why the thought of Joe and Lynne had jumped into her mind just then. Perhaps the words on the rocks had reminded her of their parents' endless journeys away from one failure or another – a job lost, a neighbour with whom they had started a war, a vague dissatisfaction with the landscape or the people. Perhaps each move had held out the prospect of a beginning for them, but when they had arrived at a new flat or a borrowed house, in the end it had just become another place in which to tear at each other.

Once, when she was about sixteen, Tina asked her mother why she and Joe stayed together.

'Because I love him!' her mother had said to her, astonished.

'It doesn't seem like love to me,' she had said.

231

'You know nothing at all of life,' Lynne had answered. 'One day you will understand.' Tina was now much older than her mother had been then, and she still didn't understand.

'I'm sad I haven't got parents I really want to be there,' Lottie answered.

'It's just as well they're not coming. You want your wedding to be a peaceable affair.'

'Have you ever been in love?' Lottie asked her sister, as if she knew what she had been thinking about.

'I don't know,' Tina said.

'How can you not know? It's easy. You either love someone or you don't.'

'It's never been as straightforward for me. My feelings for people are always hampered by a sense that I might be fooling myself, or that they might be fooling me.'

'I love Dean,' Lottie said.

'How do you know?'

'Because he feels like part of me.'

'And yet, here you are, miles away from him, thinking about the parts of quite another person,' Tina said, grinning wickedly.

'You always have to lower the tone.'

'Are you sure you're not wondering what it would be like to sleep with someone else? Isn't that why you've been acting so distracted?'

'No, I don't think it's about sex. It's more that I wonder about alternative versions of my life. I could have been a hundred different things and been with a hundred different people, and yet it has all come down to this particular set of choices. Who's to say I have chosen the best possible outcome?'

'That's exactly what I'm talking about,' Tina said. 'How's it possible to embark on anything with all your heart when your heart could be pulled all sorts of different ways?'

'When you're young – I mean, I know I'm not old now, but when you're really young – you imagine that absolutely anything might happen. You think that immense wealth, or being able to dance on the points of your feet or living in a houseboat are all within your grasp. But then you grow up and discover you're flat-footed and the thought of sharing a space with a chemical loo makes you uneasy and that you will always earn the sort of wage that makes you dread the cashpoint a week before payday.'

'I've always thought of you as someone who has made the choices she wanted to make,' said Tina. 'You always seem so certain.'

'Well, perhaps we're more similar than we thought,' Lottie said, linking her arm through her sister's. They started to walk back.

'Route Sixty-six next,' Tina announced once they were back at the car, 'and it hasn't gone unnoticed by me that it's been a good few hours since the last challenge.'

'One of these days, when you least expect it, I'm going to set *you* a challenge.'

'Bring it on,' Tina said.

'Bring what on?' Spike asked. He was lying on the back seat of the car.

'Lottie thinks it's my turn to do a challenge.'

'Only if I can set it!' he said, with a glint in his eye.

Chapter 21

JUST BEFORE THEY JOINED ROUTE 66, a coyote crossed the road in front of them and Lottie slowed down. It was so near that as they passed they could see its skin rippling and its wet muzzle. Chuck Berry was singing about not having any particular place to go and they yelled along with him.

They passed through several small towns hanging onto the glories of the past, guileless somehow in their blatant sell of something that perhaps had never quite existed. By the edges of the road broken glass glittered like mica and tumbleweed – 'It actually is a real thing then!' Lottie said – gathered in springy clumps against the bottoms of the cattle fences. Lottie was driving fast now. She felt a great rush of exhilaration, a kind of loosening and letting go. The road ran parallel to the railway track and a train was travelling alongside them at exactly the same speed, so that it seemed neither they nor the train were actually moving at all.

'Go faster!' Tina said, and so Lottie accelerated and tried to overtake it. Just before the train curved away, Tina got to her feet and waved, and was rewarded by a long pull on the horn. The sound was part of Fleetwood Mac and Lou Reed and the Eagles playing in the car, the tatty beauty of the road, the limpid light, the red and white diners with peeling leatherette benches. It was part of the shops full of plastic tat, men with massive belt buckles standing talking in twos and threes, giant fibreglass statues and abandoned, peeling Chevrolets, the flickering signs advertising Coke and cocktails and karaoke.

Just outside Seligman they stopped at a restaurant because Tina insisted on eating again.

'All I've had today is one tiny sandwich. I need red wine and red meat.'

'There's no such thing as a tiny sandwich in America,' Lottie said.

After they had eaten their fill – or at least when Tina had, which was an altogether longer process – they drove a little further, stopping at the next motel they saw.

They sat outside on the terrace as the moon came up – a perfect, pale disc. A warm breeze blew scraps of paper around their ankles. After a while, Tina said she was exhausted and had the meat sweats, and she went to bed.

Lottie didn't think she would be able to sleep. The air was full of static and her skin felt prickly.

'I'll sit out here with you for a while,' Spike said. He poured wine for her. She hadn't drunk anything earlier because she had been driving.

'Are you leading the life you thought you'd have?' Lottie asked, thinking of her conversation with Tina earlier.

'I guess so,' he said. 'I'm doing the job I always wanted to do. I've got friends and family who care about me. Except when I get bitten by snakes, I'm healthy enough. I get to travel and listen to music and watch movies and walk on the beach.'

'You've not got a girlfriend, though. Someone as nice as you should have someone to love.'

Lottie was a lightweight when it came to alcohol and the glass of wine she had drunk so hastily had gone straight to her head. A film of cloud passed across the moon. She poured another glass. She felt reckless. She thought of the long plaintive pull of the train horn and the way she had fought the car and the road, the sensation that she had been fixed there.

'I've done my share of loving,' Spike said in a self-mocking, old-movie-star voice.

'Don't you think it's strange that none of us is married?' she asked. 'Most people I know have settled down.'

'Well, you're about to be,' he said.

She didn't know what made her kiss him then. Perhaps because she thought he looked a little sad. Perhaps it was simply because she had let herself consider some of the other lives she might be leading. She leant over and put her mouth against his. If she had explained it afterwards, she would have said she had kissed him because she wanted to acknowledge the way he made her feel. Knowing him had given her the sense that things were not perhaps quite as decided as she thought they were. Just like the open spaces of America itself – that uncanny stretch that invoked astonishment and gratitude – she felt as if the borders of her life had been widened. It almost wasn't anything to do with him at all; more the way that everything seemed to have opened out. He didn't respond at all for a moment. He simply looked at her as if he was forming some sort of conclusion.

If he had explained it afterwards, he would have said he had felt unsettled, and that thinking about what had happened with Tina had made him wonder if he knew anything at all. He would have said he was a little drunk and the moon was bright and Lottie looked lovely with her valiant eyes and soft mouth and the silky blue top that slid off one shoulder. He kissed her back. He was careful. He saw her eyes widen. It crossed his mind that perhaps this wasn't what he wanted to do and that perhaps it wasn't what she wanted to do either. The road next to the motel was suddenly filled with a great roar and twenty or so bikers, lights and helmets flashing, tassels blowing like the pelt of some great noisy beast, passed by in formation.

She laughed at the sound – it was so extravagantly loud – and then they were standing together, he had his hands in her hair, his mouth was on her throat and she felt again that sense of letting go – of the curtains around the screen parting to allow the greatest possible field of vision. He tasted of wine and salt and the dusty road. She could feel him hardening against her. This was the moment to move away, to say that after all this wasn't what she wanted. They would laugh. They would blame it on any number of things. They would say to each other that it had been nothing more than a passing madness. She made herself conjure up Dean's face. She stepped back. She looked at Spike carefully. She knew that afterwards she wanted to be able to feel it had been what she wanted. This was to be her decision, not anyone else's. Spike's mouth was tender as if he knew what she was thinking, and so she put her hand on the back of his neck and pulled her to him. He was still unsteady on one leg and she felt him stagger slightly.

'Come on,' he said, and they crossed the terrace. He had left his window open and the room was full of the night air and the smell of blown paper and diesel and chlorine.

'You are so beautiful,' he said when she took off her clothes and stood showing herself to him. She felt as if she was another person altogether – someone bolder, less afraid.

'I thought you looked like a cat burglar when I saw you for the first time,' she said. She lay next to him on the bed, touching his warm chest, the narrow hollow at the top of his thigh, his yielding thickness.

'Be careful of my leg,' he said as she climbed on top of him.

And then, neither of them spoke. There was only the sound of cars passing, the headlights searching the ceiling, the road-infused air and the push and rock of their bodies.

Chapter 22

LOTTIE WOKE SUDDENLY. Spike was still beside her. It felt odd that he should be lying so close. He was an almost-stranger, despite what they had shared the night before. Sleep had brought a distance with it. It wasn't that she regretted what had happened – there had only been kindness between them – it was just that she felt suddenly exposed. She had been crying in her sleep; her face was wet. She thought perhaps she had been dreaming about Mia. Four in the morning was always a tricky hour. Not quite night, not quite day. The time when the body is at its coldest, when fights and suicides happen, when wanting wakes up or shuts down.

She had been told that Mia had died at around four in the morning, although Lottie hadn't found her until the next day. She always felt sick when she remembered what she had said to her only weeks before her death.

'Either you leave him, or I will never see you again. You choose.'

'I can't leave him,' Mia had said, her nails biting into her arm. She had been wearing a scarf but it hadn't hidden the livid red mark on her neck, nor the careful way she had been walking.

'I mean what I say, Mia,' she'd said. 'It's him or me.'

She had thought her ultimatum might bring her sister to her senses. She knew now that it had been a careless, stupid thing to say. The sort of thing people say when they think they carry more weight than they do. How had she ever imagined that the approach would have been effective? Not only had it not worked, but it had also meant that she had abandoned her sister just when she had needed Lottie the most. What she should have done was refuse to leave. She should have camped outside the house if that was what it was going to take. She recalled the numerous phone calls she had made to the police. She often did this in an effort to feel better about what she had and hadn't done.

'I think my sister's in danger,' she had said for the fifth or seventh time.

She had always been given pretty much the same reply: 'I understand your concern, but we've been to see Mia and we can't do anything if she won't tell us what's happening.'

'She's too scared to tell you,' Lottie would say, and it was true. Mia had been terrified about speaking to anyone official about her situation – she hadn't even talked about it much to Lottie herself – but this fear was insignificant compared to the terror of leaving him. This was the part of it that Lottie simply couldn't get her head around. In her world, if you didn't like something, if someone was hurting you, you opened the door and left. It was without question what she would do.

'Why the hell don't you just go?'

She had thought that if she said it often enough, Mia would wake up one day and finally decide to pack her bags. Lottie wondered now how hard she had actually tried to understand.

'He says he's going to change,' Mia would say, her lovely face hopeful, covering up the bruises and moving briskly on as if it was simply a matter of a little bit of spilled tea on a favourite dress. She had looked, on the rare occasions when Lottie had been invited to her house, exactly as she had when she had made it her business all those years ago to protect Lottie and Tina from their parents. Her face had had a kind of blank vigilance that Lottie remembered from her childhood, as if she was pretending that she wasn't waiting for the exact moment to move away from the source of harm. Mia had had an early training in how to play along and hide the fact that under her skin that used to glow like a sunned peach (it hurt Lottie to think of her skin), she would be alert to a tone of voice, to the number of bottles of wine on the table, to the speed of the footsteps up the stairs. Lottie had never allowed herself to consciously recall what she had seen at Mia's house, but now she could feel her mind nudging her forward.

She was standing outside looking at the symmetrical pots of pansies by the front door, and the shutters at the window that were never allowed to gather dust. She had rung on the bell, heard the echo of 'Waltzing Matilda' in the varnished hallway where the umbrellas and Rick's walking sticks stood in a copper stand at the bottom of the stairs. I can't think about this now, Lottie told herself. I have to stop thinking about this now. The world that had felt wonderfully expansive only hours ago now seemed confusing. I'm in a motel room with a picture of James Dean on the wall and a dodgy stain on the ceiling, my sister Mia is in the boot of the car and I have just slept with someone I hardly know when I am supposed to be getting married to someone else in a few days' time.

She thought of Dean's meticulous economies and the sacrifices they had made for the day that was supposed to be the beginning of the rest of their lives. 'I'll never feel this way about anyone else,' he had whispered at the top of the stairs, the day after he had asked her to marry him. He had looked both sure and hopeful. They had gone laughing down to a breakfast of flabby poached eggs (the devil's food, she had said into his ear, and he'd smiled and touched her knee under the table) to be scrutinised by his mother. He wasn't expecting this. It would come out of the sky at him like a meteorite. Perhaps she shouldn't tell him anything at all. Perhaps when she returned home this would all be like a dream and she would be able to resume her life exactly where she had left off. It would be like a film that gets inside you for a while but which always faded, however vivid the experience had been. You surely couldn't change the outcome of ten years of love in little over a week.

And yet she knew how she was made. The secret would eat away at her. She would not be able to keep it from him and when she told him he would certainly withdraw from her. For all his kindness there was about him, as there often is, even in the best of men and women, a kind of implacable sense, if not ownership, then certainly some more acceptable version of it.

'I wouldn't feel the same about you if you slept with someone else,' he'd once said. 'I couldn't bear not to be able to trust you. I know you never would,' he had said, with a touch of complacency which she had converted at the time into a feeling of success that she had demonstrated her love so effectively.

She had to get out. Her head ached. She needed to escape from this room and get her thoughts in order. Perhaps if she walked a little, she would fall upon some sort of resolution. She got out of bed as quietly as possible and got dressed in the shower room.

Outside, the air still had a little residual warmth from the paving stones and tarmac. She set off walking down the road. Despite the hour, occasional cars passed by, one full of shouting men who yelled something unintelligible at her through the window. She felt as if she was in a kind of a trance. The light was gathering stealthily, and she could hear the strange sizzling and booming sound of nighthawks in the sky above her. The thong on one of her flip-flops popped out and she bent to push it back in. She passed a diner, still open for business, where a man was sitting with his arms crossed on the table, looking as if he was waiting for someone. In the lighted window of a white-boarded house, a woman was brushing her hair with long, languorous strokes. As she walked, the day gathered pace as the early risers felt for the shape of hanging clothes in the half-dark and splashed water quietly on their faces so that they wouldn't disturb the people still sleeping. A man with a fridge on a trolley pushed his load silently up the slope of a driveway. A scrawny dog circled an overflowing bin. Beneath the odour of waste there was the smell of doughnuts and night-scented stock and rubber. There was the sudden sound of an alarm, intermittent and urgent.

She would have to tell Dean she couldn't marry him. She had slept with someone else, and that surely meant that she didn't feel as strongly about him as she should. Staying married was difficult enough without starting off on such shaky ground. He deserved someone loyal and true and she had proved herself to be anything but. She tried not to think of how he would look when she said the words – the bewilderment in his pale blue eyes as it sank in that she was not what he had imagined her to be. She would have to speak to him face to face. He deserved at least that. She would wait until she got home and tell him quickly, as soon as she was through the door, so that there would be no time for his pleasure in seeing her to take hold. No time for him to think that she was the same as she had been before. She knew him well enough to know that he wouldn't say very much – he had always taken his time to process information, looking carefully in words for their proper meaning, pondering a text closely and using the page margins to add pencilled notes that would help him to understand and explain things as clearly as possible. His grief would come a little time afterwards. She thought of the bent back and silent tears with which he had greeted the news of his father's death. He had made almost no sound when he had taken the phone call, and afterwards had wandered from room to room as if he was looking for something.

'He waited until my mother had gone out,' he said, and she had seen how difficult it had been for him to let himself down into grief. He had fought his tears as if there had been something shameful about them.

'He wouldn't want me to be miserable,' he had said, wiping his face, as though he was obeying his father's last command.

Lottie had always found Dean's father's determined joviality a little tiring. There were many times in life when just 'cracking on' was the foolish option. In her opinion it would have been better if Dean's father could have occasionally shown the cracks instead. Lottie's feeling of sadness deepened. She wondered what she was doing wandering along a road alone in the middle of the night. She thought perhaps she had gone a little mad. She wasn't even sure how far she had walked.

She heard a vehicle slow down behind her, and then a voice called out.

'Hey you! Where the heck are you heading for at this time in the morning?'

She turned to see Stacey's helmeted hair poking out of her truck window. How come the woman seemed to keep popping up? Lottie was hardly in the right frame of mind for exchanging pleasantries about Princess Diana with someone who seemed to have a tenuous grasp on reality. She shouted out a vague greeting and carried on walking. Perhaps if she ignored her, Stacey would drive on.

'Can I take you someplace?' Stacey asked. There was the sound of the truck pulling off the road and the door opening and being slammed shut. Lottie stopped and turned round. She could hardly leave Stacey to come scampering down the road after her. Tina would have had no qualms about telling the woman to fuck off, but Lottie just couldn't bring herself to.

'It's not safe. There's a lot of goochers around at this time of the day.'

Lottie had no idea what 'goochers' were, but thought that the word fitted Stacey herself pretty well. She realised now that she was bone-achingly tired. She wasn't really cut out for all this drama. She had always been Careful Carlotta as set down by her mother all those years ago – the person who would never take a risk or be made a fool of. It seemed she had somehow strayed out of character.

'How about I take you back to where you're staying?' Stacey asked. She peered at Lottie through dark-rimmed eyes. 'You look real washed out.'

'OK, if you're sure it's not too much trouble,' Lottie said. 'It's a couple of miles back. A motel called the White Horse, with a blue, starry arch at the entrance to the car park.'

'I know it,' Stacey said, and Lottie followed her back to the truck. She was glad that she wasn't going to have to retrace her steps in her dodgy flip-flops. Here was another sign, if she needed one, that she was losing it. Careful Carlotta would never have set out on a walk without being properly shod. She clambered into the truck.

'I'll just drive a little way further where there's a place to turn,' Stacey said. She was sporting dangling pearl earrings and a frilled-neck blouse, which looked incongruous with the black jeans and cowboy boots she was wearing. At least she has a passion, Lottie thought wearily as the road slid past. The sky was a pale, glimmering pink. She saw a telephone box with a toilet pan inside it and several shop dummies in fancy dress on the roof of a house and a bunch of gaudily painted cars with their bonnets planted into the ground like strange flowers. They passed a potential turning point and then another. Lottie began to get nervous.

'We'll need to turn soon, or you'll have gone too far out of your way,' she ventured.

'Don't worry,' Stacey answered. 'I know the routes around here like the back of my hand.'

'I really think we need to turn around,' Lottie said after another ten minutes. Stacey didn't answer, and for the first time Lottie began to feel alarmed.

'I'd like to go back now,' she said.

'You may look like her, but you sure need to work on your patience. Do you think she wanted to stand around being

249

stared at? Inside she was in turmoil, but she always managed to smile.'

'You can just stop and drop me off. I'll find my own way back,' Lottie said. She didn't have her phone with her. It was in her bag back in the room she shared with Tina. She was miles from anywhere with a woman who was living in a parallel universe.

'Hold your horses. I'm just gonna take you on a visit.'

'A visit where?' Lottie asked, by now seriously worried. She felt surreptitiously for the door handle. At the speed they were travelling it was unlikely she would be able to escape without injury, but it was possible that Stacey might have to slow down at a junction, which might give her enough time.

'Locked,' Stacey said without turning her head. 'Precaution against being jumped at traffic lights.'

'Where are you taking me?' Lottie tried to stay calm. No one knew where she was. Tina and Spike would discover her absence quite soon but they wouldn't come looking for her for hours. She didn't like to think about the explanation Spike might give to justify her wandering off by herself in the early hours of the morning, nor Tina's reaction to it.

'Why don't we just stop and have a chat,' she suggested. 'We can talk about Diana.'

'We've got hours and hours to chat,' Stacey answered.

Lottie wondered if it was possible to roll the window down and shout for help.

'No one is going to hear anything,' Stacey said, as if she could read her mind. She fiddled with the car stereo and then drummed her thumbs against the steering wheel to 'Candle In The Wind'. The song was cloying at the best of times, and these were not the best of times.

'Be reasonable,' Lottie said. 'You can't just kidnap me like this. You'll get into terrible trouble.'

'I just love that! *Be reasonable*,' she said, echoing Lottie's plea in a weird approximation of an English accent.

Lottie considered if it would be possible to knock her out with something and then take over the truck before it crashed. Perhaps there was some sort of implement under her seat. She ran her hand down the gap at the side and found nothing.

'Keep all my tools in a box at the back,' Stacey said, grinning.

It was the grinning that made Lottie perilously close to panic. It's possible that the whole decision about the wedding will be taken out of my hands, she thought wildly. At least I'll never have to tell Dean.

Just as quickly she told herself to keep a grip.

'We're almost there,' Stacey said, and Lottie saw out the window that they were back in Chloride – Stacey's hometown.

Chapter 23

'HAVE YOU SEEN LOTTIE?' Tina asked when Spike opened the door.

'I thought she was with you,' he answered. He had woken a few minutes before and assumed, on seeing the empty space beside him, that Lottie had returned to her own room.

'I don't think she has actually slept in her bed,' Tina said, looking alarmed. 'I crashed out straightaway and so I don't know if she even came back to our room. The bed's still made up. When did you see her last?'

'It's a little hard to say,' Spike said, vaguely. He was reluctant to tell her what had happened between them.

'You stayed up drinking together, right? What time did you go to bed? And where did Lottie go if she didn't come back to the room?'

Spike stared at her. He wasn't yet properly awake and his brain was not fully operational. He ran his fingers through his hair and stared at the floor.

'Well, we stayed up quite late,' he said lamely.

'Even if the two of you got totally hammered, you must have some idea of where she went afterwards,' Tina said impatiently.

'She came back to my room, because I had another bottle of wine in my bag.'

'Why are you acting so bloody weird?' Tina asked.

'I'm still half asleep,' he said.

'So, she came back for some more wine. How long was she with you? You must know when she left.'

'I think I must have dozed off,' Spike said. Tina stared at him. She obviously thought he was being shifty.

'So, you fell asleep and Lottie left at some unspecified time and never made it back to our room?'

'Um, yes,' Spike said. 'Perhaps she couldn't sleep and decided to go for a walk.'

He thought it more than likely that Lottie had woken up, had some sort of a crisis about sleeping with him and decided to find some space to think. It was the kind of thing she might do. She was probably in some diner nearby, drinking coffee, trying to get her thoughts in order.

'Who sets off walking down a road in the middle of the night? It's just not something Lottie would do. Was she really drunk?'

'Well, you know Lottie,' he said. 'She hasn't really got much of a head for drink.'

'If she was drunk it seems even worse that she went out somewhere else,' Tina said. 'Why would she not just have staggered back to bed?'

Tina was clearly worried, but Spike was in an awkward position. It was entirely Lottie's decision whether or not she told Tina what had happened; he didn't see the point of admitting it now. Besides, he was fairly confident Lottie couldn't be far away.

'I'll get dressed and we'll go out looking for her,' he said.

They drove down the road, slowing to check through the windows of shops and restaurants, incurring the wrath of other motorists as they loitered. After driving for half an hour, Tina stopped at a lay-by.

'She can't have walked further than this.'

'Perhaps we should drive the other way,' Spike said, so she turned the car round and set off back the way they had come, doing the same slow assessment of the places they passed. It was much hotter than it had been the day before and Tina could feel herself sweating. Lottie was just not given to behaving impulsively like this.

'How about we park up and walk back to the motel and go into some of the restaurants she could have stopped at?' Spike said. 'She might not be sitting at a window seat, or she could have stepped out to go to the washroom or something.' He was beginning to feel worried himself now. He didn't think that Lottie had been upset the night before. Perhaps she had woken up and regretted what had happened. He should never have taken on Tina's challenge – which he knew now had started as a pathetic attempt on his part to rile her. He hadn't really expected it all to go so far, nor that he would become genuinely attracted to Lottie. He felt more than a little ashamed of himself.

'Even when we were kids, Lottie would never have run away,' Tina said. 'I ran away once and Lottie and Mia came to find me.'

She remembered packing her rucksack, taking biscuits from the tin on the kitchen counter, scooping the contents of her pig-shaped money box into her hand and setting off into the drizzling night. She couldn't remember now where she thought she was going, only the feeling that was in her, even at such a young age, that she wanted to be somewhere else. She didn't think her parents had even noticed she was gone. It had been her sisters who, torches in hands, had navigated the stretch of common and the wild bit beyond the broken fence where she had taken shelter in an abandoned building.

'It's too damp to run away,' Mia had said, putting her arm around her shoulders. They had eaten the biscuits by torchlight and then returned home hand in hand. Mia had lain beside her on her bed to make sure she didn't run away again.

'Soon you will be old enough to go anywhere you want,' she had murmured, stroking Tina's hair. 'The world will be your oyster.' It had been all there, even then – her desire to protect, to make right, to soothe. She had been born to it and had died by it. Tina felt the loss of her anew as a series of blows, a kind of ebbing and rising pain, each punch harder than the one before. I let her go, she thought. I opened my hand and she fell through.

'Don't get upset, we'll find her,' Spike said, taking her tears for fear. He put his arm around her and she leant into him.

'She's got to be somewhere nearby.'

They stopped at each likely place and showed waitresses and bartenders and shopkeepers a picture of Lottie that Tina had on her phone. She was standing in the shop in her new orange dress, her hands at her waist – half pleased by what she looked like, half doubtful. Nobody they asked seemed to have seen her.

They retraced their steps to the car.

'Do you think we should call the police?' Tina asked.

'Let's go back to the motel,' Spike said. 'She's probably there wondering what the heck has happened to us.'

The truck drew up outside a house on the very edge of the town. In the headlights it looked to be a ramshackle sort of a place, with peeling wooden walls and an extension that had been fashioned from half a caravan that had been sliced down the middle and fastened to the side of the main building. Out front, a dog tethered to a length of chain was walking in circles as far as his restraint would allow him.

'Here we are!' Stacey announced, switching off the engine. Lottie wondered if she would have time to make a run for it when her companion opened the truck door. If she had been wearing decent shoes she would have had a better chance.

'Booger there is extremely fond of giving chase,' Stacey said. 'He doesn't get nearly enough exercise, with me away such a lot, so when I let him loose he moves like a bullet.'

'What do you want with me?' Lottie asked. She was cold and fear was making her arms and legs feel heavy. She tried to breathe deeply and tell herself she wasn't in any real danger. The woman was unhinged but she surely wasn't going to kill her.

'I just want you to stay with me a while,' Stacey said. 'We can hang out and get to know each other.'

'How about if I promise to come and visit you tomorrow?' Lottie asked.

'I don't think you're going to do that, are you?' Stacey said. 'What you are going to do is wait until I let you out of the truck and then you're going to walk nice and quiet through that door. Then we can rest up and have a lovely cup of tea.'

'If I come in for half an hour, will you let me go afterwards?' Lottie asked.

Stacey didn't answer, just opened the door and got out of the truck. As she helped Lottie down, she kept a firm grip on her arm.

On the way into the house Stacey unhooked the dog's chain and instantly the creature was panting at her feet in an attitude of pleading readiness. Lottie could see a sore on the side of its neck where the chain had rubbed and its glistening, frantic eyes.

'I'll feed you in a bit, Booger,' she said. 'I've got to see to our guest first.'

She unlocked the door and ushered her in, then locked the door behind them. After seeing the way the truck had been decorated, Lottie had been expecting something similar in the house, but when Stacey turned on the light, an extraordinary collage of images was revealed. Pictures of Princess Diana had been carefully cut out and glued and varnished to make up a mural that extended round the whole house. Every stage of her public life was represented, from doe-eyed ingénue in a transparent skirt to her wanton, leopard-skin lounge on the deck of a yacht. She looked coquettishly over her shoulder, leant despairingly against car windows and peeped dolefully from beneath the brims of a hundred unbecoming hats. She marched like an avenging angel in loafers and slid her shining shoulders out of cars and stared, with malevolent, kohl-rimmed eyes, into the camera.

'In honour of your visit, I'm bringing out my best cups,' Stacey announced, and set to with a great clattering in the kitchen area. Lottie looked around her for signs of a phone, but there was nothing in the room but a bed, a couple of chairs set around a table and a mad airborne army of Diana dolls hanging from the ceiling. There was one window but it appeared to be boarded over. She felt a sinking sensation in the pit of her stomach.

*

When they got back to the motel, Tina rushed to her room – but Lottie wasn't there. Spike went to ask the person at reception if they had seen Lottie leave, but the woman claimed not to have seen anyone.

'I can't really see the courtyard from my desk,' the woman said, 'and I can't be hopping up and down every two seconds if I hear a noise.'

'And did you hear a noise?' Spike asked.

'I might have heard someone go past at about three in the morning.'

'I think we should definitely ring the police now,' Tina said when he came back to their room.

Spike called 911 and was put through to the local station while Tina paced around wringing her hands.

'And what happened prior to her disappearance?' the police officer asked Spike. 'Was there some kind of an argument or fight? Was there some reason why she would set off by herself at that time in the morning?'

'There hadn't been a fight,' Spike said. 'But it's possible she was upset about something.' He could hardly lie to the police about the circumstances of Lottie's flight.

'Should we perhaps ring the hospitals?' he asked the police officer.

'We'll do that. You just wait there. She'll almost certainly turn up soon. People mostly do.'

'What did they say?' Tina asked as soon as he rang off. 'Are they going to start looking for her?'

'They're going to check the hospitals first,' Spike said.

'Oh my God. Perhaps she's lying in a ditch somewhere. Cars hit stray dogs and coyotes all the time. Even if the driver had known it had happened, they probably wouldn't even have stopped.'

Tina was white-faced and tremulous.

'Don't think like that. Try and keep calm,' Spike said.

Tina turned on him. 'This is my sister we're talking about, of course I'm going to be worried! What were you saying to the police person about her being upset? What was she upset about?'

'We slept together,' Spike blurted out. He didn't think he could keep it from her any longer. If Lottie didn't come back soon, he would have to explain to the police why she had gone and Tina would find out anyway.

Tina stopped her pacing and stared at him.

'You did what?' she asked, her eyes wide and shocked.

'We were both a little drunk, and it . . . it just happened,' Spike said.

'You are unbelievable!' Tina said. She spoke slowly and deliberately. 'You took advantage of her. You knew she was feeling conflicted about Dean and you swooped in there.'

'It wasn't like that. We both wanted it,' he said. 'And anyway, why the fuck should I have to explain myself to you? You've spent most of this trip forcing us together. You've only got yourself to blame that your plan worked better than you expected.'

'I *told* you to back off,' Tina said through gritted teeth. She was shaking with anxiety and fury.

'You can't just order everyone around. You had some twisted idea that you were in charge of what Lottie did or didn't do. Her relationship was never your business.'

Tina sat down on the bed and stared blankly out of the window. Spike felt suddenly weary at his own stupidity. He thought about Lottie wandering around in the middle of the night, confused and upset, and he berated himself for his carelessness.

Tina couldn't believe the relationship between Lottie and Spike had progressed as far as it had. She was certain that Lottie had never been unfaithful to Dean before, and Lottie would never have slept with Spike on a whim. It just wasn't in Lottie's nature to do such a thing, however drunk she had been. She must have decided she cared for Spike more than she had been letting on. Tina was furious with him, but beneath her anger and her fear for her sister, another feeling was uncurling inside her. Although she had never admitted it, even to herself, she realised now that she felt proprietorial about Spike and the history they had shared. The truth was that the thought of Lottie sleeping with Spike unsettled her in some fundamental way that she didn't really want to examine. Spike would not be a good partner for her sister – they were not at all compatible – but if Lottie had really chosen Spike over Dean, Tina couldn't, in all conscience, prevent it. She had set the bloody thing in motion and would have to live with the consequences. Now that she knew that Lottie had had sex with Spike, it explained why she might have set off by herself in the dark. Her sister often resolved matters that troubled her by thinking things through as she walked. But why wasn't she back by now? She must know that they would be worried about her.

Chapter 24

'I REALLY THINK IT'S TIME I went back to the motel,' Lottie said.

She had lost some of her fear of Stacey, who seemed to her now just to be terribly lonely. Over tea, and for a good couple of hours afterwards, she had subjected Lottie to her life story. Abandoned by both her parents, she had lived with her grandfather in the caravan, half of which was now the toilet block. She wasn't explicit about it – indeed her conversation was full of strange euphemisms that sounded as if they had come from the mouth of someone else – but Lottie had the impression that this man might have abused her. Lottie had talked to enough young homeless people who had left for the same reason to know the signs – the sudden spurts of anger, the desperate lack of confidence, the tendency to pick their way amongst the words of their story, pulling out the bits they could bear to think about. Lottie had been able to imagine her as a child, lonely and scared, waiting for something good to happen and knowing it probably never would.

It seemed she had first become fixated on Princess Diana on the day of her wedding to Charles. Stacey had been ten at the time. On that July day, when most of the UK had been either studiously ignoring the event, or waving flags and eating sausage rolls at street parties, when Lottie herself had only been a baby, Stacey had been sitting in a caravan, in a town full of rusting metal, watching a fairy tale princess who seemed destined for a happily ever after. Of course, the clues that no good would ever come of it had been clear for all who chose to see them – the distasteful turn of the groom's mouth, the obliterating veil, the royal family lined up like a drystone wall – but Stacey had been transfixed.

'When she spread out her dress, I could feel my own heart spreading too,' she had said, with her eyes still full of it. 'She was so beautiful. So clean and new, like a flower, like nobody I had ever seen in my life before.'

'Can't you just stay until I've done one quick delivery?' Stacey asked now. 'I'll only be gone for an hour at the most.'

'Tina and Spike will be getting really worried about me. Can't I just phone them and tell them where I am?'

'If you do that they'll come charging over and spoil our fun,' Stacey said. Her childlike eyes were pleading.

'I've been here a long time,' Lottie said.

'Tell you what,' Stacey said, sounding almost rational. 'I'll do the delivery and then I'll pick up some pizza and then we can talk some more and then I promise I'll drive you back.'

Stacey bustled around getting Booger his food, humming happily to herself. Then she left, locking the door firmly behind her.

After Lottie heard the truck start up and then drive away, she pushed against the door, but it didn't move. The boarded-up window was as securely fastened as she had feared. There was nothing for it but to sit and wait. As always, when forced into contemplation, Mia came to her mind.

She didn't know exactly what had made her go round that morning. Some instinct had started to agitate her. Until then she had been obdurate in her belief that it was only a matter of time before Mia came to her senses. Thinking about it now, Lottie saw that it had been a kind of vanity on her part to imagine that her absence or her presence would make the necessary difference. Mia had been fatally entangled; the rope that held her to Rick had gone right through to the very centre of her. Mia's mistake, if you could call it that, when all the blame and all the crime was his, was to have imagined that her love for Rick was strong enough to protect her. He saw her ability to believe not as something to be valued, but rather as something on which to cast his own endless anger.

'He knows what he's doing is wrong, but he can't help himself,' Mia had once said. 'He always feels terrible afterwards. It's only that I sometimes say and do the wrong things. He loves me. He says he'll change. He says that we can be happier than we have ever been. He says I just have to try and understand.'

Lottie had woken that day with a feeling that something was terribly wrong. She had dressed so quickly that she had left her shirt unbuttoned and forgotten her handbag. All she knew was that she had to see Mia.

The house had been quiet when she arrived. So quiet that she had almost turned away, thinking her fears foolish, but she had knocked on the door and waited and then gone round to the back, where she knew there was a key hanging just inside the shed door. Mia had told her about it once – perhaps because she knew that one day it might be needed. Everything was just as it always was – the throw on the sofa folded into a neat oblong, the silver tray that had belonged to Rick's mother with its usual prescribed gleam – except, on the bottom step, in the cream carpet, there was a rusty-coloured footprint.

At that moment, she had known.

Her mind had lost the time in between noticing it and her arrival in the room, but she could remember the blood, an extraordinary amount of it, so much that she didn't at first see Mia, lying on the floor, her face torn, her arms curved by her sides, her hands extended as though she had been caught mid-embrace.

The police had rung to say that Lottie was not in any of the local hospitals, and that now she had been gone for several hours they would send out a patrol car to go house to house in the area to check if anyone had seen her.

'Do you think she might have harmed herself?' the policeman asked.

'No,' Tina said. 'She's on a road trip. She's fine. She's getting married in ten days.'

'Although I gather, from what Spike said, that the wedding may now not actually take place?' the policeman asked, with impressive delicacy.

They were told the best thing they could do was wait it out, so Tina and Spike sat huddled together on the veranda.

'Do you think I should ring Dean and tell him what's happening?' Tina asked. 'I *know* he's going to blame me.'

'Don't you think it's a little soon?' Spike asked. 'She could still turn up at any time and we'll have scared him for nothing.'

'I just think I should. I have a really bad feeling about it,' Tina answered, and went to make the call.

'He said he's flying out,' Tina said when she came back out. 'I told him that coming all the way here when she'll almost certainly be found soon was probably an overreaction, but he wouldn't listen to me. He says he's been a bit worried about how Lottie seemed during their last conversation. His voice went all wobbly when he was speaking to me. He told me to look after her before we left on this trip.'

Tina began to cry, and Spike got up and put his arms around her. She hit him in the chest with her fist a few times, and then subsided against him. Spike was seriously alarmed. Tina just didn't do tears. Her apparent toughness had been one of the things that had drawn him to her in the first place. She had always been so self-contained and resilient.

While Spike was ringing round all the places they hadn't managed to visit in their earlier search, Tina went to the car to clear out some of the rubbish they'd collected on their travels. It wasn't that she thought this was a task that needed to be done, but she couldn't sit still. Throwing away the empty crisp packets and Coke cans and brushing grit from the floor stopped this twitching and prevented her from dwelling on what might have happened to Lottie.

She opened the boot and pushed aside the carpet covering the spare tyre well. She was relieved to see that the ashes were still intact. She touched the urn briefly, wondering, as she had before, how a life could come to only this. When she had first gone to pick up her sister's remains (such a doleful word in its suggestion of ruins, and leftover scraps) from the crematorium, she had sat in the car and opened the vaguely Grecian, double-handled container and looked inside. She had expected something the consistency of sand, and had been unsettled to discover visible fragments of bone. She had wondered if this rough-hewn debris had been the result of a hasty, incomplete process, or whether they had decided at the crematorium that the bones were necessary to provide the correct amount of verisimilitude. Perhaps people found it harder to believe the reality of their loss when all they had to hold onto was a vase of dust. She closed her eyes and leant against the door of the car.

A memory came to her. Mia was sitting cross-legged on a lawn. It was a couple of years before she had met Rick. Her hair was long and her feet were bare and she was wearing bright earrings. Her dress had been tucked into her knickers – 'My gardening attire,' she had said, laughing. Being near her had allowed Tina to be restful in a way she wasn't with anyone else. You never had to impress her or convince her, and you could say absolutely anything and she would offer only kindness. Tina had been telling her about a trip away in which she had climbed to the top of a mountain and then abseiled down. She had been taking photographs for a piece about extreme sports.

'You take such risks with your body,' Mia had said. 'But you've never really allowed yourself to love anyone. It doesn't get any riskier than that.'

She had stretched out a hand ringed around the nails with earth and stroked Tina's face.

Tina could still feel the gritty sensation of love against her skin. Stinging anguish engulfed her. It was as if something had been let loose in her that she had previously kept locked up. She couldn't lose another sister. She was culpable for Mia's death; she couldn't bear to be responsible for Lottie's. If she hadn't persuaded her sister to come on this trip, or primed Spike to flirt with her, Lottie would be at home right now, happily working out her seating plan or buying ugly shoes to match her terrible dress. She almost cried again at the thought of it hanging hopefully in the back of Lottie's wardrobe.

'I've drawn a complete blank,' Spike said, startling her out of her reverie.

'Have the police called back?' she asked.

He shook his head. 'I'm not sure they're taking it completely seriously yet. They told me that the vast majority of people return within twenty-four hours.'

'But she's in a strange country and she hasn't got anywhere to go and she's been missing for about fifteen hours, and Lottie wouldn't do that unless there was a very good reason.'

'I think they're still assuming she's gone off in a state and doesn't want to see either of us.' Spike looked away. 'They might be right.'

'However upset she is, she wouldn't scare us like this. It just isn't in her nature.'

'I must admit I thought she would be back by now,' Spike said. 'She's not in any of the hospitals, nobody has come upon her by the road or anything – I can't really think of any other reason why she would be away for so long.'

'Unless someone has taken her,' Tina said, giving voice to her worst fears.

'I think that's highly unlikely.'

'She wasn't really thinking straight. Someone could have stopped right next to her, pretending to ask the way or something. They could have got her into a car and driven off without anyone noticing.'

'Don't think about it,' Spike said, although his voice sounded shaky.

'I can't just sit here and wait,' Tina said. 'I'm going to go out and look for her again.'

'I'm not sure it'll achieve anything,' Spike said, but she had already made up her mind.

They drove the same way they had that morning. By now the small towns they passed through were gearing up for the evening. The neon signs were being switched on and the shopkeepers were pulling up their awnings and locking their doors. John Wayne was leaning on a truck and two giant inflatable dinosaurs were shifting slowly from side to side. Tina imagined Lottie's picture on the TV, the people in the bars they were passing now staring at it as they drank beer. Her own sister in one of those news items that makes everyone shudder and scrutinise the face of the missing person to see if there might be a clue written there.

'Isn't that Crazy Woman's truck?' Spike suddenly said. Sure enough, driving a little ahead of them was the white and silver livery of Diana's most fervent fan.

'Perhaps she's seen Lottie. She seems to be around here all the time.' Tina honked on her horn several times and flashed her lights, but Stacey seemed oblivious, in fact she seemed to speed up.

'We'll just have to follow her until she stops,' Tina said.

'She may be setting out on one of her long trips,' Spike said, but Tina ignored him. She tailed the truck when it turned right at the next junction.

'It looks like she's going home to Chloride.'

Stacey carried on through the town, past the shining junk and onto the road they had taken when they went to look at the painted boulders. She stopped outside a tatty house.

'No wonder she prefers to escape into fantasy,' Spike said, eyeing the pile of old furniture and the mean-looking dog chained up in the yard.

Spike and Tina drew up next to the truck and got out at the same time as Stacey jumped down from her cab. Tina shouted out a greeting and Stacey turned her head briefly, then scuttled down the concrete path to her front door.

'That's a bit weird,' Spike said. 'Normally she's all over us, or all over Lottie at least.'

Stacey shut her front door with a bang. Tina knocked loudly but there was no response.

'We just want to ask you something,' Spike shouted. He walked round to the side of the house to the boarded window. The dog followed his progress with moist eyes.

Tina rattled at the door and shouted some more, but it was clear that Stacey wasn't going to answer. Tina peered through the window of the bit of caravan affixed to the house.

'It smells really bad in there,' she said.

She took Spike's arm and led him back to the car.

'She's clearly having one of her madder moments,' Spike said, getting in next to her. Tina drove a little further down the road and stopped where the car wouldn't be seen from the house.

'What are you doing?' Spike asked.

'Let's just wait for ten minutes,' she said, 'and then we'll go back on foot. She wasn't happy to see us and I want to know why.'

This time they approached the house quietly. Tina put her ear to the door. She could hear voices.

'Hello,' she shouted loudly and banged on the door again. There was a short silence and then the sound of something crashing against the floor and a voice shouted back. Lottie!

'Open this door now or we'll call the police,' Tina demanded. There was another silence and another clattering fall of furniture and then the sound of a key turning in the lock.

Stacey looked dishevelled and out of breath.

'I only wanted her to stay for a while,' she said, as they pushed past her.

As they drove back to the motel, they asked an exhausted Lottie exactly what had happened.

'She's a poor old soul. I don't think she was actually going to harm me.' Lottie gulped gratefully at a bottle of water. 'She just wanted to talk to someone about Diana and her own life, which sounds pretty wretched.'

Spike was getting out his phone. 'We'll have to tell the police. She can't go around kidnapping people and locking them in her house.'

'I think she would have let me go in the end. If you call the police, they'll probably arrest her. She doesn't need time in prison – she needs some sort of help.'

'We have to ring the police, Lottie,' Spike said. 'Apart from anything else they're out searching for you.'

Lottie subsided against her seat. She didn't have the strength to argue, and it was probably best that the authorities knew what Stacey had done. She would tell them that she didn't think Stacey was actually dangerous, that what she needed was therapy and medication and some company. She gazed out of the window unseeingly. Tina had promised a trip to cowboy land and burgers and hats, not a spell locked up with a crazy person. This trip was definitely turning out differently to how she had imagined it.

'I rang Dean earlier in the day to tell him what was happening,' Tina said.

'Why on earth did you do that?' Lottie asked, turning to look at her.

'You were missing, Lottie. We had no idea what had happened to you. I had to keep him in the loop.'

'You'd better tell him I'm OK,' Lottie said and turned her head to the window.

'Do you want to speak to him yourself?' Tina asked.

'Not just now.'

'He's not answering anyway,' Tina reported, punching him out a hasty message. 'I hope this gets to him in time.'

'In time for what?' Lottie asked. She felt immensely weary. The roadside lights made her eyes feel sore and the man on the radio was talking too loudly about a fire somewhere. '*The roof has just caved in!*' he yelled. '*There's debris absolutely everywhere!*' 'Could you please turn the radio off?' She stole a surreptitious glance at Spike, who was driving now that his leg was almost back to normal. He felt her looking at him and turned his head and smiled at her.

'Are you feeling OK?' he asked in a quiet, I'm-addressing-this-only-to-you tone of voice, and she nodded. He touched her briefly on the leg – a friendly, consoling pat.

'The thing is, Lottie,' Tina said, 'I have a feeling that Dean is on his way to meet you.'

'He can't be!' Lottie exclaimed, looking astonished and terrified in equal measure. The thought of Dean turning up made her almost want to be back in the house from hell.

'Well, unless he gets my message in time, you'd better put your game face on.'

Later, when Lottie had showered and eaten a sandwich and got into bed and it was clear she wasn't going to volunteer any information herself, Tina asked, 'So you slept with him then?'

'I'm afraid I did,' Lottie replied. 'I'm going to have to cancel the wedding.'

Tina hesitated. She had another question to ask, and though she didn't really want to hear the answer, part of her had to know. She had seen Spike touch Lottie's leg in the car earlier, an intimate gesture, something a lover would do – and had been astonished to feel a wave of something perilously close to jealousy.

'Are you in love with him?' she asked quietly, but Lottie had already fallen asleep.

Chapter 25

'I<small>F</small> D<small>EAN</small>'<small>S</small> <small>TURNING UP,</small> I really think it's time I took off,' Spike said. They were sitting in the café next to the motel waiting for Tina to finish packing up the car and join them for breakfast before they got on the road again. The plan today was to go to the police station and make a statement about what had happened the day before and then drive to the Grand Canyon National Park, which was not far away.

'I don't think Dean is really going to come. It would be unlike him to drop everything in term time and fly out here. He doesn't do spontaneous trips.'

'I'm pretty sure he does when his fiancée is missing. I certainly would.'

'I'm not missing,' Lottie said.

'Listen, what happened between you and me, it doesn't . . . it doesn't actually have to be something,' Spike said.

'Are you trying to tell me it didn't mean anything to you?'

'Of course it did.' Spike sighed. 'It's just that it doesn't have to be a deal-breaker. If you want to, you can still go home, marry Dean and pick up exactly where you left off.'

'So, if the person you were about to marry slept with some-one else just before your wedding, you would be perfectly happy to carry on as if nothing had happened?'

'If I didn't know anything about it, I would,' he replied.

'I'm going to have to tell him.'

'The fact that you feel you have to tell him is one of the reasons I like you so much,' he said.

'So you like me, do you?' Lottie said.

'Yes I do,' Spike said earnestly. 'I think you are a beautiful, kind, marvellous, not to mention very sexy, person.'

'I can hear a "but" coming,' Lottie said.

'There's no "but",' Spike said. 'It's just that I don't want you to make a decision about Dean based on one night.'

Spike was aware of having to choose his words carefully. He liked her too much to hurt her. He thought that if she ever found out that the whole thing had started because Tina had instructed him to seduce her, she would never forgive either of them. He might only have known her for a short time, but he understood enough about her to recognise that she would feel it as the deepest of betrayals.

'Don't worry, I'm not going to turn into a bunny boiler and make you stay with me until the end of time.'

They're gazing into each other's eyes; I'm not sure I can bear it, Tina thought as she walked across the café towards them. She had spent an almost sleepless night thinking about how shocked and hurt she had felt when she had discovered they had slept together. Tina hated both sleepless nights and examining her feelings. In her opinion people spent far too much time analysing their motives when what they really should be doing was living their lives. If you kept going over and over old ground all you were doing, in effect, was walking on the spot. It wasn't that she hadn't thought about Spike over the years – there had been times when she had allowed herself to wonder what he was doing and who he was with and whether he had children – but she hadn't thought of him with any sense of loss or longing. She had been there, done that, and there was no point dwelling on what might have been. Lottie had once accused her of compartmentalising things, as if this was a flaw in her personality, when Tina herself considered it to be a positive asset. Keeping everything apart seemed to her to be the only effective way to survive. She was certain she hadn't been hanging onto the hope of seeing Spike again. Even starting the trip from San Francisco had not been a consciously calculated move on her part, since the last time she had heard news of him from Rachel, she understood he had moved away from the city.

'You've managed to get up!' Lottie exclaimed, when Tina arrived at the table. She was looking at her strangely, and Tina supposed she did look less bright this morning. She was wearing an uncharacteristically muted outfit – a loose grey dress, with her hair bundled up carelessly, so that it fell in uncombed clumps against her neck.

'Are you OK?' she asked.

'I'm absolutely fine,' Tina answered and ordered pancakes with prickly pear syrup as if to prove the truth of her words.

'Spike has decided to come with us at least as far as the canyon,' Lottie said.

'Has he, indeed?' Tina said, giving Spike a sharp look. 'Do you think that's such a good idea? Dean texted me this morning to say that he's meeting us at the Best Western Hotel near the canyon.'

'He's actually coming!' Lottie said, looking shocked. 'I never thought he would. Didn't you tell him that you found me and that I'm OK?'

'I did but he'd already set off by then. He flew into Phoenix and is now en route in a rented car.'

'Tina's right, Lottie. I shouldn't really be with you when he turns up,' Spike said, placing one of his hands on hers. Tina averted her eyes. He had always been touchy-feely; it was just that she didn't want him to be touching and feeling her sister. Tina wondered if that was the source of her agitation. It wasn't perhaps that she wanted him; it was more that she was finding it strange that he was being like this with Lottie. He only did what you told him to do, she reminded herself.

Tina wondered what Spike was thinking about it all. Was he as smitten with Lottie as she seemed to be with him? She stole a look at him and was annoyed that he seemed so relaxed. He was now sitting with his arms crossed, tilting back on his chair, his bloody ear sticking out of the thatch of his hair, which had been bleached a little lighter by the days he had spent in an open-top car. The man looked as if he was on some sort of a holiday.

She hoped his leg was still hurting.

'I'll come with you today,' Spike said, 'but as soon as he arrives I'll go off somewhere else and give you some space.'

Tina thought he had the maddeningly complacent air of someone who thought he would come out of this mess as the victor. Perhaps Lottie's godawful wedding dress wouldn't go to waste after all.

'If you were a garden implement, what would you be?' Lottie asked as she drove past the endless strip malls outside Flagstaff.

The business at the police station had taken longer than they thought it would and so they had left much later than they had expected. Up ahead was the snowy cap of Humphreys Peak, only a few miles distant and yet seeming a world away from the tangle of roads and signs and traffic. America was surprising like that, Lottie reflected – there was always something wonderful to see in even the most unprepossessing of landscapes. She felt a clench in her stomach at the thought that they were driving towards their meeting place with Dean. She tried not to think about what it would be like to see him again. I'll tell him I've changed, she thought. I'm not sure exactly how I have changed, but I know I'm not the same as I was before. I'm not the person he fell in love with anymore.

'I hate this game,' Tina said.

'I'd be a spade,' Spike interjected. He was sitting in the back of the car eating a Mountain Man sandwich of beef and grated cheese and onion.

'In your case a spade is not a spade,' Tina said sourly.

'I'd be a small trowel,' Lottie said, and Tina snorted.

'More like a hoe,' she said and Lottie glanced at her. She was definitely looking out of sorts. She hadn't slept well the night before, which was very unusual. Her sister normally went out like a light as if nothing that had happened to her during the day held any sway over her. What had taken place between her and Spike had clearly affected her deeply.

'If I have to be something, I'd be one of those big, sit-on lawnmowers,' she said finally, and Lottie smiled. Tina might not be quite herself but at least she couldn't suppress her naturally competitive nature.

They turned onto Route 180 and within a few miles they were driving on a gently undulating road that ran through a forested landscape. Blink and everything changes, Lottie thought. I'll tell Dean he deserves someone better than me.

'Just walk straight ahead,' Spike instructed them. Both Lottie and Tina (who had unwillingly capitulated) had scarves over their eyes as he led them to a lookout spot on the North Rim of the canyon. 'OK. One. Two. Three. Take off your blindfolds!'

Lottie let her scarf fall. She had been expecting a distant vista, but the canyon was right there, spread out at her feet.

Four steps further and she would be tumbling down its seamed sides, down its castles and turrets and wide slopes to the narrow crevice at the very bottom. Lottie found it hard to even take in the stretch and depth of it. She had the strangest sensation that the world had been inverted and that she was looking down an enormous mountain range rather than up at it. Even Tina seemed to have left her bad mood behind and was staring around her in wonder.

'It's so much more beautiful than I ever imagined,' she said, her eyes full of tears. Lottie was surprised. Her sister was being much more emotional than she usually was. She had sat dry-eyed through *Toy Story 3*, which was conclusive proof she had a heart of stone. Lottie put her arm around her and was aware of an initial flinch away – almost imperceptible, but definitely there – before she relaxed into the embrace. I've hurt her, Lottie thought.

When they checked in to the reception at the Best Western, there was a note written in Dean's meticulous hand waiting at the desk for Lottie. Just seeing the words on paper gave her a jolt. There was something so unmistakably particular about his handwriting that conjured up the writer more vividly than anything else could have done.

I'm here my darling. Room 23.

The curve of the 'g' and the loop of the '3' were as familiar as the smell of his skin or the sound of his voice. Spike and Tina went off to their rooms saying they would go out once they had unpacked and leave her in peace to spend as much time with Dean as she wanted. Tina gave Lottie a consoling kiss on the cheek and Spike squeezed her arm and whispered, 'Don't be too hasty.'

In the narrow, peach-coloured corridor she looked at herself in the mirror before she knocked on his door. She smoothed down her hair, which had tangled itself in the breezy car, and ran her tongue over her dry lips. For a moment she contemplated delaying their meeting, but after a panicked moment she reasoned there was little point in hiding away from him. This would have to be faced and the quicker it was done, the better.

At her knock, the door opened, as if he had been waiting on the other side for her. He didn't give her a big gushy embrace as some men might have done; instead, he stepped back into the room as she came in. It was just like him to be restrained, to wait and take his lead from her. His reticence gave her a sudden pain in her throat as if she had swallowed something too bulky. He beamed at her. He was wearing his cobalt-blue shirt, the one they had bought together for a holiday to Turkey. She remembered he had agonised about the concept of short shirtsleeves.

She could see his smile begin to fade when she didn't go immediately to him, but he wouldn't take this in itself as a particular sign of anything. They had always been a little awkward with each other after they had spent time apart. It was as if they had to get the measure of each other all over again. Sometimes she suspected that he was unsure of her at such moments, even a little resentful that she had been somewhere he hadn't with people he had never met and changed as a result in a way that might exclude him. She had always found this tendency of his endearing in the past, but now it terrified her. This time they wouldn't ease back into each other with a touch or some long-running joke or a shared bottle of wine.

'I was so worried about you,' he said. 'What happened? Tina sent me a brief text, but I didn't really understand.'

Lottie was a little relieved that they would at least have this to talk about before she had to tell him the rest.

'It's a long story,' she said. 'I was kidnapped by a raging Princess Diana fan who thought I looked like her, so she locked me in her house and fed me butterfly cakes and Earl Grey tea.'

'It must have been terrifying, even though you're making light of it. Tina said you were imprisoned in there for hours.'

'I was scared for a while,' she admitted. She sat down and patted the space on the bed next to her. It would be easier to explain what she had to if she didn't have to look directly into his face.

'What on earth possessed you to set off walking alone at that time of night?' Dean asked.

'I couldn't sleep,' Lottie answered.

'Why couldn't you sleep? Were you thinking about Mia? That's usually what gives you insomnia.'

'I've got something to tell you,' she said. She turned with an effort so that she was looking squarely at him. 'I'm so sorry.'

'What have you gone and done now?' he asked. He was trying to keep his voice light, but she heard the tightness in it. 'Let me guess . . . you've developed a taste for doughnuts.'

'I slept with someone else,' she said. Her heart pounded.

'Who? When?'

'We took someone else on the trip with us. I mean . . . it wasn't planned or anything. He's Tina's ex-boyfriend. He's going to Mexico.' She was aware that she wasn't explaining it very well. His frozen face was harder to bear than she thought it would be.

'Are you in love with him?' he asked.

She had known beforehand that this would be his first question. She knew he thought her a serious person, not given to impulsiveness, and she wondered whether this perception of her had been created by him or presented by her. It wasn't true. She hadn't taken any major risks until now, not because she hadn't felt that she was capable of such behaviour but rather because her steadiness and reliability had come to be what was expected of her. It was what she expected of herself.

'No,' she said. 'I don't think I am.'

'But you're not sure?' he said, and she hated herself for the look of hope in his eyes. She would have given almost anything to spare him this pain.

'I hardly know him,' she said.

'So you were just so attracted to him, you couldn't help yourself.' He sounded angry.

'I am attracted to him,' she said, seeing him recoil at her words, 'but that wasn't really what made me do it.'

'What did make you do it?'

'It felt as if I needed to find something out. It's hard to explain.'

'And did you? Find anything out?'

'It was partly that he made me feel beautiful. I know it's shallow. I know it's not the sort of thing you would expect me to want or need . . .' She trailed off, overcome by his look of hurt.

'And I don't make you feel beautiful?' he asked, his voice so quiet she could barely hear him. He sounded almost as if he blamed himself.

'I expect your sister was standing in the sidelines cheering you on,' he said.

'It wasn't anything to do with Tina,' she said, although she felt she wasn't being entirely truthful. She knew that Tina had wanted to cast doubt on her decision to marry Dean, that that was why she'd had a change of heart about taking Spike along with them on the trip – but she hadn't actively encouraged them to get together.

'Did he know you were engaged to be married?' Dean asked.

She nodded her head.

'The fucking bastard.' Dean got up and walked over to the window. Lottie could see his shoulders shaking as he stood with his back to her. She thought perhaps he was fighting tears. Still doing what he had been brought up to do.

'Well, you can tell him the wedding's off,' he said. 'That should make both of you happy.'

'It doesn't make me happy.' Lottie was perilously close to tears herself, but didn't want to give vent to them in front of Dean. This had been her doing and she hadn't earned the right to grieve. She thought if she saw any softening in him she would go to him, but it seemed he had made up his mind.

'I was so certain marrying you was what I wanted,' she said.

'Perhaps it's just as well you found out in the nick of time.' He turned back to her, his face suffused with anger. 'And me too.'

It was perhaps at this moment, seeing him so changed by what he had discovered, that she really understood what she had risked.

'I love you,' she said, and her whole heart was in her words. He was the same as he had always been.

'Not quite enough, it seems,' he said.

'I'm sorry,' she said again, not knowing what else to say.

'Where is he now?'

'He's gone out for a walk with Tina. He wanted to give me some space.'

'How considerate of him.' Dean's face was blazing with anger. 'Where have they gone?'

She had never seen him look like this. He was usually so controlled.

'They won't come back while you're still here,' Lottie said.

'So the plan is you see me off, then phone them to give them the all-clear?'

'There isn't a plan, Dean,' Lottie said. 'There really isn't.' She was worried about what he was going to do. This version of Dean was not one she knew how to deal with.

'Tell me where they've gone.'

'They've gone on one of the trails into the canyon. The Bright Angel, I think it's called. It's a fairly long walk. They could be anywhere.'

'Call them and tell them to come back,' said Dean. He was shaking. 'I want to meet the bastard who has wrecked my life.'

'I really don't think that's a good idea.'

'You've just given up the right to tell me what I should or shouldn't do.'

'Just stay here and we can talk some more.'

'I really don't think there's anything more to say.' Then Dean walked across the room without looking at her and went out of the door.

Chapter 26

'WHAT DO YOU THINK WILL happen with Dean and Lottie?' Spike asked.

They were walking along a narrow, rocky trail down into the canyon, stopping every now and again to let people on perilously balanced donkeys pass by, or to take in the view which stretched and contracted round each bend. As they descended, they could see the lines of passing time in the curving strata, by turns creamy white, dark purple and yellow. Below them the crease of the canyon floor seemed always to be the same distance away. Here in the shelter of the canyon the sun was fiercer than it had been up on the rim. Tina could feel it burning the tops of her arms.

'If she tells him, I'm guessing the whole thing will be off,' Tina said.

'What if she makes it clear it was just a one-night thing?' Spike asked, navigating a stepped section of the track and pausing to look out at the mounds of rock, which were shaped like jelly moulds.

'Is that what it was? A one-night thing?' Tina asked, stopping alongside him.

'I'm not exactly sure what it was.' Spike took a step onto an outcrop of rock that jutted out of the edge of the path. A foot wrong and he would bounce several hundred feet down.

'Be careful,' Tina said. 'Being the cause of a cancelled wedding is bad, but not bad enough to kill yourself.'

'You should be pleased,' Spike said. 'You didn't want her to marry him, so it's mission accomplished.'

'I just wanted to give her a chance to test her feelings. I wasn't expecting her to fall for you the way she has.'

'Do you think that's what's happened?' Spike asked. He had stopped again and was scraping the side of a stone with the penknife he had taken out of his pocket. Tina thought it was a bit like walking with a dawdling child – Spike seemed endlessly distracted.

'Well, she's been with Dean for the best part of ten years and I'm certain she never strayed from the path of true devotion – and then you come along and all of a sudden she's behaving like a moonstruck teenager,' Tina said.

'I didn't expect to like her as much as I do,' Spike said, and Tina felt her stomach clench. 'It started out as a bit of a game and I wanted to prove you wrong about her not being sure about marrying Dean, but there's something so lovely about her.'

'Can you imagine the two of you having a relationship?' Tina asked. She didn't want to hear the answer.

'Stranger things have happened.' Spike smiled. She wanted to hit him. He looked insufferably smug. 'Although of course, we live a long way apart, and I'm only likely to be with you guys for a couple more days.'

'True love can survive a little bit of geography,' she said as blithely as she was able. Somehow, the thought that he and Lottie might be together made her feel like crying. She should be happy that she had saved her sister from marrying the wrong man and that Lottie had met someone she clearly liked enough to risk everything for.

Just then a condor sailed above them, the girth of its white-flashed wings looking improbably wide at such close quarters. A moment later it was joined by a second bird. They looped around each other and then drifted down into the canyon, so that for a while Spike and Tina were standing above, watching their effortless flight.

'It's the strangest sensation being higher than the birds. It feels as if we're at the top of the world,' Tina said.

'Your shoulders are getting burned,' Spike said. 'Why don't you put your scarf over your arms?' He leant forward and untied it from her neck and shook it out and placed it around her. As his fingers touched the skin of her throat, she felt a kind of contraction – a tiny clenching shiver that took her completely by surprise. She looked at his bent head as he secured the scarf and had an almost irresistible impulse to put her fingers in his hair. She remembered the spring of it against her hand, as if recovering a lost memory. When he met her eyes, she thought he looked shocked, as if he had read something in her face that he had not expected to see there. They stood looking at each other for what seemed a long time, but then she stepped back.

'I think we should carry on,' she said, and began walking downwards.

The path narrowed as it hugged the edge of a large expanse of rock, ruddy and warm under her hand as she eased her way round. Below she could see the trail path zigzagging its way down the face of the cliff, looking terrifyingly narrow viewed from where she was standing, although she knew it was much wider when you were walking along it. The Bright Angel Creek in the flattened-out stretch of hillside, which now seemed suddenly much nearer, was marked out along its length by cottonwood trees and willows, a vivid green against the dun-coloured rock.

Tina walked on without looking behind her. She felt as if stopping might be dangerous since it would bring her into contact with Spike again. She recognised in the hammering of her chest and the bright, tender edge to her skin the feeling she'd had when she'd seen him for the very first time. She knew now that the longing had never gone away, but had just been resting under the rim of her heart. It wasn't possible. It mustn't be possible. She was almost certain Lottie was in love with him. Right now, her sister was probably breaking off her engagement and it had been her doing. She couldn't now compound her carelessness with cruelty – and in any case it seemed that Lottie's feelings for Spike were reciprocated.

'Slow down!' Spike shouted out, and she looked back to see that she had been walking so fast, she had left him behind. His leg still wasn't completely healed and it hampered his progress. She watched his uncertain approach. She could seal up her feelings. She had done it before over Mia and she could do it again.

'It's just that he wants the best for me,' Mia had said. 'All I need to do is try a little harder.'

'But you're perfect just as you are,' Tina had replied. Lottie had taken her hand and held it tightly. They were sitting on stools in a bar. Three sisters, three strawberry daiquiris and three curving top lips – the barman had hovered over them.

'The Three Graces,' he had said, doing a funny little bow that had made Lottie and Mia giggle, although Tina had rolled her eyes.

'When things are good between us, it's the most perfect feeling ever. He holds me closer than anyone ever has. In the night,' here Mia had blushed; she was always a little prudish, which meant that Tina enjoyed the sport of trying to shock her, 'in the night he's as tentative as a boy.'

'But what about the rest of the time?' Tina had asked. 'When he's not having sex with you.'

'He struggles sometimes with believing I love him,' Mia had said, a shadow crossing her lovely face. 'It's hard to prove love, isn't it?'

'You shouldn't have to prove it,' Lottie had said. 'It should be enough for him that you're there, putting up with his shit.'

'I can help him.'

'Mia, you need to understand that nothing you ever do will be enough for him,' Lottie had said, putting her arm around Mia to take the sting out of her words. 'You'll not find him, you'll lose yourself.'

But she had been implacable, as sturdily oblivious as the slopes of the Grand Canyon. 'He just needs me to keep on loving him. One day he will believe it.'

That had been the last time Tina had ever seen Mia. The period afterwards had been filled with work and trips away and a new lover. One night Mia had phoned her, but she had been at a party. She'd barely been able to hear her sister's voice; the music had been so loud. She had been too drunk to get it together to find somewhere quiet to talk.

'Can you come round? Can you come round now?' Mia had asked. Tina should have been alerted by the fact Mia had never asked this of her before.

'I'm at a party,' she had said, stupid and oblivious. Careless, the way she always had been. Mia had said something else which she hadn't been able to quite catch.

'I can't hear you,' she had said. 'I'll ring you tomorrow when I'm not wasted. I'll ring you tomorrow, Mia.'

She had rung off and had another drink, then sex with the new lover in one of the rooms upstairs.

'I'm a wasted waste of space,' she had said, laughing as he put his fingers into her.

It had been the night of Mia's murder. She had thought many times in the three years since her sister's death about what would have happened if she had left the party and taken a taxi to Mia's house. She knew that she might not have been able to prevent her sister's death, but she would have been there for her at least. She would have come when Mia called for her. She would have been a good sister. Mia's last phone call was a secret she kept to herself to pick at in the night – her unforgivable, missed chance.

Spike caught up with her, a little breathless and limping slightly.

'You're walking as if you're being chased by the devil,' he said.

'Perhaps I am.'

'My leg's giving me a bit of trouble.'

'I think we're almost at the creek,' she replied. 'When we get there I think we should eat lunch and have a rest and then start back. I don't think you're going to make it all the way down to the bottom.'

They found a shady spot by the river, where they took their boots off and paddled in the water. It was shallow but still cold enough to make their hot feet numb. Spike splashed her stinging shoulders. She poured water from the cup of the Thermos over his swollen leg. A family of raccoons foraged at the river's edge, dipping and tapping and then rolling their paws together as if they were taking a wash. They ate, and then Spike fell asleep with his head resting on his rucksack. Tina lay down and looked up at the sky, which was an unblemished blue lid over the cupped sides of the canyon. She must have dozed off too, because she was startled awake by a voice above her.

'Hello, Tina.'

She stared into Dean's face, then sat up quickly. He looked flushed and untidy. Her first thought was that he was wearing completely the wrong shoes – he must have almost slid down the trail in those smooth-bottomed brogues. Her second thought was that he had been propelled downwards by fury. You could feel it coming off him with a stronger heat even than that held in the sun-facing rocks. She got to her feet and nudged Spike awake with the side of her bare foot.

'Hello, Dean, it's very nice to see you,' Tina said, and then inwardly cursed herself for her choice of words. She was sure he wouldn't appreciate being greeted as if they were acquaintances at a party.

'Is this Spike?' Dean asked.

Spike got to his feet and looked at him warily.

'Yes,' he said, extending his hand. Dean ignored the gesture and stared at him.

'Did you at any point when you were fucking my fiancée stop to think about the fact she was supposed to be getting married in little over a week?' He spoke through gritted teeth, his fists clenched by his sides.

'I know how angry you must be,' Spike said. He was pale and looked a little shaken. 'But it wasn't as if we planned for it to happen.'

'Not the way we had planned flowers and favours and fairy cakes and the rest of our fucking lives.'

'Dean, why don't you sit down and let me get you a drink,' Tina said. She had never heard Dean swear before and the venom in his voice shocked her.

He turned to her. His pale eyes were red-rimmed as if he had been rubbing the canyon dust into them. 'You've never wanted her to marry me, have you?'

'I just wanted her to be sure she was making the right decision,' Tina said.

He ignored her and turned his attention back to Spike, who, sensing his disadvantage, was trying to put his boots on.

'Why don't we talk about it,' Spike said, in that particularly chummy, American way which only serves to inflame an already irate British man. 'I'm not even sure it was that important to her,' he continued, bending to tie up his laces.

The blow from Dean's fist knocked him off his feet and he lay for a moment blinking up at his adversary, then scrambled up, holding the side of his face.

'Well it was fucking important to me,' Dean said, and swung his arm again. This time Spike ducked to avoid the blow. Tina was astonished. The man had clearly lost his mind.

Who would have thought that Dean, whose idea of a good time was half a lager and a walk through a bluebell wood, would behave like Liam Neeson on a tough day? Dean hit out again and this time made contact with Spike's head.

'Stop it!' Tina cried, trying to get between them as they grappled with each other, but Dean was oblivious. He grabbed hold of Spike's neck and tightened his hands around it. Spike was making desperate gurgling noises.

Suddenly Dean's shoulders slumped and all the fight seemed to go out of him. He let go of Spike's T-shirt, which he'd held balled up in his fist. He stood for a moment as if he was trying to find something to say, then turned away.

'Let's walk back up with you,' Tina said, alarmed by Dean's blank stare and the dejected way he was holding himself.

'I don't want either of you anywhere near me.' Dean set off walking back up the path again. At one point his ankle twisted as one of his shoes slid on a rock and Tina's heart smote her.

'It would have been better for all of us if you hadn't come back for me in Morro Bay,' Spike said.

Tina didn't answer. She was thinking it would have been better for them all if she had not taken it upon herself to meddle. Everything was spoiled, and it was her fault.

Chapter 27

WHEN LOTTIE RETURNED TO HER room and found that Tina wasn't there, she crept into her bed, fully dressed, and cried herself into a deep and exhausted sleep.

She woke a couple of hours later, disorientated and dry-mouthed, haunted by her tumbled dreams. Mia had been in the car with them, Lottie's horse on her lap. She had smiled and waved from the window at the train they had over-taken on Route 66. In the soupy, kelp-filled sea at Big Sur she had risen up out of the water, laughing, her hair as sleek as a seal.

Lottie took a shower in an attempt to clear her head, but she felt as if she was being pulled back to the dream fragments of Mia that seemed more vivid than her hotel room.

She went down to the reception and asked if anyone had phoned for her or left a message, but nobody had. She was worried about what had happened to Dean. She wandered through the lounge – leather sofas, couples with suitcases propped up at their feet, a group of young girls in hen party sashes manically having fun – and on into the bar, with a vague idea of getting a strong coffee and waiting for the others to return.

Dean was sitting at a table by the window with his back to the room. She would have known the slope of his shoulders anywhere. He seemed startled to see her, as if he too had been pulled back from his own set of dreams. There was an almost empty glass of whiskey on the table in front of him and she could tell by the way he was holding himself that it was probably not the first. He never drank very much when they were at home. He claimed he was a morose drunk, and certainly now he looked utterly desolate. He seemed to have acquired mud or something on the leg of his trousers. She felt an instinctive desire to brush him clean – a reflex as automatic as the ready hand that catches something falling through a cupboard door. He raised his glass to her in an attempt at bitterness that made her throat close.

'Where did you go?' she asked, sitting down opposite him.

He gave her a kind of flinching look, as if what he was seeing was too vivid to look at directly. 'I went down the Bright Angel Trail as far as Bright Angel Creek and punched your lover in the face.' He was still himself enough to name the places exactly, then. He knew the names of everything; it was one of the things she had always liked about him, that and his tenderness, the way he remembered all their anniversaries, even the day they had moved in together. He had picked her up and carried her through the door and deposited her on the living room rug, which had pretty much been their only possession at the time.

'He isn't my lover,' she said.

'What is he then?' Dean asked.

'He's someone that made me wonder about the possibility of a different version of my life,' she said.

'What's wrong with the life you actually have? Or rather had, to be precise, since you've just thrown it all away.' He drained his glass.

'Don't tell me you've never, in all the years we've been together, thought about what else you might be doing or who else you might be with.'

'I've always been completely happy. Grateful, even,' he said. 'I never wanted to change anything.'

'I've been happy too. I have. It was just a kind of curiosity. That sounds terrible, but honestly I think that's all it was.'

'Well, curiosity killed the cat and our relationship,' he said.

He caught the eye of the waiter and waved his empty glass in the air.

'Don't you think you've perhaps had enough to drink?'

'That's another example of something that isn't your fucking business.'

'Why don't we go out somewhere? Let's just get out of this hotel for a bit,' she said. 'Find somewhere to sit and take in the view and talk.'

'Strangely, I don't think I'm up for sightseeing at the moment,' he said.

'What are you going to do instead?'

'I plan to get drunk and then go to bed and then get a flight back tomorrow morning. Leave you to your great adventure.'

'You can't come all this way and not see at least a bit more,' she pleaded. She couldn't bear for him to go, still hating her. The hen party had swooped into the bar, scattering bits of feather boa in their wake. The bride-to-be was as plump-chested as a chicken and basted with shimmering oil.

'Oh God, happy people!' Dean moaned. 'A bride who actually intends to go through with her wedding.' He seemed to have entered the morose phase of drunkenness. Despite his protestations she took him by the arm and led him out of the hotel and into the car park.

'Did you really hit Spike?' Lottie asked. They had stopped for take-away coffees and, by some miracle, since much of the rim of the canyon was teeming with people, who buzzed around its edges like wasps on the lip of a jam jar, Lottie had found a quiet place with a flat rock to sit on. Just ahead of them there was a tree with white, twisting branches like the antlers on a deer. Below and beyond, the intricate wrinkles and bulges of the canyon were orange and wine red. The sun's fiery line stretched from one end of the horizon to the other.

'Yes I did. Right in the face.' Dean managed a smile at last.

'Did he hit you back?'

'He tried to. He was quite pathetic actually,' Dean said, looking almost happy at the memory. 'Kept fumbling around with his boots.'

They sat in silence for a while watching as the darkness crept stealthily over one side of the canyon, extinguishing its brief brightness. The tree lost its pale glint and darkened too. Lottie felt sad. She had thrown his love away so carelessly.

'Was he better in bed than me?' Dean asked as if he knew he shouldn't need to know, but couldn't help himself.

'Of course not,' Lottie said. 'Sleeping with someone new is always a bit awkward. It takes time to get it right.'

They subsided into silence once more. Swift shadows danced across the sky, almost too quick to be seen.

'Bats,' Dean announced. 'Probably pipistrelles. They have hairy toes, apparently.' He smiled ruefully when she laughed. 'You see, I'll never be able to change. I'll always be boring on about the proper names of things. I can't help myself. No wonder you wanted someone different.'

He gazed at her for a long moment and in his look was all he had ever been and all she had ever really wanted. How could she have put this in jeopardy? What had it even been for? She thought she must have gone briefly mad.

'Can't we start again?' she asked.

He was silent for a long time, and she found she was holding her breath.

'I'm not sure I can,' he said. 'When I think of you with him, it's as if something solid has crumbled and can't be built up again.' He spoke sadly and with resignation.

'Other people get over things like this.' She took hold of his hand, but he pulled it away.

'I don't think I'm one of those people,' he said. 'I'm not sure I can love you when I'm no longer sure of your love.'

There it was, as she had suspected. He was all in or nothing. The last of the canyon's shine was snatched away and the giddy stretch of it was sucked inward into dark.

Chapter 28

'WHERE'S DEAN?' TINA ASKED, when she finally came back to the hotel. Lottie's face was sore and puffy with tears.

'He's gone to his room. He's leaving in the morning.' Lottie wiped her face with the edge of her sheet, smearing snot and mascara all over it. 'God, another thing I've spoiled. It's all I ever do.'

Tina came and sat down next to her and put her arm around her sister's heaving shoulders.

'He won't forgive me,' Lottie murmured. 'He said it was like a wall tumbling down, or something.'

'I thought you wanted to be with Spike,' Tina said, giving her sister's face another wipe with the sheet.

'I did. At least, I wanted to sleep with him and I wasn't completely sure afterwards. I was a little dazzled, I think, and he seemed to like me, and there was a moon and I felt pretty. Oh, I'm the crappest person on earth.'

Lottie gave another gulping moan and threw herself into her pillow. Tina stroked her hair, which was tangled into unruly clumps. Where on earth had her tidy, controlled sister gone? Lottie looked as if she had given up even trying to keep herself together. Tina was almost certain Lottie had her sweatshirt on inside out.

'Maybe he'll come round,' Tina said.

'I don't think he will. He seemed so certain.'

Tina felt a great wave of contrition. It was her fault her sister was suffering. As for her own feelings, they were such a conflicting bundle of emotions she couldn't say exactly what it was she wanted – only that she had to admit to a sense of relief, squashed almost as soon as it began to worm inside her, that Lottie didn't want to be with Spike after all.

'I think I should go home, even though I probably haven't even got a home anymore,' Lottie said. 'I can't possibly continue on the trip feeling like this. Dean will think me even more heartless than he does already.'

'What about the ashes?' Tina asked. 'We still have to do that.'

Here, Lottie pulled the sheet over her head and began crying again.

'We can't come all this way and not find Landing Rock,' Tina said. What an utter mess this trip had turned out to be! What would Mia think to find them so at odds with themselves and each other?

'If you come out of there I'll get you a hot chocolate,' Tina said at last, when she thought that Lottie had cried herself out. Lottie sat up wearily and smoothed her hair down.

'I think I'll live life without men,' she announced, with only the slightest wobble of her bottom lip.

Spike had decided it was best he kept out of the way, so after parting company with Tina, he found a bar near to the hotel. There was a buffalo head fixed to the wall and a man playing 'Three-Quarter Blues' on the piano. The waiting staff had tags on their chests saying where they were from. 'Yavapai County', who had ringlets and darkly pencilled eyebrows that gave her a look of permanent astonishment, served him fried potato skins and a beer. His leg throbbed and his jaw ached from the not inconsiderable blow Dean had planted on him. These were minor matters and easily soothed by salty crispness and a cold drink. It was far harder to work out what exactly he was doing in a bar near the Grand Canyon, and what on earth he was going to do about Tina and Lottie.

His motives for staying on the trip seemed to him now to be terribly unclear. He had joined the sisters partly because he really was stuck without a car, but also because he had been curious about Tina – a curiosity that had perhaps prompted his decision to set off so early to Mexico, although he would never have admitted that to her. He could imagine the derision she would heap on him if he did. Seeing her so unexpectedly at the party had triggered a desire in him that he had thought was utterly dormant to find out what had happened to her since they had been together. It quickly became apparent that she had no intention of telling him anything much at all. Her air of superiority and the way she seemed always to need men to admire her had irritated him almost from the very beginning.

When she had made her crass suggestion that he should divert Lottie from her wedding, he'd had absolutely no intention of obeying her. He had only fallen in with the plan in order to goad Tina a little, and then he had begun to like Lottie. It had salved his wounded pride to be the object of her admiration. He had thought Lottie cast in the same shape as her sister, and had realised too late how deeply she felt things, how irresponsible it had been for him to play with her affections. Now she had broken off her engagement and he felt that he was duty-bound to try and give them a chance to create something more lasting, if that was what she wanted. He owed her nothing less than that. He was pretty sure that if Tina had been in a similar situation she would never have confessed to the infidelity, but Lottie was much more truthful than her sister had ever been. Lottie would never have allowed him to stumble upon her having sex with a twat in their own bed.

If he hadn't started telling Lottie she looked lovely and putting jackets around her shoulders and all the other perfidious crap Tina had encouraged, she probably wouldn't have looked twice at him and he would have quite rightly thought her engaged and out of bounds. He had never been someone who actively sought to take women from other people, and yet despite himself it seemed he had. They had flirted, then gone a step further and then they were both enmeshed in something that really shouldn't have ever started, or at least not started in the way it had. Tina had always been trouble. It would have been better if he had hiked back to San Francisco or even taken pot luck and got on a bus heading pretty much anywhere.

On the next table, two tourists in dusty boots were holding hands across the table. The woman's ring finger glittered. They looked completely intact and untouchable, as if they were held by the air in their own private space. He thought again about that strange moment in the canyon when he had been tying Tina's scarf around her shoulders. It was so unlikely that he thought now he must surely have imagined it, but there had been a kind of tremble in her face when she had looked at him – a kind of softness that he had not expected to see again. It must have been a trick of the dusty light. If she had even the slightest of feelings for him she would never have thrown him so forcibly into her sister's arms.

'Congratulations!' he said to the couple next to him, raising his glass. They smiled at him, and although he beamed back, he felt something very close to sadness.

Chapter 29

Tina was assiduously pretending not to watch them, but every now and again she let her phone drop so that she could assess Spike and Lottie's body language. Soon after entering the Painted Desert, they had stopped by a lopsided caravan selling cold drinks, and the pair of them were now walking slowly back to the car across a stretch of blond grass. Although the hues of the canyon were still in evidence in little flashes of cerise and lilac layered in cream, they were paler versions of the colours they had left behind. Here the light was harsh and flat and the road was relentlessly straight, its central markings so even they looked as if they were being fed into a machine as they disappeared under the moving car.

Spike had told them he was planning on getting a bus from Monument Valley the next day. Tina knew that Lottie wanted to speak to him before he left, so she'd pretended she was too tired to get out of the car to give them the opportunity to be alone together. Dean had checked out of the hotel early that morning, presumably to fly back to the UK, and Lottie had accepted his departure with a sad resignation that made Tina feel very guilty.

'I thought perhaps he might have left me a message,' Lottie had said. 'I had this feeling when I woke this morning that he'd changed his mind, or at least decided to stay with me for a while so that we could have talked some more.'

'Perhaps he just needs some time by himself to think things over,' Tina had answered. She was revising her impression of Dean on an almost hourly basis. It was true what they said about still waters running deep. He might have a tendency to pomposity, and she herself couldn't stand a man who used beard oil or in fact had a beard – but there was no doubting that he felt deeply about her sister. He was behaving in an impressively erratic way.

'More likely he's rushing back to the UK to see if he can't get a rebate on the venue and the catering,' Lottie had said with a grim smile, and Tina had been a little reassured to see her fighting spirit hadn't been quite extinguished.

Lottie was making a wide encompassing motion with her arms. She was wearing a red jumper over her orange dress and green espadrilles that laced half way up her legs, and the wind was moving her hair away from her face. She looked beautiful, but Tina could see the weariness in her shoulders and in the way she walked. She fought against her baser nature, a battle she waged and lost all too often, trying not to feel jealous of her sister. At the start of this road trip she had felt sorry for her, believing her to be drearily bogged down in a life that wasn't of her choosing – and now, barely ten days later, Lottie had driven blindfolded, stolen some clogs, worn something that wasn't navy, tussled with a kidnapper, run across a night desert and had two men fighting over her. Tina felt almost dull in comparison. It was almost as if they were swapping personalities. She wondered exactly what Lottie was saying to Spike.

'Blame it on the moonlight, or the sunshine, or my utter stupidity. I don't want you to think that I didn't want to sleep with you, because I did, but the main outcome of it, apart from me wandering around in the middle of the night and getting kidnapped by a trucker, was that it made me realise how much I love Dean.'

Lottie stopped, as though to make sure he understood what she was saying. Spike thought she looked lovelier than he had ever seen her, although there were violet shadows under her eyes and her body was tight with the effort of keeping herself together. She was someone who tried to do no damage, who was earnestly truthful to herself and other people. She was an impressive person. For a moment Spike felt a kind of regret that it wasn't him that she had chosen, but he knew that there was really nothing more between them than a mutual liking and the feeling that maybe life was passing them by. They just happened to have met when they were both a little unsure that the choices they had made and were making were the right ones. Love, or the potential for it, was an altogether heavier and more twisted thing than what they had shared or would ever share. Spike thought again of that strange look on Tina's face – what had it been exactly? The more he thought about it, the more he convinced himself that it had been shock he had seen in her eyes.

'I get it,' he said. 'I really do. Don't worry, my damaged heart will survive.'

Lottie kissed him on the cheek and smiled.

'And if that man of yours has any sense at all, he'll come running back,' he added, gingerly rubbing his jaw.

They're walking quite close to each other, Tina said to herself as she pretended not to peep at them through the window. Perhaps Lottie has decided that, since Dean has gone, she'll settle for Spike instead. Maybe Spike has told her he loves her and so she's decided not to hurt him. Lottie was easily capable of doing something as daft as that. Tina tried to read their faces as they came nearer to the car, but there wasn't much to go on. Lottie looked pretty much the same as she had before, and though Spike was smiling, he wasn't giving much away. He certainly didn't look cast down, so perhaps the two of them were going to make a go of it after all.

'If you were a method of flying, what would you be?' Tina asked as they pulled out of the lay-by. She was desperate to cut through the silence in the car. It was making her uneasy.

'I'd be a hot air balloon,' Lottie said obediently, although Tina could tell her heart wasn't in the game.

'I'd be a rocket,' Spike said, settling back in his seat.

'I'd be a condor,' Tina said.

As they drove across Navajo Nation, the landscape seemed to lose its focus and become more desolate. The small towns became smaller and then seemed to disintegrate entirely into scatterings of trailers and abandoned cars. The earth was massed in throwaway heaps, the hills spreading downwards like something thick being poured slowly. There was nothing to see for miles other than signs advertising Navajo artefacts, the occasional emaciated horse and herds of sheep. A dog chased a jeep. A woman, in the middle of nowhere, was walking with her head down, her backpack loaded with tin cans. Train tracks ran parallel to the road as if there was only one way out.

'The Painted Desert sounds so much nicer than it is,' Lottie said. She felt desperately sad. All she had to look forward to now was going back to England and making a hundred phone calls saying that the wedding had been cancelled. How would she explain it? Glen Campbell was singing about being on his way to Phoenix after leaving a woman a goodbye note, and she turned it off. She didn't want to feel worse than she already did.

'When in doubt, eat sugar,' Tina said, sensing her despondency. So they stopped at a garage and filled up the tank and bought a heap of confectionery.

'It tastes wrong,' Lottie said, letting Spike take over the driving and sampling a bar. 'Like chocolate with all the chocolate taken out.'

They were not ready at all for Monument Valley. It caught them all by surprise and lifted the mood of depression instantly, as if something heavy had been plucked away. Just after Kayenta there was a small rise in the road, just an insignificant bump, and then there it was, the beginnings of the strangest and most wonderful of landscapes. As she gazed out of the window, Tina thought there would be no point at all in trying to fit what was there within the frame of her camera. Even if she used the widest lens, there was just too much of it to be contained or even to properly make sense of. The evening light made the colours of the rocks richer than any she had ever seen. They were more akin to the bright lushness of fresh paint than the shades normally seen in nature – a fiery, unholy orange, the purple of regal robes and slices of pink and green like an oil-rendered rose. And the shapes! Citadels, cathedrals, the roofs of temples, spires, columns, an Egyptian queen sitting on a throne – just fragments of things, really, and yet on a grander scale than any classical ruins. With wide stretches of flatness between them and around them, it was as if they had simply landed there or been left behind – not quite belonging under this sky and yet so calm and lovely.

'I can't believe it!' Lottie exclaimed, turning a stunned face to her sister, who caught hold of her hand and held it. Spike smiled at them both, looking pleased at the reaction and a little complacent, as if being an American meant he was partly responsible for the splendour of the landscape.

'I need to be in it,' Lottie said.

They parked and walked towards a distant fortified city within a crumbled, crenellated wall. The fact that they didn't seem to be getting any nearer to it, even after twenty minutes, reminded Lottie of the strip in Las Vegas and the sense she'd had of moving on the spot. The whole of America was a mirage. Spike had wine and so they sat, finally, in the crimson glow of the evening, and drank warm Merlot out of plastic cups.

'Where do you think Landing Rock is?' Lottie asked. 'This is all much bigger than I expected it to be. It's going to be hard to find.'

'Perhaps I should have broken the habit of a lifetime and done some research before we left,' said Tina. 'You can really see and hear Dove and Tache now though, can't you? The silhouettes of horses against the sky, whistles, gunshots, whiplashes, close-ups of faces so detailed you can see the hairs in their chins, and then the pull away to the wide, endless frontier.'

'I'm sure going to miss you,' Spike said. 'This has been a road trip like no other.'

'We'll miss you too,' Lottie said.

'Speak for yourself, sis,' Tina said. '*I'm* looking forward to getting rid of him.'

Tina turned her face towards the ruined city, which was trimmed now with a glittering golden ribbon.

Lottie looked at Spike, thinking she would make a don't-believe-a-word-of-it face in case he had taken Tina's words seriously, but he was staring at her sister.

Suddenly, Lottie understood. There was no mistaking the longing she saw there. It was as clear as if he had said the words out loud. It felt like a revelation, although when she really thought about it she was surprised she hadn't seen it before. There had been a hundred clues along the way – his decision to come along with them in the first place; his despondency when Tina got off with Greg; his anger when she danced with the handsome cowboy type in Lone Pine; the continual sparring they had exchanged throughout the trip; even perhaps, she thought now with a lurch of her heart, the fact that he had slept with her. Maybe all he had wanted was to make Tina jealous. The more she thought about it, the more certain she was. Tina was the real prize. She always had been.

Lottie got up abruptly, knocking her cup of wine over.

'I think we should find somewhere to stay the night,' she said, and the other two looked startled at the suddenness of her suggestion. Only minutes before she had been saying that she could stay in the same spot forever, or at least until it was so dark you couldn't see anything anymore. Lottie marched back to the car without saying another word, and Spike and Tina followed her, exchanging bemused looks.

'Probably Dean,' Tina mouthed at Spike, and he nodded his head. When they had almost got back to the car, Tina stopped and stared at the ground and then bent and picked up something and slipped it in her pocket.

'What's wrong?' Tina asked. Lottie had already strapped herself in and was staring fixedly ahead.

'Nothing. I just feel a bit tired, that's all.'

What a fool I've been, Lottie thought, as the car slid on through the valley, the shapes of things less vivid now as they blued into the darkness. I've thrown away love to satisfy a vain whim, thinking myself desirable, when all along I was only second best.

Chapter 30

'WHAT DID YOU SAY TO Spike when you were having your talk today?' Tina asked.

'I told him that I love Dean,' Lottie said, looking up at the wall.

'How did he take it?'

'Something tells me he'll recover,' Lottie said in a dull voice.

'He told me how lovely you are,' Tina said, remembering the stab of envy Spike's words had given her. 'If he seemed not to care, I think he was pretending.'

'He's in love with you,' Lottie said, watching Tina twist her hair and secure it to the back of her head with a mother-of-pearl clip. They were supposed to be getting ready to go out for a drink and something to eat, but ever since they had arrived Lottie had been lying on her bed, barely moving, despite Tina's entreaties that she was starving. She was always starving, Lottie thought vengefully, as she watched her sister highlight her already fine cheekbones with a shimmering stick. She looked particularly lovely this evening in a gold-coloured, boat-necked top and black jeans.

Lottie had tussled with herself about whether or not to tell Tina about her discovery. If she did, it would confirm how deluded Lottie had been to risk so much for so little, and in any case she thought it would probably only give her sister ammunition to torment Spike. There was no way Tina felt anything for him. She had spent the whole trip being rude. What purpose would it serve to tell her something she didn't need to know? It was better that Spike just went off the next day, with Tina none the wiser. But even so, the impulse to speak the truth was stronger than her pride or her misgivings about how Tina might react. Let her sister make of it what she wanted. It wasn't Lottie's business anymore. Lottie's business was to fly home with a broken heart and sell her wedding dress on eBay.

'Who's in love with me?' Tina asked, turning from the mirror.

'Spike, of course. Who else would I mean?' said Lottie crossly.

'Don't be stupid!'

'He is.'

'Did he say something?'

'No, but I saw him looking at you when we were in Monument Valley.'

Tina turned back to the mirror. 'It must have been your imagination.'

'I'm serious, Tina. I'm good at expressions.'

Tina started laughing. 'As in the time you thought Sean Bingley was keen on you and it turned out he was just trying to suppress a fart.'

'Sean Bingley *was* keen on me, actually,' Lottie said with dignity.

'God, that boy had a wind problem!' Tina said.

'Well, I've told you. What you choose to do with the information is up to you.'

'Spike and I have had our time.'

'I'm not saying you're in love with him. I'm saying he's in love with you, and just be a bit kind to him when he leaves.'

'Whatever,' Tina said. 'Now get up and get changed. There's a bison slider waiting with my name on it.'

'You go out. I'm not hungry,' Lottie said, turning herself to the wall.

'I'm so sorry about what's happened with Dean,' Tina said, a moment later. Lottie did not reply.

Tina went out into the corridor and phoned Dean's number. It went straight to voicemail so she left a message.

'Don't be a fool. She loves you.'

Spike was waiting in the lobby.

'Where's Lottie?' he asked.

His hair was still wet from the shower and he was wearing a tight black T-shirt.

'She's not feeling up to coming out,' she replied, 'so I'm afraid it's just the two of us.'

They walked past the light-trimmed succulents and the modest water feature, which was sending out a tired spume of foam. The air was heavy with imminent rain and smelt of jasmine and creosote – a lorry was ejecting tarmac out of a chute and a man was frantically spreading its gleaming silkiness across the road with what looked like a rake. The restaurant had large windows that overlooked Monument Valley, but their vantage point was wasted since it was dark outside, although you could just see the dim shapes of the rocks if you pressed your face to the glass. They ordered cactus juice and burgers.

'How are you going to find Landing Rock?' Spike asked.

'I'm not sure. It might not even exist. It could be just a bit of scenery knocked up out of polystyrene and paint,' Tina answered.

She got her phone out and showed him the screen grab she had taken from the scene in the film. 'It *looks* real enough,' she said, 'but I don't know.'

Spike studied the picture. 'It looks pretty convincing to me. There's that strange-shaped tree in front of the stone with a split down the centre of the trunk. A juniper, I think. That doesn't look like something they'd have made in a studio.'

'We *have* to find it. It's the main reason for this trip.'

'What really happened to your sister?' Spike asked. He expected she would fob him off as she had every other time he had mentioned it, but Tina looked directly at him.

'Her husband killed her.'

'Oh my God! Really?'

'He stabbed her seventeen times.'

'I'm so sorry,' Spike said. His words seemed inadequate, as words always were when something truly terrible happened.

'We told her to leave him. We told her again and again, but she just couldn't.'

'Was she scared to leave him?'

'I think she was, but I think mainly she stayed because she loved him. She once said to me that she thought her life wouldn't be worth living if she couldn't be with him. To us, on the outside, it seemed that the real problem was that life wasn't worth living *with* him, but she just didn't see it like that. I think she thought she could make him better. Mia always tried to make things better.'

'I expect you did all you could,' Spike said.

'I don't think I did,' Tina replied. 'I let her go.'

He thought for a moment that she might start crying. Her eyes filled and her face moved with a kind of deep feeling he thought he had only seen once before. It occurred to him that although she was expressive in her movements and in her sudden turns to mockery, she seldom showed so much. She shook her head, as if trying to shuck off her sadness, then took a long drink of her juice.

'Why don't we go out onto the patio?' Tina said, changing the subject and trying to sound upbeat. 'They're showing *The Searchers*, which was mainly shot in Monument Valley.'

They went outside to the covered veranda where chairs were laid out in rows in front of a projector screen. There didn't seem to be many takers for the movie; one other couple and a man with his son made up the entire audience.

'We're on the back row,' Spike said.

'Well, don't go getting any ideas,' Tina answered.

Just as they sat down, it began to rain. Heavy, single drops at first and then a drenching fall that trickled and then gushed across the packed earth around the porch. You could hear it on the wooden roof and on the ponderosa pines that lined the nearby road and on the bonnets of trucks. It almost drowned out the sweet, familiar opening strains of the film's soundtrack – Martha in her white apron stepping out of the darkness of the house onto the bright porch and holding fast to the post as John Wayne's Ethan rides towards her, the love between them never explicitly mentioned in the film but tangible here.

'Mia thought this was the saddest and most beautiful western ever made,' Tina said in a whisper.

Spike looked at her upturned face. The light from the screen touched the side of her cheek and her mouth. Her hair curled around her ear just as he remembered it. The skin of her throat and shoulders gleamed above her gold top. He felt his heart was beating as loudly as the rain. He tried to watch the film but all the time he was conscious of her beside him and of the time dripping away. He was going tomorrow. He did not think fate would throw them together a second time.

'Valentina,' he said, so softly that he thought she hadn't heard him over the sound of the rain and of gunshots and snorting horses. Then she turned her head and looked at him. Her eyes were cautious but she was smiling. He kissed her. He remembered the softness of her mouth and the way her hand held his face and the sharp, sweet smell of her.

'Let's go for a walk,' she said, pulling away from him after what seemed like a long time.

'It's still raining,' he protested, but she took him by the hand and led him down the steps of the veranda. They were almost instantly soaked to the skin but the heat in his body made the rain feel warm. He thought of his walk home from The Fillmore all those years before, when he had felt the same burn, the same longing. They wandered down the road hand in hand. The lights of the bars and restaurants were smeared across the pavement.

'I've just remembered, I've got a present for you,' she said, stopping and fishing around in the pocket of her trousers. She held the stone out to him on the palm of her hand. 'I found you a meteorite! I'm certain it's one. It latched itself onto the fridge magnet I bought in Vegas. I remember you saying they were magnetic.'

He looked into her cupped hand. Rain was gathering there and in the centre he saw a small black lump of iron with the characteristic dents or 'thumbprints' caused by the surface melting during flight. He took it from her and felt its weight – heavier than a normal stone that size would be. He peered at it closely.

'I'd have to test it,' he said, 'but I think you're right.'

'How old do you think it is?'

'I can't tell just by looking at it, but almost certainly millions of years old.'

'It was just at my feet!' she said wonderingly. 'This evening, when we were walking back to the car.'

She looked so pleased with herself that he couldn't help kissing her again. Their bodies were close together and their wet clothes clung so that it was difficult to tell where he ended and she began. A passing car honked its horn at them but they ignored it.

'Let's go back to the motel,' he said at last, when he didn't think he could bear being so near her and not touching her properly.

They ran back past the restaurant and the pool of tarmac and the fountain. In his haste his room key slipped from his wet fingers, so that she bent laughingly to pick it up and opened the door. The room was chilly compared to the temperature outside.

'I'm so cold,' she said, her teeth chattering.

'You should get out of your wet things,' he said, pulling his own soaked T-shirt over his head and then going and getting her a towel. Spike looked ridiculously handsome standing there with his hair wet and his chest bare. The old Tina would have thrown herself at him, not caring at all about the consequences, but something in her had shifted. She drew the towel around her shoulders.

'I'm not sure we should do this,' she said, and saw him flinch slightly, almost as if he had been expecting to be rebuffed.

'We don't have to do anything at all,' he said. 'Perhaps you should just go back to your room before you catch a cold.' The way he traced her face with his eyes did not match his words.

'You slept with my sister two days ago,' she said. 'This feels wrong.'

'This is a very different thing . . .' he said, trailing off.

'If she knew I was here with you, she would be really hurt.'

'She says she's in love with Dean,' Spike said. His eyes were dark. Despite her misgivings, she wanted to touch him. It felt as if her fingerprints had never really left his skin. She knew exactly what he would feel like.

'Yes, but she would still feel upset. I would, if I was her. In any case, perhaps it would be a mistake to try and recapture the past. We tried once, remember?' Tina wasn't sure whether she was trying to convince him, or herself.

Spike looked sad. 'I was a fool then, and it seems I haven't changed.'

'I have,' Tina said. 'It seems as if I've learnt to think before I do things. Perhaps a bit of Lottie has rubbed off on me.'

He smiled and something in her turned. It was as if a hand had reached down and twisted her from inside.

'There are some things that remain the same, however,' she said. 'I still can't resist a man with a cauliflower ear.'

She led him to the bed and he stood while she unbuckled his belt and helped him to take off his soaked jeans. The effort to get her own off set them tumbling onto the bed and he laughed, but when he looked at her the laughter caught in his throat. Her beautiful face was shining. She was looking into his eyes, at his mouth and he heard himself make a sound – a kind of hissing sigh as if he had landed at last after hurtling for a long time through space. He put his hand under her bra, feeling her nipple harden under his palm. She stroked him between his legs and pulled him to her.

'Condom,' he managed, and stretched across her to the bag by the bed. She took it from him and rolled it down with quick fingers. I need to slow down, he thought, but it was impossible. He felt more urgent than he ever had before. He was almost maddened by it. She was wet and then he was inside her, and all he could see was her face moving beneath him and all he could feel was a rising joy.

Chapter 31

TINA WAS WOKEN BY A soft tapping and the sound of Lottie's voice on the other side of the door calling out for Spike. She leapt from the bed and made a hasty grab for her still-damp clothes. Shit. Shit. How come she had allowed herself to fall asleep? What would Lottie say to find her in Spike's room? She claimed she didn't want anyone but Dean, but she would surely feel bad about it. Tina herself couldn't believe that she had succumbed in the way she had.

She opened the door a little way and saw both shock and relief in her sister's face.

'I didn't know where you had got to,' Lottie said.

'Give me a minute and I'll come to our room,' she said, trying unsuccessfully to smooth down her hair, which had dried in wild tufts. She shut the door again. She heard her sister pause for a while and then walk away down the corridor.

She washed her face and ran Spike's comb through her hair, then attempted to flatten out the creases in her clothes. It was still dark outside. Lottie must have been waiting up for her.

Spike stirred and muttered something. She told him to go back to sleep.

Lottie was sitting on the edge of her bed waiting for her when she went into their room. She didn't say anything at first, only ran her eyes slowly over her sister's rumpled appearance.

'I've been worried sick,' she said at last.

'I'm really sorry, it was thoughtless of me,' Tina said, 'especially after what happened to you. Although the chances of me getting abducted as well are probably rather slim.'

She laughed, but Lottie remained stony-faced. 'You had sex with him, didn't you?' she said.

Tina thought about denying it but it was unlikely Lottie would believe her. She looked like something that had been dragged through a hedge backwards. She could hardly claim with any credibility that the two of them had been having a quiet game of Scrabble until three in the morning.

'Yes, I did,' she conceded. She moved into the bathroom and began to take off her clothes again.

'Just another shag then?' Lottie asked, her voice low and mean. 'He was clearly gasping for it, the deluded idiot, and you thought, well, why not? It's his last night, so let's go out with a bang.'

'It's really none of your business,' Tina said, coming back into the room and pulling some dry clothes out of her suitcase.

'He's still in love with you.' Lottie said, in the same hateful voice. 'What's your excuse?'

'Well what was your excuse when *you* slept with him?' Tina fired back. 'At least I don't have a bloody fiancé.'

'No, you don't, and you probably never will because you're just too self-centred to care about anyone else.'

'Well, technically you don't have one now either!'

Lottie stared at her with wounded eyes, and Tina immediately regretted her spiteful words.

'I'm sorry. I shouldn't have said that. It was unkind of me.'

'Spike probably thinks you feel something for him,' said Lottie. 'He doesn't know you're as cold as ice.'

'I don't know why you're getting so wound up about this,' Tina said. She scrambled into sweatpants and a T-shirt and began to tackle her hair with the brush that was lying on her bedside table. 'It's not as if you want him. You've made that very clear.'

'But you don't want him either, do you? I mean, you wanted him enough to have sex with him, but tomorrow you'll just let him walk away without caring about his feelings at all.'

'Since when were you responsible for Spike's feelings?' Tina asked. 'And exactly how's what I've done any different from what you did?'

'I never made Spike think what we had was anything more than what it was. I was honest with him.'

'Are you sure about that? And in any case, what makes you think I haven't been honest, too?'

'I *told* you he was in love with you, and you still went selfishly ahead.'

'You really need to get a grip, Lottie,' Tina said.

'I bet you slept with him just because I did,' Lottie said.

'Don't be so childish!'

'You never could bear not being the centre of attention.'

Tina was infuriated by her sister's condemnation. Lottie always thought she knew everything.

'You weren't the centre of attention, Lottie,' she said. 'I told Spike to seduce you. He took quite a bit of persuading, actually.'

As soon as she said the words, Tina knew she had gone too far. Her hand went up to her mouth as if to cram the words back in.

Lottie stared at her. 'What are you talking about?' she said finally.

'Nothing. Really nothing. It's the middle of the night and my head is scrambled.'

'No, say what you just said again.' Lottie's voice was dangerously quiet.

'Take no notice of me,' Tina said.

Lottie stood up. 'I want you to tell me what you just said,' she repeated. Her fists were bunched at her sides and her face had gone so pale, her freckles stood out in livid contrast.

'It was nothing really. It was kind of part of the challenges . . .' She tailed off lamely.

'When did you ask Spike to do this?' Lottie asked.

'Shortly after he joined us. He didn't take me seriously. You got together because he really likes you.'

'So, knowing I was about to get married, you decided to get Spike, who would clearly do almost anything you asked, to flirt with me and pretend he found me attractive.'

'I didn't tell him to sleep with you,' Tina said.

'You are such a bitch!' Lottie said. 'What gives you the right to play with people the way you do?'

Tina was alarmed to see that tears were rolling down her sister's face. 'All I wanted to do was make you certain that you really wanted to marry Dean,' she said.

Lottie put her face in her hands.

'And I was kind of right, wasn't I? You didn't exactly fight Spike off.' Now she had started, she couldn't seem to stop, even though she knew she was hurting Lottie. She wanted to explain that it hadn't been malice, but rather concern for her sister that had prompted her actions, but the words all seemed to come out wrong.

'You know so little about me,' Lottie said, taking her tear-smeared face out of her hands. 'But you know even less about yourself.'

'You can't blame me because you were attracted to him,' Tina said, almost pleadingly.

'But I can blame you for manipulating us both and for humiliating me.' Lottie said. 'I will never forgive you.' She started putting her clothes into her suitcase in a most un-Lottie-like way – scooping up her toiletries and bundling up her nightdress and throwing everything in carelessly.

'What are you doing?' Tina asked.

'I'm getting the hell away from you.'

'Where are you going to go? It's the middle of the night.'

'What do you fucking care?' Lottie hissed and walked out of the room, dragging her suitcase after her.

Lottie sat huddled up in one of the sticky leather chairs in the hotel lobby. It was raining so hard that a pool of water had forced its way under the door and gathered on the floor by the entrance. She had been told by the bleary-eyed receptionist that she would have to wait until the morning if she wanted to hire a car. She was furious enough to take the Mustang from the car park outside and leave the other two stranded, but unfortunately Tina had the keys. Her plan was to drive to Phoenix and get the first available plane home. It was going to cost a fortune, but she could afford it since she no longer had a wedding to pay for. Ever cautious, she had insured herself against wedding disaster, and this certainly qualified as one. It didn't matter what it cost – she would spend any amount of money to get away from Tina.

Lottie did not for one moment believe her sister had had her best interests at heart and, in any case, who was she to decide who was worthy of love and who was not? She knew nothing at all about real feelings. This terrible trip had taught her an important lesson – or perhaps reaffirmed what she already knew – which was that if you lived your life as if every day was your last, you were likely to fuck up what was left of your life. Tina had always had a taste for this sort of crass, spongy philosophy, along with all those other awful life quotes dim-witted people posted on social media: *Let your smile change the world, don't let the world change your smile. Everything happens for a reason. Difficult roads lead to beautiful destinations.* Well, there was nothing beautiful about sitting in a lobby in the early hours of the morning, with yesterday's knickers on, feeling as if you had lost everything, including your pride. She gave a middle-aged man in a sweaty suit who cast a hopeful smile in her direction an evil-eyed glare.

How could Tina, her own sister, have done what she had? Lottie winced inwardly at the thought of how easily she had been duped. Was she really so weak and insecure that she had allowed herself to fall for Spike's commissioned atten-tions? She was someone who prided herself on knowing what was true, on her ability to spot bullshit – and yet she had so readily succumbed to the cheapest of ploys, all those intent looks, the oh-so-casual touches on the arm, the jaded rituals of seduction. And how could Spike have agreed to such a plan? She had thought him kind. She imagined the conversa-tions he might have had with her sister, she laughingly setting out her idea, he, not in love with the task, but in love with the puppetmaster. He was a weak bastard, along with pretty much every other man on the planet. The middle-aged man, too drunk perhaps to have registered the venom in Lottie's gaze, sat down opposite her.

'What you doing all on your own?' he asked. He had red lips and a thick neck and the air of someone who was used to getting what he wanted. 'How about you come to my room for a little drink?'

'Why don't you fuck off?' Lottie said.

He made a kind of hateful ooh-mark-her noise that made Lottie want to stab him with a knife, and got to his feet.

'There's no need to act so rude,' he said. 'I was just being friendly.'

Lottie watched him lurch away. You couldn't even sit quietly without some man getting into your space and acting as if he had a right to speak to you. As if he thought she should be *grateful* for it. Her father, as ready with his charm as he was with his fists; Rick with his unswerving belief that Mia belonged to him; Spike's sly perfidy; and even, although she had to accept culpability for her own actions, Dean's jealousy that blinded and deafened him – it seemed to her that they were all cut from the same cloth.

Lottie was glad she was angry. It stopped her feeling so helpless.

Chapter 32

'LOTTIE'S GONE,' TINA SAID, shaking Spike awake. When he opened his eyes, blinking in the sudden glare of the overhead light, he smiled and made to pull her to him, but she batted him away.

'Lottie's gone,' she repeated, and this time her words registered. Spike sat up abruptly.

'What do you mean?'

'She stormed out of our room a few minutes ago.'

'Why did she do that? She sure makes a habit of wandering around in the middle of the night.'

'We had a row,' Tina said.

'What about?'

'I told her that I asked you to flirt with her.'

Now Spike was fully awake and looking alarmed. 'Why the hell did you do that?'

'She was being all sanctimonious about me sleeping with you. I lost my temper.'

'That wasn't very smart,' Spike said, and then saw how stricken Tina looked. 'Are you OK?'

'I've ruined everything,' Tina said.

'She'll come round when I explain it to her,' Spike said, getting out of bed and pulling on his jeans. 'Let's go and try and find her.'

'I don't think she will ever come round. She looked at me as if she hated me.'

'She doesn't hate you. You're her sister.'

'The sister who has ruined her life.'

'She has to accept some responsibility for what happened. Lottie and I slept together because we wanted to and we were a little drunk. You didn't engineer that. You didn't make her tell Dean about it either.'

'But I started the whole thing. I'm sure she would never have fallen for you if you hadn't appeared so smitten with her.'

Even in her distressed state, with her wild hair and mascara-streaked face and with the urgent task of finding Lottie underway, he wanted to take Tina in his arms and kiss her so that she would look at him again as she had a few hours before. He was completely lost. He had opened himself up to her in exactly the way he had vowed he never would again and with no certainty that she felt anything for him in return. Maybe he was nothing more to her than Greg or that slimy cowboy in Lone Pine or her photographer friend who she had mentioned a couple of times in that archly casual way that convinced him he was her lover. He loved Tina for the joyful, freewheeling way she lived, the fact that she did handstands against walls and stood up yelling in cars and didn't care at all about what other people thought of her. Yet the very things that drew him to her were also the source of his pain because he knew she was enough without him. She would never need him as much as he needed her.

Lottie was asleep in a chair in the lobby, curled up under her cardigan. She woke instantly when she felt someone shaking her.

'She told me to let her sleep until the car arrives,' the receptionist said wearily, clearly inured to the strange, night-time perambulations of hotel guests. Why anyone travelled half way across the world to have such an apparently terrible time was beyond her comprehension. Home was most definitely sweet home and she couldn't wait to get under her newly acquired broderie anglaise duvet just as soon as this darn shift came to an end.

'Get off me,' Lottie exclaimed furiously, shaking off Tina's hand.

'I'm so sorry. I've been a complete witch.'

'I don't want to talk about it,' Lottie said, deliberately ignoring Spike, who was hovering in the background.

'What are you planning on doing?'

'I'm going back to England to pretend none of this ever happened.'

'You can't do that. We've got to sprinkle the ashes,' Tina said.

'You sprinkle the bloody ashes by yourself,' Lottie said.

'I can't do that. It needs the both of us.'

Spike approached nervously.

'How about you let Lottie and me have a chat on our own?' he suggested, giving Tina a gentle push.

'I don't particularly want to talk to *you*, either,' Lottie said, crossing her arms and looking pointedly in the other direction. Spike met Tina's eye and she nodded and left them to it. Spike sat down in the chair next to Lottie's.

'I honestly don't think Tina meant any of this to have turned out like it has,' he began.

'Yeah, you would say that. You are so bloody besotted that if she'd asked you to kill me, you would probably have done it.'

Lottie felt humiliated by Spike's solicitous look. He was acting as if she was ill or insane, not someone who had been mortally betrayed by the pair of them.

'It wasn't as you imagine it. OK, it was a stupid idea and I was dumb enough to go along with it, but it didn't end up where it started.' He paused as if struggling to explain himself.

'She doesn't love you, you know,' Lottie said. 'She's never really loved anyone.'

'She loves you,' he said softly.

'Yeah,' she said bitterly. 'It's really the action of someone who loves someone to concoct a plan to break up their engagement.'

Spike looked at her gravely.

'You did that all by yourself,' he said, and Lottie flinched. 'When we started this stupid game, that's exactly what it was – a stupid game that I joined in on because yes, you're right, I would probably do anything she asked of me. It felt like a kind of dare. I wanted her to see how heartless she was being. I'm not proud of myself, but I think I wanted to hurt her. And then I discovered how lovely you are and I felt genuinely attracted to you and for a while it stopped being a game and began to feel like something real. That night in Death Valley was real. At least it was for me. It felt like kindness and friendship. Not to mention you're very hot indeed when you're not scowling and behaving like a child.'

'You were a complete idiot for agreeing to it,' Lottie said. 'But what she did was cruel.'

The rain had stopped at last, and the day was gathering over the pines and the fountain and the desert landscape in promising pink strands.

'The fact is, Lottie, you chose to be seduced. You wanted an adventure. You can blame your sister for her poor judgement, even for her carelessness and manipulation, but in the end the buck stops with you.'

'She thinks she knows everything, even what's best for me. But she has no idea.'

'There may be an element of truth in what you say, but none of us is perfect.'

Lottie looked him squarely in the face.

'You really do love her, don't you?' she asked, suddenly gentle.

He nodded wordlessly.

'Well both of us are completely screwed then,' she said, getting to her feet.

'Won't you at least see the trip to its end?' Spike asked.

'I suppose I'll have to,' Lottie said. 'I still hate her, but Mia would expect me to be there.'

'Give me a hug then,' he said, smiling at her, and she embraced him tightly. Despite it all, she didn't want to part from him on bad terms. He was as heartbroken as she was.

'I won't say goodbye, I hate saying goodbye,' she said.

Spike packed his bag and took a last look around the room, which despite its standardised blandness was a place he would always remember. It would become yet another memory to torment himself with. He had to get to Mexico and work, and it was time to leave the sisters to sort themselves out. He should have gone before, but he hadn't been able to tear himself away from Tina. It would be all right. He would be able to lose himself in this project and the next one and in time he would recover. He had no choice.

He had gone to her room while Lottie had been downstairs having breakfast. Tina wouldn't sit still and talk to him. She kept moving around and going in and out of the bathroom.

'My bus leaves in an hour,' he had said, standing by the window, watching the sun stirring up the day – setting cars

343

and people into motion, making the monuments things to wonder at again.

'Do you want a lift to the station?' Tina asked, looking up at him briefly and then resuming whatever it was she was doing as if she was impatient for him to be gone.

'No, I'm fine. I've got a taxi booked.'

'Well, it's been mostly great having you on our road trip. Could have done without some of the drama, but I guess it made for a memorable holiday.' She was meticulously folding things she had never bothered folding before. She was usually a cram-everything-in kind of a packer.

'About last night . . .' he started, but she interrupted him.

'Don't worry. It was just something that happened, right? It was a perfect storm – John Wayne and the rain and an end-of-trip feeling and sex. Makes perfect sense.'

'So that's what you think it was about?' he asked, holding on for a few moments longer to the memory of how her face had moved beneath him.

'Maybe it was something that needed to be done to give us a better ending than the one we had the first time round,' she said, looking at him properly at last, her face expressionless. His throat closed up. What he had suspected was true – sleeping with him had meant nothing more to her than a tidying-up of something left incomplete, a kind of epilogue. Perhaps it was even less than that. Perhaps it had simply been a chance to assert herself over her sister. He didn't want to think that, but he could see no tenderness in her.

'When you're all sitting round the campfire, or whatever it is you do in the evenings when you're away, you can entertain your colleagues with the story of how you went on a road trip with two sisters and slept with both of them.' She turned to carefully fold a towel, edge to edge.

'Right then,' he said, holding back his anger at her words. 'I'd better be off.'

There would be time enough on the long and dreary bus ride to feel the burn and the hurt. He didn't want the last thing he ever said to her to be unkind.

'I hope you find Landing Rock,' he said. 'I hope everything works out for you,' and he gave her the kind of quick embrace you give to someone it doesn't break your heart to be parting from. She hung listlessly in his arms.

Later, on the bus, he clutched the meteorite tightly as if he was holding onto what he had left behind, feeling its scorched crust bite against his palm.

Chapter 33

'IF YOU WERE A DOUGHNUT, what kind of a doughnut would you be?' Tina asked.

Lottie, who was slumped in the front seat of the car, pulled the brim of her hat down over her eyes and didn't bother to answer. She had agreed to stay on and finish the trip, but she was damned if she was going to make Tina feel as if she had forgiven her for what she had done. She was just going to grit her teeth and get through the last three days and then she would go home to face the wreckage of her life. Her heart clenched at the thought that Dean might not be there when she got back. She supposed if it really was over, and she couldn't imagine Dean ever changing his mind, they would have to sell their flat with the iron fireplace that had taken them three days to scrape clean, and the postage-stamp-sized garden in which the clematis had been patiently coaxed to spread its velvety purple flowers all over the back wall. They had built their home together so carefully, with tester pots of paint and swatches of cloth and trips to furniture shops to contemplate one grey sofa over another. They had made their seasonal plans so that the year was punctuated with places and events to enjoy. They had built their happiness around each other, finding in their regulated life more than enough to be glad and grateful for and yet, despite all of this, some sort of greed had lodged itself inside her. An unspecific longing so apparently strong that she had been ready to throw away all that they had so painstakingly constructed. She couldn't even remember now what it was she had thought was missing.

'I'd be a custard one sprinkled with hundreds and thousands,' Tina said, and Lottie shrugged indifferently.

'I've apologised over and over again,' Tina said, fretfully, putting her finger up at the driver in the next car who was goggling at them at the traffic lights as if he was in a safari park.

Lottie made a harrumphing noise from under her hat.

'I don't know what else you want me to do. I can't wind the clock back. And in any case, some of it is your fault.'

Lottie sat up and pushed the hat back off her face. 'How like you to say sorry and blame me in the same sentence!' she exclaimed. The man in the next car took off with a screech when the lights changed and then fell back, so that he was driving alongside them. Tina glanced his way to see him waggling his tongue up and down at them.

'What the fuck?' Lottie said furiously, following the direction of Tina's gaze. She grabbed at the carton of orange juice at her feet and with one swift movement sent the contents through his car window and right into his face.

'Bull's eye!' Tina said with approval, and Lottie allowed herself the smallest glimmer of a smile.

'What did you say to Spike before he left?' Lottie asked, propelled by curiosity to break her silence.

'Not much,' Tina answered. 'He seemed in a hurry to get away.'

She thought about how awkward Spike had seemed in the hotel room, as if he was trying to find a way to let her down lightly. Perhaps he had been terrified that she was going to throw herself into his arms and tell him she loved him. Thank God she had held back and taken her lead from him, rather than done anything rash, which would only have ended up embarrassing them both. He had talked about buses and departure times as if he was longing to escape.

'You're an utter idiot,' Lottie exclaimed. 'Not only are you a manipulative old bag, but you have about as much insight as a tree slug.'

'Well gee, thanks,' Tina said sarcastically.

Lottie wrestled briefly with herself. If her sister couldn't see what was staring her in the face, why should she, betrayed and humiliated as she had been, explain it to her? Tina didn't deserve Spike or anyone else's love. She had already told her sister about her suspicions and Tina had not reacted at all. What would Tina do with the knowledge anyway, other than suck it up into her already rapacious ego? Perhaps it would be kinder to protect Spike's pride from her sister's indifference, although she didn't know why she was concerned with his feelings – it wasn't as if he had been particularly concerned with hers. In the end, her better nature, the part of herself she had always believed to be strong until Mia's death had shown her that it was a poor, weak thing, won through.

'He's in love with you. I was right when I told you so before. Can't you see it?'

Tina turned her head and stared at her sister.

'Keep your eyes on the road,' Lottie yelled, as they narrowly missed ploughing into the back of the vehicle ahead.

'What makes you say that?' Tina asked, braking inches away from the bumper. 'It's rubbish. We've been over this already.'

'He told me, you fool,' Lottie said.

'When?'

'This morning.'

Tina lapsed into silence as the traffic moved inch by inch along the congested highway. Lottie had no idea what her sister was thinking.

'He said the actual words, *I love her*?' Tina asked incredulously after a moment or two.

'Well, to be strictly accurate, he nodded when I asked him the question.'

'Are you sure he hadn't just developed a nervous tick, or was trying to get the attention of the waiter, or something?'

'Yes, Tina, I'm sure.'

'How come he slept with you then?'

'Probably because he'd been driven to desperation by the horrible way you were treating him,' she said, thinking it undiplomatic to mention that he had said she was hot. She knew that Tina thought of herself as far hotter, and she was willing to give her that.

Tina lapsed into silence again. Lottie couldn't remember the last time her sister had stayed quiet for so long. It gave her the opportunity to look out of the window at the desert populated by cathedrals and totem poles. She still couldn't take in the strange, random beauty of it. It was so huge it made her feel agitated.

'I hate the amount of time women spend talking about men,' Tina said.

'Well, when I'm not on a road trip with you, I barely mention them,' Lottie said.

'They suck up all the energy you should be spending on thinking about other things. I've hardly taken a decent picture this whole trip.'

'If you hadn't been plotting to undo me and primed your devoted hitchhiker to say nice things about my hair and skin, perhaps you would have taken the definitive picture of the American West and I would have read the three books I brought with me and done some sketches of seals and freight trains and monuments.'

'Let's stop and have something to eat,' Tina said, pulling off the road into the forecourt of a diner.

Tina ate a strange thing called a 'masher', which was a burger on a bun topped with mashed potato with a thick, beige gravy poured over the whole lot, while Lottie picked her way through a soggy Caesar salad.

'At the risk of doing what you so deride,' Lottie said, trying not to watch as her sister enthusiastically wiped up the gravy with her bun, 'what do you really feel about Spike?'

'I don't know,' Tina said.

'You don't know, or you don't want to think about it?'

'What's the point of thinking about it? We failed last time round. I don't think we really trust each other, and besides, he lives on the other side of the world. I think it's better if I just move on and forget about it.'

'So your heart didn't do a flip when I told you he loved you?' Lottie asked, scrutinising her sister.

'Stop staring at me as if you're trying to work out if I'm the main suspect in your investigation. Eat your croutons.'

'What are you so scared of, Tina?'

'I'm not scared. I'm never scared. I just don't know exactly what I feel about him and I can't see the point of tying myself to someone unless I'm a hundred per cent sure.'

'This old chestnut again!' Lottie exclaimed impatiently. 'I've told you a million times that no one is ever *sure*.'

'So you're not sure that you love Dean then?'

'Not sure the way *you* think of it. Not sure like I'm sure that eating chocolate makes me feel better, or that the world is full of horror and wonder or that I'm going to die at some point.

I'm just sure that I want to love him, although it seems I may have missed my chance.'

'You feel like that about him and yet you still slept with Spike.'

'That's what I mean. You can't be certain about what you'll do and feel or what they'll do and feel either. You just have to go for it and hope for the best.'

'I'm beginning to think you're much braver than I am,' Tina said.

'I am,' Lottie said and ducked as Tina flicked gravy at her.

'Anyway,' Tina said, when Lottie had stopped moaning and dabbing at the front of her shirt, 'we have more important things to think about.'

'I'll let it rest for the time being,' Lottie said, 'but I'm warning you that I will be returning to the subject.'

'The fact is, oh wise sister of mine, that we have very little time left to locate Landing Rock. I've spent ages trying to find it on the internet but the only mention of landing rocks is the one on the moon, which marked the place where the astronauts took their first steps, and Plymouth Rock, where the English Pilgrims arrived in America. Nothing about a place in Monument Valley.'

'So how are we going to find it?'

'Well, I'm thinking that the best thing might be to get on some horses and explore,' Tina said, smiling in anticipation of her sister's reaction.

Lottie's head shot up from her croutons. She stared aghast at Tina.

'No. Just *no*,' she said.

'Apparently, you can get a jeep down the main trails, but if you really want to get off the beaten track you have to either go on horseback or hike.'

'Let's hike then,' Lottie said firmly.

'I don't think we have either the time or the stamina to go on foot,' Tina said. 'If we go on horses we'll have a guide who'll have some local knowledge.'

'Tina, you *know* I can't get on a horse.'

Of all the many things Lottie was timorous about, horses were at the very top of her list. Her dislike had been forged at an early age when she had been chased across a field by a black stallion that had taken an instant dislike to her. She'd had some idea from her avid reading of all things pony- and gymkhana-related that she would feed it the bits of carrot she had secreted into the pocket of her shorts. In a rare departure from her usual timidity, she had climbed over the fence into the enclosure before anyone could stop her. While Mia and Tina had watched in horror, the massive creature had galloped wild-eyed, its tail beating against its flanks, making a great, snorting, roaring sound that was louder than anything Lottie had ever heard before, and she had turned and fled, scattering bits of carrot in her wake. There had been no chance at all that she would be able to outrun it; Tina could still see her bare legs desperately pounding across the grass, making vainly for the gate at the other end of the field. Mia of course had climbed over the fence too and had stood waving her arms in an attempt to draw the fire. In the end, Lottie had decided to throw herself on the ground and roll herself up into a ball with her arms protecting her head, which turned out to be the right thing to do because, having reduced her to abject fear, the horse lost interest and sashayed off with a toss of its head.

'I could see his eyes,' Lottie had said afterwards, as Mia put her cardigan around her trembling shoulders. 'It was like he could see right into the centre of me. He knew everything about me.'

'You know what I'm going to say, don't you?' Tina said, grinning, and Lottie groaned and put her head in her hands.

'It's Challenge Five-Hundred-and-Sixty-Seven.'

Chapter 34

THEY GOT UP EARLY AND after a hasty breakfast drove to the visitor centre where the jeep was going to pick them up. They had expected to be part of a crowd, but they were the only people there. It was freezing cold, as if winter had arrived during their brief sleep. Despite the anoraks and the gloves they had been instructed to wear, they shivered in the chill air, their breath making smoky plumes, their eyes watering. The sun was barely up and the mittens in the distance were still only dark shapes, although you could see them gathering the light around their bases in a kind of hazy glow. Above, the sky was still full of stars, as if the night was dancing with the day.

'Who's going to take her?' Tina asked as she pulled the urn out of the back of the car.

'I think you'd better,' Lottie said. 'I'll probably fall off the horse and scatter her everywhere.'

'It feels all wrong putting her in a rucksack,' Tina said.

'It feels wrong her being anywhere at all except with us,' Lottie said sombrely.

A large man ushered them into the jeep and they set off along the dirt track, lurching from side to side on the back seat. As they descended into the desert, the sun came up suddenly, switching off the stars. Their guide pointed out the monuments as they passed: the Elephant Butte with its curved, stone trunk; the Three Sisters – two tall, slender pillars with a shorter one between them; the Rain God's gaping mouth; the Thunderbird Mesa with a central cave just the right size for an international rescue aircraft to hide itself in.

'Each of these monuments has a heartbeat,' their driver said. 'If you stay very still you can hear it.'

'Oh my God,' Lottie muttered under her breath. She felt her own heart beating as the jeep drew to a halt by the Totem Pole. Standing at its base was a man holding the reins of what looked like three enormous horses.

'I'm not sure I can do this,' she said as they disembarked.

The jeep roared off in a cloud of dust, leaving them with their new companion – a Navajo Indian with long grey hair in a headband who introduced himself as Gilbert.

'My sister's a nervous rider,' Tina said.

'Summer is as gentle as a baby,' he replied. Lottie eyed the horse in question doubtfully. It didn't look particularly placid; she thought it had a sly, furtive air, as if it was planning on doing something bad. She couldn't imagine being able to climb up onto its massive back. Seeing her hesitation, Gilbert produced a kind of tall stool and encouraged her to step onto it. Lottie made a last desperate appeal to her sister.

'How about I ride on the back of yours?' she suggested.

'One lady, one horse,' Gilbert said firmly.

She had no choice. She avoided looking into the creature's eyes while she got up on the teetering stool. She took hold of the shifting saddle and hoisted herself on board. The sweet smell of the horse's skin and the way it glistened horrified her. She was certain its apparent gentleness was a disguise, that it was simply biding its time before hurtling into a canter. It could probably sense her fear.

'It's such a long way to the ground,' she said, and Gilbert laughed as if he had heard it all before.

'People from Great Britain know horses almost as well as we do,' he said.

'You're thinking about the Queen. Most British people have never been anywhere near one,' Lottie said, trying not to squeak as she felt the horse move beneath her.

Tina waved the stool away and mounted her horse, Billy, with what looked like expert ease. She grinned smugly when Gilbert complimented her on her technique. Lottie gritted her teeth. When had Tina learnt to ride? It was so annoying the way she could do everything so easily.

After a brief lesson on how to hold the reins, they set off. Gilbert led the way on a black horse called Prophet, who had a worrying way of rearing up on its hind legs. Tina followed right behind him and Lottie trailed after. Her horse kept stopping to nibble at the spiky grass and she gasped each time it bent its neck, convinced she was going to slide forward and fall off. It was ridiculous that they were actually allowed to do such a hazardous thing without proper training and hard hats. She was sure it was a contravention of health and safety regulations.

'Have you heard of a place called Landing Rock?' Tina asked Gilbert, rolling from side to side in her saddle as if she thought she was a flipping cowboy.

'There are many rocks with many names,' he answered, rather as if he thought it was part of his role to be mysterious.

Despite her anxiety, Lottie was amazed to be deep in this landscape of silvery sagebrush and weathered yuccas and outlandish rock masses. The soil was the colour of the bricks of a Victorian terrace. It was like no place she had ever been before – and yet, at the same time, it was deeply familiar from a hundred westerns, a hundred shots of horses making their way across this same terrain or standing in silhouette against the great big sky, marked white today in what looked like a Navajo pattern.

'Come along, slowcoach!' Tina yelled, as Lottie fell further and further behind. Her dratted sister was showing off and making her horse trot. For a while they traversed the cracked hollow of what must once have been a river and then, just as Lottie thought she was beginning to get used to the motion of the horse, the track suddenly sloped steeply downwards.

'Hey, I'm not sure I can do hills!' she yelled out. Her companions ignored her. Summer descended lazily, sure-footed on the loose stones. Lottie tried to grip the sides of the horse with her thighs, which were already beginning to chafe, but this only had the effect of encouraging Summer into a sluggish trot. Lottie pulled frantically on the reins, and after a few scary seconds when she was sure she was going to be propelled head first, the horse resumed its slow, disdainful ramble. She breathed again.

'We'll stop here for some songs,' Gilbert announced when they at last reached the bottom of the hill. Ahead were the crumbling turrets of a monolithic castle. He had wheeled his horse round and was sitting facing them. Although Lottie was extremely relieved that she had managed to get Summer to stop, she was deeply embarrassed by the thought of being sung to. She felt bad that Gilbert was obliged to provide them with the whole Native American experience just because he had been paid. Singing was most definitely something you had to feel like doing. She glanced at her sister, who was exhibiting no signs of discomfort, but instead sitting bolt upright on her horse, looking expectant. I should be more like her, Lottie thought. I would enjoy life more if I wasn't so eternally self-conscious.

Gilbert cleared his throat and launched himself into a song that he said was about happy horse riding, then another that was a lullaby and a third about herding cattle. He must have done the exact same thing with a hundred tourists, but nevertheless there was a ring of conviction in the way he sang and held himself that spoke of pride and a sense of ownership. Once she let herself properly listen, she found the songs had a sweet, melodic quality. After the recital, they dismounted and ate the dinner Gilbert produced from his saddlebag – corn dumplings as blue as a bruise, and some greasy bread that tasted of honey.

'There's no sign of Landing Rock,' Tina said fretfully as they ate. 'I've been looking for it all the way. We may have to find somewhere else.'

'Why are you looking for this particular place?' Gilbert asked.

After a moment's hesitation, they explained about the film and about Mia's ashes. Gilbert's naturally morose face assumed an even more lugubrious slant. He stood and took up a solemn position, looking out across the desert as if he was going to say something profound. Lottie steeled herself for the Navajo version of a motivational quote, perhaps something about listening to the wind or following a falling star or life being like a rainbow.

'I need to pass water,' he said and wandered off, leaving the horses' reins under some heavy stones. The horses looked unlikely to bolt; they knew the drill as well as their master. If they remembered in their blood the fierce grip of proper riders, sitting astride them bareback, the memory had been eroded by years of bearing soft-bottomed, anxiously respectful visitors, laden down with turquoise jewellery and guilt.

'I actually need to go myself,' Lottie said after Gilbert had vanished.

'Well, don't go miles,' Tina replied. 'It's not as if there are millions of people craning to catch a glimpse of your arse.'

Lottie walked around the massive slabs of the castle. From the other side, it looked less like an ancient building and more like a crouching animal – a bear perhaps, or a lion. It was part of the wonder of this place that nothing was definite, but was open to many different interpretations, depending on the cast of the light or where you were standing or even what you chose to see. It was both rooted in the earth and as insubstantial as a dream. She found a spot hidden behind a patch of ragged shrubbery and squatted to pee, looking out into the middle distance as she did so, just in case there was another singing Navajo Indian and another group of transfixed, awkward tourists. In front of her was only empty space and a juniper tree with its lower branch hanging almost as far as the ground. Beyond that was a small incline topped with a thick, flat rock scalloped around its edges, as if some idle child had passed a few hours chipping away at it. Lottie stared. It was the rock on which Dove and Tache had discovered the abandoned baby – the place where their journey had taken a turn towards an unforeseen happiness. She zipped up her jeans quickly and rushed back to her sister. Gilbert had now returned and was standing beside her.

'I've found it!'

'Found what?' Tina asked. 'The meaning of life? A marble toilet with a flush and fluffy hand towels?'

'No, you fool. Landing Rock.'

361

And Lottie caught hold of Tina's hand and pulled her back to the place, half expecting that in the short time she had been away it would have disappeared like the mirage of a dying cowboy.

'It *is* the right place, isn't it?'

Tina was staring at the stone as if she couldn't quite believe it. 'I think it is,' she murmured.

Tina could almost hear the baby's cry and see Tache's big, dirty hands picking up the swaddled bundle, Dove still on his horse telling him to move on and leave well alone.

Like everything that has been long imagined, the reality of it was different – smaller perhaps, or just more ordinary, than she had expected. Looking at the unremarkable stone Tina had the panicked feeling that it wasn't at all what she wanted it to be. She had expected to be relieved when they found Landing Rock, but all she felt was distress. They had been tricked by soaring music and a clever manipulation of the light into believing that this was a special place. They had brought Mia to what amounted to a piece of scrubland and a disintegrating tree. It didn't feel like a destination. It wasn't grand enough, solemn enough, even beautiful enough. It just wasn't enough.

'Shall we do it then?' Lottie asked.

'No,' Tina said. 'We need to find somewhere better.'

'But this is where she wanted to be!' Lottie said. 'This is what we've been looking for. I'm going to go and get the rucksack. I'll tell Gilbert to wait for us.'

Gilbert was squatting on the ground and he got up as Lottie hastily explained what was happening.

'We shouldn't be too long, I'm sorry.'

'You must take your time to lay her to rest,' he said, 'or she will follow you home. I'm in no hurry.'

'It's not what I expected,' Tina said to Lottie when she got back. 'I thought it would feel right, but it doesn't. We can't leave her here.'

'It's where she wanted to be,' Lottie said again, pulling the urn out and laying it on the ground between them. 'Look, the Three Sisters!' she said, and tried to smile. She found instead that she was crying. Now that it was time to leave Mia, she didn't feel ready.

'She asked me to come to her the night she was killed,' Tina said suddenly. She put her hands over her face.

'What do you mean?'

'She rang me up when I was at a party and I couldn't be bothered to listen to her properly. While I was getting pissed and having a shag, Rick was stabbing her to death.'

Lottie put her arms around her sister and held her. Tina's whole body was shaking hard.

'You weren't to know. How could you have known?' Lottie stroked her sister's bent head. All the anger and betrayal she had felt only a few hours before seemed to soften and spread, until it was nothing more than a little blown dust.

'I could've stopped him.'

'If it hadn't happened that night,' Lottie said, 'it would have happened on another.'

'The thing is, we'll never know.' Tina broke into loud, sobbing tears. She sounded just as she had as a child, when fury and regret for what she had done or what had been done to her finally broke through her defences. She had been a stout-hearted girl, not given to crying, so when she had shown her sorrow it had always been surprising. It was the same now. Tina was weeping with great, ragged exhalations. It sounded to Lottie as if her sister was releasing all the tears she had kept dammed up for years.

'I told Mia that I was never going to see her again if she didn't get rid of Rick,' said Lottie, in a small voice. Tina raised her head to look at her. 'So she didn't even ring me when she needed help. I made her choose between us and she chose him, so I left her to it. I hadn't spoken to her for at least a month before she was killed.'

'You did what you thought was right,' Tina said, rubbing at her face with her sleeve. 'How were you to know that she would be so fatally stubborn?'

'I thought I was being firm. I thought I would make her see what needed to be done, but all I did was abandon her when she needed me the most.' Tears ran down her face. She didn't think she would ever be able to stop crying.

'Oh Lottie, we both let her down!'

Lottie nodded. She felt the weight of Tina's words, and yet at the same time a kind of easing and shifting of pain. They could share it now in a way they never had before.

'She knew we loved her though,' said Lottie. 'I know she did. And she loved us back. She was so full of love. It made her and unmade her.'

In the distance, they heard Gilbert singing. He might have been singing about anything, about grinding corn to pollen or catching antelope, but the song sounded solemn, as though it were his contribution to their ceremony. They were grateful for the melancholy strains winding their way across the cowboy plains. Along with their confessions, his song seemed to have transformed this small monument into a suitable resting place after all. They made a little dip at the base of the tree and took turns scooping handfuls of their sister into the ground.

'She's been dead for three years, but I'll miss her forever,' Tina said when they had smoothed away their footprints so that the earth looked as it had before.

'She'll always be here,' Lottie said. 'She'll always be with us and wherever we want her to be.'

As they walked past the castle, or the bear, shadowed now along one of its great flanks, Lottie thought she could hear its heart beating.

Chapter 35

'IF YOU WERE AN ITEM of jewellery, what would you be?'
Lottie asked. She was back in her cowboy hat and in the
driving seat. It was a beautiful evening, and John Denver
was singing about Colorado. They had left the roof of the
car down to enjoy the last of the sun.

'Easy,' Tina replied. 'I'd be a turquoise and silver ring.'

'So would I,' Lottie said. The sisters held up their matching
knuckleduster bands, bought from a stall in Monument Valley
owned by Gilbert's cousin. She'd had the same dark eyes and
downward-slanting mouth that Gilbert had, and had taken
their dollars with such charm that they hadn't minded.

Gilbert had seen them back to the visitor centre with a
grave solicitude that had touched them.

'You have been my very favourite riders,' he said when
they parted, with such sincerity that they almost believed
he didn't say that to everyone. 'I hope you will soon stop
feeling sad.'

They had been on the road for most of the day, and
were now searching for a lodge just outside Moab, where

Tina had decided they were to spend the night. Lottie had pointed out several possible motels along the way, but Tina was adamant that they should continue until they found this particular place.

'Apparently it has a great view,' she said, and so Lottie buttoned her lip and kept on driving, ignoring the fact that she was longing for a cold beer and a place to be stationary for a while. After their time in Monument Valley and a further day spent hiking in the weird landscape of the Arches National Park, she wanted to rest before the last stretch of driving to Park City and the flight home. The road passed through the mountains, alongside a khaki-coloured river. The light was greenish and, for a fleeting moment, just as the sun was beginning to set, the earth became the shade of vermilion found in frescoes and in the shining insides of Chinese bowls.

'We've seen so much on this trip,' Lottie said. 'I feel full up to the brim.'

'There it is!' Tina said, indicating a ranch-style building, which suffered from a surfeit of pine. Inside, their room was cool. It did indeed have a great view of the massy, fast-flowing Colorado River. All around, holding them in, were great slices of earth, looking as if they had been smoothed to a shine by the cut of a giant knife.

'Now, I don't want you to overreact,' said Tina ominously, as she fiddled with her sponge bag in the bathroom, 'but Dean is in the bar waiting for you.'

'What?' Lottie sat bolt upright on the bed she had thrown herself down on minutes before.

'I *said*, don't overreact.'

'What do you *mean*, Dean's in the bar?'

'I've been phoning him since we last saw him at the canyon. He wouldn't take my calls for ages, but he finally cracked when I got stern with him.'

'I thought he'd gone back to the UK.'

'No. He's been trekking in the canyon for the last couple of days. He says it has helped him think. Boy does that man set store by thinking! It's a wonder he gets anything done.'

'He's *really* downstairs?'

'Yes. He texted me fifteen minutes ago to say he was.'

'I thought you didn't like him!'

'I know you do,' Tina answered, looking pleased with herself.

'God, I don't know if I can bear to see him. I feel really nervous.'

'Don't go getting your hopes up. He still seems fairly intractable, but at least he's prepared to talk.'

'It was kind of you to do this for me,' Lottie said, crossing the room and embracing her sister.

Tina wriggled away from Lottie's grateful clutches. 'Since I made the mess, the least I can do is try and clean it up,' she said. 'We've got ten minutes to make you look presentable.' She surveyed Lottie's crumpled linen trousers and shirt. Her sister's attempts to make an effort with her appearance earlier on in the trip had been abandoned in favour of comfortable practicality.

'No, it's fine,' Lottie protested, as Tina started throwing clothes out of her suitcase and spreading them all over the bed. 'I'd prefer it if he just sees me as I am.'

'Now let me see, what have I got left that's still clean?' Tina said, ignoring her sister. 'I'm not letting you go down there in one of your droopy smocks. Ah yes! This is perfect!'

'I'm not wearing that!' Lottie looked in alarm at the tiny yellow dress Tina was holding up, but she could see that her sister was in no mood to be thwarted, so she gave in and pulled it over her head with a sigh.

'You can practically see my breasts,' she moaned, tugging at it as she stood in front of the mirror.

'That's kind of the idea,' Tina answered, pulling Lottie's hair from its scrunchie and shaking it out.

'Dean's not that impressed with women who rely on their physical attributes,' she said, as she reluctantly allowed Tina to smear her mouth with some raspberry-flavoured concoction.

'I know, I know. It's your mind and soul he admires – but it doesn't do any harm to help him value what's inside you by making the outside of you equally attractive.'

Lottie laughed. 'You'll never change, will you?'

'Not in this respect, but maybe in others.' Tina suddenly looked a little sad, and so Lottie bore without further complaint the addition of some teetering wedged espadrilles and a squirt of perfume.

'Go down there and knock him dead,' Tina said, when she was finally satisfied. 'You look utterly beautiful, and if he doesn't instantly forgive you and fall into your arms, the man truly is a fool.'

Lottie licked the gloss off her lips as she walked down the corridor towards the bar. This meeting was going to be hard enough without looking as if she was dribbling. She almost went over on one of her shoes and cursed inwardly. She really needed to develop some backbone, instead of always giving in to her sister's ideas. Yet when she caught a glimpse of herself in a mirror as she passed, she was surprised by how good she looked. She straightened her back. She was wearing the kind of dress that required attitude, so the best thing to do was pretend that she had some.

The bar was decked out like a western saloon with orange, varnished wood and a long bar made for sliding shot glasses down. She couldn't see Dean anywhere. She felt her heart sink. It was crowded, and she didn't trust her ability not to fall over in her shoes, so she ordered a drink and sat down at one of the tables. Perhaps he had changed his mind and decided that he didn't want to meet her after all.

'Hello, Lottie,' he said, appearing suddenly in front of her. He had a newly ruddy look and a slightly peeling nose and was wearing unfamiliar boots. Her heart jumped at the sight of him.

'I gather you've been talking to Tina,' she said, trying to calm down. Women in dresses like the one she was wearing had to look as if they were in command of themselves.

'Yes, your sister has been very persistent.' He smiled slightly, although she could see no real humour in his face.

'Why did you decide to stay?' she asked.

He looked at her for what seemed like a long time before answering. 'I couldn't quite bear to go,' he said finally. 'I knew that if I went home it would really all be over.'

'And is it over?' she said, hardly daring to breathe.

'You look beautiful,' he said. 'Although you don't look like yourself.'

'Who do I look like?' Lottie asked.

'I would say Tina, because it's the sort of dress she would wear,' he answered; 'but that's not quite true. You look like a new version of you.'

'Is that a bad thing?' she asked.

'I'm not sure,' he said, and his mouth twisted slightly as if he was trying out a new taste. 'I liked the old version of you very much.' He was scratching the surface of the table with his thumbnail and one of his legs was doing a kind of juddering dance. She had never seen him this stressed, even when he had thirty-three essays to mark and a breakfast meeting. Walking in the canyon didn't seem to have calmed him down much.

'It's just a dress.' She wanted to reach out and touch him, but knew it was too soon.

He lowered his eyes as if he didn't want to betray his feelings too much. 'But it isn't *just* a dress, is it?'

'People don't change in a couple of weeks – not fundamentally, anyway.'

'So you *will* admit you've changed to a certain extent?' Dean asked.

'I think perhaps being away made me feel less certain about things.'

'By "things", I take it you mean me?'

'I know it seems like that, but it's really not.' Lottie bit her lip. She was struggling to explain what had happened in a way that would not hurt him and yet would be truthful. 'I thought I was just going away, rather inconveniently as it happens, to spend time with Tina and find somewhere to lay Mia to rest, but at some point I felt a kind of shift. I can't think of another way to describe it.'

'What kind of a shift?'

'I started to wonder if the life I was leading was really my choice. I felt a little as if I had been standing still. I wanted to try something new to see where I would land.'

'And sleeping with someone was your great experiment?' Dean said quietly. 'I thought you had more depth.'

'It wasn't just about sleeping with Spike. That was more of a symptom. It was bigger than that.'

'And where did you land?' Dean asked. 'What did you discover?'

'I think I discovered that I wanted what I already had,' she said.

There was a long pause. Then Dean said, 'So every time things are getting a little boring at home, you're going to make a habit of having sex with strangers?'

'There's no need to sneer at me,' she said, suddenly angry. She had been as contrite as it was possible to be and yet he wasn't giving her a chance.

'I'm just disappointed in you, that's all.'

'Can you stop being a bloody teacher for just five minutes?' She got to her feet. 'I can't talk to you when you're being like this. There's no point in this at all.'

She stalked off across the bar. There must have been a wet patch on the floor or perhaps the ridiculous espadrilles tripped her up, but there was a horrible moment when she was fighting desperately for her balance and then she slid a couple of feet and landed in an undignified heap on the floor. Her first thought was that if this had happened to her when she had been wearing her linen trousers, at least she wouldn't have ended up with at least fifty people getting a sight of her knickers. Dean was by her side almost instantly, helping her to her feet, but she batted him off and staggered to the door.

'Fuck off and go and tell your pupils what to do,' she shouted, causing a middle-aged couple at a nearby table to look at each other askance.

'She's British,' the woman said to her companion in a carrying voice. 'They swear a lot and get drunk.'

'She sure is fiery!' he replied. 'They're not as reserved as they look in those costume dramas.'

Still in the grip of fury, Lottie swung out of the hotel and into the smoky-coloured evening. After a few minutes of angry, unsteady marching, she stopped, took off her shoes and walked on the grass by the river. The earlier fire of sun in the mountains had now been extinguished, leaving the slopes an ashy grey. She sat down on a toppled log and watched the silky water filling the curving banks. It looked like liquid in a mould.

She knew she had hurt Dean and that what she had done might be too much for him to ever recover from, but she thought he could at least try. She shivered slightly in her flimsy dress. Tina was probably tucked up in bed in her pyjamas. It almost made her smile to think how things had changed. Only a few days ago she had been disapproving of her sister's decision not to take a coat to the party in San Francisco and now here she was, sitting in the middle of nowhere dressed in a square of silk. Maybe Dean was right and she had changed more than she thought.

'Take my jacket,' Dean said, with another of his sudden appearing acts.

'I don't want it,' she said, without turning round.

Why was it that men thought women were endlessly long-ing for someone to drape them in jackets, and why was it that women so often valued being looked after in this way? After all, women didn't feel the cold any more than men did.

'Suit yourself.' He came to sit next to her on the log and she pointedly moved further along and away from him. 'Your mouth is turning blue,' he said.

She ignored him. For a while they sat in silence surveying the river.

'Listen, Lottie,' he said at last, when she thought they might sit there forever, like a pair of bookends on an empty shelf, 'I can't put my hand on my heart and tell you that everything is going to go back to how it was, but it turns out that I can't actually live without you. Who knew?' He tried unsuccessfully to laugh.

'I did,' Lottie said. 'Because I can't live without you either.'

'I just need you to tell me that I'm what you want. We can work on the rest.'

'You are *exactly* what I want,' she said.

'What, even though I have a small mouth and a tendency to be pompous, even though I'm stuck in my ways, even though I find it hard to switch off from being a teacher?'

'I love you because of those things,' she said, smiling. 'When I really think about it, what happened was that I briefly became risk-averse.'

'What do you mean? Surely having an affair and putting your relationship in jeopardy is the ultimate risk?'

'But choosing you, loving you – that's the risk, silly.' She kissed him. His mouth fitted hers exactly and she held him as she always had, her hands at the back of his neck where his hair was curly.

'I'm so sorry I hurt you,' she said, when they finally pulled apart. 'I'll try never to hurt you again.'

He put his arms around her, and she felt the coldness disappear from her body, as if the sun had risen and lit up the sides of the mountains and set them burning again.

Chapter 36

Five days later

TINA WAS JUST A LITTLE drunk, and the grey silk frock that Lottie had insisted she wear clung in none of the right places. Her sister, on the other hand, glowed as if someone had polished her with a rough cloth and then dipped her in stardust. The wedding dress that Tina had so disliked fitted her body perfectly, the little pearl buttons that ran all the way from the small of her back to the nape of her neck acting like a marker for her curves. After a bit of persuasion, she had agreed to let her sister style her hair, and Tina had blow-dried it to bring out its natural curl and threaded the golden tresses with daisies. She was most definitely the most beautiful bride Tina had ever seen, although she had to admit her bar had been set rather low. If she ever made the mistake of shackling herself to someone for life, she was going to wear something memorable – bright red, perhaps, slit all the way to the waist with just a suggestion of underboob, a dress that was revealing enough to make people disapprove slightly. Although why she was even thinking about wedding dresses, she couldn't imagine. She was going to live her life exactly the way she wanted to. Being married would only ever inhibit that.

She checked the pictures on her camera and thought she had probably got the most important moments so far – Lottie, pale and tremulous at the door of the chapel; the wonder in Dean's face as he watched her come towards him; the way she had touched his arm to steady him, her face solemn despite her smiling mouth; the requisite kiss that had been so surprisingly romantic that Tina had found herself blinking a tear from her eye so she could focus her camera properly. This stuff was truly insidious. It broke even the most hard-hearted of sceptics.

When Lottie and Dean had returned to the pine lodge in Utah, their faces had been so transparently and skinlessly happy that she had felt a warm glow. She was proud of the part she had played in getting them back together. She had really grafted to make Dean see sense, going to the toilet endlessly or ducking behind bushes – on one occasion, even hiding in a broom cupboard so that she could harangue him on the phone in private. She felt she had almost made up for her manipulation of Lottie's feelings.

'I love him more than I can say,' Lottie had said, when Tina asked her for the last and final time if she was sure. 'I'm as sure as I can be about anything, and that has to be more than enough.'

Lottie and Dean were currently moving through their guests, dutifully talking to each and every one of them. Why they weren't getting drunk and having a sneaky shag in the very nice bedroom that had been booked for their wedding night was utterly beyond her. At least Dean had the nurse's outfit to look forward to, although Tina wondered if Lottie had actually packed it. You could take a horse to water, but you couldn't make her frolic in it.

Tina looked around for the champagne waiter and made a beeline for his silver salver. The Cambridge college certainly provided a pretty backdrop for the wedding, with the river slinking by and the leaves on the well-manicured trees just turning to shades of ochre and cerise. The lawn was studded with white cyclamen and the beds were full of fragrant pink phlox and wine-red dahlias. They had been lucky with the weather – a stray hot autumn day, more beautiful than any summer one because it had not been expected. She scooped up a flute and sat on one of the chairs that had been placed by the water.

'I wanted to check you were all right,' Lottie said, coming up behind her.

'I'm absolutely fine,' Tina answered. 'You look so beautiful I might even squeeze out a tear or two.'

Lottie laughed and pulled up a chair beside her, giving a relieved little sigh as she untied the ankle straps on her shoes and pushed them off.

'You know I said that I would make you do one challenge?' she asked, looking sideways at her sister.

'It's too late. The road trip's over,' Tina said. 'You've missed your chance.'

'Don't you think, since it's my wedding day, you might just indulge me?'

'Oh, OK then,' Tina said grudgingly. 'What do you want me to do? I'll tell you for nothing that while I'm perfectly happy to plunge naked into the river, risking being ejected by the steely-eyed porter, if you ask me to talk to some very grim man you've marked out for me, I'm saying no.'

'Your one and only challenge is to admit that, somewhere deep in that black heart of yours, you have feelings for Spike.' Lottie's face was almost as solemn as it had been when she had been standing at the altar. 'I know that although you've done your very best to distract yourself since you got back, you miss him. The fact that you haven't mentioned him at all tells me all I need to know.'

'You are completely and utterly wrong,' Tina said indignantly. 'He's barely crossed my mind.'

Although of course he had. She had tried not to dwell on anything Spike-related, but she had found a hundred things that reminded her of him – the way a passer-by dipped his head, or the sky being the same colour as it had been that night in the desert when they had huddled together on the blow-up mattress, a glass of red wine that tasted of blackcurrant, damson, wet rope and just a hint of soil. It made her furious with herself, but she couldn't seem to help it. It was perverse to be languishing after a man who blatantly had no interest in her. He hadn't tried to ring her or even send her a message. He was clearly happy to be alone, chasing meteorites across scrubland.

'Do you accept my challenge?' Lottie asked. 'Remember, if you say no you will have failed.'

'This isn't a fair challenge at all,' Tina protested. 'And anyway, I could just say it and not mean it.'

'You said you'd be able to tell if I'd had a poo in the desert or not – well, I'm going to be able to tell whether you're telling the truth about Spike.'

Tina groaned. 'Why have I been afflicted with a sister who thinks she's Miss Marple?'

'Time's running out,' Lottie said, lacing up her shoes. 'Aunt Philippa looks as if she's making her way towards us,' and indeed, when Tina looked up, a woman in a powder-blue suit and cornflowers on her hat was marching over. She was one of the few relatives the sisters could bear, despite the fact that she always acted as if it was a crime to run out of words.

'OK,' said Tina. 'Because it's your wedding day, I'll admit that it's just possible that I may have *slight*, almost insignificant feelings for Spike. Are you happy now?'

'There, that wasn't so bad now, was it?' Lottie got up and stroked her sister's head, then skilfully cut Philippa off at the pass. She looked back, grinning as she put her arm through her aunt's and led her to the buffet.

Weddings went on far too long in Tina's opinion. It took about two seconds to say 'I do', and yet there were hours and hours in which the guests were expected to enjoy standing pinned into lawns by their heels, waiting for incoherent speeches or undignified scrambles for flung bouquets. At least as the official photographer she had something to do other than hang around hoping some more food might make an appearance. She thought she probably should take some pictures of the guests so that there was a proper record of who had turned up to endure the day.

She captured a shot of two little girls in grubby party dresses crouched digging with spoons in a flowerbed. She took a close-up of King Ramses' head – the centrepiece of the wedding table, which had arrived from Greg that morning. A group of reunited college friends, made a little giddy by the temporary illusion that things were just the same, stood laughing in a line against a golden brick wall. A woman held a baby above her head and made it swoop, gurgling, through the air. Arms were draped around shoulders and dresses held out for examination. Heads were thrown back in laughter and tilted up to kiss. Some people posed. Others pretended not to notice the intrusion. Only one person looked directly into the lens of her camera. She took the picture before she had really registered who it was. A man in a suit, crumpled around the knees, arms by his side, his face with its sure lines just a little doubtful. She stood still and he came towards her. She could feel her body trembling although she knew no one else would see it.

'What are you doing here?' She tried not to smile, the habit of self-protection still strong. No point giving the game away.

'Lottie invited me,' Spike said. 'Which was very kind of her considering the fact that Dean probably wants to take another swing at me. I think she really had to work on him.'

'It's funny, she never mentioned it,' she said.

'I think she meant it as a surprise. A good one, I hope.'

She didn't answer, only looked at him, and he looked back and she saw the hope in his face. She felt the thud of her heart. It seemed that perhaps he wasn't indifferent to her after all.

'I gather she gave you a challenge,' he said. He smirked a little, but not too much.

'She's the most annoying sister in the world.'

He leant towards her. She hesitated, not because she wanted to make him wait but to give herself the time to choose, the time to look him in the face and know all of it and jump anyway. Then she took a deep breath and kissed him.

Later, when people were beginning to gather their bags and their children, who, high on staying up late and fizzy lemon, still ran in endless circles round the garden, and when the river had assumed its night-time glisten and the grass had turned just a little damp, Lottie and Tina danced together slowly across the lawn.

'So, is it happy ever after?' Lottie asked Tina.

'It's happy tonight and perhaps tomorrow,' Tina said, smiling. 'That's as far as I am prepared to plan.'

'It's as far as any of us should plan,' Lottie said, putting her head on her sister's shoulder.

'I wish Mia could have seen you today, looking so serene and so lovely.'

'I wish she could have seen you,' said Lottie, 'visibly swaying after five glasses of champagne, tears on your face, making your speech about how men come and go but sisters last forever.'

'Yes, I caught Dean's eye at one point and he looked like he wanted to kill me.'

They both laughed.

'Dean really didn't want Spike here. I had to tell him that I thought you and he had a real chance to be together.'

'I love you.'

'I want that in writing.'

They continued to dance even though the music had stopped.

'Mia would have approved of today, I think. I hope,' said Lottie.

'Are you kidding? She would have been right at the front, beaming.'

'We have to hold fast to each other, for us and for her.'

'Yes, let's hold fast forever,' said Tina. 'Let's never argue again.'

'Come on, Tina,' said Lottie. 'Be *realistic*.'

Lottie swung her sister round in a classic square dance move they had learnt as cowboys, and Tina smiled as she bent under her arm to end up where they had begun.

Acknowledgements

THIS BOOK WAS WRITTEN DURING a period of change and anxiety. It was difficult at times to think about a holiday road trip when life was rather bleak, but sticking at it also gave my days shape and purpose.

I would like to thank all the people who have helped me and my family navigate what has been a less than smooth ride. I love each and every one of you.

I would also like to thank my agents, Luigi Bonomi and Alison Bonomi. I hope you know how much I appreciate your support and your faith in me. I am grateful to Sarah Bauer at Bonnier for her cheerfulness and invaluable editorial insight, and to Katie Lumsden for her keen eye. Thank you also to my copyeditor, Rhian McKay, and my proofreader, Jenny Page.

Felix and Olivia and Sid and Jack bring pleasure and pride to my life and make me feel so lucky. I thank my mother, Valerie, for her wisdom, and apologise to her for not always listening.

Lastly, and as ever, I thank my husband, David, who remains true and steadfast whatever life throws at him. I intend to ensure that however long or short the road, we will live it a lot.

The Inspiration Behind
Live A Little

I AM ONE OF THREE SISTERS, and although some of our characteristics (shared and distinct) have crept into the novel,
we are not very much like siblings Mia, Lottie and Tina in
Live A Little. The road trip featured in the book is, however,
true to life.

My sister Tania and I took almost exactly the same route
several years ago in a white convertible. We wore cowboy
hats and had adventures and marvelled at the beauty of
America – although, I would like to make it clear that we
didn't pick up a handsome hitchhiker, since we were both
happily married and not even a little bit interested in sexy
geologists. My youngest sister Thomasina wasn't able to
come on the trip, but I am glad to report that she is alive
and well and didn't travel with us in an urn.

I kept a journal of our holiday while we were on route. This
was quite a long time before I had begun writing novels and
I had no idea that one day what I had scribbled down would
become the inspiration for one. I rediscovered my account of
the trip when I was clearing out my desk (a long-postponed

task) and read it for the first time since it had been stashed away amongst half-used diaries, my children's paintings and instruction booklets for now-defunct electrical goods.

I was struck by how excited I had been about everything – the smells and colours, the expansiveness of the landscape, the sheer joy of driving down a road when you are the only vehicle on it. I was also interested to see that I had recorded in detail the pleasure and (I have also got to admit) the irritations of travelling with my much-loved sister. It was as if that fortnight emphasised both the differences between us, and the ways we are alike. Being together in a car for extended periods of time made us snipe at each other about small things – a tendency to chew gum loudly or to drive too near to the vehicle in front or the need for astonishingly frequent loo or food stops – but it also made us even closer than we were before.

Tania is a very adventurous and seasoned traveller, whereas I am timorous and prone to worrying about where we are going to spend the night. Having been to fewer places (Tania also lives in America and is familiar with much of the country), I was more wide-eyed and astonished by everything than she was. Like Lottie and Tina in the novel, what we each brought to the trip enhanced it for the other – Tania experienced everything newly through my eyes, and I learnt not to be so hung up on knowing exactly where we were going. We saw many wonderful things on that trip and we learnt a lot about the places we were travelling through, but it also taught us just how much we valued our relationship.

Having and loving sisters is the most fortunate thing in the world. It makes both the good times and the bad times so much better. It frees you from having to explain yourself. It gives you the opportunity to behave badly at times, but also to step up when you have to. Above all, it bestows a kind of courage and confidence that nothing else quite can.

Thank you, Tania, for the road trip and for so much else (I forgive you for trashing my best shoes in Las Vegas), and Thomasina, it will be the three of us next time.